OUT OF BOUNDS

Emma pulled up in front of his house but didn't turn off the engine. "What do you want me to say? You know you're good-looking. You know you're a good kisser. Do you need me to tell you it was nice? Okay, I admit it was nice. All my girl parts were groovin' with your boy parts. But it didn't mean anything, and we both know that."

Bobby's gaze clashed with hers. "I think we need to talk. You better come inside."

"I'm not going inside your house. I'm going home. And we're going to forget this ever happened."

"In my experience that never works."

Her hands gripped the steering wheel, knuckles white. "Did you know there's a betting pool in the department on how long it'll take you to get me into bed?"

Anger rushed through him so strongly that blood roared in his ears. "No, I didn't."

"Well, now you do."

Emma put the car into gear—a cue to him to get lost. Bobby opened his door.

"I always seem to piss you off."

"Nobody is winning that bet," she said.

He stepped out of the car, closed the door, and watched her drive away.

Avon Contemporary Romances by
Michele Albert

OFF LIMITS
GETTING HER MAN

MICHELE
ALBERT

Off
Limits

AVON BOOKS
An Imprint of HarperCollinsPublishers

AVON BOOKS
An Imprint of HarperCollins*Publishers*
10 East 53rd Street
New York, New York 10022-5299

Copyright © 2003 by Michele Albert
ISBN: 0-380-82056-0
www.avonromance.com

First Avon Books paperback printing: September 2003

Avon Trademark Reg. U.S. Pat. Off. and in Other Countries, Marca Registrada, Hecho en U.S.A.
HarperCollins® is a registered trademark of HarperCollins Publishers Inc.

Printed in the U.S.A.

10 9 8 7 6 5 4 3 2 1

For Gail Russo Shamasna,
Bobby's first champion . . .

One

Nursing a vicious hangover—and inexcusably late for work, judging by the captain's glare dogging his heels—Bobby Halloran ran the office gauntlet of ringing phones, clacking keyboards, and yakking detectives to the sanctuary of his office desk.

Without bothering to remove his sunglasses, he sank onto his chair, wincing at its grating creak, then raised the steaming take-out cup of coffee in his hand, gulped half of its contents down in one swallow, and shuddered.

Nothing like kicking off a brand-new day to the bitter taste of burnt coffee laced with a chemical chaser of Styrofoam.

Unfortunately, neither the caffeine jolt nor his slightly scalded tongue did a damn thing to send his headache packing, much less dull the stale, ashy taste in his mouth. He'd given up cigarettes five years ago, but still slipped in a smoke when he was shit-faced or deep in a funk.

He wanted to be home in bed with a pillow over his face, and just to make matters worse, the greasy smell of the egg and sausage McMuffin he'd bought on his way in made him queasy. Grabbing a bite to eat had seemed like a good idea at the time, and now he couldn't shove the bag out of his way quick enough.

What the hell had he been thinking last night? Drowning his sorrows in booze had never worked, and if he'd had a reason to believe drowning his guilt would work any better, he couldn't remember it in the light of day.

As clipped, determined footsteps cut across his thoughts, Bobby cautiously looked up—and groaned inwardly.

Well, hell, now his rotten morning was complete: Earnest Emma had arrived in all her perfectionist glory to make him feel even more inadequate than he'd been feeling just five seconds ago.

She slowed as she approached, and regarded him with that same flat, dispassionate look she always wore, a look that said she found him as appealing as something she'd just scraped off the sole of her shoe. "Late night?"

Not in the mood for small talk, he only grunted. And downed more coffee.

"Looks like you fought the bottle, and the bottle won." She moved to her desk. "You're not going to throw up, are you? Because it's really way too early in the morning for me to deal with that."

"I'm good."

Barring bright lights, loud noises, or sudden jostles. Or a whiff of that McMuffin.

"I've got Tylenol, if you need it."

"I'm already on that part of damage control." Then, belatedly realizing she'd thawed enough to offer him help, he added, "But thanks."

She'd already dismissed him, though, and didn't bother acknowledging his thank-you as she sorted her phone messages, presumably by priority, and then tapped them into a tidy square.

Most cops were control freaks, but Detective Emma Frey took the freak part of it soaring to whole new levels.

In a rare moment of whimsy—or maybe just a burst of temper over his latest fuck-up—the captain had assigned the newly arrived Frey to the desk next to Bobby's. He didn't know much about Frey, beyond that she'd relocated from the LAPD's Hollywood Division, and she'd barely registered on his radar so far. He hadn't talked much with her since she'd started work a little more than a week ago, and every time he ran into her, she looked exactly the same: crisp, cool, and relentlessly serious in brown suits that fit right in with her brown-haired, unobtrusive looks.

But even with his morning-after impaired powers of observation, he couldn't miss the chip on her shoulder the size of the Superdome.

"Hey, look who finally decided to grace us with his presence. Glad to see you put your detecting skills to good use and managed to find your way to work this morning, Halloran."

Bobby looked up to find Captain Derrick Strong, head of the First District Investigation Unit, staring at him with an undisguised irritation.

"Sorry. I got tied up in traffic." Which was mostly true; because he'd been running late, he'd missed the ferry, got on the Pontchartrain Expressway instead—and ended up ensnarled in rush-hour congestion.

"Right. Which is why you're still wearing your sunglasses."

Reluctantly, Bobby removed his dark glasses and slipped them into his shirt pocket. The hard fluorescent

light lanced clear through his eyeballs, which jump-
started the throbbing in his head, then triggered an uneasy lurch in his belly.

Strong took in the reaction, and his dark, thick brows
pulled together in a straight line. "You missed the morning briefing, but Frey can fill you in. We had a busy
weekend."

Nothing new in that. The First District encompassed
some of the roughest parts of New Orleans, including
the Lafitte and Iberville housing projects, always fertile
grounds for sprouting all sorts of weedy, pernicious
vices.

"And you're also just in time to catch a case."

"Jesus, I hope it's not a murder. My stomach's not up
to blood or brains yet. At least not before one more cup
of coffee."

"Then consider this your lucky break for the day."
Strong tossed a file on Bobby's cluttered desk. "An apparent burglary with heavy property damage in the Esplanade Ridge area. Delgado started the preliminary
work, but she's going on maternity leave tomorrow, so
I'm transferring the case over now. You two can pick up
where she left off."

Bobby straightened from his slouch, suddenly wary.
"What do you mean, 'you two'?"

"Take Detective Frey with you. Show her the ropes,
seeing as how she's new."

Bobby toward Frey, whose thin-lipped look of dis-
pleasure revealed she wasn't exactly bursting at the
seams with excitement at this unexpected development,
either.

"Captain, I believe I can manage this alone." Frey
shot to her feet, then obviously thought better of it. She

hesitated, but instead of sitting down again, she parked her trim behind on her desk's edge, her every muscle so taut Bobby half expected her to go *twang* when she moved. "I'd like the chance to show you what I'm capable of. And as you recall from my interview file, I grew up here. I know the area, I can——"

"I appreciate the fact you're eager to make a good impression, and since you're so gung-ho to prove your credentials, here's your chance. It's your case." Strong fixed his gaze on Frey, and her face blanked. "But I'm the one giving the orders here, and you either take Halloran with you, or you can spend another thrilling week reading procedure manuals and helping out everybody else with their overloads."

A sudden, faint edge of hostility hummed between Strong and Frey. Intrigued, Bobby leaned forward and waited as his captain and his new "partner" stared each other down.

Frey looked away first. "Yes, sir. I understand."

Bobby thought she put a slight, bitter emphasis on the word "understand," but he didn't have time to dwell on it, as Strong had turned back to him. "There's a small problem, though. The reason I said it's an apparent burglary is that we don't really know if anything was taken. The renter seems to have pulled a disappearing act. She was hanging around when the responding officer arrived, but while he was on the radio, she booked. And since you know this chick, Halloran, you can save time by smoking her out of her usual haunts and get her in here to make a statement. Or at least tell us if anything was stolen."

"Who is she?"

"Chloe Mitsumi." Strong grinned. "Remember her?"

Bobby rubbed at his eyebrows. "She's hard to forget."

"I bet." Strong turned to Frey, who was frowning. "Chloe Mitsumi, our victim, is a party girl whose brother is serving a life sentence in Angola for a whole list of badness, among them drug trafficking and murder. Halloran helped put him there, and the sister was something of a pet project with him for a while. You know where to track her down, right?"

The question was directed back to Bobby, who nodded as he took a quick sip of his coffee. "Yeah. She lives for the bar and club scene. I'll find her."

"What else do we know about her?" Frey asked, all brisk and businesslike, although plainly not happy that he already had the edge in "her" case.

"She's a hot mama Asian cupcake who's five feet and ninety pounds' worth of trouble." Strong's grin turned wolfish. "And she likes flashy clothes and high heels."

"She's not trouble," Bobby said, too tired to keep the edge of irritation out of his voice.

The captain shrugged. "If you say so, but I think we can at least agree she's ninety pounds of pure attitude."

Frey arched her brows. "Actually, I was asking what we know about her convictions or charges, not her fashion sense. Or lack of it."

"Oh." Strong looked amused. "Well, let's see . . . she's been arrested a few times on misdemeanor charges, including possession of narcotics—"

"She smokes a little weed now and again," Bobby cut in. "Stays away from the hard stuff."

"Still protecting the lady?" Strong cocked his head at Bobby. "Presumably she isn't in any trouble at the moment; she's just a swinger living for the good times and the nightlife. But what we don't know is if she still has ties to her brother's former associates, which might account for the break-in. According to Delgado, the place was trashed."

"She probably pissed off another one of her loser boyfriends." Bobby pushed himself to his feet, then swallowed, fighting back a spurt of nausea. "Okay. We're on it."

"And don't screw up. I need you functioning on all fronts, Halloran."

Catching his supervisor's skeptical expression, Bobby nodded gingerly. "I'm good."

Strong's stance eased, and he sighed. "Look. You've got over fifteen years of police work behind you, so I shouldn't have to remind you that you're a cop, not a missionary. Or a miracle worker. Get over it."

A tense silence followed, and Bobby could feel Emma Frey's curious, weighing gaze on him. Well, hell. If she stuck around long enough, she'd hear all the dirt. The old, the new, and the really juicy stuff.

Then Strong turned to Frey, and she pushed away from her desk, suddenly wary. "As for you, don't make trouble, and remember what I said. You're the primary, but you defer to Halloran's judgment until I say otherwise. You clear on that?"

"Yes, sir."

After pinning them both with a scowl, Strong spun and walked away. Several seconds passed before Frey turned to him. "So, Halloran . . . let's go find your party girl."

Despite never having passed more than fifteen minutes in her presence at any one time, he noticed the woman had an uncanny knack for rubbing him the wrong way. Man, he so did *not* look forward to sitting with her in a car or working with her for hours on end.

He donned his sunglasses again, then drank the last dregs of his coffee and tossed the empty cup, along with the breakfast sandwich, into his trash can. "She's not my anything."

Flashing him a cool look, she snatched the report off his desk. "That's not what it sounded like to me, but whatever. It's not like I really care one way or another."

"A word of warning here, Frey: I'm *not* in a good mood, so don't yank my fucking chain and we'll get along just fine."

She didn't so much as blink. "What did Captain Strong mean by that miracle worker remark?"

"None of your damn business." He walked toward the door, trusting her to follow, and trying not to wince at the renewed assault on his senses: burnt coffee, rattling casters, slamming file drawers, the rise and fall of voices and laughter, humming printers, and the *tappity-tap* of fingers on keyboards.

God, it was going to be a long day.

Frey caught up with him within seconds, easily matching his stride. Bobby gauged her height at around five-ten, and considering her athletic build, he was willing to bet those pants hid a great pair of long legs. Earnest Emma might not be exactly hot babe material, but the way she wore her brown hair, pulled back in a ponytail, emphasized her keen dark eyes, full mouth, and smooth, fair skin. She had to be in her early thirties, but he assumed the lack of smile lines meant she wasn't the chirpy type. Nor was she the chatty type; she didn't say a word during the walk to the garage, and he didn't feel a need to change that.

When he stopped at his assigned unmarked car, Frey

asked, "Do you want me to drive? I'm not entirely sure where we're going, but I can—"

"I'll drive. I know where Chloe lives—it's a house off Esplanade, near Bayou St. John." Without thinking, Bobby opened her door, only realizing he'd done so when surprise flashed across her face. Pretending not to see it, he walked to the driver's side, climbed into the car, and started the engine.

As he'd expected, the drive was awkward, the silence broken only by the static buzz of conversation from the radio. He listened absently to it, through his hangover haze, and concentrated on the traffic while his companion stared straight ahead, hands folded in her lap, back straight.

Not that her aloofness mattered. Making nice with Emma Frey would be as much fun as humping a razor-sharp barbed-wire fence, and he didn't need any more of that kind of fun.

Still, he knew what it was like to be the odd man out, and taking out his problems on her wasn't right, no matter how shitty he felt or how much she rubbed him the wrong way.

The silence—and his guilt—gathered steam until he couldn't stand it any longer. "Look, I'm sorry for jumping all over you back there. The mother of all hangovers is banging around inside my head, and I'm . . . It's been a bad week. It's not like I have anything personally against you."

She made another one of those little shrugs. "Forget about it."

Fine. He'd do exactly that.

By the time he turned onto Esplanade, though, she'd

managed to annoy him all over again. She'd looked over Delgado's report at least three times, and made several calls. Definitely a Type-A, workaholic personality. The kind that put the "anal" in "analyze."

Hell, yes, she was everything the perfect detective should be, and Bobby could see how Strong might find it entertaining to team them up.

Since it looked as if he'd be spending a lot of time with her, he'd be doing himself a big favor by turning on the charm and persuading her to thaw a little and open up—but right now he was too weary, still riding too close to the edge of last week's fallout, to muster the energy to even try.

Bobby shook off another spurt of guilt—and the flash of images it brought. Several minutes passed before he glanced her way. "I heard you worked in Hollywood."

"That's right."

"What was it like, with all the movie stars and tourists? We get plenty tourists here in New Orleans, but not many big-name celebrities."

"It's not that much different." Her expression remained aloof, but she spoke carefully, as if choosing each word. "Except sometimes we'd arrest people with higher profiles than your average wife-beater, drunk, or junkie."

"Did you ever bust any movie stars?"

"Yes."

He waited for her to elaborate, but when it became clear she wouldn't, he changed his tactics. "So why'd you come to New Orleans?"

Frey smiled, and it surprised him to realize she had really pretty eyes—even if the emotion he glimpsed inside them wasn't friendly. "You haven't heard? I find that hard to believe."

What the hell? "I must've missed the memo. Care to fill me in?"

"I testified against several officers, who are now serving time in prison. You could say I wasn't feeling the love in the workplace, and so I decided it was time for a change of scenery." She stared out her window, as houses and trees flashed by. "And that's all I'm going to say about it. If you want details, go talk to Strong."

Great, a rule-book-thumping do-gooder; just what he needed to further complicate his life. Strong had to be laughing his ass off right about now, no doubt about it.

After a short silence, Frey turned toward him. "I know about you. A few of the guys were quick to bring me up to speed."

For some odd reason, her abrupt change of subject amused him. Or maybe it was her defiant tone; he wasn't sure. "And did it scare you?"

Frey made a noise of annoyance. "Cut the crap, Halloran. You know what's going on here."

A couple of possibilities had already occurred to him, but he wasn't feeling particularly magnanimous this morning. "Maybe. Tell me anyway."

Again, her finely curved brows shot upward. "Some old-timers are having a little fun with the new girl, and they think it's worth a few laughs to throw us together and see what happens. I'm a rules-and-regulations kind of cop and you . . . you're the guy who's known for his ability to finesse the rules."

She put a slight emphasis on the word "finesse."

"A friend of mine describes my approach as creative

law enforcement. I like the sound of that better." Bobby glanced over his shoulder, pulled into the passing lane, and hit the accelerator. The engine purred with power, speeding past other cars. "And you're probably right. Even if they were dirty, you ratted out fellow cops. That's not going to automatically put you on the top of the blue brotherhood's favorite persons list."

"I'm well aware of that." Her voice was quiet, controlled—and vibrating with anger.

Officially, hazing and initiations weren't supposed to happen, but they did anyway. Nobody would ever fess up to it, but she'd been handed a test. Would she meet expectations without complaint? Act like a man about it, so to speak, suck it up and take it on the chin? Or would she make like a crybaby, kick up a fuss, and stir up trouble like a poor, weak little girl?

Bobby didn't envy her situation; either way, she was fucked. And, now that he thought about it, he didn't like being used in such a prank. Sure, he messed around and played practical jokes as much as anybody else, but something about this struck him as mean-spirited.

Then again, maybe if she'd come across a little friendlier, less remote and prickly and defensive, she might've met with a warmer reception.

"For what it's worth, I didn't know anybody was planning on giving you a hard time."

"I am so tired of this shit." He could hear both frustration and annoyance in her voice. "I left L.A. so I wouldn't have to keep proving over and over that I'm a good cop. All I want is to do my job, and for once I wish people would just look at me and see—"

Aware she was perhaps revealing more than she'd like, Frey cut herself off with a sigh. "It doesn't matter. And let's get something straight, Halloran. I'm not playing along. This is my problem, not yours, and since I really don't need help to work a burglary or find some bimbo who's probably sleeping off her latest drunk on a girlfriend's couch, if there's something you'd rather be doing, don't let me hold you back."

Everything she said made sense, but his own dark mood, coupled with the snotty tone of her voice, pissed him off anyway. "You have something against me?"

"As I said, I've already heard the lowdown on you, and maybe your lone gunman style works well for you, but that's not how I operate. My charges stick because I don't take shortcuts, and I don't hotdog."

Anger surged, but he held it off. "That sounded an awful lot like a 'yes' to me, darlin'."

"I need to make a point by clearing this case, and prove I'm competent and trustworthy. I'm not jeopardizing it by having you do something impulsive or questionable. I may be the butt of a departmental joke, but you can bet I'll be the last one laughing. Are we clear on this?"

Bobby turned onto the street where Chloe Mitsumi lived, a block off Esplanade. "Sure."

He didn't blunt the edge in his voice, and she took in a long, slow breath, the stiffness in her shoulders easing slightly.

"Really, I don't have anything against you." She sounded a little less icy. "I'm sorry for coming across as such a hard ass, but this is important to me. More important than I can ever begin to explain."

Points to the woman for being direct; he admired that. And as his mother always said, if you tried hard enough, you could find something nice to say about anybody.

If Frey had been a man, he'd have given as good as he got. Unfortunately—or fortunately, depending on how a body looked at it—his mother had also brought him up with a heavy dose of old-fashioned manners when it came to dealing with women. Not even fifteen years as a cop had completely cured him of his protective habits toward women, including those who didn't need even an iota of protecting, and who'd sooner bust his balls than accept his help.

Like Earnest Emma, sitting right here next to him.

Wonder of wonders, in spite of his aching head and foul mood, he still managed to keep that lid on his temper. "I can deal with that."

Frey regarded him with surprise and suspicion. "So no hard feelings?"

"That you don't want to go slummin' with me?" He pulled up to the curb in front of an old double-gallery house that had been converted into apartments. Turning to her, he flashed his widest, most harmless smile. "Darlin,' I'll be so good you'll think I'm a goddamned choirboy."

Two

As Emma briskly walked up the sidewalk to the old house, with its peeling white paint and genteel air of decline, she shot a surreptitious look at the man ambling along beside her, his hands shoved deep into the pockets of his black leather coat.

Choirboy?

No chance of that, even if he had the looks for it— pretty in a way only a man could be pretty and still wholly, potently male. It almost made her teeth ache, all that golden blond, ooey-gooey goodness.

The day she'd met Halloran, her knee-jerk response was that he probably skated along on his physical appeal, because it didn't seem likely he'd been gifted with intelligence as well as a face that would've given Botticelli wet dreams. And, as she'd quickly noticed, his taste in clothes didn't exactly scream "take me seriously," either.

Halloran stopped abruptly, interrupting her musings, and Emma turned as he brought his hand close to his mouth, blew out a breath, and then inhaled.

"Oh, man." Grimacing, he looked at her. "Got any gum?"

Resisting an urge to roll her eyes, she patted her blazer's pockets. Finding a half-empty pack of cinnamon gum, she tossed it over to him.

He caught it neatly, again flashing a wide, disarming grin that was an odd mix of sweet and bad-boy sexy, especially with his blondish beard stubble and the visible ravages of one humdinger of a hangover. "Thanks."

"I'm sure anybody you question this morning will thank me, too."

She continued toward the house, but not before sneaking another peek at Halloran, faintly resentful at how he made her feel like a plain sparrow fluttering along beside a strutting, glorious peacock.

Most men in his shape would be lucky to match their socks, but Halloran looked as flamboyant as ever in casual black pants, a shirt sporting a retro bowling print in electric shades of red, blue, and yellow, and a skinny red silk tie. His short leather coat, which nicely accentuated his broad shoulders, concealed his shoulder rig, but not his detective shield.

Good thing, because without it he didn't come across very coplike. The majority of detectives she'd known were understated types who blended into the woodwork, and she'd been advised early on in her career not to dress to draw attention to herself. Obviously, Bobby Halloran had skipped over that part in the rule book.

Or, more likely, he didn't care, which just underscored the doomed nature of this "partnership." On top of all that, Emma found the entire physical package completely distracting, and, good God, distractions were the last thing she needed right now in the craze-o-rama that was her life.

Since she couldn't get around working with him, she might as well strike up a conversation. "So this is it?"

"Yup. And that must be the landlord. What did you say his name was again?"

"You should've looked over Delgado's report," she said tartly, sizing up the beefy, seedy-looking man on the porch.

"No disrespect to Rosie, who's a damn good cop, but I'm here to form my own opinions. So what's his name?"

"Herb Demaris."

"It don't look like Herb's happy to see us."

True enough, and the landlord, wearing an expression ripe with annoyance, tapped his foot on the porch as she and Halloran climbed the steps, which creaked with their every step.

"Hello, Mr. Demaris." Emma motioned to her badge. "I'm Detective Frey. We talked a short while ago on the phone."

Demaris, wearing paint-splattered jeans and a ragged Mardi Gras sweatshirt, was a middle-aged man with a barrel chest, bushy gray hair, and an old-time handlebar mustache. He peered at her as if his eyes couldn't quite focus, then at Halloran, and frowned. "Who's he?"

"Detective Halloran. We're both here to look at the vandalized apartment."

"I don't understand. The cops were here for *hours* yesterday."

"The case was transferred to us this morning. We need to quickly look over the scene for ourselves."

"And will this be it? Because I've got a hell of a mess in there that'll take days to clean up. And the repairs are going to cost me plenty, too. I need to get started as soon as possible."

"We won't be long. We really appreciate your help," Emma politely assured the man, cuing in to his stiff posture and obvious discomfort.

Guns and badges did that to people. Early on in her career, it had been a heady rush to have that kind of power and intimidation. Now it was just another part of the job she took for granted.

"So you don't mind if we take a look around?" Halloran asked, more out of courtesy than any real need for permission.

"No, but make it quick." The man scowled. "I'll show you the way."

With Halloran close behind her, Emma followed Demaris inside. It had started out as the home of a wealthy family back in the days when rich plantation owners built summerhouses in the city. Remnants of antebellum elegance still existed in the architectural details, high windows and ceilings—and the curving staircase where hoop-skirted Southern belles had once descended, faces flirtatiously hidden behind fans, to meet their waiting beaux. Similar to many older buildings in New Orleans, it wore a patina of age and smelled faintly musty, with a hint of dust and mold.

The Mitsumi apartment comprised the northwest half of the first floor. Not that she could miss it, as the mangled door hung off its hinges and fingerprint powder liberally smudged the beige paint on either side of the doorframe.

"Guess we can narrow down the method of entry to a

crowbar and heavy boots," Halloran said dryly, poking at the splintered gash by the doorknob and plate.

"I was going to nail a tarp over it until I can get the door fixed," the landlord offered, standing aside.

Emma nodded, although not really interested in his repair plans, and gingerly pushed the door aside, hoping it wouldn't crash to the floor. She became aware of an unpleasant odor, and as she stepped into the apartment, the stench of spoiled food hit her full on.

She glanced at Halloran, hoping the smell wouldn't send him running for the azalea bushes outside. He paled, lips thinning and nostrils flaring slightly, but other than that he showed no signs of distress.

Probably because he'd had lots of practice working crime scenes the morning after a bender.

"You came down to the apartment after receiving a complaint of loud music, is that correct?" Emma pulled out her notebook and pen, and turned to Demaris, who stood poised at the threshold, as if afraid to cross it.

"Right; nothing out of the ordinary. So I came downstairs to tell Chloe to knock it off, and found the door like this. I went inside, saw what had happened, and turned off the music. Then I called the cops."

"And the apartment was empty when you entered?"

"Yes, thank God. It never occurred to me the guys who did this might still be around. I still get the shakes when I think about what could've happened if I'd surprised them."

"Right. Keep that in mind if you encounter a similar situation again." Emma noticed Halloran slowly circling the room—still wearing his sunglasses. Turning back to the glum-faced landlord, she asked, "Have you heard from Ms. Mitsumi since yesterday?"

"For the third time, no." Demaris sounded more weary than impatient. "As I keep telling you people, Chloe's a big girl. She doesn't check in with me. And she doesn't exactly keep regular hours, anyway."

"And to the best of your knowledge, she wasn't living with anybody at the time?"

"Not that I was aware of, and she's never been the discreet type, if you know what I mean."

"I don't. Could you please explain?"

A dull red slowly tinged the man's cheekbones. "She's a screamer."

Okay; image coming through, loud and clear.

Emma glanced at Halloran, curious to see his response, since he allegedly knew the woman. But he was hunkered down beside a toppled-over curio cabinet, unmindful of the glass shards beneath his polished black shoes, and peering over the top of his sunglasses at scattered knickknacks.

She turned her attention back to Demaris. "I looked over the statement you made yesterday. You provided the names of several of Ms. Mitsumi's friends, as well as contact information on her place of employment. Is there anything else you'd like to add at this time? Either about the victim or the break-in? Anything you might've remembered later, or forgotten to tell Detective Delgado?"

"Nope. I don't socialize with my renters. All I care about is if they pay their rent on time. I don't keep track of their social calendars or sex habits."

He sounded certain enough that she didn't see any need to question him further. With a perfunctory smile, Emma handed him her card.

"Thank you, Mr. Demaris. I appreciate your taking

the time to talk to us again. If you should hear from Ms. Mitsumi or happen to think of anything else that might be useful to us, no matter how minor it seems, please give me a call."

Understanding that he'd been dismissed, the man backed out, his relief palpable. After his footsteps faded away, Emma gingerly made her way through the debris toward Halloran.

"What are you looking at?"

"Nothing much. Whoever hit this place had a good time busting up things." He held up what looked like one of those little ceramic cherubs her mother liked collecting—except this one was headless. "They're not worth much, she couldn't hide anything inside one, so why break them?"

"Good question."

Emma surveyed the wreckage of the living room, still sensing the lingering shreds of fury in the air, the frustration that had driven the intruders to destroy the apartment. No piece of furniture had been left untouched; even the curtains had been slashed. Books and CDs had been dumped from their shelves, and the TV screen was shattered. The stereo, because it had been used to disguise the sounds of destruction, was untouched, although the speaker covers had been dismantled and crushed.

"It's a good thing she wasn't home when these guys broke in, otherwise we'd be responding to a homicide. Or at least a nasty assault." Emma pushed a wisp of hair from her eyes. "I take it you've been here before. Give me a tour."

Yes, she was fishing—and not being subtle about it—

but she really wanted a better idea about Halloran's past relationship to Chloe Mitsumi, although from the captain's hints, she figured it had been an intimate one.

Halloran smiled, which pretty much confirmed her suspicions, and stood. "No call for a tour. It's an apartment, not a palace. There's no more than the usual: living room, kitchen, bathroom, bedroom."

Nodding, Emma moved to the center of the living room, looking around, but nothing in the mess provided any obvious red flags or clues. Yet she was still very aware of the heat of Halloran's body beside her, and the expensive, spiced scent of his cologne she could smell even with the sour stench wafting from the kitchen.

Halloran finally took off his sunglasses and hooked them on his shirt pocket. "Yessiree, somebody wanted something real bad. Let's see what the rest of the place looks like."

Together, they walked into the kitchen, where drawers and cupboards had been emptied, and a few plates and glasses broken. After another quick, wordless survey, Emma picked her way over the scattered remains of congealed liquids and spoiling food, and headed into the bathroom. It looked just as bad, with makeup, styling products, and tampons scattered across the floor, countertop, and tub. Packages of birth control pills—and hey, the same brand as hers—had been opened and dumped. On an apparently artistic whim, one of the intruders had smeared lipstick over the white tile walls in vivid slashes of crimson, rose, and dark purple.

"Somebody had a sense of humor." Halloran motioned at a smiley face drawn on the mirror. "Kinda warms the cockles of your heart, don't it?"

Pursing her lips, his solid presence still uncomfortably

close behind her, Emma headed to the bedroom, which seemed to have sustained the most damage. Somebody had slashed all the clothing—and it was expensive clothing, too. Leathers, silks, linens . . . even the dozens of shoes and boots hadn't escaped damage. The ripped mattress had been shoved aside, and hundreds of photographs lay scattered across the floor, along with the wilted remains of potted plants and dirt.

She picked up the photo of a woman in a little black dress, who radiated a blatant come-hitherness even in a picture. Small-boned and exotic, with her hip-length black hair, full mouth, and dark, upturned eyes, the woman had the whole Oriental-mystique and Dragon-Lady-femme-fatale routine down pat.

Emma showed the photo to Halloran. "Chloe Mitsumi?"

"The one and only."

Emma pocketed the photograph, wondering at his droll tone, then looked around again. The room's two tall windows, both liberally dusted with fingerprint powder, caught her attention. "The windows are closed."

Halloran stepped up beside her. "Yeah, so what? It's January."

"Delgado's report said the north window was open." She looked over at him. "Somebody must've closed it."

"The landlord, or one of the uniforms. Probably to keep out insects and animals, considering all that food in the kitchen."

"Or somebody came back in here after our guys left."

Emma picked up a purple leather skirt from off the floor and traced the holes in the slashed lining. Halloran likewise examined a pair of jeans that had the pockets turned inside out. Putting it aside, he hooked the strap of a red lace bra on his finger and held it up. "Look at this."

"Slinky." Emma arched a brow. "Not your color, though."

"Pay attention, Detective Frey." Halloran made a *tsk-tsk* sound. "The cup linings have been slit."

At that, the significance behind all this damage suddenly made sense, and she met his gaze over the ruins of the bed.

"You thinking what I'm thinking?" he asked.

His long-voweled, deep drawl washed over her like warm caramel, thick and sweet. More than a little unnerved by her reaction, Emma looked away, shaking off the feeling, and dropped the leather skirt to the floor.

"They were searching for something small enough to hide in a bra, the lining of a skirt, or in a package of food." She sighed. "Great. I was sort of hoping they were after a multi-ton pink elephant. I could use a lucky break."

To her surprise, Halloran gave a short bark of laughter, quickly followed by a wince. "Hey, don't make me laugh. It hurts."

"It could be somebody she knew," Emma added. "Somebody with a grudge. She sounds like the kind of girl who might easily get on somebody's bad side."

"She's no Miss Manners." Halloran tossed the bra aside. "She runs with a wild crowd, but generally keeps out of serious trouble."

"Unlike her brother."

Halloran shifted his focus directly to her, and for the first time she noticed how bloodshot his eyes were—and that he looked deeply, heavily tired.

A rush of sympathy washed over her, quickly followed

by guilt that she'd been so sharp with him earlier. It hadn't been necessary, and it wasn't as if her bad luck were his fault. What would it hurt now to be a little nicer to him?

"He was one mean sonofabitch, but he was a good brother," Halloran said, interrupting her little burst of self-reproach. "He took care of his sister, and always kept her clear of his business. For her part, Chloe had an impressive set of blinders where her brother was concerned. I don't think she's involved in anything illegal, unless it's petty shit like smoking a joint or two."

"You're sure of this?"

"Nothing in life is ever absolute, darlin', but I'm pretty sure."

Since Halloran called even the grandmotherly cleaning woman "darling," Emma ignored it the same way she ignored his lapses in grammar, which she suspected were as much of an act as the pretty-boy schmoozing.

Emma turned back toward the living room. "I think we've seen enough. I'll wait to hear if any prints come back, though I'm doubting there'll be much to work with. It sounds like half of New Orleans partied here at one point or another, and Delgado was sure the intruders wore gloves. Let's go."

"Where to?"

"I want to talk to the other tenants and neighbors again, but first we need to find Chloe Mitsumi. What do you think? Should we try the boutique on Magazine where she works?"

Halloran caught up with her in the hall outside the apartment. "At this time of the day, that'd be my first choice."

"Hope she gets a hell of a discount, because she's going to need a new wardrobe." Emma took a final look around her, at the door hanging off its frame, the slightly shabby elegance of the old house. "The uniforms and Delgado already contacted most of the neighbors and tenants. We'll come back to them later. You can follow up with the neighbors, I'll take the other tenants."

One side of his mouth—a nice mouth, with a full lower lip—curved in a smile. Then he popped his cinnamon gum. "Sounds good."

Considering that it would take days to contact all of the woman's acquaintances—having Halloran might not be such a liability after all—her first priority was to find Mitsumi, verify her safety, and then question her.

Solving the case would be easier if she could establish not only a motive, but whether or not anything was stolen. Also, there had to be a reason why Mitsumi up and disappeared after discovering her trashed apartment.

"Does it concern you that this woman's gone missing?" Emma asked as they walked down the porch steps.

Again, he popped his gum in a steady rhythm. "Chloe can take care of herself."

If that wasn't a provocative statement, she didn't know what was. "Really?"

"Really." Halloran winked—winked?—at her. "But I agree we need to find her. Otherwise, we ain't got shit to work with."

As she neared the car, Emma headed for the driver's side, but Halloran swiftly maneuvered his way there first, to her annoyance.

"Remember, you defer to me," he said. "That means I'm driving, and you're not arguing."

Since he hadn't left her a choice, Emma headed back to the passenger's side, yanked the door shut, and buckled her seat belt as he hit the accelerator and muscled his way into traffic. From what she could hear on the radio, the bad guys were hopping today, and she listened to the transmissions—until she suddenly realized that Halloran was taking a strange route toward Magazine.

When Armstrong Park whizzed past her window, she asked, "What are you doing?"

"I'm taking a quick detour to the Iberville projects. There's somebody I need to see over there first."

"Halloran, we need to find Chloe Mitsumi. That's our—"

"This won't take long. Promise." Again, he flashed that beguiling half-smile. "Just make sure your badge and gun are visible. It can get a little rough down here."

He drove with a sureness that told her he knew exactly where he was going, and she tensed, more alert, as they passed through run-down blocks of public housing. She and the angelic-looking Halloran didn't exactly blend in with the project's predominantly black residents. Even the youngest children, playing in the streets or on patchy bits of lawn, could pick out an unmarked police car, and stopped what they were doing as Halloran drove past. Older residents watched from porch steps or lawn chairs, sometimes nodding a greeting. Clusters of young men and women stood on street corners or next to parked cars, rap music blaring from boom boxes, and Emma could almost feel their stares as the car passed them. A squad on routine patrol drove by, and Halloran raised a hand in salute to the other officer.

Finally, he pulled up before a square, multistory brown brick apartment building indistinguishable from those surrounding it. Poverty and hard times hung over the place like a cloud, despite the bright morning sun.

"What's going on?" she demanded as he turned off the ignition.

"A follow-up on a domestic assault. Just wait here." He slammed the car door shut behind him, and walked toward the complex's main door with long, unhurried strides.

Emma quickly got out of the car. Like hell would she stay behind. She was his partner—no matter how reluctantly, and if only for a short time—and partners watched each other's backs. Period.

Ahead, Halloran reached the front door as it swung open to reveal a short, thin black man who was talking over his shoulder, presumably to someone behind him.

Halloran stopped short. "Hey, Raymond. Just the man I've come to see."

The man whipped his head around, eyes widening. "God*dammit*!"

Immediately, he tried to slam the door shut, but Halloran lifted his foot and kicked it open, hard.

For a split second, Emma was too startled to react. Then, as Halloran disappeared inside, she swore under her breath and ran forward, taking the steps two at a time.

Back him up back him up . . .

With that litany pounding urgently in her head, her gun almost clear of its holster, she stepped into the entryway and quickly scanned the scene.

Halloran had Raymond by the front of his shirt, and two other men stood to the side, frozen in place. Raymond was loudly cursing and protesting, spittle flying, neck corded in rage.

Behind them and down along the hallway, several doors opened as curious tenants poked their heads out to see what was going on.

Emma held up her shield, shouting, "Police. Stay inside!"

The sound of slamming doors and clicking locks immediately echoed down the hall as Raymond struggled uselessly in Halloran's white-knuckled grip, glaring. "What the fuck you doing, man? You got no business—"

"Shut up," Halloran said pleasantly—then he hoisted the man up into the air, ignoring his choking gasps and kicking feet, and threw him into the opposite wall.

Raymond hit with a meaty thud and a grunt of pain before sliding to the floor, head drooping.

Too stunned to do more than stare, Emma didn't react until Halloran lunged forward. She grabbed the back of his coat, but he effortlessly shoved her aside and against the wall. With a wince at a stinging pain in her shoulder, she quickly regained her balance and moved toward him again.

And . . . now what?

She had no idea what was going down here, but every instinct told her to at least act as if she were supporting him, to show a united front with not even a whiff of weakness.

Raymond, his eyes rolling in fear, saw her come up behind Halloran. "Get him off me!"

"You have a problem following orders, don't you? I said, shut up." Hunkering down, Halloran grabbed the man's shirt again and yanked him forward until they were eye to eye.

Emma hovered uneasily at Halloran's back, her gaze darting between the scene in front of her and Raymond's two friends, who still hadn't moved a muscle. For a brief moment, an eerie quiet filled the hall, except for the sound of labored breathing and the distant, muffled wail of a baby.

"Now listen up, because I'm only gonna say this once." Halloran smiled, deep dimples creasing his face as he continued in a soft, growling drawl. "She dies, you sonofabitch, and I promise I'll be coming after you."

After releasing Raymond, who flopped back against the wall, Halloran stood, briefly catching Emma's gaze. Cold fury glittered in his eyes, and a dark, violent current of tension radiated outward from every rigid line of his body.

A tingle of fear slithered up her spine, and the angry protest on the tip of her tongue died away.

Halloran turned, breaking the uneasy moment, then straightened his tie, smoothed back his hair, and walked past her as if nothing of consequence had just transpired.

As he headed out the door, Emma faced the man sprawled on the floor, still spitting curses, and his two companions, who watched her in silence, flat-eyed and sullen. She slowly backed toward the door, hand on her gun, not turning her back on them until she'd cleared the building. Even then, she kept checking over her shoulder as she followed Halloran.

She caught up with her sunny-haired lunatic as he reached the car, and snapped, "What the *hell* were you doing back there?"

"Just taking care of business. Forget it." Avoiding her glare, he slid into the car, cranked the ignition, and the engine roared to life.

Emma stalked around to the other side, and after

buckling her seat belt, she leaned toward him. "Forget it? I don't think so. You kicked in a door and roughed up some brother, who's probably going to call down to the station house and—"

"Raymond won't be calling anybody. Don't concern yourself. It's a personal issue."

"Nothing's personal when you're on company time— and especially not when you involve *me*!"

Halloran pulled away from the curb, looking far too relaxed for someone who'd just thrown a man into a wall. In fact, it looked as if that burst of violence had left him feeling one hundred percent better. Color had returned to his face, and a renewed vitality seemed to shimmer around him, like a glow.

"I told you to wait in the car," he said calmly. "If you'd listened to me, then you wouldn't have been involved, right?"

Emma didn't argue that particular point, suspecting it would do her little good. But the second they returned to the station, she'd ask Strong to cut her loose from Halloran.

"Sorry for pushing you back like that," he said after what seemed like hours, although it couldn't have been much more than five or ten minutes. "I didn't hurt you, did I?"

"No." Her hands were shaking slightly, more from shock than fear. That violence had exploded from out of nowhere, taking her completely by surprise, and part of her still couldn't believe he'd thrown a man into a *wall*. "And you're just damn lucky they didn't kick your ass or shoot you before I got there. God, you scared me half to death."

She dies, you sonofabitch, and I promise I'll be coming after you . . .

That threat, along with the captain telling Halloran earlier to "get over it," provided a fairly clear reason behind the hallway incident. She hesitated, then asked, "So who'd he beat up?"

Emma studied his profile as she waited for an answer, amazed all over again that beneath his handsome, stylish facade lurked a capacity for such casual brutality.

"C'mon, Halloran. You owe me that much."

He shrugged, unperturbed. "His girlfriend. It's your usual domestic battery situation, and it's not the first time. Me and Raymond, we've had more than a few confrontations. Guys like him, the only language they listen to is violence—and it's the only thing they respect."

"That doesn't justify a use of force. What you did back there goes against everything we stand for. We're the good guys, remember?"

Halloran didn't respond. Instead, he rolled down the window to let the January air rush through the car's interior. Registering the welcome relief of the cool wind, it dawned on her that she was, quite literally, hot with anger, and a quick peek in the side mirror showed her flushed cheeks.

It surprised her that he'd noticed—and quietly done something about it. Not that she'd thank him, considering he was the reason for her rocketing blood pressure, and since it appeared Halloran had closed the subject, Emma let the car fill with her silent disapproval, figuring he'd get the message without her having to say another word.

The remainder of the ride passed in an awkward silence, but she'd calmed herself down by the time they reached their destination on Magazine Street, a shopping mecca that bustled with traffic and people.

Chloe Mitsumi worked in the Wild Orchid, a trendy and expensive boutique that was definitely *the* place to be seen—unless, apparently, you were Chloe Mitsumi.

"I'm sorry," said the store's manager, a sleek, forty-something woman named Leena Bondurant. "Chloe called me at home early this morning and told me what happened. She's terribly upset, as you can imagine. She asked if she could take the next few weeks off, to find a new place and take care of matters with the police, her lawyer, and her insurance company. I'm sure she's terribly overwhelmed, so of course I agreed. It's the least I could do."

The woman's words added weight to Emma's suspicion that Chloe was deliberately making herself scarce. She glanced at Halloran to see if he'd caught that bit of disturbing news, but he wasn't listening. He was far too busy checking price tags on a rack of slinky evening dresses.

Maybe if the situation at hand didn't involve destruction, death, or threatening bodily harm, it wasn't worth his full attention.

Turning back to the manager, Emma pulled out her notepad. "She said she was going to contact the police, her lawyer, and her insurance company?"

Bondurant nodded. "Something like that. It was early, and I wasn't exactly taking notes."

"So you have no idea where she is right now?"

"No. I'm sorry. If I did, I'd tell you. Why? Is something wrong?"

"We need to talk to her, and we're having a little trouble contacting her to leave a message." Emma took out a business card and handed it to the woman. "If she calls again, or if you see her, can you please tell her to contact me immediately?"

"I certainly will." The manager paused. "She's not in any kind of trouble, is she?"

Picking up on the caution, Emma asked mildly, "Why do you ask?"

"I know she likes to have fun, but I wonder about the people she parties with. Don't get me wrong, I like Chloe very much. She's been with us over three years, and she's an excellent worker. She's great with customers, rarely calls in sick, and she's always on time and willing to do extra little jobs. But sometimes I worry . . . You know about her brother, right?"

"Yes, I'm aware of that situation. Do you believe she is in some way involved with his prior criminal activities?"

Bondurant shook her head, looking shocked. "Oh, no. No. Chloe hated her brother with a passion."

This was news. She'd assumed, from Halloran's earlier comments, that the two had been close.

"Every once in a while these young men come in to see her." The woman shrugged, looking a little uncomfortable. "Maybe it's nothing, and I've only seen them around a few times since Chloe's been with us, but I noticed because they're not the kind of people you'd normally see in a store like this."

"What do you mean?"

Halloran had asked the question. Without Emma noticing, he'd moved in close behind her—apparently he'd been paying attention, after all.

"Well . . . let's just say they appeared to embrace a rougher kind of lifestyle."

"How many were there? Do you remember what they

looked like? Were they in any way dressed the same? Any distinctive tattoos?" Halloran's interest was plainly piqued, which in turn piqued Emma's. "Would you recognize any of them if you saw them again?"

Bondurant blinked, flustered by his rapid-fire questions. "There's two or three of them, and they're usually black, but every now and again there's this Asian-looking guy with them. They're full of attitude and loud, like they want to cause trouble. They made me nervous, and the other customers, too. But I don't remember details, and I don't know that I'd recognize them if I ran into them on the street. Sorry."

Emma jotted down the information. "When was the last time they came by to see Ms. Mitsumi?"

"Last Tuesday. It was the first instance in at least six or seven months."

"How did Ms. Mitsumi act around these men?" Emma asked. "Did she seem comfortable with them? Afraid? Angry?"

"She was pleasant enough, but in a distant kind of way. I never got the impression she considered them friends, just people she knew in passing."

"Did you catch any names?" Emma persisted.

"No, I'm afraid not. I kept my distance. They made me nervous."

"That's fine. You did great." Halloran smiled at the manager, who smiled back, her demeanor suddenly less reserved, her expression softening—almost flirtatious, in a discreet sort of way. The woman inched closer to him, cutting in front of Emma to do so, as if she'd completely forgotten her presence.

Note to self: From here on out, have Halloran question all the women . . .

"You've been very helpful, Ms. Bondurant." In his drawl, "Bondurant" sounded melodic, seductive.

From behind the manager, Emma tipped her head to catch Halloran's attention, injecting as much skepticism into her look as possible. In response, he cranked the charm even higher.

Emma almost laughed, and she had a sneaking suspicion that was his intent. Aware he'd upset her, he wanted to coax her out of her bad mood.

Unfortunately for him—though fortunately for her—she was mostly immune to schmoozy charm.

"If you do talk to Ms. Mitsumi and pass on Detective Frey's message, would you also mention to her that Detective Halloran would like to talk to her? She knows how to contact me."

"I certainly will, Detective. Can you leave me your number just in case?"

No doubt to make note of it for her own purposes.

Then, as if suddenly remembering Emma's existence, the manager turned, looking a little sheepish, and Emma managed to blank her "I'm gonna puke" expression just in time.

"And thank you, too, Detective Frey. I hope you'll help Chloe straighten out this mess. That poor girl. After all the grief she's been through, she hardly needs this."

Emma nodded, then signaled Halloran to follow her out the door.

"So what's the plan?" he asked as they crossed the street to where he'd parked the car—illegally, if they'd been anybody but the cops.

"I thought I'd make a few calls to see if someone knows where she is, check back on the prints, then write up my notes."

"I'll drop you off at the station. I have a couple other appointments this morning."

Emma eyed him. "Does it involve beating up any more people?"

If he was offended by her question, he didn't let it show. "Nope."

His nonchalance didn't sit right with her. It was as if he'd completely moved on after what he'd done: out of sight, out of mind.

Well, she didn't work that way. This man was trouble waiting to happen, and she could not—would not—open herself up to that kind of pain again.

When they were in the car and on their way back to North Rampart, Emma turned in the seat toward him. "I told you I testified against bad cops, and yet you roughed up that guy in front of me anyway. I don't doubt he had it coming to him, and then some, but . . ."

Her voice trailed off as she watched for a reaction, even a glimmer of remorse, but saw nothing.

Frowning, she quietly got to the point: "Aren't you even a little concerned that I'll go to Strong and report what you did?"

As he stopped for a red light, Halloran looked at her from behind his dark sunglasses and shrugged. "Truth is, Frey, I can't seem to care."

Three

Emma pushed through the station house main doors and slowly headed to her desk, still mulling over Halloran's last words to her: *I can't seem to care . . .*

It wasn't so much what he'd said, though that was disturbing enough, but how he'd said it that bothered her. Not angry or loud with puffed-up bravado. Not defensive, or even a careless, unemotional brush-off.

No, he'd sounded painfully weary, almost . . . resigned? Emma couldn't put a finger on the exact shade of emotion in his voice, but she couldn't stop thinking about it, either, or shake off this sense of unease and worry.

Dammit, she wanted to put as much distance as possible between herself and that man, *not* feel sorry for him. And the sooner she prevented any softer emotions from undercutting her instincts for self-preservation, the better.

Giving free rein to emotions led to nothing but grief. She'd seen it, over and over, in her parents' deteriorating relationship, in the selfish, nihilistic attitudes of the los-ers she dealt with on a daily basis, month after month, year after year—even in her own late, unlamented, and pathetically naive quest to see justice served, no matter what the personal cost.

And in the end, it had cost her plenty.

As she approached her workstation, Emma took a deep breath and strode briskly past the other occupied desks. That way, she wouldn't have to acknowledge the speculative looks, suspicion, judgment, or even flashes of pity. She'd been working hard and keeping to herself for over a week, and yet wisps of silent disapproval still trailed after her wherever she went.

On the positive side, it wasn't as bad as in L.A., where a lot of people had been downright hostile. She'd accepted that the fallout from the scandal would inevitably follow her no matter where she moved, but going home to the city where she'd grown up had appealed to her need for comfort and familiarity, her itch to wipe the slate clean and start over. With luck, a little time, and distance, she'd soon ease back into her old routines and get back to what she did best: locking up the bad guys.

Closing the Mitsumi case was exactly what the doctor ordered. If nothing else, focusing on that would keep her from obsessing too much about what people were whispering about her.

She sat at her desk, crowded with hand-me-down case reports, thick procedural manuals, her computer, phone, coffee cup, another half-empty pack of Dentyne gum, and a small vase of limp flowers with its "Welcome!" card still attached.

After opening Delgado's report, she tried rereading the notes and examining crime scene photos, but she couldn't concentrate. She was too distracted by a prickling awareness of being watched, even as she wondered if maybe, out of knee-jerk habit, she was seeing hostility and distrust where none existed.

"Frey. You're back already. How'd it go?"

Emma turned to see Strong, coffee cup in hand, perched on Halloran's desk. Despite his polite smile, she sensed he didn't much like her, but she respected him, if for nothing else than after twenty-five years of working his way up through the ranks, he ran an efficient department. He struck her as a pragmatic, reasonably fair man. In his early fifties, he was trim, attractive, and still married to his wife of thirty years.

For a cop, that was damn near miraculous.

"It went well."

Judging by the look on his face, he'd expected a different answer. "No trouble?"

She was tempted to ask a few blunt questions about her "partner." Instead, she avoided his gaze—and the actual implication in his question.

"We still haven't located the victim, but she contacted her employer this morning to ask for time off, so she's around. I've left messages for her to call me. Whoever trashed her place was after something in particular, and I'm hoping she has the good sense to come to us before they find her again."

Strong nodded. "That's what Delgado thought, too. By the way, where's Halloran?"

"He said he had a few appointments and would check in later." She hesitated, curiosity still warring with caution, then casually asked, "Does he have a drinking problem?"

"No more than anybody else in this department."

Strong didn't appear concerned, or surprised, by the question. "As far as I know, anyway."

"It's just that I wasn't sure." Even to her own ears, she sounded overly defensive.

"Hey, it's okay. He was looking a little rough this morning, and I don't blame you for wondering. But you say you two hit it off, then?"

This time, Emma met his gaze. "Did you think we wouldn't?"

"I wasn't sure how you'd mix. He can be bullheaded, and you've got this sharp edge . . ."

He trailed off in a leading way, and Emma realized he'd handed her the perfect moment to request Halloran's removal from the case.

Do it; get it over with, quick and easy . . .

Emma hesitated, then said evenly, "Thanks for your concern, but we did fine."

Strong quirked a brow, and after a moment, he nodded. "Stay on top of this one. I don't like the sound of it. Keep me updated—and find that woman."

As Strong walked away, Emma slumped back in her chair, already doubting her impulse to keep quiet.

And where had that come from, anyway? She sure hadn't held back to protect Halloran. No, it had been about pride, stubbornness—or, most likely, a reluctance to stir up even a speck of trouble so soon after her arrival. With any luck, none of this would come back later to bite her on the ass.

Luck? As if she'd had any of *that* lately.

A wave of good ol' self-pity washed over her, tempting her to jump right in and wallow, if only for a teeny bit. What had she done to deserve this long streak of bad luck? She paid her taxes on time—and didn't even cheat—and sent cards out promptly for holidays and birthdays, flossed her teeth daily, always wore clean underwear, defrosted her freezer, changed her oil regularly, didn't kick puppies or pinch babies—

"Hey, girl. What's the matter? You look like you just lost your best friend."

Emma jumped, startled, but when she saw who stood next to her desk, she relaxed again and smiled.

Alycia Chatman was one of several detectives who'd made her feel welcome from the start. She was a small, slender black woman with broad shoulders, a lot of hair in tiny braids, thickly-lashed dark eyes, and a generous mouth that smiled a lot. She was also happily married to a patrol cop in the Fifth District, and had two teenage kids.

"I was just thinking that my life sucks right now," Emma admitted sheepishly. "Bad me. I know."

Alycia quirked a brow. "It didn't go well, huh?"

Figuring a number of nearby ears were tuning in, despite appearances to the contrary, Emma lowered her voice. "He's crazy. And way too pretty."

"That sounds like Bobby, all right." Then, her amusement fading, Alycia leaned closer. "Got a minute? There's something I need to talk to you about."

On a renewed sense of dread, Emma sighed. "I'm going to hate this, aren't I?"

"Most definitely. Which is why we're going outside. I need a cigarette break anyway."

Emma followed Alycia outside, where the earlier sunny weather had given way to a gray, bleak sky, and she buttoned her blazer at the first touch of cool air.

The North Rampart building was relatively new, so the "no smoking" rule was enforced with some diligence. A number of cops loitered outside in the brisk January breeze smoking, but Alycia walked past them. Finally, a few blocks away, she stopped and leaned against a street lamp, backed by a long line of cars parked curbside. She fished a pack of cigarettes from her jacket pocket, tapped one out, and lit it.

Emma watched the ritual with mild fascination. "I feel this overwhelming urge to point out that smoking will kill you."

"Yeah, but not before this bleeding ulcer in my gut gets me first. Or high blood pressure blows out the old ticker."

"Gee, I love being a cop. We're such an upbeat bunch."

"Ain't that the truth." Grinning, Alycia blew out a stream of smoke. "So let's talk about Bobby."

Not about to make the first move, Emma only raised a brow, waiting.

"Okay. I'll go first." Alycia's grin widened. "I'll be honest here. Blond, blue-eyed Southern boys don't generally trip my trigger, but I have to say he is one fine-looking man."

"No arguments from me."

"And he don't go too long between girlfriends, either." Alycia took another long drag. "Though they don't seem to stick around for long."

Ah, gossip: the most treasured pastime of every police department, large or small.

Although *hugely* curious, Emma did her best to act nonchalant. "His love life really isn't any of my business."

"It is when there's a betting pool based on how long it'll take him to get in your pants."

At first, she didn't think she'd heard right. But there was no mistaking the faintly disgusted expression on Alycia's face. After a brief spurt of anger, the sheer absurdity of it hit her, and Emma burst out laughing.

Alycia flicked away her cigarette ash. "Okay, that wasn't exactly the reaction I was expecting."

"Oh, I'm pissed, all right, but *please*. Are they crazy? It's not as if a man like that is ever going to give me a second look."

"You're an attractive woman, Emma, so don't you go disrespecting yourself, or—"

"I'm not, but let's be real here. Halloran strikes me as a guy with a definite 'type,' and I'm not it."

Alycia fell silent, for so long that Emma started fiddling, smoothing non-existent wrinkles from her blazer, suddenly aware she had nothing to do to keep her hands busy.

"Let me tell you something about Bobby." After a final drag, Alycia stubbed out the butt and tossed it aside. "Despite what you might hear, he's a good cop, and a good guy. He's always been decent to me, so I have no issues with him. He just naturally gets along with women, and that bothers some people. I've been around him long enough to know he's the kind of man who wears his heart on his sleeve. When he's happy, you know it. When he's messed up, he tries to hide it, but you know it anyway."

This wasn't anything Emma hadn't already figured out for herself. "I'm not sure I'm getting your point."

"My point is, you could do worse than having him covering your back. Don't let a few ignorant assholes make up your mind for you. It's not Bobby's fault some of the guys resent how women are always checking him out, or think he dresses like he's queer, and so they tell stories about him to make themselves look better."

"When we were over at the projects this morning, Halloran kicked in a door and threw a man into a wall. Just because he felt like it, as far as I can tell. I'm thinking he and I are going to have a few . . . trust issues."

"That's Bobby. He pushes it hard to the limit sometimes, I know." Alycia nodded, her expression growing thoughtful. "But you might want to give him the benefit of the doubt."

"Why? Just because he's a cop?"

Alycia sighed. "I don't need to tell you police work can be a dirty, nasty business. We deal with shit most people can't even begin to understand, and I'm not saying wearing a badge gives us the right to do anything we want. I sure don't have to tell you that a few cops sometimes go too far and make the rest of us look bad."

No; that was one subject Emma understood loud and clear.

"But we're only human. We have bad days. We get sick and still go to work. Our boyfriends cheat on us, and we still stop a guy from smacking his girlfriend around. Our kids drive us nuts, the dog next door keeps us up all night . . . and we still gotta deal with some pissant creep who just beat on a baby." Alycia's voice stayed calm, and even. "Can you honestly tell me you've never said something you shouldn't have to an asshole you're arresting, or gotten a little too rough because, just for a second or two, you got so much disgust in you that you can't keep it back?"

"No, I can't," Emma admitted. "I understand what you're saying."

"Good. It helps to remember none of us are perfect."

Emma rubbed at her forehead, trying to ease the steadily rising tension. "Can I ask one more question?"

"Sure."

"Will Halloran hold back on me?"

"As much as he can get away with."

"Meaning?"

The other woman arched a thinly plucked brow. "Meaning when he's in a mood, he tends to run with scissors and not play nice with others."

"Wonderful." Emma tipped her head back, staring up at the sunless sky, then blew out a breath, cheeks puffing. "Is he dangerous?"

"Usually only to himself. A few years back, he got shot."

A chill prickled just under her skin, raising goose bumps. "I'm not sure I want to ask this, but how?"

"He got caught up in a private vendetta, and by the time he figured out what was going on, it was too late to do more than ride it out. It caused him a lot of trouble at the time, and he was suspended for six weeks for failing to follow proper procedure."

"He seems to have that problem."

"Yeah, but not always." Alycia shifted. "And in case nobody's told you yet, the guy that shot him was Jacob Mitsumi."

"Uh-oh." In an instant, her already worrisome case took on a deeper, darker significance. "My mysteriously missing victim's brother."

"Uh-huh. I thought you ought to know." Alycia pushed away from the lamppost. "You ready to go back in?"

"My blood pressure's getting a pretty good workout today, but I think it's mostly back to normal."

As the two of them strolled back toward the building, Alycia said, "I sure don't envy you having to deal with all this shit, but if you ever need to talk about it, you're welcome to come to me. Sometimes it helps to talk."

A sharp, icy breeze cut through Emma's wool blazer and cotton shirt, and she shivered. "I still can't believe somebody would be stupid enough to bet money on Halloran noticing the color of my eyes, much less getting me in bed."

"Are you gonna talk to Strong about it?"

"And tell him what, that a few of the guys are being mean to me?" Emma gave a rueful laugh. "I don't think so."

"That's exactly what those morons are counting on. You know that, right?"

Emma nodded. "But thanks for the support, and the heads-up. I really appreciate it, Alycia."

"In a lot of ways, it's still a man's world out there, and believe me, being black *and* a woman, I know how hard it can be. We have to work long hours, deal with all the bullshit that comes our way, and still go home and be wives and mothers, housekeepers and chauffeurs."

Catching the commiserating look Emma sent her way, Alycia smiled. "It's not right that we have to work harder and prove ourselves more, and maybe someday things will change, but for now it's how we earn respect. So I get why you don't want to say anything, but remember it's not everybody giving you a hard time, okay? My best advice is to ignore it. Eventually, these guys will get bored and find somebody else to pick on."

All good points; theoretically, she had every right to register a complaint. Ten years ago, or even five years ago—when she'd been younger, more idealistic, and less patient—she *would* have complained. Now she chose her battles. Maybe she'd grown more cynical and pragmatic over time. Or maybe she'd finally wised up enough to realize not every fight was won by charging headfirst into the opposition, full of all the sound and fury of righteous indignation.

Some fights weren't worth the hassle in the long run, either. Reputations were hard to live down—as she'd painfully learned—and difficulties with coworkers and frequent transfers looked bad on a personnel jacket. Promotions often depended on staying on the good side of the desk cop who happened to be your supervisor, and since she believed success was the best revenge, she intended to achieve exactly that.

And besides, a few guys acting like Neanderthals were nothing compared to what she'd endured before hightailing it out of L.A.

"You're awful quiet," Alycia said as they approached the main doors. "Are you thinking, or getting mad?"

"Not as mad as I probably should be," she admitted. "I think I'm all angered out for the day—it's actually kind of funny, if you think about it."

Seeing Alycia's narrow-eyed skepticism, Emma couldn't help smiling. "Really. I mean, in just one morning, I've been handed a case with no suspects or motive, and a victim who doesn't want to be found; the guy I'm working with is all testosterone and trouble; I'm stuck with this hazing nobody will ever admit to; and now I'm the star attraction in a betting pool on when I'll get screwed by my so-called partner. Literally. But you know what? I don't care."

And, boy, didn't *that* sound oddly familiar?

"Good girl." Alycia briskly patted Emma on her back. "Never let the bastards get you down."

Flushed with a renewed determination, Emma swung the door open with more force than necessary, but it felt good anyway. "What's done is done. I'll deal with what I can't avoid, and blow off the rest. I'm going to clear my case and show these pricks exactly what I can do. I'm going to be a good little cop and do my job with a big, sharp smile."

Alicia let loose with a rich, full-throated chuckle. "Now you're talking. Go get 'em, tiger."

Four

Bobby made his way through the massive maze that was Charity Hospital, paying little attention to his surroundings. He'd walked these halls so many times, night and day, that he could probably find the ER or trauma unit blindfolded. He tuned out the constant hum of voices and rhythm of footsteps, the rising and falling tides of weeping and whispers, beeping and whirs of machines, the smells of disinfectant and sickness and death.

God, he hated the place.

It didn't help that he'd spent time here as a patient himself, although that was only one of the reasons why the nurses here at the trauma ICU knew him by name, and waved him in with nods or smiles.

The on-call resident, leaning against the nurses' station desk and reading a chart, looked tired and far too young for such responsibility. She looked up with a frown when he stopped in front of her, and he read her ID tag: Dr. S. Carrolton. When he displayed his shield, her frown deepened.

"Hi. Can I help you with something, Detective Halloran?"

"He's here to see Juleen," said Andrea Thurber, the head nurse, a phone headset tucked between her ear and shoulder and cradled against a tidy blond braid.

"Um . . . the assault that came in last Wednesday. Right." Dr. Carrolton stood a little straighter, tucking a strand of brown hair behind her ear, as if suddenly aware she wasn't looking her best. "She's not having a good day."

"Has she regained consciousness at all?"

"No. And her condition's deteriorating—impaired cardiopulmonary function, brain swelling . . . it doesn't look good." Carrolton paused, then added, "I'm sorry."

Bobby nodded, understanding the medical shorthand. "Can I see her?"

Carrolton shrugged. "Sure."

Catching Bobby's questioning look, Andrea covered the phone receiver with her hand and whispered, "She's alone. It's okay."

As Bobby walked away, the resident called after him, "You know, it would help if you'd stop these assholes *before* they beat their women to a bloody pulp. We can patch up bodies only so many times before they break for good."

Anger flared, only to smother beneath a rush of guilt as Bobby met the resident's flat, I've-been-up-for-eighteen-hours-straight stare. He couldn't blame her for that frustration; he'd been in her shoes too many times himself. "I'll try to remember that for next time, thanks."

Turning, he headed to a small room packed with the full range of high-tech equipment medical science had to offer, and all of it useless against the inevitable. She lay on the bed, small and still, on a ventilator and hooked up to a catheter, IVs, and monitors. As the machine breathed for her, her chest rose and fell with a sharp, mechanical precision, and even the bandages couldn't hide the extent of the damage.

If there was any dignity in dying, he sure as hell couldn't find it here. Eyes and nose still swollen, her mocha-colored skin had a grayish cast to it, where it wasn't bruised or scabbed over.

She'd been barely fourteen when he'd had his first run-in with her five years ago over her hooking. Back then, she'd been a mouthy, defiant, pretty little thing . . . but she wasn't so pretty anymore.

A nurse came in to check the IV, casting a curious look at Bobby, then left without a word. Probably because he looked like he'd snap her head off if she so much as said hello.

Slapping Raymond around had provided a moment of gratification, but it had long since faded. Seeing Juleen like this made what he'd done feel all that more futile. And stupid.

There wasn't anything he could do for girls like Juleen; he'd seen hundreds of them since he became a cop, and he'd see hundreds more. He shouldn't be this frustrated or angry. It wasn't smart; it wasn't productive.

And he knew Strong was right: All he could do was say a prayer for the lost ones, then take down the animals who got off on beating the shit out of their wives and girlfriends and kids, and trust in the system to do the rest.

For a long while, Bobby stood by the bed, listening to the *click-hiss-click-hiss* of the ventilator. The sound put him on edge, made his head throb like a bitch, and the dryness of the room aggravated his eyes, which already felt as if they were coated with sharp sand. His eyes burned, and he rubbed at them, briefly wishing he could lose himself in the peace of a dark, quiet room.

The thought brought an immediate stab of guilt—and disgust. Some big, brave cop he was, wanting to run away and hide. No matter how messed up his head had been for the past few months, it was nothing compared to what Juleen Moss had suffered, and the least he could do for her sake was do his damn job.

Or at least get it *right* this time. God, he'd been so sure of himself when he'd persuaded her to press charges after the last beating. He'd dotted all his *i*'s, crossed all his *t*'s, followed every procedure, did everything by the book. It had been an airtight case, and he'd even gotten it on the court docket.

Then she'd backed out—and to show his appreciation, Raymond had beaten her senseless. Not that he'd admitted to it, and not that Bobby had enough evidence yet to prove it. Raymond was smart, and claimed the john she'd been with had beaten her. It wouldn't be the first time for that, either, although Bobby knew better. So did Raymond; that flash of white-eyed terror in the hallway earlier told him as much.

Good. Raymond deserved to know even a small part of the helpless terror this girl had felt.

Anger flared again, only to fade into the flat, nagging sense of helplessness that had shadowed him these past few months, night and day, and he didn't even know what he'd hoped to accomplish by coming here.

Last week, the nurses told him to talk to her, that she might understand something of what he said. But what could he possibly say? Promises and excuses no longer mattered to her—and he didn't believe she could hear him, anyway.

Wherever Juleen was now, it had to be a better place and he had no wish to disturb the peace she'd found in what little time was left to her.

Finally, he turned and headed out of the ICU. Andrea, vibrant and colorful in raspberry-pink scrubs, was munching on a package of Sprees as he passed the nurses' station. Even a whiff of the candy's fruity tang made his stomach knot, but he slowed when she motioned for him to stop.

"Did you have a nice visit with Juleen?"

Bobby shrugged. "She's not too talkative today."

"A broken jaw and practically zero brain activity will do that to a girl."

"Has her mother been by?"

"She visits a couple times a day." As if sensing what he wanted to know, Andrea leaned forward and said softly, "Mom's doing as well as can be expected, and the rest of the kids are coping okay. They've brought Juleen's baby with them a couple times."

The baby. Damn, he'd forgotten about the kid. He needed to call Protective Services and find out what was up with all that.

He blew out a breath. "Has Raymond tried to come by?"

"No. Which is too bad, because we have a new crop of nursing students who need to practice inserting catheters, and I'd love to turn them loose on that man's worthless dick."

Bobby laughed; he couldn't help it. "I wish I were that

creative. I'd just shoot him on sight if I thought I could get away with it."

"You sure wouldn't find me complaining. You'd do the world a favor by taking out that sorry sack of shit before he brutalizes or kills some other girl." Andrea rolled her shoulders and sighed. "If you want to make my day the next time you come by, Bobby, tell me he's behind bars for good. Or six feet under."

Smiling, hands still in his pockets, he slowly backed toward the door. "I'm working on it, darlin'."

"Promise?"

"Cross my heart and hope to die."

Five

Emma spent a few hours talking with a number of Chloe Mitsumi's friends, none of whom knew where to find the woman—or would admit to it. When Emma returned to her desk shortly before noon, Alycia grabbed her arm and hauled her off to lunch, which turned out to be an impromptu baby shower for the departing Rosario Delgado, who was a blunt-talking and friendly woman. At the restaurant, the three of them were joined by a small group of female officers and a female detective from a neighboring district. Once Emma overcame her initial dismay at not having a baby gift, she enjoyed their little estrogen fest over salads, coffee, and pastel baby gifts.

"Emma came from L.A.," Alycia said as dessert arrived, then lightly touched Emma's shoulder. "Hollywood."

Even to cops, the name "Hollywood" conjured glamorous images of movie stars and movers-and-shakers, and Emma fielded a barrage of curious questions not unlike the ones Bobby Halloran had asked earlier. Only this time, she didn't feel defensive, even relating a few tales of actors caught in compromising positions with prostitutes, and more serious shop talk on high-priced call girls and escort services.

Then one of the women asked, "Why'd you leave L.A.? Sounds like you enjoyed it there."

Immediately Emma tensed. It was an automatic, defensive reaction—and she couldn't help it. After a moment, she said, "I was involved in an internal investigation that resulted in several officers being convicted and sent to prison. A lot of people resented me, and I just wasn't comfortable working there any longer. When the NOPD offered me this job, I took it."

The woman who'd asked the question looked embarrassed, then concerned. "Sorry to hear that. Must've been rough for you, but you did the right thing."

The sympathy seemed genuine, and Emma relaxed, smiling a little. It came as a huge relief that none of the women looked at her with disapproval, but she felt a twinge of guilt because she'd expected the worst in the first place. Going on the defensive every time somebody asked about L.A. wasn't helping her make friends.

Picking up on Emma's discomfort, Alycia leaned across the table and asked Rosario if the baby had dropped yet, and the conversation soon turned to labor and delivery, sex, and then finally men, and if the other restaurant patrons were offended by the raucous laughter and explicit conversation, nobody had the guts to complain.

Emma didn't participate very much in the girl talk, but smiled and laughed at the stories, all the while thinking that, for the first time since she'd moved back to New Orleans almost two weeks ago, her life felt almost normal again.

By the time they left the restaurant, the weather had turned from cloudy to rainy, and Emma ended up soaked and thoroughly chilled just running from the parking garage to the station. Her good mood faded a bit when she not only failed to find Halloran back at his desk, but found no messages from him, either.

When she approached one of the detectives—a freckled strawberry blond name Brian Mottson—he grinned in a way that wasn't exactly friendly. "What's the matter, Frey? Bobby ditch you already?"

"If I knew, I wouldn't be asking the question, would I?" It took an effort, but she kept her voice cool and even.

"You gotta watch that boy. He's tricky."

"So I've heard. I take it your answer is no, you haven't seen him."

"Not since you left this morning. Check with Strong. Maybe he called in."

She nodded her thanks and sought out her captain, who reacted with impatience to her question. "Bobby's been working on a series of muggings near City Park and said he'd be back later this afternoon. Christ, if you need him, page him."

"Thanks. I'll do that." With Strong still staring at her, Emma added, "I'm thinking I can make the rounds of a few bars and dance clubs, ask questions about the Mitsumi woman."

"You don't need my permission to do your job." Strong picked up a pen and pulled a pile of paperwork toward him, clearly dismissing her. "Go."

Emma wasted no time in getting out of the office, and immediately set out to poke around whatever clubs and bars she could find that opened early. New Orleans was a party town, and it would take hours to work through

Chloe Mitsumi's known hangouts. Emma had taken the woman's photo with her, even if Madame Barfly didn't strike her as the low-key, forgettable sort.

She drove along familiar streets, glad to be out and doing her job again. After a while, she cracked the car window to let in the cool, fresh air. The tension that had seemingly taken up permanent residence in her shoulders lately began to ease, and she couldn't help smiling as she half listened to the radio traffic.

Yes, indeed. Damn good to be back in the saddle, patrolling the streets and, whenever possible, making the lives of evildoers everywhere a little less comfortable.

Within an hour, however, frustration blunted her good mood. At one popular Warehouse District bar, the manager not only recognized Chloe, but cheerfully informed Emma another detective had been by earlier, asking the same questions.

"Blond? Youngish?" Emma tried to keep the chill out of her voice, but judging by the suddenly wary look in the manager's eyes, she wasn't entirely successful.

"Yup. He came by a couple hours ago."

With a polite smile, Emma murmured her thanks, then stalked back to the car and slammed her door shut in a burst of temper.

What was Halloran trying to prove by going behind her back like this? Did the weasel really think she wouldn't find out?

Then, realizing what she was doing, she forced herself to calm down. Again, she was jumping to the worst possible conclusions. It was entirely possible Halloran had returned while she was at lunch and, instead of waiting for her, had decided to continue working on his own caseload, stopping by a few bars on his way to check on

Mitsumi. Maybe he'd figured this sort of thing wasn't worth leaving her a message or going through the huge inconvenience of paging her, and—

Whoops. There was that pesky cynicism again, rearing its ugly, sharp little head.

She pulled out her notebook and thumbed to where she'd jotted down his pager number. She paused, torn between trusting him to eventually update her and wanting to demand an explanation right this very second.

"Oh, hell," she muttered, and put the notebook away. If she had to expend any energy on chewing him out, she might as well wait until they were face-to-face. When they met again, she'd ask for a rundown on the details of his bar search. That would be a more effective—and professional—way of reminding him this was *her* case and he'd better keep her in the loop so she wouldn't waste time asking questions where he already had.

The final few bars she checked gave her the same results—Chloe Mitsumi had been around, but not within the last couple days—and by that time, it was getting late. Emma headed back to Esplanade to question several of the neighbors who hadn't been around when Delgado and the patrol cops had gone door to door. Those she found at home had nothing useful to offer: It was too dark, nothing looked suspicious, they'd been asleep, been out, or didn't think anything of the loud music or what had sounded like one heck of a good party. She handed out her card as if it were candy, hoping somebody would eventually call her with even the tiniest tidbit of useful news.

Or, best of all, Madame Barfly herself would give her a jingle.

At five-thirty, Emma called it quits for the day. She returned to her desk, nodding politely to the detectives still hanging around, and returned phone calls and completed some paperwork. It was nearly six-thirty, and still no sign of her "partner," when she decided to head home and play catch-up with Halloran in the morning.

On her way to her car, however, she spotted Halloran walking toward her, his red tie and open black coat flapping in the breeze. He saw her, too, and slowed, looking like he wanted to avoid a confrontation.

No *chance of that, pretty boy.*

Emma stopped short. "I figured you'd left for the day."

He held up his hand, nodding. "I know. Sorry. I meant to call, but I lost track of the time, and then I had to cool my heels over at the courthouse for longer than I expected. You heading home already?"

"It's after six-thirty."

"Yeah, but I thought you wanted to find Chloe."

"I do." She pinned him with her best don't-shit-me stare. "How did your search for her go? And don't bother denying it, Halloran. While checking a few bars earlier, I found out another detective was asking questions about Mitsumi. I'm told he was a blond, on the youngish side. Good-looking, according to one female bartender. Gosh, guess that would be you."

Halloran returned her stare, blank-faced. "So you didn't find her, huh?"

"No," she retorted. "Did you?"

"Can't say as I did."

He moved closer, acting not the least bit guilty, much less offering any apology. Not that she'd really expected one.

"But you want to find Chloe, right?" he asked.

Emma narrowed her eyes, shifting the strap of her attaché higher onto her shoulder; the blasted thing weighed a ton. "Duh."

His lips twitched. "Okay, I deserved that. But what I mean is, how much do you want to clear this case?"

"Haven't you heard a word I've said to you all day? You know I—"

"How much?"

The sharpness of his voice startled her. "Bad enough to taste it."

As she spoke, his gaze dropped to her mouth, and his lips slowly curved in that wide, sweet smile that made her heart beat faster, as much with alarm as . . . well, as anything else.

Disguising her discomfort beneath sarcasm, Emma asked, "Is that answer good enough for you, Halloran?"

"How about you call me Bobby, and I'll call you Emma? If we're working together, we may as well call each other by our first names. What d'ya think?"

Every now and again his deep drawl thickened. Briefly, she wondered why, then shrugged it off. "What I think is that you talk a lot but rarely say anything. I've got a long commute, I'm hungry, and I really don't have the patience for a round of twenty questions."

"Darlin', this town don't come alive until after the sun goes down, so if you want to find Chloe, we're gonna have to do it on our own time."

Emma gave him a doubtful look. "Shouldn't we request overtime first?"

"What's the problem with a couple off-duty cops hitting the bars together? And if they happen to run across somebody they need to talk to . . . hey, it's a lucky break, right?"

The friendly, congenial pretense didn't wash with her,

but he was good at answering her questions with questions, countering her arguments with logic. She could push back, but he had a point. Checking bars off-duty couldn't hurt, and it wasn't like she had plans for the night. Besides, if she refused, he'd undoubtedly go off on his own anyway—and she couldn't have that. "How come you're so cooperative all of a sudden?"

"I want to make sure Chloe's okay. So what do you say, are we gonna do this or not?"

"All right. You talked me into it."

"Okay." He seemed taken aback by her abrupt acquiescence, but the reaction came and went so quickly she couldn't be sure. "If she's hitting her usual haunts, it won't be until after eight. I can pick you up around seven-thirty."

"Do you really think she'll show? If she's spooked, wouldn't she want to hide instead of going barhopping?"

"Chloe moves in mysterious ways." He shrugged. "It's worth checking into, that's all I'm saying."

Emma didn't quite trust him, but as long as he was helping her—and she could keep an eye on him—she'd play fair. "I'll see you at seven-thirty, then." She waited as he pulled out his notepad and a pen, then gave him directions to her apartment in Kenner, and her telephone number as well.

"Okay. Got it." He moved past her, heading in the direction of the station. "Catch you later, darlin'."

She watched him go, taking in his broad shoulders and how he moved with an unhurried grace, as if strolling through a park under a blue, sunny sky without a care in the world—quite a difference from his earlier revolving guises of morning-after zombie, scary-eyed brute, and flirtatious Southern boy.

Hello, will the real Bobby Halloran please stand up?

Unease pricked, and on a sudden impulse she called after him, "Bobby!"

He stopped, then turned, and something about the hard expression on his face, the tension in the way he stood, set off her inner alarm. Maybe it was only the evening shadows, the gloomy weather, or her own overstretched nerves, but she sensed . . . a wrongness here. "About tonight—"

"Don't worry; if there's one thing you can count on, it's that I know how to have a good time even at work."

Oh, boy. Obviously they were coming at this from totally different perspectives. "I'm looking for Chloe Mitsumi, not a good time, and there'll be no drinking tonight, either. I mean it."

Anger—and something darker—flashed across his face, swiftly banked. Finally, an honest emotion, even if it did raise the hairs on her arms.

"Are you calling me a drunk?" he asked, his voice eerily soft.

"Are you?"

Silence settled between them, heavy and thick. Outside, distant thunder rumbled, signaling an approaching storm.

"You sure don't pull any punches, I'll give you that, but I am *really* not in the mood for this." He stared at her for a long, discomforting moment. "Look, just be damn sure you're ready when I get there. And wear something that says you might know what it's like to have a little fun, no matter how much you have to fake it."

Embarrassment, mixed with an unexpected pang of hurt, shot through her, and her defenses kicked in before she could even think twice: "Fuck you, Halloran."

"Kinda busy right now." Blond brows arched, he walked backward away from her, hands deep in the pockets of his coat, his fallen-angel smile a gleam of white in the shadows. "But maybe later, if you ask real nice."

Six

"You wish," Emma muttered.

Ugh; too standard. So was: *Dream on* and *Not even if you were the last man alive on the planet.*

Courtesy of her simmering resentment, Emma's drive home flew by in a blur—and here she was, almost at her apartment complex, and *still* trying to come up with a witty retort to his crude comment.

Was she pathetic, or what? Because finding the perfect put-down wouldn't mean jack at this point, although it might soothe the sting of remembering how she'd simply stood there as he sauntered away, her mouth hanging open in that oh-so-intelligent, gasping fish look.

Why couldn't she ever come up with clever, ego-shriveling comebacks until hours after the fact?

Emma parked her car in the lot, then stalked into her apartment, snapped on the lights, and glared at the clock. Thank God she had time for a shower, because she *really* needed to relax.

She avoided looking at herself in the bathroom mirror as she stripped down, not feeling particularly attractive at the moment, or in the mood to wonder what Bobby

Halloran saw when he looked at her. She could tell herself a thousand times over that her appearance didn't matter, that her competence and her worth weren't dependent upon a model-perfect face or a killer body, but she was only human, and his little dig had hurt.

Turning on the shower, Emma waited until steam whirled lazily from behind the curtain before stepping inside. As the hot water ran down her face and body, easing away the day's stings and tensions, she thought back on the fleeting, dark look that had crossed Halloran's face when she'd told him there'd be no drinking. Admittedly, she'd hit his sore spot first—yet another bad habit of hers, giving in to her inner bitch when feeling defensive—and all he'd really done was bite back.

Sighing, she reached for the shampoo. "Great. What a pair we make."

With any luck, though, they'd get through this case without inflicting any major damage on each other. All she had to do, no matter how on edge or stressed, was to count to ten before shooting off her mouth.

After she'd finished with her shower, Emma headed to her closet and mulled over her noncop wardrobe options: sexy, trashy, understated yet elegant, or casually sophisticated?

She decided on understated. Until she developed a better feel for the situation, not drawing attention to herself was the smartest way to go—especially since "covert" wasn't a word she'd use to describe even Halloran's everyday attire, and at least one of them should be able to blend into a crowd.

With the possibility of trouble in mind, Emma pulled out a tan, washed linen suit. The pants were tailored but full, with plenty of running room, and the jacket's zipped front and boxy cut was not only casual-dressy, but easily disguised the slim shoulder holster she used with her personal handgun. A rusty red camisole added a dash of color—it was also low-cut, and, combined with the miracle of a push-up bra, revealed bar-appropriate cleavage when she partially unzipped the jacket.

She finished off her look with a pair of low-heeled black shoes, the kind she could run in without worrying about breaking an ankle, and a simple gold necklace and ear studs.

After checking the clock again—she had fifteen minutes before Bobby arrived—Emma returned to the bathroom to do her hair and makeup. She kept her hair loose, styling it into a no-fuss, no-muss look, then hairsprayed the hell out of it. Nighttime bar scenes called for extra makeup in dark, dramatic tones, and she decided on coppers and crimsons.

She'd just tossed all her necessities—shield, makeup, gum, wallet, pager, cell phone, and keys—into a small bag when a knock sounded on her door.

Emma peered through the peephole, and held back a smile at the sight of Halloran mugging for her, all rude tongue and waggling eyebrows. The man had his moments, to be sure.

She unlocked the door and swung it open. "You're on time."

"Yeah. But don't let it go to your head. It'll probably never happen again." He didn't bother disguising his thorough survey of her, and his gaze lingered on her breasts and lips before he looked over her shoulder, angling for a peek at her apartment. "Are you gonna invite me in?"

Maybe later, if you ask real nice . . .

"No." More flustered by his earlier remark than she cared to admit, Emma grabbed her bag. "You said be ready. I'm ready. So let's go bimbo-hunting."

As she fell into step beside him, Emma noted that he'd shaved and showered, and a freshly scrubbed soap scent mixed with the darker, spicier smell of his cologne. She might not like him very much, but couldn't deny he looked as swoon-worthy as ever, wearing a gray tie with a red-and-gray-striped shirt tucked into pleated black pants. He still had the black leather coat, and the soles of his shoes sported a thick, heavy tread—in case he had to kick in any more doors or, for the sake of variety, a few heads.

To her chagrin, he caught her checking him out. "Like what you see?"

Considering his ego hardly needed boosting, she ignored his question. "You armed?"

"Always. I feel naked without a gun."

Now, there was an unfortunate choice of words. Suspecting he was deliberately teasing her, Emma glanced at him. Sure enough; he was smiling, well aware of her thoughts, and as if on cue, a naked vision of him played out across her mind—in wide-screen Technicolor.

Stupid, unpredictable, irrational hormones . . .

As they headed outside, Halloran gave her a sideways glance. "You look nice. I'm liking what I'm seeing."

He'd directed the comment to her breasts, but her annoyance only lasted a second or two; no fair getting mad at him for noticing what she'd deliberately played up.

"I'm so thrilled to hear it, I don't think I can contain myself."

"Yeah," he said wryly. "I noticed."

Emma stopped at the edge of the parking lot. "Which one is yours?"

He pointed to a Ford Expedition parked in the NO PARKING zone. Emma sent him a faintly disapproving look, which he pretended not to notice, and she bit back her retort with an effort and walked toward his SUV. It gleamed under the light of a nearby street lamp, all shiny and brand-new, and definitely his kind of transportation: muscular, utilitarian, and a flashy red.

He opened the door for her, which again caught her off guard. "You *do* know I'm capable of opening my own car doors, right?"

"Don't get excited. It's just another of my many bad habits—and maybe I'm trying to make up for how I acted earlier."

"Earlier" covered a broad spectrum of questionable behavior on his part—not to mention her own—but making a big deal out of the simple courtesy of opening a car door wasn't necessary, especially now.

Truce, his actions seemed to be asking, and she granted it by murmuring her thanks, then busied herself with the seat belt as he walked around to his side. The car's interior was as pristine as its exterior, with the telltale extras she'd expect to find in a cop's personal vehicle.

"Nice car," she said to break the ice.

"Thanks. I just bought it—the first new car I've had in years."

Not sure where to take the conversation from there, Emma didn't respond, and Bobby didn't rush to fill the silence. Instead, he turned on the radio, keeping the volume low, and had them on the highway in minutes.

Softly intimate strains of music filled the SUV's dark interior, and with the added warmth of his body and heady scents of cologne and leather, Emma was acutely conscious of his nearness. She'd spent a good portion of the morning riding around with him, but doing so now felt very different—and not quite in a way she welcomed.

Just five minutes in his presence, and already her female senses had snapped to attention; spinning her from unease to raw curiosity to this belly-deep, instinctual awareness of a powerful, attractive male sitting inches away.

Stupid, stupid hormones.

As the seconds crawled by, Emma tried to think of something else to say. Something friendly, yet not *too* friendly. Finally, she squared her shoulders and asked casually, "So where are we going first?"

She suppressed a small sigh at her less-than-brilliant foray into conversation. Thankfully, he didn't notice—or maybe he was just used to women making fools of themselves around him.

"It depends on Chloe's mood, and we have no way of knowing what that is. If she's feeling sure of herself, she'll be in young sophisticate mode, hanging at one of the classier bars. If she's feeling urbane, it'll be the Quarter. If she's playful, she'll be in one of the Warehouse District hot spots. If she's in a bad mood, she'll head to some of the more offbeat, rougher bars."

"Which means we could spend hours looking for her."

"This is the city that never sleeps." Unlike her, he didn't appear unhappy over the prospect of a night-long prowl. "I thought we'd hit bars in the business and Warehouse districts first. Start with the Howlin' Wolf, because that's one of her favorites, then try Check Point Charlie's, the

Mermaid Lounge, Tipitina's . . . and there's also dance-club meat markets. We'd probably find her at the Metro, but they're only open on Saturdays, so our best bet's Club 735 on Bourbon. We can also try a few Faubourg Marigny bars. She likes Rubyfruit Jungle."

"Isn't that a lesbian bar?"

"I don't mind a little girl-on-girl action."

Emma laughed; she didn't intend to, it just slipped out. Oh, yes, Bobby Halloran had his moments. "Wow. Now, there's a surprise."

He grinned, all sunny and deceptively wholesome—maybe spending a few hours in his company while tromping through noisy, smoky bars wouldn't be as boring as she'd thought. If nothing else, she could entertain herself by watching him switch between personalities and trying to guess which one of them—if any—was the genuine article.

Seven

At midnight, Emma found herself sitting in a dark dive that smelled of fryer grease, burnt coffee, and old vinyl, and watched Bobby tuck into a plate heaped with fries, a monster-sized hamburger, and the biggest pickle spear she'd ever seen in her life.

She'd ordered coffee, but after the first sip she'd pushed it aside, not all that keen on dissolving her stomach. As Bobby plowed a thick, crispy fry through a mound of ketchup, she leaned her elbow on the booth's table and rested her chin on her palm. "That's a lot of food."

He grinned. "Enough to fuel me through a few more bars."

The notion didn't excite her. By eleven, she'd already reached her saturation point on trolling clubs and would've called it quits if Bobby hadn't still been operating at full steam ahead—and if a mule-headed part of her hadn't refused to be the first to cry uncle.

"You look bored," he added.

"I wanted to find our party girl, question her, and get to bed at a reasonable hour. Unfortunately, luck isn't on our side tonight, and we keep missing her. Hanging out in bars isn't my idea of a good time."

Bobby slouched back in the booth seat, and his knee brushed hers. More than a little flustered, she shifted so that her legs didn't touch his—and didn't miss the amusement shining in his eyes.

Was he trying to flirt with her, or was he just dense?

"So what exactly is your idea of a good time?" he asked, dipping another fry in his ketchup.

The fries looked really good, and her stomach suddenly growled. She hadn't been hungry when he'd ordered, but now the flavorful smell of his food made her rethink her decision.

"A dinner party at home with a small group of close friends. I've never been comfortable in social situations with people I don't know. It's exhausting, smiling and talking, trying to act casual."

"Are you telling me you're shy?" Surprise crossed his face. "You sure don't act like it at work."

She continued observing the fry-and-ketchup ritual, because it was easier than meeting those direct, blue eyes. She'd watched him work through a half dozen bars tonight like a politician on campaign, effortlessly charming every woman he encountered. He'd never understand, but she answered anyway. "When I'm working, it's not personal, and going undercover just means I'm acting. I don't care if the sleazy john I'm busting likes me or not. Bars and parties are different; they're not my usual territory and I don't feel in control."

"Why do you need to be in control?"

She looked up, a sarcastic retort on the tip of her tongue—until she saw the genuine curiosity in his eyes.

"Because I'm aware that I try too hard. I end up saying all the wrong things, people start looking at me as if I'm some mutant life-form, and then I just want to go away and hide. So if I'm careful, I won't say anything stupid. Of course, I don't exactly wow anybody with my sparkling personality, either."

Her explanation came out sounding a lot more honest than she'd intended, and judging by the look on Bobby's face, she'd surprised him, too.

Maybe she could blame the blabbing on her tired feet, or that he was just easy to talk to, like a priest or a bartender—or a smart cop who knew how to get answers out of people.

"An only child?" he asked after a moment. "Or the eldest?"

She smiled. "Stop profiling me, Bobby."

"Just curious." He moved his plate toward her. "Have some. I've noticed you keep eyeing my fries, and there's plenty to share."

Emma hesitated, not wanting him to think she was too cheap to buy her own food, but when he pushed the plate closer, she gave in and took one.

Another answer would pay him back for the fries, and they'd be even. "After my parents divorced, I left New Orleans to live with my mother. We moved around L.A. a lot because she didn't have great job skills or much luck with boyfriends. Then she got smart and lucky, married a really nice guy, and had another baby when I was fourteen."

"I bet that didn't make you too happy."

"Not one bit. I'd just started classes at another new school, and I wasn't the most secure kid to begin with, so I resented my sister for sucking all the attention away from me. But Lindy was such a happy baby, and it wasn't long before she had me wrapped around her little finger." Emma let out a long sigh. "She's graduating from high school this year. It makes me feel old."

Well; wasn't she chatty all of a sudden. "Sorry. I didn't mean to run off at the mouth like that."

"Not complaining. I know you've just moved here, and haven't had a lot of time to hang out," he said, still comfortably slouched back. "I wondered if you might be lonely."

Great; he was being nice to her because he felt sorry for her, and she was glad the dim lighting hid her flush of embarrassment. "I'm not lonely at all, but thanks for the thought. And what about you? Do you have brothers and sisters?"

"An older sister and two younger brothers, and they've been keeping Grandma and Grandpa busy with grandkids. I have a big family, and we're close, even if we don't see each other a lot these days."

"Is your family from around here?"

"Nope. I hail from Mobile, Alabama."

"I thought that drawl of yours sounded Alabamian."

"And not even fifteen years in New Orleans has mellowed it any. My friends tell me it gets worse when I'm angry or moody."

Which would explain those changes in tone she'd noticed earlier.

"I've got family all over, even a couple cousins in Los Angeles," he added. "I wanted to get out of Mobile for someplace more exotic. I considered Houston, Miami, San Francisco, even Phoenix. But I had an uncle here who said he'd help get me a job in the police department, so this is where I settled."

It was nice, having a normal conversation with him. They'd gotten off to a rocky start earlier, largely because of her bad mood, but this chatty bonding moment boded well for them working together during the remainder of the case.

"Did you become a cop because of your uncle?" she asked.

"My father was a cop, too. It runs in the family. And I liked the whole mystique, being one of the good guys. How about you?"

"Job security. There's always a need for cops, and the benefits are decent." The fries were delicious, crisp and seasoned—and he really didn't seem to mind that she kept snitching them. "I considered going to law school, but changed my mind and graduated from Caltech with a criminal justice degree."

With their store of small talk exhausted, a silence settled between them and Bobby finished off his burger as she continued to pick at his fries.

"Are you settling in here okay?" he asked finally. "Need help with anything?"

"It's nice of you to ask, but I'm doing okay. I haven't met a lot of people yet, but with this job . . . well, you know how it is. Cops tend to hang out with other cops, date them, marry them."

He nodded. "You married? Divorced?"

"Neither, but there was this guy . . . another detective. We were together for a few years, but we're not anymore."

"What'd he do to you?"

The question took her by surprise. "Why do you think he did anything to me?"

"Call it a hunch."

Emma sent him a sharp look. "Maybe you should be asking what I did to him."

"Okay, I'll bite. What did you do?"

"Technically, nothing." She picked up her coffee, but after another glance at its thick blackness, she put it back down. "The trial I was involved in was a nightmare. Things got really ugly, and I guess he came home to one too many harassing messages on the answering machine . . . or maybe it was the 'die bitch' written in red marker on the wall outside our apartment door that sent him packing."

A short silence followed, and she regretted mentioning it at all. It had put him on the spot, and what did she expect from him, anyway? A medal?

It wasn't like her to be so open, and to cover her discomfort, Emma gave a small shrug. "Ancient history—and another reason why I'm here. This was the first job offer to come along, and at the time I wasn't in a picky mood."

"I'm sorry. It must've been hard."

She sighed. "I don't usually whine like this to people I hardly know. I hate it when people do that to me, because I never know what to say. Are you about ready? We need to get back to looking for Chloe Mitsumi."

"Yeah, I'm ready. I need to go to the john first, though."

He slid out from the booth and headed toward the restrooms, just as a rowdy group of couples walked in, obviously ending a night out at the bar with a round of junk food.

The girls were giggly, bumping and brushing against each other as well as their boyfriends, who were loudly showing off. Attractive and bright, sparkling with a self-confidence only the young and idealistic could carry off without looking arrogant. She smiled, thinking they looked like a pack of well-dressed puppies.

They also blocked the way to the bathroom, and Bobby patiently made his way through them, smiling and talking—and flirting back with a sweet young thing in a red leather swing coat that probably could've paid Emma's rent for a month.

What really caught her attention, however, was how Bobby Halloran exuded confidence and power, with a hint of danger, even when doing nothing more than walking down a dingy hall of a greasy spoon. He made the younger men look like little boys, and the gazes of the young women followed him until he disappeared inside the men's room.

Emma had no idea how he did that, but if he could patent it, he'd make a fortune. Nor would she mind if a little of his magic at putting people at ease rubbed off on her, even though she'd long since accepted she was simply one of those quiet, introspective types who also happened to excel at reading people and putting together puzzles—a trait that did wonders for clearing cases, but not much for her social life.

Oh, well. The last thing she needed right now was a man to complicate her life.

A few minutes later, Bobby returned. The light nearest their booth shone down from behind him, and the pale color of his hair and silky sheen of his shirt gleamed. Between his golden looks and the energy that practically shimmered around him, it was no wonder he always seemed to light up a room whenever he walked in.

After leaving a generous tip, he picked up the check,

then leaned against the wall. Emma was uncomfortably aware of him as she slid across the bench—she hated those sticky, squeaky vinyl seats—and she didn't miss how his gaze lingered on her breasts. The low neckline had shifted as she'd wriggled out of the booth, revealing more of her cleavage—and a peek at the white lace of her bra.

"Nice shirt," he said, then surprised her by helping her into her coat.

And was it her imagination, or were his hands lingering on her shoulders?

Emma took a step back. "It's old . . . I've had it for years, but I like the color."

His slow smile told her he was well aware how his closeness and touch affected her. What the hell? Maybe he was part of that stupid betting pool after all, and would earn a hefty cut if he succeeded in getting her into bed.

As soon as the thought came to her, Emma dismissed it. He didn't strike her as the sleazy womanizing type. As far as she could tell, he just liked women, which Alycia had pointed out to her earlier.

"You sure don't know how to take compliments gracefully," Bobby said as they headed to the register to pay his bill. "Don't you think men find you attractive?"

"Not in the way they'd find women like Chloe Mitsumi attractive."

"Why do you say that?"

What an idiotic question; did men just not get it? "Because women like her make ordinary mortal women like me feel more than a little inferior."

"Yeah, she's beautiful and not afraid to flaunt it, but you turn heads in your own way."

It almost sounded like a compliment, if not for the "in your own way" part. "Tall women usually do. What's your point?"

"That you're nice-looking. Is this a problem?"

This whole night just kept getting stranger all the time. "Are you hitting on me?"

"You have to ask?"

Shooting him probably wasn't an option. Emma counted to ten, willing her blood pressure lower, then asked, "Ready to get back to work?"

"You bet. You think you can keep up with me?"

"Absolutely," she said, with as much chill as she could muster. "Let's go, partner."

Eight

What a bust.

No Chloe. No booze. No fun—except for getting a rise or two out of Emma, which had been fun, if in an admittedly twisted kind of way.

Bobby swung through the door of his house, letting it slam shut behind him as he rubbed at his brows. Almost two-thirty in the morning, and he was beat. Hell, beyond beat. Keeping up with Earnest Emma had been a trip, and halfway through the night he was convinced the woman was a damn robot. His ears were still ringing from the blaring music of a dozen or so bars, and after pushing through and around hundreds of people in crowded spaces stinking of perfume, spilled beer, and cigarette smoke, he needed a long, hot shower.

And the real kicker? Chloe always seemed to be one step ahead of them. Unlike Emma, who figured her as some airhead party girl riding a streak of good luck, he knew better. He might not know yet what Chloe was up to—or why—but she'd obviously landed herself in serious trouble this time.

Once in the kitchen, he threw his coat on the table, followed by the holster and his gun.

There'd been way too many hours in this day; he'd only managed some three hours of sleep in the past twenty-four hours, and the next twenty-four weren't looking much better. While he had no idea how long he could maintain this pace before his body got even with him, with the way things were going he'd find out soon enough.

Right now his body wanted more food, preferably something on the salty side. He and Emma must've walked through at least ten miles' worth of bars, and at midnight he'd finally bullied her into stopping to grab a quick bite to eat—which was the point where he'd first picked up on a developing pattern: If he wanted something from Emma, he had to piss her off first, *then* he'd get it.

Interesting, and worth thinking about when he wasn't feeling so wrecked.

He scrounged around in the cupboards and, finding nothing interesting there, tried the freezer. After a long contemplation, chilly air wafting around him, he settled on a frozen macaroni and cheese entrée.

Nice and salty, and loaded with carbs, baby. He needed all the energy he could get.

After popping the mac and cheese in the microwave, he splashed some Jack Daniel's in a glass over a few ice cubes, figuring it would relax him enough to help him catch a few hours of sleep. Drink in hand, he headed to the living room, turned on an end-table lamp, and played back the three messages on his machine, hoping one of them was from Chloe.

The first was a hang-up, the second from Andrea at Charity, updating him on Juleen's condition—downgraded from grimmer to grimmest.

The third message was from a friend: *"Hey, Bobby, it's Diana. What's up? I haven't heard from you in ages and I'm calling to make sure you're not dead."*

Bobby smiled down at his glass. Although recently engaged, she wasn't too busy or caught up in the new man in her life to forget old friends.

"Okay, I lied. Actually, I'm calling because there's an antique car show in town next month, and I was wondering if you'll go with me. Jack's flying out to Boston for a guest lecture that weekend, so I'll be all by my lonesome. If you're interested, call me back. Unless you're dead, in which case you're off the hook for being such a lousy friend. Buh-bye, darlin'."

Still smiling, he turned on the TV, slipped a DVD in the player, then headed back to the kitchen, admitting he *had* been a lousy friend lately. Too caught up in work, in other head stuff, he'd spent less time hanging out with his friends. It wasn't avoidance, exactly, though lately he'd begun wondering if that might not be some small part of it.

Lost in thought, he stood by the microwave and watched the digital numbers count down.

All his friends were coupling up. No surprise; they were in their early to later thirties, prime time for settling down with the one you wanted to be with, for making a baby or two, or at the very least buying a house.

Still, it was getting harder to watch, because even if he had the house part covered, the rest of it was beginning to look mighty elusive.

In his life, women generally came in two flavors: those

who thought a cop boyfriend was romantic, and those looking for shelter from some sort of personal storm. Neither kind worked out in the long run.

What he needed was a woman who didn't mind being alone for dinner, who changed arrangements at the last minute without a fuss, didn't resent the calls that came at all hours of the night, knew when to offer comfort and when to give him space, and who didn't let the fear of what might happen to him out there on the streets rule every part of a relationship.

Women like that existed; he even knew a few of them. Unfortunately, they were already married, or nearly married, to other guys—or they were cops.

And his last relationship with another cop had worked out *so* well.

Frowning at that less-than-happy reminder, he took another gulp of whiskey as Emma Frey's serious, intense face drifted to mind.

A nervy bundle of surprises and puzzles, that woman, and with defensive shields so thick it would take a better man than him to ever chip his way through. Still, she wasn't half bad to be around when she relaxed a little and smiled—and seeing her dressed up had been a pleasant surprise.

All night long, his attention kept straying toward her breasts, and that brisk, aggressive walk of hers made them bounce in a way he couldn't help but appreciate. She carried herself like a queen, and Bobby watched men taking notice, even though Emma herself was unaware of it. He'd liked how her looser hairstyle gentled her face, and he'd really liked her shade of lipstick—a dark, shiny red that had him wondering if she'd taste like chocolate-covered cherries.

That particular possibility had kept him occupied during the many long silences as they drove from one bar to the next, but considering she didn't like him—and he still wasn't sure how he felt about her—his chances of ever finding out if she tasted like cherries were slim to zilch.

The beeping microwave pulled him back from his reverie. He removed the plastic dish, careful of the hot steam . . . and heard the unmistakable click of his front door opening.

Bobby went still as footsteps came his way in a slow, steady *tap-tap, tap-tap*.

Putting aside the dish, careful to make no noise, he leaned over the table, slid his gun from its holster, and silently moved toward the kitchen entrance.

The footsteps stopped.

Taking a deep breath, he quickly stepped out from the kitchen, gun raised. "Don't move!"

A split second later, he lowered the gun and sank back against the wall.

Chloe Mitsumi stood a few feet away from him, smiling, arms upraised. "Hello, gorgeous."

"Dammit, you're lucky I didn't shoot you!"

"I see that. How about you put that thing away before you hurt somebody. Namely, me."

"*Jesus,* Chloe." In the wake of a fading adrenaline rush, he let out his breath, returned the gun to the table, and then touched the back of his hand to his upper lip, wiping away a film of moisture. "What the hell are you doing here this late?"

"Bunches of little birdies told me you were looking for me. I was in the neighborhood, and your front door was unlocked." She moved closer in a loose-hipped, languorous walk. "*Tsk-tsk,* Robert. In your line of business, you should be more careful."

"In my line of business, a locked door wouldn't stop the kind of people who'd want me dead. Remember that before you bust in here again without knocking." He walked into the living room, taking in her appearance. "Let me guess: Dominatrix Night at the Crow Pit, and the more black leather, the lower the cover."

Unperturbed, she struck a provocative pose, opening a fur coat to reveal a curve-hugging leather dress with a short skirt. A large, medieval-style marcasite cross hung between her breasts, and she also wore lacy stockings and a pair of heels with broad leather straps tied in a girlish bow around her ankles. Even in four-inch heels, though, the top of her head barely brushed his chin.

"Sarcasm is such an unattractive trait in a man. You don't like my dress?"

Best to sidestep that one. "Sit down. We need to talk."

Chloe shrugged, and he noticed she'd changed her hair to a geometric, Cleopatra-ish style. While long in back, the locks of hair framing her face had been bluntly cut to brush her shoulders, and her bangs skimmed the tops of her brows in a ruthlessly precise line. Dark red lipstick highlighted a mouth he knew from personal experience could send a man straight to heavenly bliss, and the smoky grays and deep reds of her makeup accentuated the slant of her eyes and high cheekbones.

She dropped down on his couch and crossed her legs, revealing a generous length of thigh, her pale skin showing through the black lace pattern of her stockings. "So what do you want to talk to me about?"

"I think you know."

"It occurs to me the list of possibilities is on the short

side." She looked around, settling more comfortably on the couch. "Don't let me stop you from whatever you were doing. I'm in no hurry to get home."

"Especially since home is trashed?"

"I have places to stay." She examined a fingernail, painted metallic silver. "I smell food. Go get it, then come back and sit with me. We'll catch up on old times."

He hesitated, then gathered his mac and cheese, whiskey, and a bag of chips, and carted it all into the living room. By the time he returned, she'd started the DVD.

"You still watch *Cowboy Bebop*?" She patted at the empty place on the couch beside her, smirking. "It's nice to know some of my influences on you actually stuck. Maybe not the ones I would've preferred, but hey . . . a girl can't be that choosy."

As if she'd ever been the choosy type. He sat, lowering the volume of the jazzy opening song. "I just like it."

"Mmmm . . . the world-weary bounty hunter struggling to fight the good fight, haunted by his past, unable to escape his destiny," she intoned dramatically, and reached for his whiskey. After taking a drink, she returned the glass to the coffee table, pressing herself against him in the process. "It's dark and depressing."

"It's all about karma." With a glare in her direction, Bobby moved the glass out of her reach. "No good deed goes unpunished. I can relate."

"Ol' Spike had a death wish." Her voice had an uncharacteristic edge. "Can you relate to that, too?"

"It's just a cartoon."

Chloe gave him a long, unreadable look. "And I still don't like this episode. I much prefer happy endings."

"Real life isn't about happy endings. I get hit over the head with that lesson at least a couple times a week."

"Sarcastic *and* fatalistic." She made a pouting face. "Ever think of quitting your job? You're not much fun anymore . . . which is too bad, because you do know how to have fun, as I fondly recall."

"And fun's what you're all about, right?"

"Not all of us believe we need some kind of heroic purpose to our lives to justify why we're still breathing."

"Hey, we're here to discuss your fucked-up life, not mine, and I'm too tired to fight with you." Especially about a conflict of opinions they'd never resolve—the reason why, after a few months of hot and heavy sex, they'd drifted apart. "And if you really need an answer, I watch *Bebop* for Faye. I have a weakness for purple-haired femme fatales."

"Liar. It's not her hair that's got your attention." With a knowing smile, Chloe snitched a chip and munched it. "So how's life been treating you?"

"No complaints. And yourself? Make any enemies lately?"

"Always business with you, never pleasure." She leaned close again, rubbing the fabric of his sleeve between her fingers. "I like this shirt. It looks good on you . . . though it'd look even better *off* you."

Plucking her hand away, he returned it to her lap. "Bad idea."

"Not even for old times' sake? It was good, Bobby. You know that."

Hell, yes—but still a bad idea. "I'm not interested."

"You're not interested in helping me? But isn't that what you *live* for?" She sat back, fixing him with an amused, mocking look. "Or . . . maybe it would be easier on your Southern chivalry if I were wearing something pretty and white instead."

Her words hit him on his already raw nerves, and as he surged to his feet the derisive look on her face dissolved into sudden wariness.

"Don't you do this," he said, his voice tight with controlled anger. "You know how I . . . you know, all right? Don't think you can just walk in here and throw it in my face like it's some kind of joke. If you want my help, you play fair. If not, you can get the hell out of my house."

"I'm here *because* I know what's going through your head, so I'll save you the trouble. I don't want you riding to my rescue, Bobby, and I don't want your help." She tilted her head up, plainly pissed. "I don't know who trashed my place, or why anybody would want to. Nothing was taken, nobody has threatened me. You wanna hear my theory? It just some random bad luck. You know—shit happens."

"And pigs fly."

She recrossed her legs, mouth set in a hard line. "I don't want the hassle. I'm sorry if that's not what you want to hear, but I'm not making any statements, filing any complaints, or pressing any charges, so there's no point in you wasting any more of your precious time tracking me down."

"I'm not the only one trying to find you."

"Oh, yeah . . . that chick detective." Chloe pulled a small stack of business cards from her coat pocket and slapped them down on the coffee table—all were Emma's. "The one who's blitzed every bar in town looking for me. Is she one of yours?"

"She's my partner. Temporarily."

"Call the bitch off."

"No can do."

"Why not? Just be you . . . turn on that sweet, sexy smile, take her aside, whisper a few sweet nothings in her ear. Don't tell me you've lost your touch, lover man."

Temper wearing thin again, he said tightly, "It's not like that."

"Really?" Chloe looked intrigued. "Isn't she pretty enough to bother with?"

The question, as unexpected as it was irrelevant, made him hesitate. "She sure doesn't look anything like you."

Chloe laughed. "Ever the gentleman, always mouthing the right words. I've missed having someone like you in my life."

He couldn't say the same. "Let's get back to business. There was another cop looking for you, but it wasn't Detective Frey and it wasn't me." Even if Emma had assumed so. "This guy was youngish and blond. I don't know who it was. You got any ideas about it?"

She gave an exaggerated shrug, pushing her breasts against the leather and half burying the cross in cleavage—and, man, there had to be something sacrilegious about that.

"I haven't a clue and I don't care. Would you sit down? You're hurting my neck. And stop asking so many questions. I mean it, Bobby."

"Whoever broke into your apartment might want to hurt you." He sat, though more at a distance this time.

In the brittle silence that followed, Chloe fished a pack of cigarettes from her coat pocket, lit up, and threw the pack on the coffee table. "Got an ashtray?"

Bobby stood, shooting her a look of irritation, and

fetched one from the kitchen. When he was sitting—again—he helped himself to one of her cigarettes.

After a moment she tossed him her lighter, brows arching. "I thought you gave up that little vice."

"I only smoke under extreme emotional duress. Or when I'm drunk off my ass."

Her brows inched even higher, though it hardly seemed possible. "So which one are you now?"

"The first, thanks to you, and working my way to the second, if you'd leave my whiskey alone." He returned the lighter, and watched as she slipped it back into her pocket. "Is that real mink?"

"I may be a self-absorbed, amoral bitch without any useful purpose in life, but at least I'm an ecologically friendly one." Smiling thinly, she blew out a stream of smoke. "It's very fake."

Bobby digested that, along with her tone of voice. "Okay, I get that you're mad at me. What I don't get is why. I just want to keep you safe."

Her gaze shifted past him to the TV. "I've been keeping myself safe for years without you, so unless I'm doing something illegal by not wanting to be bothered by the police, you need to back off. Now."

"It doesn't work that way."

"Then make it work that way." Her voice was sharp, cold. "Go harass real criminals and leave me the hell alone."

Getting Chloe to cooperate had always been an exercise in patience—and he was fast running out of his short store of that. "Are your brother's people still watching over you?"

"Can I have another drink?" She pointed to his nearly empty glass. "Those chips were salty."

"I can get you your own glass if you want."

"No, thanks. I've had enough for the night." She picked up his glass, even though he hadn't said yes, and took a small sip. "And speaking of which, can I use your bathroom?"

"Answer my question first."

She rolled her eyes, then stabbed out her cigarette in the ashtray. "Yes, my brother still spies on me. Not that it matters. I don't visit him, I don't call him, and I throw away his letters without opening them. Every now and again one of his pet dogs will stop by and give me grief about it. I smile and tell them to go to hell. They laugh, pat me on the head, and tell me to be a good girl. That's about the extent of it. Now can I go pee?"

"You know where the bathroom is."

With a glance at the TV, she pushed up from the couch. "I don't want to watch this part, anyway."

Chloe walked into the kitchen, and Bobby turned his attention to the screen just as the climactic gun battle in the cathedral began. It never failed to amaze him how fictional bad guys couldn't shoot worth shit, but the good guys never missed a shot. In his experience—very painful personal experience—the bad guys hit what they were aiming for more often than not.

And even though he'd watched this scene at least a half dozen times before, he still followed the action as the stained-glass window shattered and Spike fell in slow motion, amid shards of glass and to the accompaniment of sweet choral music, and all the while flashing back to a mysterious woman loved and lost—in these stories, there was always some woman screwing up a man's life.

Emma's face came to mind again, and the low-necked red top she'd worn. He passed a pleasant moment or two dwelling on that recollection, finishing off his smoke, until he realized, with a jolt, that Chloe had been gone for an awfully long time.

Muting the TV, he called, "Chloe?"

No answer.

Immediately suspicious, he pushed up from the couch and quickly headed through the kitchen to the bathroom, which also led to his bedroom, not sure what he'd find—though Chloe naked in his bed was a strong possibility, in view of her mood tonight.

The bathroom door was shut, and he gave the wood a sharp rap with his knuckles. "Chloe? Answer me, or I'm coming in."

Only silence followed his threat. Swearing softly, he turned the doorknob. Locked; but he'd mastered a handy trick for opening the old-fashioned lock.

He gave the knob a quick, hard upward twist. With a audible pop, the door swung open on an empty room— and an open window that might be too small for him to squeeze through, but not for a five-foot-tall, size-zero nuisance who was, by now, long gone.

The cheery yellow curtains fluttered and flapped in the breeze, almost as if mocking him, and a sharp sense of unease spread through him. "Okay . . . this can't be good."

Nine

All through the morning's short briefing, Emma was aware of Bobby's presence as he sat behind her, quietly drinking coffee while everybody provided updates on active cases.

Considering she hadn't fallen asleep until around three, it was all she could do not to yawn. Prowling the frenetic bar scenes, especially in the goading presence of one Robert Halloran, had left her wired, and even though her weary body had been ready for some shut-eye, her brain refused to shut down.

"Frey. Any news on your Esplanade Ridge break-in?"

Emma straightened, hoping Strong hadn't noticed her inattention. "So far, not much. I've yet to locate the occupant of the apartment, although the landlord has been cooperative and filed a complaint for damages. Halloran and I are still working on finding the victim. We've been systematically checking her known whereabouts. Other than that, no suspects, no motives, no nothing. We still don't know if anything was actually taken from the apartment."

Strong nodded. "One more thing from the hot sheet.

District Five is requesting assistance on a homicide. Last week, a couple kids found a man in a car, shot through the back of his head. Name's Willie Farmer, and he's got a long record of petty shit, mostly nickel-and-dime drug possession and trafficking. The primary on the case hasn't turned up any solid leads, so they're asking around in the hopes somebody's heard anything about this guy."

"I know him," came Bobby's low drawl. "He used to work the streets for Jacob Mitsumi. I arrested him a couple times. He was never a player, just an errand boy, and dumber than a box of rocks. Unless he's moved up on the food chain, killing him would be kinda pointless."

"Maybe they did it for fun," said Mottson, the red-haired detective who'd given Emma a hard time yesterday. He yawned, looking thoroughly bored.

Bobby shrugged. "Could be. Who was he working for when he was killed?"

"Baby Boy Duvall," Strong answered.

"Now, there's a nice, upstanding guy," Alycia murmured, turning to Emma. "Not as bug-crazy as Mitsumi, though. Maybe Baby Boy knows who trashed the sister's apartment."

"We should check it out," Bobby said, giving Emma a look that said they'd talk about it later. "Who's the primary on this case?"

Strong looked down at his clipboard. "Gary Giacomo. You know him?"

Bobby nodded. "Yup. We'll give him a call."

After the briefing ended, the detectives wandered back to their desks to begin the day's work, and Emma tensed the second Bobby fell into step beside her.

He looked better than he had yesterday morning, all

chipper and fresh-faced, wearing navy pants, black suspenders, and a loud, distracting floral tie with a pale blue shirt that brought out the arctic blue of his eyes.

She'd worn one of her better suits, a chocolate brown pants-and-jacket combo with an ivory silk tee that made the most of her smallish breasts. The colors looked nice with her brown eyes and paler skin tone, but once again, she ended up feeling sparrowlike next to Bobby.

And why had she bothered sprucing up in the first place?

"Are you going to talk to me or not?" Bobby asked.

"I will, when I have something to say."

"You could always try 'Good morning, Robert.'"

Emma held back a smile. "Don't be a smart-ass. And I'm not sure yet if there's anything 'good' about it. Maybe you're used to operating on four hours of sleep a day, but I'm not." She tossed her notepad on her desk, found a bare spot for her coffee cup, and then dropped down on the chair with a groan. "And did I tell you I hate bars?"

He sat as well. "You did great."

"Hardly. We didn't find Chloe, remember? In my book, that qualifies as a failure."

"You may need to reinterpret your book, darlin'."

"Stop calling me that." As she picked up her cup, Emma glared—but just a little. "And what are you talking about?"

"Chloe came by to see me last night."

She very nearly sprayed her desk with a mouthful of coffee. "Seriously?"

"Seriously. I was having a drink and getting ready to watch cartoons when she just waltzed on in—and believe me, she's damn lucky I didn't shoot her on the spot."

Emma blinked. "You were watching cartoons?"

His gaze briefly shifted to some point beyond her shoulder. "Focus on the important stuff, Emma."

Right, like her case. Still . . . Bobby Halloran watched *cartoons*? Such as, what? The Roadrunner, the Simpsons, the Powerpuff Girls?

And since when had she become so easily distracted?

"So where is she now?"

"I have no idea."

Her elation deflated. "I don't understand."

Bobby scowled—and if she wasn't mistaken, a faint red tinged his cheekbones. "She snuck out my bathroom window."

"What?"

At her yelp—pitched at least an octave higher than her normal voice—several nearby detectives, including Mottson, turned to stare at her, then exchanged knowing looks with each other.

Ignoring them, Emma scooted her chair closer to Halloran and dropped her voice. "You let her get away?"

"I wouldn't say it happened like that. We were talking, I was trying to get a few answers out of her, and she was being her usual pain-in-the-ass self. She asked to use the bathroom, I let her, and by the time I realized she'd been gone a long time, it was too late to go after her."

Emma made a sound of disgust. "You let her get away."

"How was I supposed to know? I've never had a woman crawl out a bathroom window to get away from me!"

As far as excuses went, it was pretty weak, and not

even his defensiveness disguised that. Emma sighed. "Okay. So she tricked you. But did you get *any* answers?"

"She mostly talked about how she doesn't want you or me harassing her, and she asked me to tell you to back off."

"Wait a minute. We want to find the people who destroyed her apartment and belongings, and *we're* harassing *her*?"

"Like I said, Chloe moves in mysterious ways." Bobby finished off his coffee. "She claims not to know who broke into her apartment or why, says nothing was taken, nobody's threatened her, and she feels it was a random break-in."

"And you believed her?"

"Hell, no." He swiveled back and forth in his chair, full of pent-up energy, with no way to work it off. "Plus, the whole slithering out my bathroom window at three in the morning tells me she's lying through her teeth."

"Why didn't you mention this in the briefing?"

"I had my reasons."

She sat back, giving him a long, assessing look. "I hope your almighty ego wasn't one of them."

His eyes narrowed, and she noticed his lashes were two-toned; dark brown, with paler tips. "Remember how you ripped me a new one for asking questions about Chloe without telling you what I was doing?"

The tone of his voice put her on the defensive— again—but this time she quashed the urge to bite back. "You know how important this case is to me, and why, but you cut me out of the loop anyway. All I'm saying is that I didn't appreciate it, and you should—"

"It wasn't me."

"Oh." She stared at him, exasperation building, and then demanded, "Why the hell didn't you tell me that yesterday?"

"Maybe I was pissed you thought so little of my personal integrity."

"Oh, please. You were in a bad mood, I'd made you mad, and you just wanted to be a pain in the ass."

He shrugged, not denying or confirming it. Emma checked around her, and although she didn't see anybody obviously listening in, she leaned closer. "So if it wasn't you, who was it?"

Bobby raised his hands. "Chloe says she doesn't know, either. She could be lying. I figure it might be Giacomo, following up on Willie Farmer's murder."

Which made sense, and it was likely Giacomo hadn't heard yet they were looking for Chloe as well. "So you're going to call him, or should I?"

"You can. It probably doesn't tie in to Chloe's problem, but we don't know that for sure."

"Was she friends with this Farmer guy?"

"That'd be pushing it. Willie was one of her babysitters, so there is a connection." He sat forward, stretching. "Chloe admitted her brother still keeps tabs on her through his old crew. I figure they're the guys the store manager saw talking to Chloe, so I'll track down a few of them and ask some questions."

Emma nodded, absently chewing on her pen cap. "Okay, let's recap the situation. We have a woman with a trashed apartment who doesn't want to be 'bothered' by the police, a petty crook murdered execution-style, and a once-dangerous drug dealer twiddling his thumbs in Angola, but still in contact with former associates.

These former associates have been seen hovering about the ex-boss's sister, who just happens to be the one with the trashed apartment. It has a certain . . . circular symmetry to it."

"That it does."

"Except for the alleged blond, youngish cop looking for our party girl, who may or may not be Giacomo. Is Giacomo blond?"

"Bottle-blond," Bobby said, deadpan.

Emma grinned. "Okay, so it probably was Giacomo, unworthy bottle-blond that he is. But there's a possibility one of her brother's people could've been looking for her, pretending to be a detective."

"Except WASP-like and coplike isn't how I'd describe any of Jacob Mitsumi's boys. Most of the guys hustling or muscling for him were Asian, though he employed a few blacks, Cubans, and white trash for the sake of variety. He wanted to form his own Yakuza in New Orleans, except he was too crazy to pull it off."

Just what New Orleans needed, a Japanese version of the Mafia.

"Thank God for small favors, huh?" Emma kept her tone light, but as he'd rattled off all this information, her respect for him ratcheted up a notch or two. Maybe he'd never be her favorite person, maybe he'd always bounce her emotions from one extreme to the other, but he wasn't quite the pretty-boy slacker she'd pegged him for.

"Then I guess we should get to work." Emma leaned back. "You're more familiar with these people and the victim's history. After I call Giacomo, tell me what I can do to help."

Surprise crossed his face, but he didn't make a big deal out of her deferring to his experience; not even one smart remark. He simply nodded. "The first thing is to find Chloe. You up for another round of barhopping tonight?"

Emma sighed. "Do you really think we stand a chance now that she knows we're looking for her?"

"You have another suggestion?"

She didn't. "All right. It can't hurt to give it another shot."

"I'm guessing Chloe believes that after telling me she won't cooperate with the investigation, we'll drop it. And technically, if she doesn't want to file a complaint, we don't have much of a case."

"Maybe she trashed the place herself. Insurance fraud." Emma didn't really believe that, but she had to at least raise the possibility. "We could use that as justification to bring her in."

"Despite what she told her boss, she doesn't have insurance; I checked. And she's not breaking any laws by cutting up her bras or breaking her own dishes." Frustration flickered in his eyes, then vanished as he yawned. "Anyway, the only thing we've got is property damage for the door and cleanup costs. Probably most of the repairs are covered by her security deposit and the landlord's insurance; anything beyond that would be small-claims shit."

"It still feels off to me, and that she walked into your house at an ungodly hour of the morning is just—" Emma cut herself off, waggling her hand in a vague motion of unease. "I don't like it. She could've called and left us a message to get lost. Why bother with the face-to-face chat?"

"When we find her, we'll ask. And last night she was in a mood, looking aggressive as hell. We won't find her

hanging out in the nice bars with clean-cut office work-
ers. Goth, punk, techno, biker bars . . . pick your favorite flavor of sin and that's where we start."

"I don't like any of them."

Leaning back in his chair, Bobby raised his arms above
his head, fingers laced, and stretched again. "Life's a
bitch, ain't it?"

Emma couldn't help but admire how his shirt pulled
tight across his muscles, though she tried not to be obvious about it. After a moment, she smiled ruefully. "I like
the open-and-shut cases better, but if they were all easy,
I'd just get bored."

He smiled back; a full, generous smile that hit her
midchest, a little like a burst of heat, with tingly threads
slowly spreading outward.

While she'd *never* allow herself to develop any sort of
crush on him, she wasn't blind to his appeal: good-
looking, charming, with a powerful physical presence, a
wild reputation, and a hint of a shady past—what
woman wouldn't find a man like that intriguing, at the
very least?

And despite what people whispered about her, she *was*
only human.

"My, my," came Alycia Chatman's amused voice.
"Don't you two just look all cozy."

Emma twisted around, feeling guilty—even if she
hadn't done anything to feel guilty about. "Halloran and
I are talking about the Mitsumi case."

"Uh-huh. Sure you are."

"Be nice, Alycia," Bobby said amiably. "Is there something you wanted, or are you just here to give me shit?"

"Both, as usual." Alycia grinned as she sauntered
closer to lean against his desk, then turned to Emma.

"Two things. First, me and Car are having our annual Mardi Gras cookout next Sunday. Bobby's coming, and I was wondering if you wanted to come, too."

"You mean me and Bobby? Together?" Emma asked, startled.

"Well, no." Alycia looked at her thoughtfully. "Unless you two got something going I don't know about."

"What's the matter, Emma?" Bobby said, his drawl deepening. "Ashamed to be seen with me in public?"

He was joking, of course. Or was he? Emma glanced at him, unable to tell by the tone of his voice. He was smiling, but it didn't quite reach his eyes.

"No, it only sounded like Alycia was . . . Oh, never mind."

Alycia laughed. "I was just trying to save myself some extra work by reminding Bobby at the same time I invited you. I throw a first-class barbecue, by the way. There's great food, lots of drinks, stimulating company, and a game of basketball, District Five against District One. It can get . . . wild."

Interest piqued, Emma straightened. "Basketball?"

"Uh-huh. And don't forget the stimulating company," Alycia said, her tone coaxing. "Or my secret-recipe baked beans."

Emma tamped down a flutter of excitement. A chance to meet a few people outside of her department *and* a game of basketball, too—it was the best offer she'd had in months. "I'd love to come. Thanks."

"Good! And how about you, tall, blond, and sexy . . . with the emphasis on *tall,* for the honor of District One? You can still squeeze me into your busy social calendar, right?"

"I don't know . . . I may have to shuffle around a few

girls, but I think I can swing it. No way could I let you down or miss one of your parties. Besides, Carter owes me a rematch, the rat bastard. He plays dirty."

Alycia rolled her eyes. "Funny, he said the same thing about you last night. All right, we'll see you Sunday afternoon. The eating starts at three; with any luck it won't rain, and the bad guys will hold off killing, raping, and stealing long enough for us to have some fun."

Emma rolled her chair back to her desk, grabbed her pocket calendar, and opened it. "Do you need me to bring anything? And where—"

"No to the first, and I'll get you a map later. Now, the other thing I'm here for is to see if you want to take a break. I need a smoke, and I was hoping maybe you feel up for a little girl talk."

Oh, boy. Emma hoped this was just girl talk; no more bad news. The stress of these past few days alone was enough to last the rest of the month. Glancing at Bobby, she said, "Sure. I think we're done here?"

He nodded, and rolled back to his desk. "For now. There's a few people I need to talk to, so I may be gone awhile. Page me if you need me. And if I come across anything interesting, I'll get ahold of you. Good enough?"

"Good enough."

"Look at that. Acting like a team already." Alycia appeared impressed, and as Emma stood, she leaned closer and murmured loudly, "And won't that disappoint certain people."

"I heard that." Bobby picked up his phone, not looking in their direction. "Why does everybody act like I'm so difficult to work with? I'm a nice guy."

"Sure you are," Alycia said with a wink, as she and

Emma walked past his desk. "You're just misunderstood."

Bobby's laughter followed them. "Damn right. And I'm telling ya, nobody understands my pain."

Ten

By the time he'd dragged himself home at the end of the day—after running down belligerent gangbangers who didn't want to talk to him in the first place, answering pages for pointless questions, filling out reports, and arguing with a prosecutor who hated his guts and never failed to give him a hard time—all Bobby wanted was to strip off his clothes, take a shower, crawl into bed, and sleep for at least six hours straight.

Except Emma was dropping by in less than an hour. He'd offered to pick her up again, but she'd refused, pointing out it'd be wasting time to drive all the way to Kenner, then back to New Orleans. Having already gone a couple rounds with his least favorite prosecutor, he wasn't up to arguing with her, too. So he'd agreed and given her directions to his house.

Which, he suddenly noticed, was a mess.

Not a pigsty level of mess, but cluttered, dusty, disorganized—everything that would be anathema to a perfectionist like Emma.

Cursing under his breath, he hastily began picking up.

He should be showering, but he couldn't leave his dirty socks lying on the floor, or that pile of discarded mail scattered across the coffee table when it should be in the trash, along with the empty chips bag on the floor by the TV. Or—*shit!*—his laundry still in the basket on the recliner, a wrinkled, jumbled mess. Grabbing the basket, he threw it into his bedroom and shut the door. She had no reason to go there anyway, so he'd be safe. And since he hadn't bought a dishwasher yet, it was a good thing he'd washed that week's worth of dishes before leaving for work, otherwise he'd have to stash them in the oven or the fridge crisper.

He straightened a few pillows, his stacks of DVDs and CDs, rinsed out last night's—or should that be this morning's?—whiskey glass, and put it in the sink, thinking one dirty dish wouldn't look too bad.

Then he made a quick, final survey to make sure he hadn't missed anything embarrassing. The place looked passable. He didn't have time to dust or vacuum, but maybe she wouldn't notice the water rings or film of dust on the tables, the cigarette butts in the ashtray or the dust bunnies in the corners—

Who was he trying to fool? Of course she'd notice. She was a *detective*; homing in on the little details was what they did for a living.

Ah, to hell with it. Why should he care one way or another what she thought of his place? Especially since she'd refused to let him into her apartment last night. Maybe her place had looked worse.

He gave a derisive snort at the thought, knowing it was more likely he wouldn't find even a speck of dust, and every pillow would be perfectly aligned, every water spot on every glass rubbed off. She was probably one of those people who used an old toothbrush to clean the grout around the bathtub.

Rubbing at his eyes, he sighed. He really needed a shower, especially now that he'd worked himself into feeling irritable *and* inferior as well as tired.

After treating himself to the hottest shower he could tolerate for as long as he could spare, he emerged from the bathroom with his skin nearly parboiled. Unmindful of the wet footsteps he left on the floor, he headed into his bedroom, tossed the towel on his bed, and then stood in front of his closet, naked, rubbing his knuckles absently along his belly as he decided what to wear.

He'd take his cue from Chloe—which immediately alerted him to the fact that he needed to tell Emma to wear something sleazy, if she had any such thing in her perfectly organized closets.

Bobby glanced at his alarm clock. Too late to call; she was probably halfway to his place by now.

It didn't matter; they'd make do, no matter what she wore. As he searched through his closet, he pulled out his old black leather pants, a narrow black leather tie, and one of his newer silk shirts, also black. After he dressed, he retrieved a pair of scuffed motorcycle boots from underneath his bed and blew off the dust. Once he added his leather coat, he'd look right at home in any bar from grunge to punk.

Bobby headed back to the bathroom and roughly towel-dried his hair until it stuck straight up, which was the look he wanted, anyway. He opened his medicine cabinet and poked through bottles of Tums, Mylanta, mouthwash, and aftershave, a box of condoms, and dental floss before he found a tube of industrial-strength hair gel. He glopped some of the stuff onto his palm, then slathered it through his hair, spiking it with his fingers.

The goop dried into concretelike stiffness that wouldn't flatten even in hurricane-force gales.

Before leaving the bathroom, he quickly tidied it, even closing the toilet lid. He also double-checked to make sure his bedroom door was shut tight, then headed into the kitchen, slid his gun into his back holster, and clipped his shield and pager to the side of his belt. The wallet barely squeezed into his back pocket, and with not much spare room in his pants, he'd have to stash his keys and cell phone in his coat pockets.

Bobby glanced at the clock again, thinking he had time enough for a quick drink, but as he reached for the whiskey, a knock sounded—a brisk, hard rap that had Emma written all over it.

He headed to the door and swung it open to a view of long, long legs, deep cleavage, and a whole lot of black lace hugging more curves than he'd seen in way too long. "Holy shit . . . Emma?"

Eleven

The door opened as Emma raised her fist to knock again. She began to say hello, but all she could do was stare at the godlike man framed in the doorway.

"Holy shit," the godlike one whispered in a reverent tone. "Emma?"

For her part, she'd been thinking *Heaven help me,* but *Holy shit* worked, too. Several seconds passed before she found her voice. "Yeah, it's me . . . and hey, you look good."

The High Priestess of the Understatement, that was her.

Some men cleaned up nicely, but Bobby Halloran badassed up even better. All that black leather and silk and golden hair—he should've looked washed out in such dark colors, but instead he looked delectable. Pounceable. Lickable. Kissable. Bedable—oh, hell, just plain able, ready, and willing. A hot, liquid rush of pure lust shot through her, head to toe; a sure sign her baser instincts were firmly in the driver's seat.

The pants fit him—*all* of him—like a second skin, and

she struggled to keep her gaze from slipping downward. The sheen of his shirt caught the light, its softness clinging to the contours of his belly and chest in a way that made her ache to pet him as if he were a big, sleek cat. Even his hair looked like he'd just rolled out of a lover's bed, and with his darker brows, pale eyes, and strong jaw, he was dangerous, angelic, and vitally male—a daze-inducing paradox of six feet and one hundred eighty pounds of unadulterated sex in leather and silk.

"You look damn good, too." Bobby folded his arms across his chest and leaned against the doorjamb, his gaze still locked somewhere south of her face. "Jesus, Emma, men are gonna walk into walls when they see you, starting with me."

"Is it too much? I was worried the skirt would be too short."

Frowning, she looked down at her dress: black stretch lace, lined in red Lycra. It had long sleeves, a plunging neckline, and a very short skirt that she'd tried disguising with black hose. Her shoes were low-heeled, but the faux-barbed-wire ankle strap was attached to a buckle with a mildly kinky—if nonfunctional—lock-and-key charm. If necessary, she could easily kick a little ass in the stretchy skirt, but she hadn't thought it would look out of place in the meat markets, dives, and clubs they'd go trolling through tonight.

Now she wasn't so sure.

"The skirt's just fine, but you better come inside before you cause any traffic accidents." Bobby stood aside, smiling as she brushed by him. "And if you don't mind my asking, just where the hell are you hiding your gun?"

Emma patted a metal mesh bag partially hidden beneath the black velvet jacket draped over her arm. "Here. It didn't fit anywhere else."

"No kidding."

As Emma walked into his house—one half of a double shotgun cottage—she looked around, curious. Cozy, lots of wood and pale tones, not overly decorated or neat, but comfortable. Lived in, in that way a man's spaces often looked, with well-worn furniture in dark blues, a big TV, expensive stereo system, stacks of sports magazines, a sloppy scattering of a week's worth of newspapers, and the usual debris of daily life.

"Nice place."

"I inherited it from my great-uncle last summer. He was a thirty-year veteran of the NOPD. I keep meaning to rent out the empty side, but I never seem to get around to it, even though I could really use the extra cash."

Emma turned as he shut the door, and watched him shrug into his coat, buttoning it to hide the holster— and, to her disappointment, covering the clingy silk shirt and tight, leather-clad rear.

"You can sit down if you want." A sheepish expression crossed his face. "I was so busy checking out your legs that I forgot my manners. Sorry."

His blunt compliment warmed her cheeks—and it frustrated her a little, too. Hadn't she been worth a second look before baring most of her legs and boobs? "I think we should be on our way."

"Okay." He slipped his keys and cell phone into his coat pockets. "Are you hungry? We could stop at a drive-thru on our way to the first club."

"Good idea. You seem to have a hollow leg, and this

way I can avoid your dragging me to some greasy dive at midnight."

Bobby chuckled as he opened the door. "Greasy dives are the best that late at night, and even better after a couple beers. But there's a Taco Bell on the way to Punk Amok, which is the first place we're checking."

"Any reason for that decision?"

"Yeah. I read the bar stamp on Chloe's hand. If she was hanging there last night, maybe we'll get lucky tonight."

"We can only hope." Emma brushed past him as he held open the door for her, her body lightly touching his. "You know, you do have your good points, Detective Halloran."

"Why, thank you, Detective Frey." His gaze lowered to her cleavage. "And so do you."

"Pig."

"In every sense of the word, darlin'."

With Bobby giving directions, Emma drove—she'd brought the car, so she won that battle by default—to the nearest Taco Bell. Unlike burgers, tacos weren't road-friendly fast food, so she only ordered a drink, then headed toward Tchoupitoulas Street as Bobby ate his dinner.

The targeted club, only a year old, was located not far from Harrah's Casino, so if the party animals grew bored with mirror balls and glam punk rock, they could stampede down the street a few blocks and immerse themselves in the equally glittery allure of slot machines and blackjack.

Halfway through the last of the three burritos he'd ordered, Bobby asked, "Did you go shopping before picking me up?"

Not an unexpected question, since black stretch lace and red Lycra wasn't her usual look.

"Right up until I made detective, I worked undercover with Hollywood Vice for prostitution enforcement. I was an escort, a call girl, your basic 'ho on the boulevards,' and I can slut it up with the best of 'em. I kept some clothes in case I'd need them later for other undercover work. I suppose tonight fits that criteria." Emma glanced down at his pants—and struggled not to stare at his groin, where the tight leather didn't leave much to the imagination. "So what's your excuse?"

Bobby took a moment to finish chewing. "Maybe I like confounding expectations."

"You've worn those to *work*?"

"Hell, no." He smiled wolfishly, which told her he'd at least considered it. "But I don't have an aversion to bars. I like parties, and besides, I was a child of the eighties and into the punk scene for a while. I got a kick out of shocking and pissing off people."

His grin widened, faintly nostalgic. "I used to live for the Sunday afternoons when my mother hosted her church group meeting. These nice Baptist women would come over to our house, and I'd walk in and freak 'em out, then sit down and talk, all 'yes, ma'am' or 'no, ma'am.' Confused the heck out of them."

"Sounds like you were every shade of brat."

He didn't bother denying it. "After a while, though, it only worked on the new visitors, because my mother's older friends were on to me. But you know what the funny thing is?"

Emma shook her head.

"When they got over the initial shock, those church ladies enjoyed flirting back with the scary-looking kid sitting in his mother's front room."

She smiled as she imagined Bobby, some twenty years younger, alarming groups of suburban wives and mothers, only to turn right around and charm their stockings off.

"This doesn't surprise me. I bet you gave them quite a thrill, too—a small, safe taste of walking on the wild side, even if you must've been practically jailbait. Shame on you."

"And it probably explains why I had a thing for older women when I was in my twenties."

And this was a little more than Emma really wanted to know about his sexual history.

After a moment, she added, "There couldn't have been much of a punk scene in Mobile in the eighties . . . How old are you, anyway?"

"Thirty-seven," he answered. "The heyday of punk was already on its way out by the time I got into it, and no, there weren't many kids who looked like me. The local cops pulled me over a lot, which didn't go over too well with my family. Except for Uncle Walt. I always had a good relationship with Uncle Walt. Probably because he lived in New Orleans and was used to all kinds of weird shit, so nothing I did made a dent."

Emma gave him a narrow look. "And what kinds of things did you do?"

"Mostly we hung out in parking lots or alleys, smoking, drinking, talking about the best music to listen to while screwing our girlfriends, and in general being loud and obnoxious. Except for underage drinking and driving too fast, I never did anything illegal, just stupid."

"Oh, come on. No pharmaceutical experimentation?"

"Maybe a little." He grinned, not in the least apologetic. "And now look at me: I'm a cop. Ain't life full of surprises?"

She couldn't argue that. "So what made you do the big lifestyle turnaround?"

He shrugged. "It was just a phase, and eventually I grew out of it."

Hmmm, now *that* was arguable. As far as she could tell, he'd traded in one attitude for another, and he was still shocking and pissing off people. Only now he did it from behind the authority of a badge.

Bobby finished off his last burrito, crushed the wrappers into a neat ball, and stuffed the wad of trash back into the take-out bag—and it earned him a few extra points for making an effort to keep her car neat.

"A club like Punk Amok brings back warm, fuzzy memories of safety pins, leather, body piercing, the burn of hair dye in my nose, and listening to music so bad it should've stripped paint off walls."

Certainly her suburban L.A. childhood had been a world apart from his.

"Anyway, getting back to answering your original question, I've had these pants for years. They're vintage, they're so old, and it's a point of pride that I can still fit into them."

And on behalf of every woman who'd ever bemoaned her widening hips and the tolls of gravity, she gave him a cranky look. "That's disgusting. Especially considering the food I've watched you eat the last couple of days."

"The Halloran men are blessed with fast metabolisms."

"Just another reason for me to hate your guts." Catching the flash of wariness in his eyes, she hastily added, "I'm kidding! Come on, I may not exactly trust you, but I don't hate you."

"I'm glad we cleared that up." He sounded curt, as if she'd definitely offended him. "Turn here."

Why was it, the moment things started going well, she always had to go ram her foot in her mouth?

Following his instructions, Emma turned into a parking lot next to a small brick building with a neon sign proclaiming: PUNK AMOK. The lot looked nearly full, but she eventually found a parking spot at the farthest end.

She turned off the ignition. Silence filled the car. Finally, she turned to him. "How long are we going to stick around and wait for Madame Barfly to make her appearance?"

"I don't know. I'm hoping we get lucky . . . and what do you mean, you don't trust me?"

Hearing the annoyance in his voice, Emma resisted her knee-jerk reaction to reassure him. "Look, I won't rag on you about the same thing over and over if you stop acting like you haven't given me plenty of justification for worrying you might do something reckless at best, or downright dangerous at worst."

His face blanked. "And if I do, will you stop looking at me like that?"

"Like what?" Her turn to sound wary, indignant.

"Like you're afraid of me." His lashes lowered, shuttering his gaze. "Whenever I get near you, you look like you're expecting me to bite you."

Oh. *That.*

"I'm not afraid, it's just—" She cut herself off with a sigh. "You don't always respond in ways I'd expect. It's kind of unnerving, like I'm always waiting for the other shoe to drop."

That should do the trick. Accurate, yet vague enough to keep him from homing in on the other reason she was always on alert near him.

"It's not like everything we do fits neatly into a training scenario. Sometimes you need to wing it." He didn't sound defensive or angry, simply matter-of-fact. "When you worked in L.A., did everything always go according to procedure? Didn't you ever find yourself in a situation where you were reacting out of instinct instead of reacting as a cop?"

"No. I can't say that I ever did."

"All right. Fair enough." Obviously not the answer he'd wanted, and he frowned. "But the thing is, I won't put you in danger. You don't have to be afraid I'd ever let you down like that on the job."

As much as she wanted to believe him, Emma *didn't* trust him not to do something risky or impulsive in the heat of the moment, reacting purely on emotion. Charging into that building in the projects had been reckless. The fact that he hadn't seen anything wrong in what he'd done—and worse, hadn't cared about it—still left her feeling unsettled.

Looking away, she opened her door. "I never said you'd get me hurt, and now's not the time to argue about this. Come on. We should get in line."

For a moment, it seemed he might argue anyway, but she didn't give him a chance. She swung out of the car and headed toward the main entrance, waiting for him to catch up to her. When he did, hands in the pockets of his coat as usual, she couldn't tell what he was thinking. Halfway to the main door, she realized she'd forgotten her coat, but decided against going back for it. It was cold, but the line to get inside wasn't long, and it'd probably be hot inside the club, anyway.

She slung the long purse strap over her shoulder as she made her way briskly across the blacktop, aware of Bobby beside her, his heels clicking in counterpoint to hers. After a short wait, they walked through the doors and into a dark, smoky interior shot through with colored lights that streaked and arced erratically from one end to the other.

At the moment, no live band was thrashing away on the small stage, only a DJ playing oldies, lost in his work, jamming to the tunes and oblivious to the frenzied light show. Synthesized, percussion-heavy music assaulted her ears, so loud the pounding beat vibrated through her body.

The current choice was a husky-voiced female growling something about lust. Figured.

"Joan. All right." Halloran spoke loudly over the noise, looking pleased, then he swiveled his hips in a suggestive bump-and-grind as he sang along—but when he took her by the shoulders and tried to pull her onto the dance floor with him, she balked.

"Stop that!"

"What? Don't you like Joan Jett?"

"I don't want to dance."

He gave her a sour look. "Is there anything you do want?"

Emma ignored the unsubtle dig. "Yes—a table or a place to sit while we wait for our party girl to show up."

"That's not what I meant."

"I know." Not interested in waiting for him to rouse himself enough to move on his own power, she clamped her hand around his arm—a little taken aback at the hard strength of his biceps beneath the warm leather—and pulled him after her through the crowd.

He didn't resist, not until a slinky blonde in pink satin zigged, then zagged, out of her way to bump into him with her breasts. Not surprisingly, he stopped. Emma sighed—but didn't let go of his arm.

"Whoops, sorry," Slinky chirped, a blatantly suggestive invitation in her eyes. "You okay?"

"Not a problem."

"You sure? I'd love to make it up to you in any way I can."

Oh, please; they did *not* have time for this crap. Reluctantly, Emma pulled Bobby closer so they looked more coupleish instead of buddyish. Ignoring his arched look, she said tightly, "Get lost. He's with me."

"Poor baby." Slinky pouted in a fake way that made Emma want to knee-cap her. Then, with a wink, she brushed past Bobby, making sure her breasts had a chance to say good-bye, too. "And so sorry to hear that, but if you change your mind, come find me."

When Bobby finally shifted his focus from the woman's shiny, undulating rear, his smile faded. "Why are you looking at me like that? What did I do now?"

His defensive tone made her feel both guilty and peevish, and she sighed. "Never mind. Just try to remember we're working, okay? Ten seconds in the door, and you're already having way too much fun—and all I'm getting is a headache from these stupid flashing lights."

"You really need to get out more and learn to enjoy the moment." He wore a faintly pitying expression, which didn't help her mood any. She pinned him with a stony stare, and after several seconds, he surrendered with a low curse. "All right, all right . . . go find a table. I'll buy a couple drinks."

"But no—"

"Alcoholic drinks. I *know*."

As he stalked off, color a little high, Emma put her height and crowd-control training to work and pushed through the living wall of bodies. She'd hoped to find a table near the bar, but every single one was already occupied or aggressively staked out. Giving up, she surveyed the rest of the place.

It wasn't much more than an open room with a bar and a scattering of tall tables to one side and a stage on the other, and a sizable dance floor shoehorned between the two. There was no ceiling, just exposed pipes, ducts, and metal beams hung with lights and speakers. A tubular, industrial-style balcony circled the main room, angling up, then down again—almost as surreal as a Tim Burton movie set.

Weirdness aside, it would provide a great vantage point for checking out the action below. She headed toward the nearest stairway, and had one foot on the lowest step when a hand touched her shoulder. "Hey, baby, hold up. Wanna dance?"

Turning, Emma saw a dark-haired, thirtyish man in studded black leather gloves, jeans, and a tight white T-shirt. He had a barbed-wire tattoo ringing his biceps, a gold chain around his neck, and an eyebrow ring. He was cute, and already well on his way to feeling no pain.

Smiling, she shook her head. "I'm with someone, but thanks."

Genuine regret crossed his drink-softened features. "That's too bad. I like your dress. You've got a nice ass and great legs."

Emma blinked. She supposed it was a compliment. "Thanks," she repeated stiffly, then shrugged off his hand and made her way up the steps, knowing the punkish James Dean look-alike was staring up her skirt.

Once on the main balcony, she searched out a spot that provided the best view of the club, as well as the rest of the balcony. She would've preferred an area less crowded, but didn't have a lot of options. Below, she scanned the room for blond hair and black leather—which didn't help much, since that was roughly *the* look for a retro punk rock club. Finally, she spotted Bobby, drinks in hand, making his way from the bar—and watched as a number of women impeded his progress by stopping him, smiling and flirting. He glanced around as he smiled and flirted back. Finally, he looked up, spotted her impatient wave, and nodded an acknowledgment.

Still, it took him another ten minutes before he joined her at the balcony rail. He handed her a glass of Coke and a cocktail napkin. Small cup holders and shelves hung at regular intervals from the balcony rail, where partyers could deposit drinks and munchies, and, not feeling thirsty, she slipped her drink into one of the holders. Several minutes passed as she and Bobby stood side by side, looking down at the people on the dance floor and at the bar.

While some wore casual clothes, most had dressed to imitate the popular rockers of the eighties, which resulted in a lot of leather and Lycra, studs and buckles, big jewelry and big hair. The flashing laser lights, in multiple colors, lanced through a thin haze of smoke, and the music was so loud the metal railing and balcony vibrated beneath Emma's hands and feet.

Leaving her coat behind had been smart. It was stuffy, and Bobby threw off major heat. Emma eased away carefully, so he wouldn't notice and jump to the wrong conclusion. Or the right one, for that matter—she couldn't imagine anything more embarrassing than for him to discover she wasn't any more immune to his appeal than half the female population of New Orleans.

Focus on the work, Em.

She poked him with her elbow to get his attention. "Any sign of our girl?"

Bobby shook his head, and the lights reflected off his fair hair in pulsating tones of blue, red, and green. "I asked the bartender if he'd seen her yet. He said no, but that she usually shows up around eight."

Emma nodded and checked her watch. Another thirty minutes to the magic hour. She was glad for the loud music; it gave her an excuse to avoid talking with him unless absolutely necessary.

Not that it helped to ease her discomfort. He leaned casually beside her, and even though she tried to put a little distance between them, he'd moved closer, and now his arm pressed intimately along hers. His hands rested on the rail, large and square, long fingers tapping along with the beat—and to add to her discomfort, a nearby couple was making out with enthusiastic tongue and hand action, unconcerned over who might be watching.

With some wistfulness, Emma wondered what it would be like to be so unselfconscious, so caught up in a moment, that you didn't care what people thought.

Although she tried not to stare, she couldn't exactly avoid noticing. The man and woman were completely lost in each other, kissing and rubbing and touching . . . and it reminded her, with a pang of envy, how much she missed kissing and making love. It had been nearly a year since her detective ex-boyfriend had walked out on her, unable to deal with the fallout and stress of the trial.

When the going gets tough, the tough sometimes bail.

Almost a whole *year* without any sex at all—and here beside her, warm and smelling absolutely lickable, stood a man who probably made her sexual experience look like G-rated Disney fluff. No wonder she was having hot flashes.

"I'd almost swear that boy don't need to breathe." Bobby's amused drawl sounded so close against her ear that she shivered. "And if his girlfriend don't take it easy on his belt, we're gonna have to arrest them."

Emma turned to him—and immediately regretted it. He was watching her intently, with a heat that ruffled her poise and stirred up a mix of messy, inconvenient responses she really didn't need stirred up.

"Only if there's actual penetration. Otherwise, I don't care what they do."

A wave of hot desire washed over her, to her chagrin. She was a *cop*; she'd witnessed shenanigans far more explicit than this without even batting an eyelash, much less getting all worked up, and it wasn't as if she'd only ever had sex in total darkness or only while lying on her back.

But it had been so long, and that alone was enough to make her squirm.

"Looks like fun."

"Bobby." Again, she risked a glance his way, and this time didn't avoid the pale eyes nearly on a level with her own. "Behave."

He arched a brow as his gaze dropped to her lips, then slowly tracked lower. "I'm just saying."

Bastard. Unwilling to play along, much less do her part in marking that stupid betting pool as "paid," Emma turned away, concentrating on everything but Bobby and the private little sex show to her left.

It didn't help, and the dancers below were generating enough friction from bumping and grinding that Emma half expected them to burst into flames. The mating game was in full play at the jammed bar, too, and more and more people were walking through the main doors—none of them, unfortunately, being Madame Barfly.

Damn, but she was really beginning to resent that woman.

The DJ started a new song, one she recognized—Billy Idol's "Rebel Yell." The crowd responded with an enthusiastic howl, and soon two-thirds of the bar was pumping fists into the air and screaming *more-more-more* along with Billy.

After a while, it became impossible not to swing her shoulders or tap her fingers to the powerful, pumping beat—or resist the sheer pull of its energy, especially when the air itself vibrated from the loud music and the force of hundreds of feet stamping on the floor below and the balcony around them. The electric excitement infused her blood and body, building and burning, and not giving in to it ached in a way that was a lot like having sex, wanting to come, but unable to pump high enough or hard enough to fall . . .

Emma squeezed her eyes shut to stop the thought—and wouldn't Bobby have a good laugh over that? Hoping he wasn't picking up on any let's-have-at-it-like-bunnies vibes she might be giving off, she turned to walk somewhere—*anywhere*—when he suddenly grabbed her upper arm.

"Hey!" Surprise, along with the pain of his fingers digging into her skin, made her gasp. "What are—"

His mouth closed over hers, cutting off her protest, and then he kissed her. No chaste peck on the lips, but a very real kiss that stopped just short of his tongue invading her mouth.

Still caught in the sensual pull of the music, enticed by the warmth of lips tasting sweetly of Coke, she responded on instinct, her mouth yielding beneath the pressure of his. And when he ran his hands down her back to cup her bottom and pull her hips against his, any thoughts of protesting vanished.

Bobby shifted, raining soft kisses from the line of her jaw up to her ear, and she shivered as he whispered, "Touch me. Kiss me back like you mean it."

She didn't need to be told twice. Even as she fleetingly wondered what the hell was going on, she slowly slid one hand over to clutch his shoulder, then angled her head so that he could more easily reach her neck.

Eyes fluttering shut as he rubbed her bottom again, Emma almost gasped when he kissed the sensitive spot just beneath her earlobe.

"Look over my shoulder," he whispered roughly. "To your left."

Relief, followed by sharp disappointment: Of course he hadn't been suddenly seized with an irresistible passion for her. He was working—and she should be working, too.

When his mouth returned to hers, Emma kissed him back as she looked over his shoulder—and tensed.

Chloe Mitsumi stood a few feet away, in a tight pair of purple crushed-velvet hip-huggers with a lace-up fly. She also wore a tiny black T-shirt that bared her arms and most of her flat little belly.

And she wasn't alone.

As Billy Idol faded away, Bobby ran his hands upward along Emma's sides, brushing her breasts . . . oh, God, this felt much, much too real.

"Yes, it's Chloe," he whispered after kissing his way to her other ear. "Do you see the man with her?"

Wiry, Asian, good-looking, and dressed slickly in a dark suit. Pretending to come in for another kiss, she looked him right in the eyes. "Yes."

"I know him, he knows me, and he's not a nice guy. He worked for Chloe's brother." His lashes lowered a fraction, enough that she couldn't read his expression, and then he moved in for another kiss as Debbie Harry's sex-soaked voice belted out an urgent command: *call me, call me* . . .

Emma had to fight the need to close her eyes and melt against his warm body. A moment later, he broke away and leaned his forehead intimately against hers. "I don't want him to see me, but I want to know what he's doing. Okay?"

Standing so close, with his hands still on her rear end, she didn't dare let him see her eyes. She couldn't hide that she liked what he was doing to her.

"Okay?" he repeated.

She nodded shortly.

He cupped her chin, thumb brushing her lower lip, and as he moved his mouth toward hers he whispered, "I'm going to kiss you again so you can get a good look at them, then tell me what he's doing."

This time, his kiss was softer, and it helped—a little—to keep her focused on Chloe and Mr. Slick.

As Bobby's lips moved up the line of her throat, she murmured, "They're talking."

"Are they arguing?" His hands were on her bottom again, kneading and rubbing, and her knees went weak. Dammit, how was she supposed to concentrate? "Is she trying to get away from him?"

From beneath lowered lids, Emma watched Chloe and her companion—and sucked Bobby's earlobe into her mouth, satisfied to hear his sharp intake of breath as his body went rigid. Served him right; he was having a little too much fun at her expense, and she had no intention of letting him gain the upper hand.

"She doesn't look upset." She kissed his lobe, then nibbled. "Just impatient. Like she doesn't want to talk with him."

The very picture of hip boredom, Chloe alternated between tossing back her long hair, sipping her drink, posturing a little, or nodding to whatever Mr. Slick said to her.

Then he must've pissed her off, because she straightened from her languid slouch, brows lowering in a fierce frown, and jabbed wickedly long nails at the man's chest as she snapped something in response.

Emma moved against Bobby, shifting so that she could nuzzle his chin, then kissed along his jaw to his ear, smelling leather, soap, and that heady, dark scent of his cologne. "All right, now she's mad; she's poking him in the chest and looking like she wants to rip out his guts."

"And what's he doing?"

Again, as his breath brushed against her ear, goose bumps prickled along her skin. Emma lowered her arms and slipped them beneath his coat to wrap around his waist, fingers spread along the small of his back, just below his gun, and then rested her head on his shoulder as if cuddling.

Taking her cue, Bobby wrapped his arms around her in a tight embrace, then angled his head to bring his ear nearer to her mouth.

"He's smiling, but he looks pissed, too," Emma answered, as Bobby began to sway on his feet, gently rocking her from side to side. "He's getting in her face. She's not impressed."

Something Emma couldn't say for herself. She was quite impressed by the feel of Bobby in her arms, the lean strength of his muscles beneath her hands, the comforting warmth of his body against her, the soft texture of his silk shirt, and the denser, smooth leather outlining his tight rear to perfection.

And he smelled so, *so* good.

Then, through the haze of her own desire, came the realization that he was getting into their pretend make-out session, too, because while she might be able to hide her response to him, he couldn't hide his. Not with the unmistakable hardness of his erection pressed against her lower belly.

Emma pulled away slightly, meeting his gaze. One side

of his mouth quirked up and he murmured, "Sorry about that."

But he didn't look sorry at all, and before she could take refuge in the safety of their cuddle—and hide her face in his coat—he kissed her again.

No sham emotion this time, and with the feel of his arousal against her, Emma couldn't hold back any longer.

Why fight it? His kisses turned her knees weak, burned down deep inside, and he made it so easy to lose herself in his kiss, in the powerful shelter of his arms.

Wrong, so wrong . . . but she wanted it; wanted to know what it would be like to kiss a man who'd satisfied the likes of that sensual creature in the purple hip-huggers and peekaboo shirt. When it came to sex, maybe she'd never be in the same league as Chloe Mitsumi—but she could fantasize right along with the dreamiest of dreamers.

Then Bobby's hands skimmed the bottom swell of her breasts and all further thought scattered. His kisses grew more urgent, more insistent, and before she even realized what was happening, she'd opened her mouth to let him inside, tongues sliding and caressing, tasting sweet and hot.

She struggled against letting her eyes drift shut, knowing she had to keep Mitsumi and her companion in view. But they were just talking again, nothing happening, and Emma couldn't resist sliding her hands lower, down the smooth, silk-covered curve of his back, and lower yet, cupping Bobby's tight rear with a throat-deep sigh of satisfaction.

He responded with a low groan, and pushed his hips

against her, deepening his kiss, his hands just under her arms, thumbs caressing the sides of her breasts.

God, she wanted to climb up along the lean length of his body, wrap her legs around his waist, and—

Bobby suddenly broke the kiss, and as he pulled back a fraction, their gazes locked. Changing shades of emotion flashed across his face: confusion, surprise, wariness—and a raw physical lust amplified by parted lips and erratic breathing.

The expression in her eyes probably mirrored his, which seemed to be asking: *What the hell is this?*

As if she had an answer. Emma focused again on Chloe—and just in time to see Mr. Slick lose his patience.

Sucking in her breath shakily, she took Bobby's face in her hands, as if intending to kiss him again, and said, "He just grabbed her by the arms, and he's dragging her toward the stairs. She doesn't want to go with him, and her cool's looking a little shaken."

Bobby eased back, face hardening. "We're following."

He waited several seconds, and then, locked in what anybody would see as a drunken, let's-go-screw-in-the-john embrace, they started for the stairs. He kept his head bent, nuzzling her hair, still hiding his face.

Not that it mattered. Mr. Slick didn't even bother looking behind him. Now he had Chloe by both arms, pushing her along like she was a chair he wanted to reposition. She didn't resist much, but judging by the sullen look on her face, she was waiting until she reached the main floor, rather than the stairs, to try and get away.

Smart: less chance of getting hurt, and bouncers were around to lend a hand. All she and Bobby had to do was wait for Chloe to start screaming.

But Bobby had other plans; the second his foot left the last step, he released Emma and ordered, "Grab Chloe. The other one's mine."

Before she could even react, he'd shoved through the crowd after Mr. Slick with a ruthlessness that left a lot of pissed-off people in his wake. Setting her jaw, Emma followed, digging in her bag for her shield.

Chloe began struggling in earnest. She twisted around, maybe to yell for help, and saw Bobby closing in. With the music blaring, Emma couldn't hear anything, but she didn't have any trouble reading the woman's lips: *Oh, shit*!

Mr. Slick glanced back when Bobby clamped his hand on his shoulder. His eyes widened, and his lips formed an even cruder curse.

Bobby flashed that wide, angelic smile, and Chloe yanked free, ducking, just as Mr. Slick spun and punched Bobby in the face.

Blood splattered as Bobby crashed back against a crowded table, sending beer pitchers and mixed drinks flying. Booze-drenched women shrieked, their boyfriends shouted in anger.

A split second later Bobby was on his feet again, smile widening to a feral grin, blood dripping unheeded from his nose. The music eased up long enough for Emma to hear him say, "Thanks. I was really hoping you'd do that."

Bobby slugged Mr. Slick, sending him stumbling into the crowd behind him. Bobby was on top of him in a heartbeat. More screams and angry cursing erupted, and then two men—either drunk-mad, aroused by the smell of blood, or simply excited by the violence-charged moment—rushed Bobby. He ducked at the last second, and the men collided. They staggered, bellowing insults at each other, spit flying and neck muscles corded, traded a couple of shoves, and then started whaling away with their fists.

More men moved in, whether to stop the brawl or join it, it soon didn't matter as a dozen men, and several women, started shoving, punching, kicking, and rolling on the floor to the accompaniment of shrieks and huge speakers blaring Iggy Pop, wailing electric guitars, and maniacal drumbeats.

Emma glanced away from her embattled partner to the flash of purple threading sinuously between leather-and-Lycra-clad bodies, clearly headed toward the exit.

At the same moment she decided Bobby could hold his own, he dodged a punch, glared her way, and yelled, "Grab her, dammit!"

Shield out, Emma ordered people out of her way as she shoved through the gathering crowd. Her runaway party girl never slowed, but she glanced back once—and when she saw Emma charging after her, she immediately whirled forward again and ran full steam for the doors.

Chloe Mitsumi might be small enough to wriggle through tight spaces, but Emma's legs were a lot longer, and she quickly closed the distance. She caught up to the woman at the doors and lunged in front of her, blocking her escape.

Rocking on her stiletto-heeled boots, Chloe Mitsumi stumbled to a halt, annoyance flashing across her face.

Breathing hard, Emma all but shoved her shield up the woman's nose. "Detective Emma Frey. I need to speak with you, Ms. Mitsumi."

Madame Barfly rolled her eyes, which were heavy on the black liner and purple eye shadow. Then she smiled thinly. "My, my. Aren't you the tall one. Bobby didn't tell me you were some Xena clone."

At the mention of Bobby's name, Emma glanced over at the brawl, and winced as Mr. Slick's fist connected with Bobby's kidney.

"Maybe you should go rescue him," Chloe said.

"He's a cop; he can handle himself." At least she sounded convincing. "And the bouncers will break up the fight soon, anyway. Come outside with me now."

"Unless you're arresting me, I don't have to talk to you, and I don't have to go anywhere with you. I know my rights, so don't even bother trying to bullshit me."

The DJ abruptly cut the music, and a loud roar shuddered through the club. Emma glanced back again, and saw Bobby fall, still wrestling with Mr. Slick, in the middle of the melee. More people joined in the fight, even as the bouncers struggled to bring the situation under control.

Catching a quick movement from the corner of her eye, Emma whipped back around, yanking Chloe to a halt by her shirt. The woman turned slowly, a mix of malevolence and glee on her doll-like face.

"Running away from cops? A really bad idea." Disgusted that the ditz found all this amusing, Emma added tersely, "I mean it. Don't move. I have a few questions—"

Another roar, and a high-pitched, chilling scream, and no matter how badly she wanted to restrain Chloe—who was already inching away, daring Emma to stop her—Bobby was in trouble. She had no choice but to help break up the brawl before somebody ended up hurt. Or worse.

Anger pounding through her, Emma started backing

away. "I need to help stop this fight. It'll take a few minutes, so please wait here."

Chloe's dark brows arched. "Well, sure. Since you asked so nicely."

As Emma hurried toward the fight, she checked to make sure Madame Barfly was cooperating—and watched as the key to her case rabbited off.

"Ah, *shit*!"

Torn between saving Bobby's ass and going after Chloe, Emma hesitated, but only for a second. Fueled by frustration—and a need to smack her idiot partner upside his head—she ruthlessly pushed and shoved her way to the fight, shield up.

She kept shouting "Police!" until the word finally pierced through the haze of drunken violence. People began pulling back, except for those too far gone to understand what was happening, but it was enough to give the bouncers the chance to add their muscle to her authoritative commands.

Bobby stood, looking a little worse for wear, and when Mr. Slick jumped to his feet, ready for another round, Emma kicked him in the back of his knees, knocking him down again. With her knee pressed against the small of his back, she twisted his arm behind him, and glanced at Bobby.

Hunkered down beside her, he wiped at his nose, and when she saw the unholy lights of excitement dancing in his eyes, she scowled. "Get my cuffs. They're in my bag."

As Bobby helped her cuff Mr. Slick, she leaned toward him and hissed, "You shouldn't be allowed out anywhere without a damn *leash,* Halloran!"

Surprise crossed his bruised face, then his eyes narrowed. "Maybe you didn't notice, but he hit me first."

"Because you shoved me," said Mr. Slick, his voice muffled against the booze-drenched floor.

"Shut up," Emma and Bobby ordered at the same moment. Then, above the now-subdued din of the club, Emma heard the wail of police sirens.

Lovely. She couldn't wait to explain this mess to a couple of uniforms.

"Hey." Bobby touched the back of his hand to his nose, then looked down. "I'm bleeding."

"No shit." After hoisting Mr. Slick to his feet, Emma picked up a cocktail napkin off the floor and handed it to Bobby. "Who's this guy?"

"Stuart Yamada." Bobby pressed the napkin to his nose with one hand and seized Yamada's collar with the other, directing him toward the nearest exit. The bouncers watched, uncertain about letting him pass.

"He's a cop, too." Emma gave them a brief, reassuring smile. "We'll be outside if you need us. The other officers will deal with the situation here. Tell them Detective Emma Frey told you it was all right."

The bouncers nodded, and as she and Bobby walked toward the door, Bobby looked at her over Yamada's head. "Where's Chloe?"

"Gone."

"You let her get away?" His tone sounded faintly mocking; probably how she'd sounded yesterday when she'd asked him the same question.

"It was more like she walked away while I went to rescue your sorry ass!"

"There's nothing sorry about my ass, darlin', and it didn't need rescuing."

Yamada made a face of disgust. "Are you trying to impress the bitch?"

Bobby rapped his knuckles against Yamada's head. "Show the lady a little respect, Stuart."

Two patrol cars, sirens grinding down but still in full light-show mode, pulled up by the main doors. Two uniforms approached, one from each car, hands near their belts. Both Emma and Bobby made sure their shields were visible.

The first officer, a stocky blond woman with French braids, raised a brow when she saw the blood on Bobby's face. Then she took in his clothes, as well as the lack of Emma's hemline, and exchanged glances with the other officer, an older guy with short gray hair and a bit of a paunch. Emma read his nameplate: D. Ferria.

"You guys working undercover?" Ferria asked.

"Something like that," Bobby answered.

Ferria eyed Emma's dress with dry amusement. "As far as I can tell, Detective, there's not much of you under cover."

Not in the mood for cop humor, Emma ignored the comment.

The woman motioned toward Bobby's nose. "Broken?"

"Nah. Just bloodied up a little."

"So what's going on? Who's he?" Ferria motioned to Yamada.

"Somebody I want to talk to, but he got confused about the preferred mode of communication." Bobby grinned; hardly a comforting sight with all the blood. "And then a fight broke out. It's not too bad—the bouncers have it under control, but you should go on in and check it out."

Ferria nodded, and judging by his bored expression he'd broken up more bar fights over the years than he cared to count.

"Do you mind if we use the back of your squad to talk?" Bobby asked.

"No problem." Ferria's gaze dropped to Emma's hemline again, but this time he only shook his head, and spoke into his radio as he jogged inside the club.

"I'm going to be more persistent than Officer Ferria." Emma eyed the handcuffed Yamada. "What's the deal with this guy?"

"Like I said, he was one of Jacob Mitsumi's crew. We managed to get convictions against some of them, along with Mitsumi, but they're like cockroaches. Squash a few, and even more crawl out from the sewers. And you can tell they're his boys by this." Bobby roughly shifted Yamada around and, paying no heed to the man's colorful protests, pulled open his shirt.

"Hey, Halloran, I didn't know you felt that way about me."

"Shut up," Bobby ordered, but it was automatic, without any heat. Then he pointed to Yamada's chest. "See this?"

"I work out," Yamada said smugly. "Pecs of steel."

Tuning out the man's attempts to get a rise out of them, Emma peered at the tattoo beneath Bobby's finger. "A red dragon?"

"That was Mitsumi's street name. He had a red dragon tattooed along the entire length of his back."

Emma winced. "Ow."

Bobby pulled the man's shirt back together—and Yamada exploded into action, elbowing him hard in the belly. Bobby doubled over with a grunt as Yamada yanked free and rammed his shoulder into Emma's chest.

Caught off guard, she stumbled backward and fell. The sting of pain as her palms scraped along the pavement hardly registered, but when she saw the ragged holes in her overpriced pantyhose, her temper snapped.

As Yamada scrambled past her, Emma kicked her leg out, tripping him. He went down with a painfully loud smack on the blacktop. Climbing back to her feet, Emma marched over to Yamada, hauled him up by the back of his coat, and "assisted" him to the side of the squad car with a shove. He sprawled across the NOPD's crescent-and-star insignia, shaking his head groggily.

"Spread 'em, Stuart." She nudged his ankles with her heels until he'd widened his legs to the point of minor discomfort. "Do you have any weapons on you? Anything in your pockets that could cut me?"

"No," he muttered, breathing hard. "Fuck, that *hurt*!"

"You better not be lying. You already wrecked my pantyhose, so I'm not too happy with you right now." She quickly searched him, and as she patted up the inside of his thighs she added, "And if you hit me like that again, I swear I'll kick in your balls so hard that you'll be chewing on them for a week."

Yamada tensed, and glanced down at her hands, resting just below his groin. Alarm flickered across his face, warring with his bravado. "Whoa, baby, that's harsh."

Halloran walked closer, hand rubbing his belly, and wearing a deceptively easy smile. "Ain't she something? And I think she might be meaner than me. If I were you, I'd think about cooperating."

"Well, well . . . what's this?" Emma patted along the unmistakable outline of an automatic weapon in the front pocket of Yamada's pants, then removed it—but without giving Yamada the satisfaction of showing her disgust at having to touch his erection as she did so. "Looks like a gun. And . . . uh-oh, it's loaded. Stuart, I'm disappointed. You lied to me."

Bobby's smile broke into a wide grin. "Somebody's going to central lockup tonight. What are we at now, six times that I've arrested you?"

"Yeah, we had us some real sweet moments, but you know, if we keep this up, I just worry you won't respect me no more in the morning. By the way, the Dragon sends his regards. How's the shoulder?"

The humor left Bobby's face in an instant. "Get in the car."

He wasn't gentle as he stuffed Yamada into the back of the squad, and Emma made a mental note to quiz Bobby more thoroughly on his relationships with Mitsumi and the sister.

After pushing aside a bunch of forms and Ferria's half-eaten candy bar, she sat in the front passenger seat, then shifted around and asked, "What were you talking about with Chloe Mitsumi?"

"I was checking up on her, seeing how she's been doing. Just a friendly chat. She's hot for me."

Emma leaned closer and turned her scraped palms, still oozing blood, toward him. "You attacked two police officers, were carrying a concealed weapon, and assaulted a woman and attempted to force her against her will to leave with you, which sounds like attempted kidnapping to me. Things aren't looking good for you, so can the smart-ass commentary."

Yamada turned toward the window, refusing to look at her.

"Were you talking to Chloe about who trashed her apartment? Do you know who did it? What they were looking for?" Bobby asked. "My nose hurts like hell, Stuart, so don't bullshit me none. You answer my questions."

"Or what?" Yamada affected an exaggerated tone of boredom. "I'm already going to lockup. There's nothing else you can threaten me with."

"Are you trying to make me mad?" Bobby asked softly, and a shimmer of violence suddenly crackled in the air. "Because I gotta warn you, that's not such a smart idea."

Yamada's gaze slid briefly toward Bobby, and he shrugged. "You know you can't do anything to me, Halloran."

A muscle in Bobby's jaw tensed, and he took in a long, slow breath before asking, "Do you remember Willie Farmer?"

Yamada sneered. "He's a stupid asshole."

"Yeah, and now he's a *dead* stupid asshole. Somebody put a bullet through his brain last week. You know who did it?"

"Nope."

"You know why?"

"Maybe you should read me my rights. If you're accusing me of gunning down some dickwad, I want my lawyer."

"We're not saying you killed Farmer. All we want is to protect Chloe Mitsumi from the people who destroyed her apartment, but she's not being cooperative. We're concerned about her," Emma said, going for reasonable and calm, since Bobby already had the scary hothead routine covered. "We just want to know if you can help us with that."

"Especially since the Dragon will find a way to smoke your ass if anything happens to his baby sister," Bobby drawled. "Right?"

At that, Yamada scowled, plainly not happy at the reminder. "Willie went to see Chloe. What I heard is that he was delivering a message to her from Mr. Mitsumi. Since she won't open his letters, he sent Willie to talk to her."

"What was the message?" Emma asked.

"That's between Mr. Mitsumi, his sister, and Willie. I don't know."

Emma frowned. "So you're saying that somebody demolished Ms. Mitsumi's apartment over a *verbal* message from her brother?"

The silence lengthened, and finally Yamada sighed. "I guess whoever hit her place thought Willie left something with her."

"Who broke in?" Bobby's nose had started bleeding again, and he pulled the crumpled napkin out of his coat pocket. "And what did Willie give her?"

"You gone deaf?" Yamada shifted on the seat, and the scent of his fear gathered in the confines of the squad. "I already said I don't know who busted up her place. It wasn't any of my guys, I can swear to that."

"You're lying, Stuart," Emma said quietly, noting beads of sweat forming on his upper lip. "You know who broke into her apartment."

Yamada met her gaze squarely, his dark eyes flat and

cold. "Let me spell it out for you, Detective. You can threaten me, beat on me, lock me up, but there are people out there who'll kill me if I give them a reason. Question time is over. I'm not saying one more fucking word."

Twelve

By the time the uniforms hauled Yamada off to lockup, and Bobby and Emma had squared away matters at the club, it was nearly midnight—and raining, the drops hitting the windshield in a rhythm that matched the steady throbbing in his nose. Emma had been quiet as she drove him back to his place, but Bobby sensed she was building up to some kind of blowup.

Most likely she was mad about how he'd kissed her on the balcony. He wasn't sure how he'd explain it away, because he didn't know what had happened, either—although that dress she was almost wearing might account for a major part of his reaction to her.

Maybe he'd get lucky and she'd just yell at him for starting a fight. That he could deal with; he'd spent half his life in trouble over one thing or another.

As if on cue, she asked abruptly, "Can I ask you a personal question?"

Dread knotted his gut; it was that kiss, all right, and he was about to catch major shit about it. "Depends on how personal, darlin'."

"Were you and Chloe Mitsumi lovers?"

Huh. So much for thinking his kiss had ruffled her. Even more wary, he answered carefully. "A few years back. We weren't together for long."

"But long enough that she felt comfortable walking through your front door at nearly three in the morning?"

"I'm not sure what you're getting at, but me and Chloe stayed on friendly terms. I always stay on friendly terms with my ex-girlfriends."

Emma picked up on the wry note coloring his voice, and glanced away from the road with a small frown. "So you still see her?"

"Not in a dating kind of way. I ran into her at a bar last November, and we had a good talk. Nothing seemed out of the ordinary."

"What's her relationship to her brother? Her boss said she hated him, but I got the impression from you that they were close."

Before leaving the club, one of the bartenders had given him a plastic baggie filled with ice, and he pressed it to his nose. While not broken, it hurt like a bitch and he'd have one hell of a black eye by tomorrow. "It's complicated."

"I'm good at complicated. Explain, please."

"They were the kids of a mixed marriage, which was a lot harder for people to accept back in the late sixties and early seventies."

"Neither side of the family approved of the marriage?"

"You got it. Chloe's parents were a couple of California radical types into the free love and drug lifestyle, and they died in a drunk-driving accident when Chloe was two and Jacob eight. Mom's family didn't want the kids, so they ended up with dad's parents in Little Tokyo, where Jacob fell in with a bad crowd. Eventually, he took off, and Chloe joined him after he'd settled in New Orleans. He never let her near the business side of his life, and watched her like a hawk. After a while, she got tired of that."

"So she rebelled in a way that would piss him off the most."

Bobby nodded. "Even though she didn't want to admit what he was involved in, his trial and conviction were hard on her. To you and me, guys like Mitsumi are bottom feeders, but to Chloe, he was all she had left."

"Are you trying to make me feel sorry for her?"

"I'm just answering your question. People used Chloe to get to her brother, including me, and that hurt her." Catching her questioning look, he added, "I was investigating a murder; I followed her into a women's bathroom one night and pinned her to a wall as I asked her questions. She didn't like that much."

"This was the case that got you suspended, right?"

"Yeah . . . and it also got me shot."

Emma fell silent for a long moment. "So let me see if I have this right: You bullied her, sent her brother to prison, then slept with her."

Bobby looked down at his hands, flexing them to ease the dull pain in his knuckles. Damn; Yamada had a skull thick as a chunk of concrete. "It wasn't as twisted as you make it sound, Emma."

"So why'd you do it? Because you felt sorry for her?"

He had to hand it to her; she knew how to hit a raw nerve on the first try. "She was going through a bad time, and I wanted to help."

"You could've done that without sleeping with her."

Although his temper was wearing thin, Bobby smiled. "With Chloe, there wasn't much sleeping going on. We were too busy having lots of dirty, kinky sex."

He thought that would shut her up, but he misjudged her. Again.

"You still could've helped her without screwing her."

"I didn't help her out with the expectation that she'd owe me a few months of sexual favors." Anger edged his voice. "It just happened. I mean, come on. She likes to have fun, she's beautiful, and she's not a bad person. I liked her, and I still do. We had a good time—and that's all it ever was between us."

Or all he was willing to admit right now.

"So what's the deal with you and her brother?"

"He nearly killed me, and hurt a good friend of mine, not to mention he was a vicious bastard who headed up a gang of killers, dealers, and pimps. You name it, he did it. Plus, he was crazy."

Emma braked for a stoplight. "He's obviously still doing business of some sort out of prison."

"Nothing much, more like keeping up with the latest news. His inner circle was very loyal to him, though, which is why they're still looking after Chloe. Even if she doesn't want it."

"I bet Mitsumi wasn't thrilled when he heard you were banging his baby sister." A small, rueful smile curved her lips. "You sure do like pushing those limits, don't you?"

"It's a free world."

"Did it ever occur to you Mitsumi might just be pissed enough to suggest one of his boys take you out of the picture?"

"It crossed my mind a few times, but I didn't worry about it."

She sighed. "So where does Willie Farmer fit into things?"

"I already told you he used to be one of Mitsumi's gofers and regularly watched over Chloe. She hated most of her brother's goons, but she was a little nicer to Willie. Maybe because she felt sorry for him."

"So she'd listen to whatever he had to say, including a message from her brother."

"Probably."

"I don't think she's as innocent as you'd like to believe. I've got a feeling she's a player."

Bobby shook his head. "Chloe drinks, parties hard, and maybe sleeps around more than she should, but she hated what her brother did. She wouldn't get caught up in that kind of thing."

"You'd be willing to bet your life on it?"

"Yes."

"Well, I'm not. We need to bring her in for questioning, so no more playing nice. Tomorrow I'm asking Strong to alert the patrol division to keep an eye out for her." As she turned onto the road that led to his cottage, she glanced his way. "She was counting on you to call off the investigation, hoping her past relationship with you would make certain of it. That's why she came to you. You know that, right?"

"I used her once, so I can't complain that she's returned the favor. It makes us even." He wanted to drop the subject of Chloe, itching to ask Emma why she'd kissed him the way she had at the club—because that hadn't been any chaste nibble. Instead, he asked, "What are your plans for tomorrow?"

"Talking with Giacomo, if he ever returns my call, then I'm trying Chloe's friends again to see if they've seen or heard from her. Nothing came back on the prints, and a guy living a few houses down was on parole for a couple burglaries, but he was out of town during the break-in. The landlord told me he closed the open window, so nothing to follow up there, either. I'm thinking I should double-check with the responding officer, since he's the only one who talked with Chloe before she split."

"Sounds like a plan."

She let out a long sigh. "I sure hope so. I'm tired of trolling clubs."

"You didn't have fun tonight?"

Bobby wasn't sure what he meant to accomplish by dragging up the subject, but it was bugging the hell out of him. He'd really enjoyed kissing her, and she'd seemed to have already filed it away as just another night on the job. He needed to know the score—especially since he could've sworn those hungry kisses weren't faked.

When she didn't respond, he added, "It looked to me as if you didn't mind kissing me all that much."

Even in the dark interior of the car, he could see her chest rise and fall as she took a deep breath. "Don't go there, Bobby."

"Why not? It happened."

"What do you want me to say?" She pulled up in front of his house, double-parked, and didn't turn off the engine. "You know you're good-looking. You know you're a good kisser. Do you need me to tell you it was nice? Okay, I admit it was nice. All my girl parts were groovin' with your boy parts. But it didn't mean anything, and we both know that."

Stung, he shifted to face her. "I wouldn't say that."

"Oh, please." She sounded thoroughly disgusted— not the usual reaction from a woman he'd kissed. "You didn't give me a second look before tonight, so *don't* expect me to be flattered that you bothered to notice me only after I'd bared most of my breasts and wore a skirt nearly up to my ass."

Bobby went very still as heated anger—and embarrassment—took hold. "It wasn't like I stood a chance in hell of *not* noticing. And now you're, what, upset because I said you're attractive?"

"All this, the dress, heels, and makeup—it's not real. It's not me."

His gaze clashed with hers. "I think we need to talk. You better come inside. I have some antibacterial cream you can put on your knees, and—"

"I am not going inside your house. I'm going home. And we're going to forget this ever happened."

"In my experience, that never works."

Her grip on the steering wheel tightened. "Did you know there's a betting pool in the department on how long it'll take you to get me into bed?"

Stunned, he stared at her, and finally said quietly, "No, I didn't."

Her gaze searched his, looking for lies, for any sign that he thought it was funny. "Well, now you do."

Jaw working, he struggled to maintain his calm. "Who?"

"I didn't ask, and it doesn't matter. Nobody is winning the bet." She hesitated. "And I don't want you making trouble about it. Sometimes the best way to deal with things like this is not to give anybody the satisfaction of knowing how much it hurts."

"I'm sorry."

She shook her head, and although she smiled, perhaps to reassure him that she didn't hate his guts even after all this, it looked tense. "That's why we forget tonight ever happened. I've been under a lot of stress, emotions running high, and if the wrong mood hits at the wrong time . . . sometimes it leads to stupid things. Kissing you instead of *pretending* to kiss you was one of them. We'll get over it."

Ouch; straight through the heart—but points to her for honesty.

Bobby opened his door, pausing before he stepped out. "I always seem to piss you off."

Another long, tense silence. Another long, soft sigh. "I'm really tired, Bobby. Let's call it a night, okay? See you tomorrow."

She put the car in gear—a cue to him to get lost—so he stepped back and watched her drive away. Then he turned and walked slowly up his porch steps, really beginning to feel the late hour and the night's kicks and punches.

His bruised nose throbbed dully, and he rotated his bad shoulder, wincing at a sharp stab of pain—a hot shower, a handful of Tylenol, and sleep were the best medicine for that chronic problem.

Inside, he switched on the lights and saw the answering machine light blinking. As he crossed the room, he stripped off his coat and holster and tossed them onto the couch, then hit the Play button.

Dim sounds of traffic, a chatter of conversation . . . the call came from a pay phone by a busy street. Then Chloe's voice filled the room: "I told you to back off, Bobby. I'm serious—leave me alone. Stop following me. And stop asking questions."

A horn blared on the recording, and when her voice came again, it sounded clearer, as if she'd moved the mouthpiece closer. "Keep this up, and you're going to cause trouble . . . and not just for me. I'll be okay if you back off. It's not worth it, Bobby. I swear it. I've got things under control, so please, for once, listen to me."

Then she hung up.

For a long moment after, Bobby stood in silence, feeling both Emma's rejection and Chloe's resistance like a one-two punch to the gut. Finally, still massaging his shoulder, he headed into the bathroom and ran the hot water until steam filled the room.

Once in the shower, he leaned against the tile wall, grimacing at another twinge of pain. As he closed his eyes, he dropped his head back, letting the hot water run down his body, easing away the aches and knots of tension, no longer fighting the heavy weariness pulling at him, wanting to find, if even for only a few moments, a mindless, numbing peace.

Thirteen

By noon, Emma already wanted to file the day away as a total bust—and it had kicked off to a bad start when the captain called her and Bobby into his office and proceeded to chew them out. Rumors of the Punk Amok ruckus had reached Strong before he'd even noticed Bobby's black eye.

Bobby tried claiming full blame for the incident, despite the fact she'd gone along willingly, but before she could tell Bobby to stop trying to protect her, Strong zeroed in on the truth and bitched them out equally.

And then, when Emma admitted Chloe had gotten away, it looked for a moment as if Strong wanted to bang his head on his desk in frustration.

"Find that woman," Strong had ordered through clenched teeth. "Haul her ass in here for obstruction of justice or indecent exposure, I don't care what, but you get this case wrapped up without making my department the joke of every other district!"

Bobby quickly made himself scarce by heading off to question a suspect in custody for his City Park muggings case, and Emma set about contacting as many of Chloe Mitsumi's friends as she could find.

After a quick lunch break with Alycia, she returned to her desk to write up her notes, and had just sat down when her phone rang. "Detective Frey."

"Hey, this is Detective Gary Giacomo from Five, returning your call on the Willie Farmer shooting."

About damn time. "Thanks for getting back to me. So quickly."

A short silence. "I've been busy as hell, and as far as I'm concerned, ol' Willie died of natural causes, so he hasn't been at the top of my priority list."

"I wouldn't call a bullet through his head natural causes."

"In the world Willie Farmer lived in, it is," Giacomo said dryly.

What a guy.

Figuring there wasn't much cause for polite chatting, Emma pulled out her notepad and pen and got to the point: "When I was looking for Chloe Mitsumi earlier this week, I heard there was another detective asking questions about her. That must've been you?"

"Sure; I'm following up on leads, and I've got witnesses who saw Mitsumi talking with Farmer a few hours before he ended up dead. Then I hear from my DIU commander you're working on the Mitsumi apartment break-in, and I'm thinking we should share information, since there's a good chance my case and yours are connected."

Very true, but she'd made detective by being a creative thinker, tenacious, and intensely competitive, and it went against the grain to share cases with a cop from outside. She had every intention of doing whatever was necessary to clear the case, but did wanting the lion's share of the credit make her an awful, selfish person?

Oh, well. At least he wasn't a Fed.

"I'd be happy to cooperate in any way I can."

"So you got anything for me?" Giacomo asked.

"Until I find Mitsumi, I don't have a thing. Sorry."

"I hear Bobby Halloran's helping you on this one."

Emma tensed. "That'd be correct. Why?"

"Has he talked with any of Jacob Mitsumi's old crew?"

"Yes. He didn't turn up anything useful."

"Tell him to ask about *netsuke*."

"*Netsuke?*" she repeated in surprise, her voice rising loudly enough that several detectives—including her perennial favorite tormenter, Mottson—swiveled in their chairs to stare at her.

"I talked with this knuckle-dragger who used to be one of Mitsumi's bodyguards. Apparently he talked to Farmer, too, and Farmer rambled on about treasure hunts and *netsuke*. I guess *netsuke* are—"

"Miniature Japanese carvings. I know what they are." And this case just kept getting stranger and stranger. "So Chloe has the *netsuke*?"

"That seems to be a point of confusion, one I'm hoping to clear up when I find her."

"Good luck in that. She's slippery and sneaky. Can you tell me the name of the knuckle-dragger you questioned?"

"Lew Watkins. Bobby knows him."

But it wasn't Bobby's case, it was hers—and with an effort, she tamped back her impatience. "Tell me where I can find Watkins. I want to talk to him."

Silence. "Finding him is the easy part, but talking to him—not gonna happen."

Unease stirred. "What do you mean?"

"Lew Watkins is occupying a table at the morgue. A couple fishermen found him near an old shack on Lake Pontchartrain early this morning, sitting in his car, and shot through the back of his head."

"Shit." Emma tipped back in her chair. "Thanks for the info. It's been very helpful. If I pick up anything new, I'll give you a call."

After hanging up, she frowned at the piles of papers and folders on her desk, thinking her simple alleged burglary was shaping up to be something other than simple—and rapidly turning ugly.

"What's the matter, Frey? In over your head on this one?"

Emma looked several desks over at Mottson, leaning back in his chair, grinning at her—but it wasn't a friendly grin.

"Excuse me?" Emma asked coldly.

"Sounds like that Mitsumi cupcake's giving you a run for your money. Maybe you need help from more experienced detectives."

"Mottson, are you always this much of an asshole?"

Before Mottson could respond, Bobby ambled into the office, a can of Coke in one hand, a Butterfinger in the other—a small, envious, mean part of her hoped someday that spectacular metabolism of his faltered, just a bit—and smacked Mottson on the head with the candy bar as he passed by.

"Mottson's only an asshole on days that end in *y*. Unfortunately, he has a brain, and since we need all the brains we can get, we put up with him."

"You're confusing me with yourself, Halloran," Mottson retorted, but he sounded more amused than offended. Then, after a galling wink at Emma, he turned back to his own work.

As Bobby sat at his desk, his gaze caught hers and she quickly turned away. Here was irony: She'd been so intent on keeping him at a distance and preventing any awkwardness that she'd only made it worse. Maybe she should simply hop into bed with him, mark that bet "paid," and get the whole nasty business out of everybody's system, including hers. Then, with that little detour into the wilds of her primal urges out of the way, she could get her life back on track.

Ugh.

"What was that?"

Halloran's voice cut across her exasperated thoughts and she sighed. Loudly. "Nothing."

"You said, 'Ugh.' Why?"

"None of your business." A too-familiar heat spread upward as she added briskly, "I just got a very interesting call from Gary Giacomo."

"Is that so?"

Emma swiveled her chair around, pretending she didn't notice his intent stare. "You said you know him?"

"Not well, but I worked with him some years back. He gets the job done. What'd he have to say?"

"He has witnesses claiming Chloe talked with Willie Farmer shortly before he was killed. Also, he questioned one of her brother's ex-bodyguards, a guy named Lew Watkins. He said you'd know him."

Bobby opened his soda can with a loud, fizzling pop. "I tried to find him the other day to talk to him, but didn't have any luck."

"He's dead," she said flatly. "Like Farmer, he was found in his car with a bullet to the back of the head."

"When?"

"This morning. And that's not all—Giacomo said Watkins claimed to have talked to Farmer shortly before Farmer died, and said Farmer rambled on about treasure hunts and *netsuke* figurines. It appears Chloe has, or had, the *netsuke*."

Bobby took a bite of his candy bar, brows lowering. "Back up a second here. Net-ski-what?"

"*Netsuke*," Emma repeated, more slowly. "Japanese carvings of stone, wood, or ivory, antique and highly collectible. I saw some in a museum in L.A. years ago, but I don't know much about them except they're usually no bigger than a couple inches—which makes them small enough to fit in a pocket, a box of crackers, or even the inner lining of a bra cup, though that might be pushing it. This could be why Chloe's apartment was demolished—the intruders were searching for something very small."

"Sounds like a good possibility. And I know a private investigator who can help us with these net-things."

Emma made a face. "I hate PIs. They always have agendas. I don't trust them."

"This one used to work with Sotheby's. She specializes in antiquities and collectibles. Generally, her agenda is the same as ours: stop the bad guys. Besides, she's a friend, and I trust her."

His tone brooked no argument, so Emma nodded. "All right. Let me know what your friend has to say. Maybe they're worth tons of money. In the meantime, I'll see what I can find out about the Watkins killing."

"By the way, you're not the only one getting interesting phone calls. I came home last night to find a message from Chloe on my answering machine."

And he was only now telling her this? Curiosity won out over annoyance, and Emma sat forward. "And?"

"She told me to back off, that she was safe and had things under control."

"But you don't believe her?"

"I believe that *she* believes it." He leaned forward as well, closing the distance between them, to Emma's immediate discomfort. "But I also get the feeling she thinks I'll be in danger if I pursue this case, and maybe she was trying to tell me that the other night, too, but she didn't want to be too obvious about it because she knew I'd just see it as a challenge."

Emma scooted back to a safer distance. "I'm not sure I'm following you."

Bobby took a sip of his soda. "The night she came by, she told me I should keep my doors locked, made a comment about me having a death wish, and then said I shouldn't ask too many questions."

Unease prickled along her skin. "What did she mean by death wish?"

"We were just watching something on TV." He shrugged. "But it was the way she said it that caught my attention, and putting that together with her warning last night, I'm getting the sense she's trying to protect me."

Emma mulled it over. "From what? You're a cop. This is what you do."

"I know, but we have a personal connection, no matter how ex it is, and maybe she's worried I'll get myself in trouble."

"Like *that's* never happened before, so I'm sure she has no basis for her concerns."

Bobby looked irritated. "What it means is this: Willie passed on a message to her before he died, and she knows who trashed her apartment and why. She's making a point to avoid whatever's going down, but doesn't feel she's in any serious danger—but that I am. We just don't know why."

This didn't sound good at all. "What do you think about that?"

He shrugged, unconcerned, then asked, "Have you had a chance to talk with the uniform who arrived at her place first?"

"Not yet. He's on swing shift today, though, and I left a message for him. Why?"

"I want to ask him what Chloe was doing when he got there, and what happened before she disappeared. She must've seen or heard something to spook her."

"You mean in addition to the fact somebody demolished her apartment and everything she owned in the world?"

He smiled a little. "Well, yeah."

"All right. Here's something else I picked up today. I questioned a few of Chloe's friends. None of them know where she is, and I didn't get the sense they were lying. One friend said Chloe dropped by for a visit the day after her apartment was ransacked. Apparently, Chloe wanted to pick up a box of clothes she'd left with the friend when she moved to her last apartment, because it didn't have extra storage room."

"So? We saw what was left of her other clothes. It'd make sense she'd need spares."

"These particular clothes have been at the friend's house for over four years." Emma waited as he processed that. "From what I've seen, Chloe lives for the latest fashions. I think it's odd she'd leave clothing with a friend, one who lives in the same city she does, for four days, much less four years."

"Did the friend say what kind of clothes they were?"

"Nothing exciting." Shoulders slumping, Emma pulled out her notebook. "A bunch of fancy evening wear and a fake fur coat."

"Wait a minute—was the coat black mink?"

Emma flipped back through her notepad. "Yes. Is that important?"

"She was wearing a fake mink coat the night she came by my place."

"And you think this means something?" Emma asked doubtfully.

"Hell, I don't know, but it's worth keeping in mind. If these *netsuke* things are as small as you say, they could fit in a coat pocket."

Emma rubbed at the growing knot of tension between her brows. "I just want to go on the record to say I'm stumped."

"I hear ya." He let out his breath. "We really need to sit down and have a long talk with Chloe."

"Strong's issued a BOLO, and alerted the other districts as well, so everybody will be on the lookout for her. It's only a matter time until somebody smokes her out."

"And let's hope that's us, and not whoever put a bullet through the heads of Willie Farmer and Lew Watkins."

The weariness and frustration were catching up to her, and she gave a snort. "Well, if that happens, she'll only have herself to blame. It's not like we haven't tried to help her."

"Don't say shit like that. I know this isn't personal for you, but it is for me. I care about what happens to Chloe."

The cold tone of his voice stung. "Are you implying I don't?"

Bobby slouched back in his chair, eyeing her as he emptied his Coke in a few quick gulps. "Do you?"

"Of course."

His brows arched, and for some reason, that stung, too.

"Look, Halloran, I know what people say about me. Even you." She held his gaze. "I don't mingle, joke around, gossip, or go out of my way to make friends, so people say I'm all about the job, all about keeping my percentages high. Victims are just file numbers, their tragedies nothing more than puzzle pieces for me to put together. I'm uptight, calculated, cold, unfeeling—does that cover everything, or did I miss a dig?"

He stared at her, his expression unreadable, then rolled his chair closer, casters clattering on the floor. "You're wound a little too tight, but it's because you're afraid of making mistakes, not because you're cold or unfeeling. I was feeling plenty of heat and passion last night."

She turned away. "Bobby, I don't—"

"Want to go there, I know. You made that pretty clear last night, too," he said quietly, finishing her sentence for her. "I still think you're wrong, but I'm gonna respect it for the time being."

At that, she raised her head, glaring. "Isn't that mighty generous of you."

"Yeah," he said dryly, "it is, considering what a pain in the ass it is when I gotta walk on eggshells around you and at the same time beat past the thick walls you've put up. Emma, is it such a stretch to think I might find you attractive?"

She glanced around uneasily, hoping nobody had overheard him, then lowered her voice to a near-whisper: "And how am I supposed to answer that without sounding arrogant, or utterly pathetic?"

"You could try the truth."

Looking down, face hot, she murmured, "Yes, it is too much. Like I said in the car, you don't even know me. You don't—"

"And you know me? From where I'm sitting, it looks like you're raggin' on my ass over not making assumptions about you, but it's okay for you to make assumptions about me."

His sharp comment bothered her, but it was probably more accurate than she cared to admit. "I don't pretend to be anything other than what I am, but you . . . every time I see you, you're wearing a different face. What are *you* afraid of, Bobby? That if you let people too close they'll see the real you?"

"If you listen to the gossip, my problem is that I let too many people too close. One of these days, you'd think I'd learn."

She had no response to that, as he'd probably expected. With a final hard, cold look, Bobby clattered back to his desk, finished off his candy bar, and tossed the wrapper in the garbage. Then he stood, pulling on his coat.

"I'm going to see my friend about the *netsuke*. I'll be back later."

Fourteen

Bobby slid into the seat of his car, scowling, and not even sure why he was upset with Emma's refusal to acknowledge what was right in front of her face: She was attracted to him, he was attracted to her, and he couldn't see any reason not do something about it.

Didn't the woman own a damn mirror? She was sexy, smart, sincere, dedicated—what wasn't to like, once a guy got past that chip on her shoulder? And it pissed him off that she didn't feel she was attractive.

As he fished out his cell phone from his coat pocket, temper cooling, it occurred to him that Emma's reluctance to hook up with him might have nothing to do with her hang-ups and everything to do with his.

It wasn't as if he hadn't given her plenty of reasons to be wary of him, as she'd bluntly pointed out last night—and just now, with that wearing-different-faces thing.

He wanted to pretend he didn't know what the hell she meant, but he did—and worse yet was knowing Emma didn't trust him. It hurt in a way he couldn't even begin to put into words, and said something about him that went against everything he tried to make of himself.

He couldn't remember being this edgy or pumped up over a woman before, and even if he didn't know exactly how or when it had happened, she'd hooked him, hard. Too bad Emma didn't feel the same.

Then he realized he was glaring at his phone as if this were all its fault.

Hey, get a look at this: Badass Bobby Halloran, the scourge of District One, moping in the front seat of his car in a parking lot because a girl doesn't want to date him.

With a snort, he punched in the number to Diana's office. Before driving into the Quarter—not his favorite place to drive—he wanted to make sure Diana wasn't in Rome or Manhattan or wherever she jetted off to on a moment's notice. Once he had learned she was in, he headed for the Quarter, stopping first for a bribe. He found a parking spot a couple blocks away from her St. Philip Street office, then walked through the ever-present crowd of tourists and into her swanky, English-lord-style office, bearing gifts in the form of a donut box.

He smiled at Luna, Diana's black-clad secretary, who was typing to the rhythm of a CD's pounding beat. "Hey, there. How's my best goth princess today?"

She produced a lip curl worthy of Elvis himself. "In the throes of PMS."

"Warning noted." Leaning closer to hear the music— lots of violins, darkly ominous, but seductive—Bobby asked, "What's that you're listening to?"

" 'Kiss of Death,' by Vamptastic. They're a local band." Luna sat back, plainly waiting for him to make a smart-ass comment. "You like?"

He grinned. "I like."

"You scare me sometimes."

His grin widened.

"Which is kind of a turn-on, actually. In case you were wondering." Black brows arching above the smoky-dark colors of her eye shadow, she added, "Anyway . . . the boss is expecting you, so take your shiny, happy-people self right on in. But leave the donuts."

"Why?"

"Toll for entering the den of the ogress."

"I'm telling Diana you said that."

"Be my guest." Her mouth twitched in what, for Luna, passed as a smile. "I'm hormonal. I fear nothing."

It made him laugh, but he left the box on Luna's desk before thumping on the closed door and walking into Diana's book-packed office, which was decked out in navy and dark red colors. It even had real leather chairs, and smelled like café au lait, books, and money. Lots of money. Not for the first time since he'd met Diana Belmaine, he wondered if he really was in the wrong line of business.

"Hey, beautiful." He grinned when she looked up. "Remember me?"

"Bobby!" A wide smile curved her mouth as she peered at him over the top of her reading glasses then tucked a lock of blond hair behind her ear. "You're not dead!"

"Not yet." He shut the door behind him and then headed to the big, comfortable wing chair in front of her desk. After leaning across her desk to give her a quick kiss on the cheek, he sat down.

Diana was wearing a hot pink sweater with black pants—dressy to most people, but a casual look for her.

She truly was one of the most beautiful women he'd ever seen, and yet he'd never been attracted to her that way. From the moment they'd met, he'd known she was way out of his league. Hell, she even *smelled* expensive and classy.

He eyed the huge diamond engagement ring on her finger. "When Jack stakes out his territory, he sure doesn't hold back."

Diana touched the ring, smiling. "It's endearing, in a primitive you-my-woman kind of way."

"How's the wedding plans going?"

"Slow. We're still in the negotiation stages." Seeing his questioning look, she added, "We're negotiating on whether we keep his cottage or my condo. So far, I'm winning—it's not like all my stuff will fit in Jack's tiny place. And there's all these other things to deal with, like last names and bank accounts and—"

"Kids?"

Alarm crossed her face. "We haven't even negotiated to enter negotiations for children."

Bobby grimaced. "Sounds to me like celibacy is a whole lot less trouble."

At that, she smirked. "You keep telling yourself that, sweetie. And by the way, speaking of trouble, what happened to your face?"

"I ran into a minor communication problem."

"Looks to me like you ran into a fist. More than once."

"Pretty much. Hey, I did get your message the other night," he said, rapidly changing the subject to avoid a Diana-style lecture on his need to be more careful. "Sorry I haven't called back."

"I figured work was keeping you busy, especially with Mardi Gras coming up soon." Diana took off her glasses, tossed them onto the desk, and sat back. "But I was worried about you. It's not like you to blow off your friends."

"I know." He glanced around the room, uncomfortable. "It's been a crazy few weeks."

After a brief silence, she asked, "So what's up?"

"A couple things. First, I did want to get back to you on the car show. My schedule's clear, so unless somebody gets stabbed or robbed, it looks like a go."

"Good. And we can catch lunch while we're at it."

He shifted, resting his ankle over his knee. "I'm also looking for information on a case. You got a minute?"

She sat forward. "I'll always make time for you, Bobby. Let's hear it."

"Do you ever work with *netsuke*?"

"You bet. What in particular do you need to know about them?"

"That's the problem," he admitted. "I'm not sure. The case involves a vandalized apartment, and it's possible the people who busted up this place might've been looking for *netsuke*. The partner I'm working with right now says these things are worth money."

"Since when are you working with a partner?"

"It's temporary. She's new, and I'm showing her around."

"A 'she' partner." Interest lit Diana's shrewd blue eyes. "Is she nice?"

"Christ, no." His face warmed, and he scowled. "So tell me, are they worth a lot of money?"

Diana's lashes lowered, but not before he glimpsed a

flash of amusement. "It depends. You can pick up nice pieces starting at around a hundred bucks, but some can bring in up to a hundred grand. Modern pieces are collectible, but antiques are the most popular. They date between the seventeenth and late nineteenth centuries, with the most valuable pieces produced out of Edo, Kyoto, and Osaka during the Genroku period."

As if he had a clue what in hell the "Genroku period" meant, but he kept quiet as Diana nattered on with enthusiasm. How nice, to love your job that much. He had a dim memory of feeling that way once.

"*Netsuke* are usually one to two inches in size, and very detailed. Most were made out of ivory and wood, but you'll also see shell, bone, horn, and even metal or precious stones, though these are more rare."

Didn't sound so impressive to him. "So they're just little statues?"

"They're actually toggles, and were used to secure objects hung from the *obi* of a kimono. Once the Japanese adopted Western dress, the *obi* fell out of use, as did the need for *netsuke*."

His confusion must've been obvious, because Diana stopped. "You do know what an *obi* and kimono are, right?"

"Sort of . . . I saw an Akira Kurosawa movie a few years ago, and one of my uncles was stationed in Japan for a while. He brought home a couple costume dolls for his wife."

"Quickie lesson, then: *kimono* robes are held together by a broad waist sash called an *obi*. Women often carried little personal items around in their wide sleeves, but men usually hung their *sagemono* from a cord that was tucked into the *obi*."

Bobby sighed. "Hold on. What's a *sagemono*?"

"Objects hung from the *obi*—a pouch, smoking pipe, writing tools, *bokuto* sword, that sort of thing. These were secured to the sash by the *netsuke* toggles, and a sliding bead, called an *ojime*, was strung between the cord and *sagemono* to tighten or loosen it. The *netsuke*, *ojime*, and *sagemono* functioned together as a sort of hanging pocket. Kinda like a fanny pack." She wrinkled her nose. "In concept, anyway."

Bobby frowned, rubbing at his jaw. "You got any pictures?"

"Of course."

Diana walked to her bookshelves, pulled out a book, and returned to her desk. Perching on its edge, she thumbed through the book, and then handed it to him, opened.

"The most popular form of *netsuke* are figurative . . . animals, people, mythological creatures, stylized masks. They're called *katabori*."

The photo showed a rabbit, a smiling fat man, and what looked like a deer standing on its tiptoes. "These actual size?"

"Yes."

"Huh." Maybe a little impressive, after all.

"Another kind of *netsuke* are *sashi*, which are long and thin—like this bean pod." She pointed at the next page. "There's also the round and flat *manju*, and a two-piece style called *kagamibuta*, which is a lid and bowl." Diana leaned back, palms on her desk. "Do you have any idea what kind of *netsuke* are involved?"

Bobby shook his head. "I'm not even sure it's a credible source, since it's coming from guys who aren't exactly upstanding members of society."

"Ah." Diana pursed her lips. "Then there's another style to consider."

"As if I'm not confused enough already." Bobby made a face. "Like what?"

"They're a subset of the figurative *katabori* called *shunga,* and you'd probably find these quite interesting. They're erotica."

He snorted. "Now we're talking."

Diana looked amused. "*Shunga* can be subtle or explicit. Most are carved out of a single piece of ivory or wood, but sometimes they come in two pieces and are, shall we say, interlocking."

Bobby started laughing.

"The interlocking variety tends to be larger in size than the standard *netsuke.* Naturally."

"Naturally." Grinning, he asked, "Got any pictures of those?"

"Which you'd want to look at for artistic purposes only, right? And to better protect the world from scum and villainy?"

"Absolutely."

She obviously didn't believe him for a second. "Yes, I have pictures." Taking the book from him, she paged through it, then turned it to face him. "The most common *shunga* are these phallic mushroom figures."

Bobby stared at little people hugging large mushrooms that, sure enough, looked like huge erections—which would explain why all the little people were smiling. Diana reached over and turned a page, and he sat forward, whistling. "Giddyup, geisha girl."

She tilted her head to one side. "It is rather acrobatic."

"I'll say. This could give *Penthouse* a run for its money."

"*Tsk-tsk,* don't let collectors hear you say that. This is *art,* not porn." She retrieved the book, despite his protest, and shut it. "Much of the explicit *shunga* is modern, and made in China out of inexpensive resins, since the ivory trade is mostly illegal these days. Sometimes, though, you can find nicer pieces made out of mammoth ivory."

"Mammoth ivory isn't illegal?"

"No, because mammoths are already extinct."

"Wait a minute. Wouldn't that make it more rare, and in more need of protection?"

Diana shrugged. "I don't make the rules, I just work with them."

That, at least, he couldn't argue with. He stood, rubbing absently at a lingering twinge in his shoulder. "Thanks for the help. If we find these *netsuke,* would you be willing to look them over and tell me if they're valuable?"

"Sure. As far as I know, I'm around for the next few weeks. After that, I have to fly to Manhattan on a consulting job, but it's only for a couple days."

"All right. I'll give you a call." He headed for the door. "By the way, I brought donuts. Luna wouldn't let me through the door until I gave them to her, but if you hurry, you might get one before she eats them all."

Diana rolled her eyes. "She's in a mood. Her and Mike had a falling out, and she's wallowing in calories. I can relate, but I hope they patch things up soon before she gains a gazillion pounds. Or I have to drug her."

Bobby grinned. "We'll talk soon. Say hello to Jack for me—and good luck on those negotiations."

Fifteen

After Bobby left the station house, seemingly taking with him all the energy within the entire building, the rest of the day crawled by for Emma. Fortunately, Strong assigned her another case—an armed robbery at a convenience store—to keep her busy. Unfortunately, she finished up at the scene within an hour. In no hurry to rush back to the office, she grabbed a bite to eat, took a relaxing, mind-clearing walk, then returned to her desk a little before three. With time to spare before the swing shift reported for duty, she called Chloe's ex-landlord to see if she'd been by to pick up any of her belongings.

"No." The landlord sounded friendlier than he had before. "But she did leave me a message and said I could throw out everything."

Not the response she'd expected. "Even the clothes? Some looked as if they could be repaired easily."

"Yup, even the clothes."

After hanging up, Emma sat back and doodled on a message slip as she mulled this over. It sounded as if

Madame Barfly was expecting to run into a lot of cash sometime very soon. Or just run, period.

Glancing at the clock, she debated waiting for Bobby, then decided he could as easily come looking for her over in patrol. She stood, gathering her notepad, pen, and files, just as Bobby walked in, looking more than a little damp—and absolutely gorgeous.

Why was it men looked so good wet and scruffy, while she just looked . . . dumpy?

"Raining again?" she asked casually, her pulse jumping as he walked toward her in that lazy, easy way of his.

"On and off. Sorry I'm late. I had some follow-up on an assault case that's been hanging over my head. Ready to go talk to whats-his-name?"

"Officer Doug Delisle. He's brand-spankin'-new, right off probation. So go easy on him," Emma said sternly as they headed for the patrol department. "How'd it go with your antique expert?"

"It was . . . an eye-opener. *Netsuke* can be worth anywhere from a hundred dollars to a hundred thousand."

"Maybe that's what it's all about," Emma said, jotting down this new information. "It would make sense as a 'treasure hunt,' though Chloe's brother doesn't sound like the art thief type."

"It's not his usual MO," Bobby agreed.

"And it's strange he'd wait until now to send his sister on a so-called treasure hunt, isn't it?"

"I'd say it's strange, yeah."

Emma scowled. "This is giving me a headache. Maybe we should take a trip to Angola and have a chat with Jacob Mitsumi."

Bobby grunted, which Emma translated as a lack of enthusiasm for her idea. "Also, I called Chloe's ex-landlord," she continued. "He said she left a message telling him to throw away all her things, even the salvageable items. Sounds to me like she's expecting to come into some money—or getting ready to leave town."

He said nothing to that, either, and by that time they'd reached the desk sergeant, and Emma asked after Delisle.

"He's waiting for you in the briefing room," the sergeant said without looking up.

Raising a brow at the surly behavior, she said, "Thanks."

Delisle was the sole occupant of the small, dingy briefing room, impatiently tapping a pen on the table, and stood when she and Bobby walked in.

After the introductions, Bobby took a chair opposite the younger man and Emma perched on the table next to him. "I know you're on duty, so I'll make this quick. Can you recap what happened when you responded to the Mitsumi break-in?"

"Like I said in my report, when I got there, she was with the landlord, and they were arguing about the damages and her moving out."

"So she didn't appear frightened at that time?" Emma asked.

"Nope. Just pissed off. I told her to wait on the porch, and after I secured the scene, I came back out to talk with her and the landlord."

Bobby propped his feet on the table. "What questions did you ask?"

"The usual: if she'd seen anything, knew anything."

"By then you were also busy keeping the scene secure?" Emma asked.

"Right. I was with dispatch again, getting an ETA on

my backup, telling the neighbors to stand back, when I noticed Ms. Mitsumi was gone. One minute she was there, being cooperative, not giving me any reason to think she'd take off, and the next she was gone."

"You didn't have a chance to look for her?" Bobby asked.

"No, sir. Not until my backup and Detective Delgado arrived."

Emma looked up from her notepad. "Do you remember if Mitsumi was carrying any packages?"

"Not that I can recall, no."

Well, that would've been too easy. "What was she doing when you last saw her?"

"Just standing on the porch."

Bobby tipped his chair back. "Facing the house, or the street?"

Delisle frowned, thinking. "The street."

Bobby glanced at Emma. "And there was a bunch of people in the street, rubbernecking?"

"Yes, sir. Maybe fifteen or so."

"Did you notice anybody in the crowd acting suspiciously?" Emma asked. "Or anything out of the ordinary?"

Delisle shook his head. "Not that I can recall, sorry."

Again, she and Bobby exchanged looks, then she said, "Okay, that's all we need to know. Thanks for your time, Delisle."

After the young cop left, she and Bobby headed back to their desks. "Chloe might've seen somebody in the crowd she recognized as dangerous."

"That's as solid an assumption as anything else we've got," Bobby agreed.

"Great; that's all I need, more assumptions. I'm no

closer to clearing this case now than when I started it. I think I have even *more* unanswered questions—and I was serious about talking to Jacob Mitsumi."

Without looking her way, he dropped into his chair. "Your call, partner, it's your case, your time to waste."

Sixteen

Sunday arrived partly cloudy, but warmer than usual, and nearly perfect for a party. After such a long, frustrating week, Emma looked forward to Alycia's cookout, especially now that she was finally settling in at work. Not everybody was slapping her on the back like a lifelong buddy, but at least more smiles and greetings were coming her way, and she'd found a friend in Alycia and Rosario—and maybe that detective she'd met at Rosie's baby shower lunch, a tiny blonde named Sophie who had a mouth like a Marine.

After dressing in jeans, a long-sleeved T-shirt with a sweatshirt, and her new Nikes, Emma set about baking a huge batch of chocolate chip cookies. Alycia had insisted she didn't need to bring anything, but Emma didn't feel right about that, and in addition to the cookies, she'd bought a twelve-pack of beer. She was dropping chunks of cookie dough onto a baking sheet—more than a few chunks of dough ending up in her mouth—when her phone rang.

She hastily wiped her hands clean, then gingerly picked up the handset. "Hello?"

"Emma? It's Patti."

"Patti . . . wow, this is a surprise!" In more ways than one, considering Patti was her ex's sister. "How are you doing?"

"Just fine. And before you ask, I called your mom to get your new phone number. I hope you don't mind?"

"No, not at all. It's nice to hear from you." While Patti sounded as chipper as ever, Emma wondered why she'd called. They'd been friendly, but things had cooled after Dennis left—and a sudden, unpleasant thought came to her. "How's Denny? Is he okay?"

"Don't worry; everybody is healthy and in one piece, including Dennis."

Thank God; even though they'd parted under bad circumstances—toward the end, they'd fought constantly—she didn't wish him ill.

"I'm glad to hear that," Emma said.

"And you're doing okay? Your mom says you're back to work."

Patti was a sweetheart, one of those genuinely kind people, and the concern in her voice was sincere. Emma smiled, hearing it. "I told Mom half the truth. You know how that is, she'd get all worried and flustered if she knew I'm still living out of boxes, and that my first real case at work is turning into a pain in the ass. But things are going really well. A lot better than I expected."

"That's good to hear. Dennis will be happy to know that . . . and, actually, it's because of Dennis that I'm calling." Patti sounded faintly embarrassed. "He wanted to call you himself, but was afraid you'd hang up on him."

Not an unfounded fear; a month ago, she probably would have slammed the phone down. Now, thinking about talking with Dennis made her feel oddly nostalgic, and just a little sad.

"Tell Denny if he calls, I won't hang up on him. I promise."

Silence. "Really?"

Patti sounded cautious, and Emma suppressed a sigh. "You only heard his side of the breakup. I don't hate him."

At least, not anymore. For a while there, she might've hated him, but that had quickly passed, and eventually so had whatever feelings of love she'd still had for him. And acknowledging the truth of it brought a feeling of both relief and acceptance.

"He wasn't sure, and I know he feels bad about what happened, how he just walked out like he did. I love him, but even I have to say that was a shitty thing to do. I think he wants to . . . maybe apologize or something."

About six months too late, but Emma understood. "You can give him my number, Patti. But tell him not to call until later tonight. I'm heading off to a cookout with some people from work."

She tried to sound diffident about it, but hoped Patti would pass this bit of news back to her brother. While she didn't want to rub Denny's face in it, she wanted him to know she'd landed on her feet, and her life was going on just fine without him.

No dummy, Patti picked up on that. "Oh. Have you met someone?"

"Yes."

And, to her surprise, she wasn't saying it just to be bitchy or to make her ex squirm a little. It was the truth.

"I'm happy for you, Emma. I really am. I wish things had worked out with you and Dennis . . . I always thought the two of you were great together. But things don't always work out the way we'd like."

"No, they don't," Emma agreed quietly.

Breakups were hard on others besides the couple, but it was tough to remember that while in the throes of a crisis or a bout of self-pity. Guilt pricked her, and she wished she'd called Patti before now, and Dennis's folks as well. They'd always been good to her.

"Well, I won't keep you, since you have plans." Patti injected a note of brightness in her tone. "You have fun at your cookout, and I'll pass on your number to Dennis. You take good care of yourself, okay? A lot of us still care."

Sudden tears stung her eyes—and when had she gotten so blasted emotional? "Thanks, Patti. Same to you. And tell your mom and dad I said hello."

After hanging up, Emma stood by the phone. It took a moment, but she finally realized that funny little turmoil of feelings inside her meant those old wounds *were* healing. How nice, to have good turmoil for a change.

Her mood considerably improved, Emma finished baking her cookies, then, after checking her appearance one last time, packed everything into her car and drove to Alycia's house.

The Chatmans lived in a modern two-story tan house in a newer neighborhood, across the street from a small park that came with a playground gym and a basketball court—which explained how the friendly interdistrict competition had started.

A number of cars were already parked curbside and in the driveway—though she didn't see Bobby's red SUV— and she ended up parking by a mailbox four houses up from Alycia's. She walked up the driveway to the sounds of a party in full swing, and despite her best intentions, she tensed a little as she rang the front doorbell.

She hoped she'd find a few familiar faces she could hang out with at the start—and with any luck, nobody would think it was funny, after a few beers, to bring up the L.A. incident, or to put her on the spot about "the bet."

Just as she was going to ring the bell again, the door swung open to reveal a teenage girl who looked strikingly like a baby-faced Halle Berry, right down to the short, feathery black hair and luminous caramel-colored skin.

"Hi," the girl said, smiling. "I'm India Chatman."

Emma smiled back. "Emma Frey. I work with your mom."

"Come on in. I'll show you where you can put your things. You got here right on time. Everybody's out back, and Dad just fired up the grill . . . and are those chocolate chip cookies I smell?"

"Fresh out of the oven," Emma said, following the girl into the house. "You want one?"

"Actually, I want them *all,* but I'll settle."

Emma laughed, and put the cookie plate and beer down on the kitchen counter, which overflowed with food, beverages, paper plates and napkins, and the usual party-time flotsam and jetsam.

"I'll put this beer in the cooler," India said, taking the twelve-pack. "You can go on outside."

"Thanks." The girl couldn't be more than fifteen, but Emma admired her maturity and poise. "Has anybody ever told you that you look like Halle Berry?"

"A few times." India grinned, then snitched a cookie. "I'm on doorbell duty, but if you want, I can take you outside and introduce you to a few people. Mom told me you're new and might not know everybody."

"I'll be fine, thanks." Grabbing a can of Mountain Dew, so she could keep her hands from fidgeting, Emma headed out the door to the backyard, where several dozen people had gathered, along with nearly as many kids, ranging in age from infant to teenager. She instantly searched for familiar faces, spotting Alycia beside a solidly built, laughing man tending the smoking grill, who had to be her husband, Car.

Another quick survey showed Mottson, his arm around a pretty brunette who looked much too refined for him, and Captain Strong with an attractive gray-haired woman who must be his wife. The enormously pregnant Rosario Delgado sat by her husband and toddler son—and that, including herself and Alycia, was the grand total of the District One detectives who'd made it to the cookout.

No Bobby on the horizon, and she couldn't decide if that was good news or not.

"Hey, Emma!" Alycia motioned for Emma to join her. "You found us."

With a polite nod at Mottson, Emma walked over to Alycia, who patted her husband's burly chest and said, "Emma, this is Carter, my husband. Car, this is Emma Frey, the new girl I told you about. She used to hook for the LAPD Hollywood Division."

"The hooking was strictly work-related." No sooner were the words out of her mouth than Emma wanted to kick herself. Alycia was joking, not being serious.

Car's dark brows shot up as he shook her hand. "Either way, it's a hell of an introduction, Emma. Pleased to meet you. I'm putting on the steaks and kabobs in about fifteen minutes, so help yourself to any drinks or snacks, and go on and introduce yourself. Most everybody here is from the Fifth, beat cops like this old dog right here."

Car was hardly "old." In his mid-forties, he was broad but fit, and handsome in a comfortable, solid way. She liked him.

"I brought beer, by the way," Emma said. "And chocolate chip cookies."

"Uh-oh." Alycia looked alarmed. "You didn't leave them anywhere near India, did you?"

Emma smiled. "Yes, but I made four dozen, and I think there's a limit to what even skinny kids can eat."

"Honey, you obviously have no teenage chocoholics in your house," Alycia said wryly. "Nothing'll stop that girl from eating every last crumb if she thinks she can get away with it."

"And speaking of people with no self-control," Car said in his deep, gravelly voice. "Where's Halloran?"

Realizing both Alycia and Car were looking expectantly at her, Emma widened her eyes. "Haven't a clue. It's not my turn to be his keeper."

"C'mon, now, he's not such a bad guy." Car winked at Emma, then raised his voice as he continued, "Halloran grows on a body after a while. But don't ever trust him. That boy cheats."

Before Car even finished his sentence, before she even turned around, Emma knew she'd find Bobby standing behind her. A sudden charge in the air, a tingling of a deep, female awareness—some part of her simply knew.

"Takes a cheater to know another one, Chatman, but you know I'd never pass on your steaks."

Emma turned, and Bobby stood only a step or two behind her, all but glowing in the sunlight. His worn, frayed jeans hugged his contours almost to the point of indecency, and an old olive drab T-shirt stretched tautly across his chest and biceps. His scruffy athletic shoes had seen better days, and as she watched he slipped a gray sweatshirt over his head, smoothing it absently over his belly in a way that had her wishing she could do it for him.

Then she noticed he'd donned a sporty pair of extra-dark sunglasses. God, was he hungover again?

Probably; last night had been Saturday, after all, and most people had things to do and places to be. She'd spent the night at home watching *Crocodile Hunter* on Animal Planet—and thinking, as she always did, that Steve Irwin was a cutie, but one of these days somebody was going to grab a tranquilizer gun and pump him full of Ritalin.

"Hey." Bobby grinned at her. "Not gonna say hello to me?"

"I was working up to it." She raised her Mountain Dew. "I just got here . . . haven't even had a chance to open my can."

A single brow arched above the frame of his sunglasses. "So are you asking for help in opening it?"

While Emma couldn't see the expression in his eyes, he sounded amused, and she popped the top of her can, more than a little annoyed with herself for letting him fluster her. Again.

Crikey! Look 'ere, the rare and elusive Los Angelian Wallflower has left the security of 'er nest to mingle at the communal watering hole. But watch how this creature, who's able to bag badass bad guys without breaking a sweat, loses all faculty for intelligent speech when she's approached by an attractive male . . .

"Thanks, but I've got it covered," she said coolly. "And what's with the sunglasses? Another hangover?"

A long moment passed. "You know, Emma, in an ass-backward kind of way, you're good for me. My ego won't ever get out of hand with you around."

Oh . . . crap. "Sorry. I didn't mean for it to sound—"

"The sun's out." He motioned with his stubble-rough chin toward the sky. "Bright sun makes the eyes hurt. Dark glasses make the eyes feel better. Amazing concept. Think you can grasp it?"

"I think I can hate you, after all."

"Ooookay!" Alycia spoke a shade too brightly, and Emma, remembering they had an audience, turned. "Glad to see you two working at the whole breaking-the-ice thing, but before you start breaking anything else, may I suggest that Bobby introduce Emma to everybody here?"

What the hell? The last thing she'd expected—or wanted—was being publicly paired up with Bobby. Within minutes, everybody stuffed into the Chatmans' nicely landscaped backyard would immediately jump to conclusions of the most lascivious sort.

Alycia ignored the wide-eyed look of alarm Emma sent her way, and added, "I'd do the introductions myself, but I am the hostess with the mostest, and right now what I need mostest is to help Car get these steaks on the grill and start setting up the food table."

"No problem," Bobby said. "You do your thing. I'll give Em the grand tour."

And when had she become just plain "Em" to him?

As he reached for her shoulder, she stepped away. "Don't. People will get the wrong idea."

He didn't move, but slid his sunglasses down the

bridge of his nose so he could better see her. No anger there, just a whole lot of impatience—and the black eye was starting to fade. "Yeah, like you might be friendly or something. Can't have that, now, can we?"

"You know what I mean, Bobby."

"I gave up worrying a long time ago about what other people think of me. I suggest you do the same before it makes you crazy."

Not bad advice—and not the first time she'd heard it.

Emma sighed. "I want so badly to make a good impression, but I keep screwing up, don't I?"

"Just be yourself, Emma; it'll make things a lot easier."

He moved off, and after a moment, she followed. After he'd introduced her to the other Chatman offspring—Tanique, a year older than India—he stopped next to a knot of men from District Five. Most were patrol officers, except for a tall blond man with quiet, collegiate good looks, who smiled and shook her hand as Bobby said, "Emma, this is Gary Giacomo. Gary, Emma Frey."

She smiled back. "We talked on the phone the other day. How's the Farmer case coming?"

"So-so. And you? Find the Mitsumi woman yet?"

Yes—and promptly lost her again. "No luck so far."

Bobby steered her to the next group of people, and one introduction followed after the other until it was time to eat. He sat on a folding chair beside her, Styrofoam plate on his lap, tucking into his food with gusto while he talked and joked with those around him, including a few kids.

Alycia and Car also made an effort to include her, for which she was silently grateful, even if the conversations

were only the usual joking, shop talk, and gossip, with
forays into sports or political subjects, the eternal mystery of men relating to women, the upcoming Mardi
Gras, and the ingredients of Alycia's secret-recipe beans.
After a while, convinced nobody was going to suddenly
get on her case about the L.A. scandal or tease her about
getting horizontal with the Lothario of the First District,
she relaxed and chatted with the other officers and their
families.

Alycia was right; some might never accept her, like
Mottson, but for the most part her little bit of notoriety
was already losing interest. And Bobby was right, too—
she only had to be herself, and the rest would come.

Of course, it helped that for the first time in a long
while she felt like she knew who she was and what she
wanted. Glancing at Bobby, she caught him watching
her, a small smile on his face, and she smiled back even
as a familiar warmth—and a tingle of pleasure—stole
over her.

She probably shouldn't make a big deal about it, but
she'd almost forgotten that flirting could be fun. And
what harm could it be, to flirt with him a little?

Then, after plates were scraped clean, bottles and cans
emptied, and everybody fed, Car stood on a picnic table
and bellowed: "It's showtime!"

Emma turned to Bobby for a translation. "Time to
play ball," he explained, with a wide—and alarmingly
predatory—grin.

From the tabletop, Car began the noisy negotiations
of picking players, hollering for volunteers, bullying the
reluctant, and encouraging the acquiescent. Before long,
Team Five was hurling good-natured insults at Team
One—who, as it turned out, were in short supply.

"Now, c'mon," Car urged. "We need one more player. Alycia, baby—"

"Nuh-uh, no way, and never." Alycia vehemently shook her head. "Me and sports don't mix. You know that."

Biting the proverbial bullet, and all but vibrating with excitement, Emma raised her hand. "I'll volunteer."

As Bobby turned to stare at her, a broad grin creased Car's face. "You sure? You know how to play?"

Holding back a smile, Emma nodded. "I'll manage."

Car still looked doubtful. "These guys play rough."

"I can take care of myself."

"All right, then." Car clapped his hands together for attention. "We got us a ball game. It's off to the court and may the baddest badasses win."

The guests migrated en masse across the street to the park, although a few of the wives with smaller children stayed behind to gossip and relax, and Bobby trotted up to Emma. "You're tall. That'll be a plus."

"What's the matter, Halloran?" she asked lightly. "You don't think a girl can't keep up with the big boys?"

He shrugged, a wicked glint in his eyes. "There's a reason us boys rule the planet."

"And considering the state of the planet, I wouldn't be too proud of that." Emma smiled at his teasing. "You know, if women were in charge, there wouldn't be wars. We'd talk about kids, chat, and swap makeup tips, then negotiate world peace over coffee and chocolate cake."

"Yeah," Bobby said, as they joined the others at the court. "But where's the fun in that?"

Before she could come up with a good retort, one of the District Five guys yelled, "Yo, Halloran . . . heads up!"

He tossed a ball toward Bobby, and Emma effortlessly intercepted it and batted the ball toward her. Bobby went utterly still as she dribbled figure eights around her ankles, fast and smooth.

It had been a while, but she hadn't forgotten how to play—and outside of a police station or interrogation room, the one place where she felt at ease and in charge was a basketball court.

Emma jogged toward the hoop, dribbling, then jumped and threw the ball one-handed. It arced, high and sweet, before plunging through the net with an airy swish.

Catching the ball as it bounced toward her, she turned to find everybody was staring at her with astonishment, Bobby included.

Car broke the silence first: "Uh-oh."

Emma grinned, adrenaline still pumping, flushed with satisfaction. "Caltech women's basketball, shooting guard, and All-Conference in 1992."

The Division Five guy who'd first thrown the ball looked disgusted. "I think it's more like, 'Oh shit, we're totally fucked.'"

"Hey, what's new?" Mottson called out with a huge smile.

"Suck me," retorted the Division Five guy, scowling.

With the crude talk, and maturity levels dropping in direct proportion to the number of alcoholic beverages ingested, things were shaping up to be a typical boy's night out—which Emma found to be familiar and, oddly enough, comfortable territory.

"It's been a while," she said, a little embarrassed over showing off. "I don't play much anymore."

Bobby slung an arm around her shoulders. "You're

full of surprises, Em. How come you didn't say anything?"

She stiffened beneath his touch, then forced herself to relax. Mottson might've looked intrigued, but nobody else was whipping out their checkbooks. Bobby was right; ignore that stupid bet. Besides, he was warm and she liked how he smelled. "It never came up in conversation."

A renewed bout of haggling followed Emma's surprise demonstration, and Bobby was swapped over to Car's team to even the odds. Team One included the gangly Mottson as center, since he didn't need to do more than stand around and catch rebounds, with Emma as shooting guard, Captain Strong as the small forward, Rosie Delgado's husband, Lenny, as point guard, and a young uniform named Jensen, who had an ex-military bearing and build, as power forward.

Team Five claimed a tough-looking black guy named Holland as center, and he was about six-four and powerfully built—he could probably squash Mottson like a bug, and without even breaking into a sweat. Bobby was the power forward, Car the small forward, Gary Giacomo the point guard, and matching Emma as shooting guard was a skinny guy with a loopy grin introduced to her as Zug. He didn't appear too impressive, but she wouldn't assume he was as uncoordinated as he looked.

Emma leaned toward Lenny Delgado. "So what are the rules?"

Bobby, overhearing the question, laughed. "Rules? There aren't any, except to win."

She glanced at Lenny for confirmation, and he shrugged. "That's about it."

"So," she said slowly, looking at Bobby. "I can double dribble, travel, knee you in the balls?"

"No on the first two—we follow the basic rules of the game—and as for the third, give it your best shot, darlin'."

Rosie Delgado, playing the part of the official time-keeper, sat down on a chair as everybody took their positions on the court and the two centers crouched, ready for the tip-off. Rosie raised a stopwatch. Emma tensed, waiting.

"Go!" Rosie bellowed.

Both teams exploded into motion, and within a minute, Emma had been knocked down, nearly run over, and had an elbow rammed in her ribs hard enough to bruise. For a bunch of upstanding law enforcement officials, they sure played fast and loose with the rules of the game—not to mention just plain dirty.

Recovering from her surprise, she gave as good as she got. When Zug shoved her, she shoved back. When Bobby was all over her trying to block her shots, his hips brushing against her bottom, she ignored his intimidation attempts. When Strong called her a moron for having her shot intercepted, she told him to shut up and do his job next time, and when Giacomo knocked her down, painfully, she retaliated by tripping him.

"Hey! Foul," somebody yelled, and Rosie halted the game before the rough play threatened to degenerate into bone-breaking violence.

Bobby, bent over, was breathing hard between gasps of laughter. "Emma, what the hell do you think you're doing?"

"What I do best—following the rules. In this case,

cheating." She glared at Giacomo. "Try that again, and I will rip your guts out. One slow inch at a time."

Bobby stopped laughing and whacked Giacomo on the shoulder as he straightened. "She's right, man. Hit her like that again, and I'm gonna kick your ass, teammate or not."

Emma rolled her eyes. "Knock it off, Bobby. If he needs his ass kicked, I'll do it myself."

"You and what army, Frey?" Giacomo demanded, and although he smiled as he spoke, the look in his eyes was cold and deadly serious.

"Cut the macho bullshit." Emma scowled. "And reality check here: It's just a game."

Strong faced her, hands on his hips, and for a fifty-something guy, he looked damn good in sweatpants and a T-shirt. "I can't believe you said that, Miss All-Conference 1992. The game is all. There is only winning."

"Do, or do not," said Zug, in a decent Yoda impersonation. "There is no try."

"True." Lenny lazily scratched his lean belly beneath his T-shirt. "By the end, we're a bunch of fuckin' mad dogs, man."

"Free throw goes to Five," ordered Rosie—not only the official timekeeper, but the referee as well. Probably because nobody would dare punch out a pregnant woman during any fights over a foul.

Giacomo took the penalty shot, and scored easily. After that, Emma slipped into the swing of the game, along with everybody else, and passed a thoroughly enjoyable hour in the most cutthroat game of basketball she'd ever played in her life.

And the most sexual.

Every time she moved, Bobby was behind her, brushing against her. Every time she turned, ball in hand, searching for a teammate to throw it to or make enough of an opening to take the shot herself, she found Bobby's chest, his arms, or his grinning face in her way. He'd lost the sweatshirt twenty minutes into the game, and the sweat-dampened T-shirt adhered to his skin and the lines of his muscles as if it had been painted on.

Nice chest—except when it blocked her way to the basket.

Swinging her elbows to clear a path, she twisted, jumped, and took her shot. The ball barely missed, bouncing off the rim, but she was still in position close enough to jump and grab it again, despite Bobby's octopus hands.

But when his hand landed on her ass—and the sparkle in his eye told her it was no accident—Emma lost her temper.

She lobbed the ball at him, hard. Bobby, not expecting it, didn't duck in time, and it smacked him on his forehead.

"Ow!" He stood there, hand to his head, stunned and plainly offended. "What the hell was that for?"

"Hey, Frey, this is basketball, not bowling," Mottson said, panting heavily as Rosie called the foul. "We don't get any points if you knock him down like a bowling pin."

"Then the next time he grabs my ass," Emma said through her teeth, "I'll shove the ball down his throat!"

Strong shot an exasperated glare at Bobby. "You're never gonna rattle her that way, so give it up already. The only way you guys will win is by getting the ball through the net."

Was *that* what Bobby had been up to? Trying to fluster her enough so his team would win?

Emma started laughing; she couldn't help it. Maybe she should be out for his blood, but she just found his on-the-fly strategy funny as hell. "Halloran, that has got to be the lamest cheat I've ever encountered in my life."

He had the grace—or the survival instincts, most likely—to look guilty. "It was worth a try. Tell you what, you can grab my ass as much as you want if it'll make you feel better."

"Mine, too," offered Zug with his goofy grin. "I know it'll make me feel better."

"Knock it off." Car elbowed Zug, then turned to Emma, grinning. "On the other hand, you did whack my guy on the head. Bobby gets a foul shot."

"What about him putting his hands all over my backside?" she demanded, her voice inching up an octave or so.

"Hey, Rosie," Car called. "Did you see Bobby acting badly?"

"What I saw was Bobby just acting like the spaz he is." Rosie looked amused. "Seriously, if he grabbed her, I missed it."

"That's not fair!" Emma protested. "He clearly—"

"It helps to remember this ain't like college basketball," Lenny cut in, smiling. "It's more like . . . a friendly kind of war."

Emma knew when to give up, at least protest-wise, but her competitive fires were roaring hot—and Car Chatman's team was doomed. She'd sink them so low they'd never get up.

The massive Holland, grinning along with everybody else, tossed the ball to Halloran. "Make us proud, man. Even if you really ain't one of us."

Bobby moved up to the free throw line, with a cheeky wink at Emma, and rotated his shoulder. She'd noticed he did that a lot, as if the physical activity aggravated an old injury. Then she remembered he'd taken a bullet in his shoulder a few years back. Damaged muscles and nerves took time to heal—if they ever did.

Bobby easily made the shot, which left Team One only twelve points ahead. Definitely time for her to get serious.

She'd never played so hard, and by the last five minutes, the game degenerated into a free-for-all, with Team Five only two points behind. In a singsong voice, Rosie began counting down the time. At the fifteen-second mark, Emma stole the ball from Giacomo and drove down the court, Giacomo hot on her heels. She barely stayed out of his reach as Strong, Lenny, and the ex-military kid scrambled to cover her as she went in for the killer jump shot and sent the ball swishing down through the hoop.

Michael Jordan, baby, eat your heart out.

The small crowd cheered, regardless of which team they'd been rooting for. Grinning, breathing hard, Emma gave a little victory leap—and came down onto a body that hadn't been there a scant second before.

Knocked off balance, she hit the concrete facedown, hard enough to knock the air out of her lungs. When the bright lights stopped flashing and she could breathe again without wheezing, she rolled over onto her back. The concerned faces of Strong and Jensen, the ex-military kid, loomed over her. Despite her protests, they helped her sit up slowly—and then she looked past Strong to see Gary Giacomo's shirt in Bobby's fist, the two men face-to-face.

Shit.

Scrambling to her feet, she waved aside Jensen's hand and ignored Mottson's nasty grin, and hurried to Bobby. By the time she got to him and Giacomo, Holland and Car had already intervened—Holland forcibly holding Bobby in place, and Car pushing Giacomo back.

The spectators, half of them kids, had fallen silent, and Emma said with quiet urgency, "Bobby, don't. I'm sure he just got carried away by the moment and didn't mean to hurt me."

Giacomo turned. A cold hatred flashed in his eyes, then disappeared as suddenly, replaced by a bad-tempered sullenness most likely aggravated by a few too many beers.

Still, that look had taken her by surprise, and she stopped short.

Bobby reluctantly backed off. Halfway through the game, he'd removed his sunglasses, and the dark bruise beneath his eye stood out against the high color of his face.

"Emma, are you okay?" At the touch of a hand on her shoulder, Emma turned to see Alycia, her face full of concern. "You fell awfully hard there."

"I'm fine, thanks." Emma blew out a breath as Bobby stalked in one direction, and Giacomo in the other. "I'm more upset with Bobby . . . I swear, every time I turn around, that man's starting a fight. Does he do this a lot?"

"He can be hotheaded," Alycia said. "But that's just Bobby."

"I've been hearing that a lot lately," Emma muttered. "Don't you ever worry that one of these days he'll . . ."

She let the words trail off, not liking the direction her thoughts were taking her.

Never one to let things drop, Alycia asked, "Worry about what? That he'll go too far and hurt somebody?"

Exactly. Emma sighed. "I don't know. Maybe."

Alycia made a pooh-poohing motion with her hands, but it didn't chase away Emma's unease. Especially since the possibility of Bobby losing his head and hurting somebody was only part of her worry.

The it's-just-Bobby excuse seemed to be everybody's way of brushing off his behavior, and at first she'd gone along with it. But now she wondered if his peers and friends might very well watch him run to the edge of a high roof, saying, *Oh, that's just Bobby*—right up until the moment he jumped.

"I'm going to go talk with him and see if he's okay." Squaring her shoulders, Emma turned from Alycia and made her way toward Bobby. He stood by a picnic table with a few others, guzzling a bottle of water and unaware of her approach.

A cell phone jingled, and half the cops, Emma included, patted their pockets. It wasn't hers, and as she looked up, Bobby pulled out his Nokia and answered.

Several seconds later, his expression altered, going from lingering anger to a stony blankness.

"Okay, calm down . . . I'll be right there." He turned, frowning when he saw Emma, then his mouth tightened as he added more quietly, "I'll take care of it."

Switching off the phone, he slipped it into his back

pocket, picked up his sweatshirt and sunglasses, and strode over to Alycia and Car. Emma followed.

"Sorry," he said tersely. "I have to go."

"Trouble?" Emma asked, and the guarded look in his eyes, the sudden tension of his body, warned her something was very wrong.

"Personal." He turned his back to her before she could ask any more questions. "Thanks for another great cookout. I'd stay and help clean up, but this really can't wait."

"Go on." Alycia said, although he'd already backed away, car keys in hand. "It's not like there won't be enough helping hands without you. See you Monday."

Without looking back, Bobby left at a run. Emma watched him a moment longer, still troubled, then turned—and caught Strong staring at her with an intense, unreadable expression.

Bobby pushed through the door to the Trauma ICU, his temper under better control than it had been when one of Andrea's nurses called to tell him Raymond had forced his way into Juleen's room.

The first thing he saw as he walked in were two hospital security guards standing by the nurses' station, talking with Andrea and several other nurses. Unfortunately, Raymond was nowhere in sight.

Andrea waved him over and introduced him to the security guards, who regarded him with dubious expressions as they took in his dirty jeans, sweat-stained T-shirt, and black eye.

Ignoring the looks, he asked impatiently, "Where's Raymond?"

"He left," answered the older security guard, his tone terse.

"He sure did." Andrea folded her arms across her chest. "The second I told Megan to call you, he suddenly became a lot more cooperative."

Bobby turned to the guards. "You didn't try to hold him here?"

"We're not authorized to use physical force unless an individual is acting violently," said the younger guard stiffly. "He was verbally abusive, and we informed him we'd escort him out of the hospital if he didn't leave on his own."

"Did he threaten anybody?" Bobby asked.

"Oh, yeah," Andrea answered. "He was a real sweetheart."

"I need a pen and something to write on." After Andrea handed him a legal pad and pen, he jotted down the names and contact information for the security guards, then asked, "Did he get into her room?"

Andrea nodded. "Yes, but he didn't do anything to her. Things didn't get ugly until I tried to make him leave, that's when he started shouting."

"About what?"

"The usual righteous crap. That she was his wife, which is a *lie,* and that we had no right to make him leave. Then he started in on how he was as much a victim as Juleen, and the police and her family were lying and trying to put the blame on him because no one wanted to admit she'd been hooking, blah blah blah."

"Did he get physical with you or any of your staff?"

"No."

"Damn." He scowled. "That figures."

202   Michele Albert

The trouble with Raymond was that for such a low-life piece of shit, he had an uncanny ability when it came to looking out for his own ass.

Andrea looked disappointed. "Does this mean you won't be able to do anything?"

"Probably not," Bobby admitted. To the security guards he added, "Too bad he didn't punch out one of you. Nothing personal, you understand. It would just make my life a little easier."

The older guard smiled. "I know what you mean. I used to be on the force myself. She didn't have a restraining order against the guy, huh?"

"I tried to get her to file one, but she changed her mind."

"I wish we could help, but he was just acting like a typical asshole."

Which, of course, wasn't against the law. "I'll see what I can do with this. Maybe it'll help later down the road."

After the girl died, but Bobby couldn't bring himself to say it.

"So you're done with us?" the older guard asked. And when Bobby nodded and thanked them again, they left.

Andrea sent a few lingering nurses on their way, and as they wandered off, she smiled and leaned over the countertop. "They think you're cute—and they're very disappointed you didn't ask for any phone numbers."

Bobby ran a hand through his hair. "Thanks, but I don't think a girlfriend is what I need right now."

"That's not a very guylike reaction. So what would you say you need these days?"

"An uninterrupted night's sleep would help." He slumped against the other side of the desk, elbows resting on the counter, chin in his hand. "For a straight week."

Andrea tipped her head, studying him. "Is that a shiner you're sporting?"

He shrugged, ducking his head. "I got into a fight the other night. All in the line of duty."

"I've noticed you have a habit of getting banged up in the line of duty." She hesitated, then asked, "Are you okay? I don't mean to pry into personal matters, but you're looking a little rough."

Bobby pushed away from the desk, ripped off the paper with his notes, then returned her pad and pen. "That's because I just left a basketball game. I probably don't smell too good, either. Sorry."

"That's not what I meant."

"Yeah. I know." Catching her concerned look, he said, "I'm okay. It's stress . . . a drawback of the job, which I'm sure you understand. I'll deal with it."

In the past, whenever he'd felt down, he always pushed himself back on track; no need to worry or embarrass anybody about it. Andrea didn't look convinced, but she was in the medical profession—it was her job to poke and prod at hurts, real or imagined.

"How's Juleen doing?" he asked, changing the subject.

"The same. Sometimes they go fast, other times they can linger for a while. In a way, it's better if they go fast. It's so hard on the families when it's slow like this. You can see that little spark of hope in their eyes whenever they look at you, and it never gets any easier." She paused. "I guess you know what it's like. You've probably done your share of breaking bad news."

"That I have." Bobby backed toward the door, suddenly needing to get away from this place. "But knowing

I can maybe squeeze a little justice out of it all . . . hell, some days a spark of hope is the only thing that keeps any of us going."

Andrea smiled. "You're a good guy, Bobby."

"Oh, yeah. A real prize." His voice carried more of an edge than he intended, so he blunted it with a wink. "I better head home. Call me when things change with her."

Emma stood in her kitchen, fresh out of the shower and wearing her favorite old terry robe, and contemplated the neat row of tea boxes in the cupboard. She wasn't in an Earl Grey mood, or a chamomile. She wanted zing. Maybe a lemon herbal—or Constant Comment. She loved how a steeping cup of Constant Comment filled her kitchen with a subtle, spicy orange tang and made her feel cozy and settled.

Right now, she could definitely use some cozying and settling. Decision made, she put a mug full of water in the microwave and was digging around in the drawer for a spoon when her phone rang.

She glanced at the clock—it was after ten P.M. on a Sunday night, and any call this late couldn't be good. With a sigh, she picked up. "Hello?"

Static silence.

"Hello?" Emma repeated, more forcefully.

Fear spiked, and she couldn't help flashing back to another apartment, another city, when the hang-up calls and threats first started.

Then a man said, "Emma? It's Denny."

Hearing his familiar voice came as a shock, even though she'd known he would call, and she sank down on the nearest chair. "Hi."

"Is this a good time?" Even over the phone line, she could feel his tension, and an odd warmth washed over, as if a last, icy little place inside her had finally thawed. "Patti said she talked to you, and that I could call. But if it's not—"

"It's okay, Denny. I'm just making tea."

"Constant Comment, or Lemon Zinger?"

She smiled; after four years together, he knew her well. "Constant Comment . . . and I see your detective skills are as sharp as ever."

Another brief, awkward silence followed. "Some things you just remember."

Beneath the discomfort in his voice, she could hear a sadness, too, and knew this talk wouldn't be easy on either of them. "Yes," she said simply. "You do. How's it going with you?"

"Good. Keeping busy. You know how it is . . . in L.A., violent crime's a way of life." He paused. "How are you doing? Patti said you're back to work."

"Yes, and settling in. Things are a little hectic, but with just moving and a new job, I expected that."

"I'm glad things are working out for you."

"Thanks. I appreciate that, Denny. I really do."

"Yeah, I wanted—" He sighed. "Christ, this is hard. Emma, I wanted to talk about what happened. I shouldn't have waited this long, until you moved half the country away, but I just . . . I'm sorry for what I did, for not being there when you needed me most. I was wrong, and a damn coward, and I want you to know how sorry I am. I hurt you."

Nearly a year's worth of pain, summed up in three little words. "Yes, you did. And I'm sorry, too, that things didn't work out better between us. I believe you never meant for us to end that badly, and I'm not mad anymore. If it helps at all, Denny, I forgive you."

"Thanks. And yeah—it helps." Another sigh. She could see him, sitting in that big, ugly green chair he liked so much, running his hand through his dark hair, the way he always did when he was upset.

But this time, no little stab of pain or regret came with the memory.

"Like the saying goes, Denny, life goes on."

"I know. And Patti said you've met somebody."

Briefly, Emma closed her eyes. "Yes."

"Somebody from work?"

"Another detective." She was only a little guilty for letting him think she was dating again. But it was so much easier than trying to explain the relationship—or whatever it was—between her and Bobby.

And it let Denny down more gently, because in the pauses and tone of his voice, she slowly realized he'd hoped for a reconciliation.

As if to confirm her suspicions, Denny said, "So you're saying there's no chance you and me might talk things through."

The microwave beeped. Done.

"I don't think so. I just don't feel that way about you, Denny. Not anymore."

"Right." He paused. "I knew the answer, but I had to hear it. I wish you the best, Emma. I really do, and again . . . I *am* sorry. I wish I could take it all back."

After four years and all they'd shared, it felt as if she should have more to say. "I know. I wish you the best, too. You take care of yourself, okay?"

"Sure. Maybe I'll talk to you again soon."

He wouldn't; they both knew it. "That'd be nice."

"I gotta run. It's late, tomorrow's Monday. Good-bye, Emma."

She swallowed, then whispered, " 'Bye."

After he hung up, she sat for a long time, staring out at nothing. She kept expecting to cry, until she realized there was nothing left to cry over. Finally, she went over to the microwave and reheated the water and, as she waited, thought about Bobby, and how quickly things had heated up between them when they'd kissed.

Maybe she wasn't at the point where she could let another man in her life, but she wanted to—and that was as good a place as any to start.

Seventeen

Strong rubbed his brows, his expression pained—a look Bobby knew all too well—and asked, "So you don't even know where to *look* for the Mitsumi woman?"

Emma traced a stain on the carpet with the toe of her shoe. "No, sir."

"Why not? And how is she keeping ahead of two of my supposedly best detectives?"

Bobby rotated his shoulder, which was still giving him trouble after Sunday's basketball game. He'd already taken two Tylenols, but maybe another couple might do the trick. "Because she's smart, and I've been too easy on her."

Emma glanced his way, her expression closed. This morning, she looked all professional and proper in a brown suit and turtleneck sweater—but he'd liked her better in jeans and a sweatshirt, all sweaty and flushed with exertion. There was a mother lode of passion deep inside that woman, just waiting for some lucky guy to bring it to the surface.

And there was nothing he liked better than a challenge.

Then Strong sat back, glowering, and Bobby forced his thoughts away from how hot Emma looked before he landed himself in even more hot water.

"I figured that had something to do with it. And here's another problem for you both to chew on," Strong continued. "I just heard about a body found early this morning in a car near the train station, shot through the back of the head. You know this guy, too. Stuart Yamada."

Bobby caught Emma's grim look. "What was he doing out of jail?"

"His lawyer posted bail. He didn't do anything more than punch an off-duty cop and carry a gun. We couldn't keep him locked up forever."

"Who's handling Yamada's murder?" Emma asked.

"Jim Tarkenson out of the homicide support office," Strong answered. "With Yamada, Farmer, and Watkins all former associates of Jacob Mitsumi, and all killed in different parts of the city, they're taking over the investigation."

Bobby rubbed his thumb along his chin—realizing he'd forgotten to shave—then sat back. "A gofer, a bodyguard, and a shooter . . . not much in common between them."

Emma straightened. "It's Chloe, Bobby. Accept it. A group of men came to see her at work a week before her apartment was hit, and if the boutique manager can ID Watkins, that connects *all* three dead men with Chloe, and that's not looking good for her."

Bobby knew Chloe wasn't responsible for any killings, but he wouldn't argue about the "not good" part. "There's other factors to consider, like the *netsuke*. It's more likely Chloe got caught in the middle. In wouldn't be the first time. Did Emma tell you about the *netsuke*?"

"Yes, this morning, before you got in." Strong frowned. "I can see guys like Yamada and Watkins getting killed over money, drugs, or guns, but not art. They might have the muscle and firepower to fence high-priced art, but without Mitsumi, they don't have the brains or organization."

"It's possible there's trouble brewing between our Yakuza-wannabes and another gang," Bobby pointed out. "The treasure hunt angle means something valuable is up for grabs—first come, first served. Could be drugs, and somebody's intent on taking out the competition."

Strong leaned back. "I haven't heard any reports of increased gang fighting. All things considered, it's been a quiet couple of months."

"I think we need to question Jacob Mitsumi," Emma said. "He apparently started the ball rolling by sending Willie Farmer to his sister with a message."

"I was just going to suggest that," Strong said. "Halloran?"

Coldness settled over him, and the ache in his shoulder suddenly seemed to worsen. "I doubt we'll get anything out of him, but maybe he'll let something slip. We can try. You up to a road trip, Frey?"

"You bet."

"When do you want to head out?" Strong asked. "I'll give the warden a call so they know to expect you."

Bobby stood. "How about right now?"

"What's the status on your other cases?"

"I have two suspects in custody on the City Park muggings. The evidence is solid, so I don't see any trouble bringing charges against either of them. And as I see it, finding out what's going on in the Mitsumi case is a priority if we got dead gangbangers piling up."

"That's what I'm thinking." Strong turned to Emma. "You clear to be out of the office for the day?"

She nodded. "My only open case is the convenience store assault, and a suspect is in custody on that one, too. The victim made a positive ID, and it looks like an open-and-shut deal. It won't take me long to close it out."

"So what are you waiting for?" Strong sat forward, grabbing a stack of printouts. "Hit the road. Get me some answers. Make me a happy man."

The trip to the Louisiana State Penitentiary in Angola took nearly three hours, one way—not the ideal way to pass time in the presence of a moody man Emma couldn't get out of her system, no matter how many rational excuses she considered as trees, cars, and towns whizzed past.

And if she hadn't been able to deduce Bobby's bad mood from his silences, the fact he was dressed all in black was a dead giveaway.

He'd insisted on driving, claiming long trips "relaxed" him, and figuring his nerves were stretched as tightly as hers, she didn't argue. Unfortunately, the only means by which certain parts of her would ever relax involved Bobby, a bed, and bare skin—although as the miles passed and the minutes ticked by, the bed and bare skin became more and more optional.

Once upon a time, she'd been proud, even a little arrogant, of her self-control and practicality—until it dawned on her that her current jitters had nothing to do with practicality and self-control and everything to do with having never run head-on into the right kind of temptation.

Or the right kind of man, one who turned her world

on its head and set her nerves to sizzling with a look or a touch. She'd listened with a skeptical ear to tales of love at first sight, and laughed inwardly at people who'd talked about "hot looks" and "melting kisses."

She wasn't laughing anymore. Feeling pulled in different directions between the physical, the emotional, and the sensible was uncomfortable, scary, and painful.

"You've been awfully quiet," Bobby said as they neared the prison. "Is something wrong?"

"No, I'm just wondering about this guy we're going to see. And his sister." She paused. "How come you didn't you tell me she was more fox than sex kitten?"

"You wouldn't have believed me, or said I was too personally involved to see her clearly."

He was right, and she should've known better. Birds of a feather flocked together, as the saying went, and both Bobby and Chloe Mitsumi had perfected the art of benefiting from people's tendency to judge the book by the cover, even when some people should know better.

Like her. So much for her fancy-schmancy detective skills.

"So why don't you want to talk to the brother?"

Emma already had a good idea why, but she wanted to hear his answer. Between what she'd read about Jacob Mitsumi from the files and what little Bobby had told her, she didn't need to be a genius to know the Red Dragon was Bobby's bête noire, and facing the man who'd shot him wouldn't be a walk in the park. But the only hand they had to play was Mitsumi's devotion to his sister, and she fervently hoped it paid off.

"Why? Because I hate him."

Ask a stupid question . . .

"What happened between the two of you? I'd really like to know, Bobby."

He kept his focus on the highway. "Back before I made detective, I was in charge of a team of officers helping vice raid one of Mitsumi's warehouses. One of my officers was a good friend, and I was half in love with her, too."

This story didn't sound like it had a happy ending. "What was her name?"

"Dulcie Quinn. She was a good cop, and when I cleared my team to go into the building, she was one of the first through the door. As it turned out, the building wasn't as secure as we were told, and one of Mitsumi's guys took a baseball bat to her. Broke her back."

"Oh, my God," Emma whispered.

"She lived, but ended up with chronic back pain and had to leave the force. She took it hard, and I took it hard, because I'd been the one to give the order. She was feeling sorry for herself, I wanted to help, and one night we got drunk and ended up in bed."

This had an oddly familiar ring.

"I know what you're thinking," Bobby said, his face flushing a dull red. "And you're not far off. My friends give me a hard time about always needing to help out 'damsels in distress,' as they put it. Hell, even Strong knows I'm a sucker for women going through hard times."

"Do you always sleep with women whose lives are messed up?"

"No, but it happens more than it should, I know that. Sometimes, it seems like the only women I attract are cop groupies and women looking for a guy to lean on.

The groupies don't like the long hours or my moods, and the other ones move on when things improve."

Emma stared at him, almost as shocked by his admission as she was bothered by it. To be fair, she could see how the lines between emotional and physical comfort could get a little fuzzy, but he still should've known better. "This sounds to me like an easy enough habit to break."

"Well, yeah, except I'm not real good at asking for a psych profile before I get involved with a woman."

"But if you keep . . . how will you know when you fall in love for real?"

"Damn good question. I'm just hoping I'll know it when I feel it." He glanced at her, one side of his mouth curved up. "Why are you asking? Thinking of asking me out yourself?"

Exasperating man; he was trying to distract her. "I'm impressed by your ability to flirt in almost any situation."

"It takes practice."

"And you've had plenty of practice."

"Could be," he agreed.

"I bet Chloe still taught you a thing or two."

"Maybe I taught her a thing or two," Bobby said wryly. "You know, for someone who doesn't like it when I ask personal questions, you sure aren't shy about asking about my sex life."

He had her there, and she had the good sense not to argue.

"Is there a reason why you're so curious about me and Chloe?"

"Morbid, prurient curiosity?"

"At wanting to give me a try yourself?" At his brief

look—direct and intense—a long, liquid tendril of need twined through her. "All you gotta do is ask, and I'm yours for the taking."

Not the smoothest of come-ons, but effective. Distressingly so. "You're serious?"

"Absolutely."

"That wouldn't be a good idea. And I know you're dodging the talk about Jacob Mitsumi, so stop it. What happened later? Alycia told me you were caught up in some personal vendetta and that's how you got shot."

"Vendetta, my ass." He laughed. "I got played. By a male stripper."

"Oh. How embarrassing."

"No kidding." He grimaced. "After Dulcie was hurt, I went gunning for Mitsumi and finally, one night, I got called to a murder of a drug dealer. Turns out Mitsumi killed him after Chloe's birthday party, and the guest of honor at her party was a male stripper who also witnessed the murder. I figured I had the case nailed, and all I had to do was keep my witness alive. I took him to stay with Dulcie, because I knew she'd want to help, but the guy wasn't too pleased about it."

"I bet. You definitely violated a few of his civil liberties."

"It gets better. Turns out the stripper was really a construction worker whose brother was killed in a drive-by shooting ordered by Mitsumi. The kid just got in the way, but the brother, Julien, decided to take the law into his own hands. Julien used Chloe to get close to Mitsumi, and set up a plan to kill him. Things went bad, somebody else ended up dead."

Amazed, she stared at him. "Did you know any of this at the time?"

"Not at all. I knew Julien was up to something, but after a week, I had to let him go. And by this time, he'd started something with Dulcie, she was upset with me for letting him go, and the next thing I knew, I was in a shoot-out with Mitsumi in a crowded strip club. My supervisor wasn't too happy about that part of it, though I didn't pick the time and place."

"Was anybody else hurt?"

"Just me, and that's only because I was trying to get Julien out of the way. And you know what's ironic?" When she shook her head, he grinned. "If Mitsumi hadn't shot me, I don't know if we would've won the conviction we did. So even though I screwed up, I still got my man."

"And it nearly cost you your life."

"Nah. I lost a lot of blood and I hurt like hell for months, but it wouldn't have killed me."

He made it sound like a scrape. "Your shoulder still bothers you . . . when we were playing basketball, I noticed you favor it."

"I'll never have full range of motion back, but close. Some days it bothers me a lot. It's just something I live with, and it makes it hard to let go of the hate."

"What happened to the brother, Julien, and your friend Dulcie?"

"They got married, had a kid, and last I heard, there's another one on the way. I consider them among my best friends, and Julien helped me with the remodeling at my cottage."

Listening to him talk about the past, she couldn't help but remember her conversation with Denny. "Sometimes the bad things in our lives are really blessings in disguise," she said quietly.

"Sometimes, yeah."

Emma wanted to talk about last night's call, but wasn't sure if it was a good idea. She must've sat there looking at him too long, indecision plain on her face, because he added, "If there's something you want to say, go ahead."

"I was . . . my ex-boyfriend called me last night."

"The one who left you high and dry because of a few crank calls?"

Maybe she shouldn't have said anything after all. "Yes, that one."

"How'd it go?"

"Not too bad. I hadn't talked to him in months, so it was a little awkward at first." She looked down, smoothing the wrinkles on her pants. "I'm glad we talked, though. The way he ended things left a lot of issues open between us."

Bobby glanced at her, his expression strangely tight—and distant. "He wants to get back together with you?"

Emma heard something else besides anger in his voice; maybe she was crazy, but he sounded a little jealous—and she wasn't sure what to think of that. "I think maybe he wanted to."

"Do you?"

Definitely more than anger on her behalf. "No. I don't love him anymore," she said. "But it was good to tie up those loose ends I'd left behind, and without any more arguments or hard feelings. Denny regrets how he ended things with me, and he needed to let me know that. He's a good man. He just wasn't the man for me."

Several seconds passed in silence as the flat Louisiana countryside flashed past before Bobby asked, "You feel better about it, then?"

"I guess so. I wanted to talk to somebody, maybe so I could get a better handle on how I feel. I thought about calling my mom, but I wasn't up to dealing with her fussing over me, and I thought about calling Alycia, but I figured she'd be really busy after the cookout, and . . ."

And what? She let her voice trail off, still uncertain she should've brought it up with Bobby. Maybe he'd think she was trying to tell him she was a free agent now and was encouraging his attentions.

"And you told me because I'm sitting here," Bobby said.

"Kind of," she admitted. "But I thought you wouldn't mind. For a guy, you're pretty good at listening."

She shouldn't have let him know she didn't mind his attentions. Getting involved with him now really would be a bad idea, even if her less pragmatic self wondered if an affair might be exactly what she needed, anyway.

By that time, Bobby had stopped at the prison gate, which curtailed further chitchat. After they were cleared, he drove to the parking lot. Once he turned off the ignition, he faced her, his expression solemn. "Ready?"

She nodded, although at this point her confidence about prying any useful information out of Jacob Mitsumi was flagging.

The chill wind cut through her heavy sweater as they walked toward the main doors, and Emma regretted leaving her coat behind in the car.

Noticing her shiver, Bobby moved closer—and immediately the edge of sexual awareness came rushing back. It hadn't really gone away since the night he kissed her at Punk Amok. It always hovered, just under the surface, and the second she didn't have the excuse of work to throw up between them as a barrier, that little itch soon inched up on her, impossible to ignore.

Bobby stopped before they reached the door. "Want my coat?"

Without waiting for an answer, he shrugged it off and draped it over her shoulders. The leather carried his warmth and the scent of his cologne, which filled her senses as she took a long, deep breath. His intimate closeness felt far more like an embrace than a friendly concern for her chill.

"I was serious earlier, about you and me. Why do you say it's a bad idea? Was it something I said or did?" he asked quietly, and when she turned her head away, he took her chin in his fingers and raised her face to his. "I really want to know."

An honest question deserved an honest answer, even if what she really wanted was to lean into him, feel his arms close tightly around her and completely envelop her in the warm, spicy cocoon of his body and coat.

She focused on his lower lip, thinking he had a truly kissable mouth. She could kiss that mouth for hours, and imagined how it would feeling kissing every part of her—

No going there.

"It's not that I'm not attracted to you, Bobby, because I am. You know that," Emma said, keeping her tone calm and even. "But you're a big risk. I'm at a point in my life where I'm not sure I'm up to taking any risks— and I'm afraid you'll end up getting yourself hurt or killed, or do something that I won't be able to excuse away or pretend I didn't see. I've had a bellyful of hurt lately. I don't want any more, and from where I'm standing, you're a heartache just waiting to happen."

He looked at her for a long moment, as if he might argue, then he turned and headed toward the door. She followed, more slowly, but once inside the prison they had no more time to talk about private matters.

After they checked in their guns and passed through security, one of the guards settled them in a private interview room. A short while later, another guard brought Jacob Mitsumi into the room.

He wore his black hair tied back in a short ponytail, and was taller than she'd expected. Although he was slender in build, his jumpsuit revealed the powerful sinews and tendons of his arms, no doubt a by-product of the prison farm's physical labor. A lot of women would've found him extremely good-looking, but Emma couldn't see past the cold, mad-dog glitter of his eyes.

Bobby sat close enough that she could feel his muscles tense—and if hate had a feel and a smell, it was the tension eddying through this room like a deadly electrical current, with its stale-sweat scent.

Thank God the long arm of the law had held these two men apart, otherwise by now one of them—or both—would be dead.

Bobby fired the first salvo: "Enjoying your stay in the state hotel?"

"Hey, no complaints. How's the shoulder?"

Bobby flashed that angelic smile she'd come to recognize as trouble. "Not bad, thanks for your concern."

"Too bad I didn't hit a little lower and more toward the heart."

"Yeah, because then you'd have fried as a cop killer."

"True, but you still would've missed all the fun of that, and I'd get the last laugh. I like the black eye. It's a good color on you." The man cocked his head toward

Emma. "Who's the ball-buster? She doing your dirty work for you these days?"

Before the mood turned even uglier, Emma sat forward. "I'm Detective Emma Frey, and we're here to talk to you about your sister."

Concern—or fear—flickered in Mitsumi's black eyes, but it came and went so quickly, Emma couldn't be sure. "Chloe's no part of my life."

"That remains to be seen," Emma said evenly. "She's in trouble, and it looks like it's related to you."

"Not possible. I don't talk to her, she won't see me. And in case you haven't noticed, I'm in prison. It limits my social contacts."

She ignored his sarcasm. "In the past few weeks, Willie Farmer, Lew Watkins, and Stuart Yamada have been killed, each shot once in the back of the head. All were last seen talking to your sister."

"So? They know my sister and keep an eye on her for me. She has this bad habit of getting involved with the wrong kind of men."

The barb was directed at Bobby, who just smiled.

"Your sister's apartment was also vandalized," Emma added. "And everything she owned was destroyed. We want to protect her, but she's missing."

A good cop knew when to lie, when to embellish, and when to shoot straight. In this case, whatever made Chloe's situation sound worse would be her best chance to get her pathologically overprotective brother talking.

Mitsumi remained expressionless, but he'd gone very still. Finally, he turned his attention to Bobby, and the two of them stared each other down across the table, poker faces in place, neither one giving an inch. Emma waited; and as long as Bobby stayed quiet and didn't cause her trouble, he could sit there and radiate menace to his heart's content.

"We want to help your sister, Mr. Mitsumi," Emma said. "But we can't do that without your help. How about you tell us what's going on so we can get to her before she's hurt? Or worse."

"Chloe is no longer a part of my life. Her choices are her own."

"Maybe, but somebody is seriously limiting those choices for her. She hasn't done anything wrong, and shouldn't suffer for your mistakes."

"She's made her choice," Mitsumi repeated, still staring at Bobby. "She's on her own now. There's nothing I can do for her."

Reading between the lines of Mitsumi's answer, Emma suspected Chloe had acted against his wishes, and he'd washed his hands of her. It was also obvious he was highly pissed that his sister had been involved with Bobby.

"What's the deal with the *netsuke*, Mr. Mitsumi? What do they have to do with Chloe?"

She didn't expect an answer, so it surprised her when Mitsumi finally turned away from Bobby and smiled at her. "It's all about numbers. Little numbers, big numbers . . . sex and greed and betrayal."

"You sound like a bad soap opera," Bobby snapped. "Cut the bullshit. Chloe's life is in danger—"

"You really think so?" Mitsumi asked. "People always forget to watch their back doors. Why is that?"

Again, the gunslinger stare-down between the two men, almost as if they were conducting an entirely wordless conversation—and Emma didn't appreciate being left out of the loop.

"And why," Mitsumi added softly, "do people trust so blindly? The truth changes, depending on where you're coming from. And in a different shade of light, allies become enemies, and enemies become allies. What will be, will be . . . life or death can't touch me now. I've moved beyond that."

Emma's patience bottomed out. "I'm not buying in to this born-again mystic shaman shit. And your riddles don't interest me."

Mitsumi leaned toward her, still smiling. "I was bored. Now I'm amused. Life's all a game, a search for a prize, and the winner takes all."

"I told you he was fucking crazy." Bobby stood. "Let's go. We're not getting anything useful out of him, and he doesn't give a shit about Chloe."

"Crazy" didn't even begin to cover it; "megalomaniac" might. Emma stood as well, ignoring Bobby's hand on her arm, and tried one last question: "Where are the *netsuke*?"

"You'll have to ask Chloe that one." Mitsumi's smile broke into a wide grin. "She has them."

Eighteen

"What happened back there?" Emma demanded as she walked toward the car, her strides matching Bobby's.

"Nothing. He's crazy, is all."

She grabbed his arm, pulling him to a stop. "He was giving answers, but in code. I don't have a translator handy for deciphering Red Dragon psycho-speak, but I think you do. What's going on?"

"I don't know," he retorted, brows drawn together. "And that's the goddamn truth, whether you believe me or not."

"Not details, maybe, but you have an idea. Don't you?"

He pulled away and started walking again toward the car. Emma followed, right on the heels of his black boots.

"Alycia told me you'd hold out on me. She said you'd get into a mood, and that would be the end of it. She was right."

"Alycia doesn't know jack about me."

"I don't, either. And, come to think of it, nobody does. Maybe that's what Mr. Mystic Dragon meant with all that mumbo-jumbo about allies and enemies, truth and back doors. Maybe you know a whole lot more about this than I want to admit, but I've been too naïve to see it. Again. I have this . . . little problem with expecting people to act with the same code of honor that I do."

At that, Bobby swung on her, his face tight and hard. "Code of honor? Do you really believe in shit like that?"

Taken by surprise, it took her a moment to find her voice. "Don't you?"

"Honor's nothing but a pretty, soft word in an ugly, dog-eat-dog world, and there's always a bigger dog waiting right around the corner to bite you on the ass."

The low, hard tone of his voice raised the hairs on the back of her neck, and when he took a step toward her, she moved back. At that, his eyes narrowed, even as one side of his mouth curved in a grim smile.

"For every bastard we put away, a dozen more pop up to take his place," he continued. "And those are just the ones we know about. We fight every single day to keep people safe, but it's a war we won't win—ever. Because in the end we're still predators, and it's human nature to prey on each other. That is what I believe. Do with it what you want, I don't give a damn."

"If that's how you feel, then why are you still a cop?"

For a moment, his face appeared to soften—but only for an instant. "Lately, I ask myself that question every morning when I roll out of bed. I used to have all the answers, Emma. I don't anymore. I just . . . don't."

Her confusion must've been obvious, because he added quietly, "I've been a cop my whole life. I don't know how to do anything else. Be anything else. If I don't have that anymore, what do I do?"

Emma didn't have an answer, and after several seconds passed in silence, Bobby climbed into the car and let the engine idle as he waited for her to get in. Finally, she did so, and closed her door—but still too stunned to look at him.

As they passed back through the prison gate, though, she turned to him. "I won't believe it has to be that way. I have to believe whatever we do makes a difference, no matter how small."

"Good for you. Whatever keeps you kickin' and taking a lickin'."

Something must've transpired during that prison interview room to plunge Bobby into a mood this black and cold. From the moment they'd teamed up, she'd sensed a darkness in him, but nothing that had, until now, led her to believe she was working with a ticking time bomb.

Halfway back to New Orleans, he started up a conversation as if nothing had happened—but it was an act. She might have missed this defensive response early in their relationship, but not anymore.

So she faked right along with him, laughing at his jokes and dry commentary, trading impersonal chitchat—and catching a look in his eyes every now and then that let her know he wasn't any more fooled by her faux nonchalance than she was by his.

What should she do? Approaching other detectives for advice on how to handle a partner teetering on the edge didn't feel right just now. She didn't know any of them well enough—except for Alycia, who'd probably say, *Oh, that's just Bobby. He'll snap out of it*. And, more importantly, if Bobby was having personal problems, she didn't want to compound them by adding grist to the gossip mill.

Dealing with trouble was hard enough in private; dealing with it in a fishbowl was a thousand times worse—an experience she knew all too well.

The only other option was talking to the captain, but she had no idea how Strong would react. Would he pull Bobby off duty? Suspend him? Or just wave off her worries as unimportant?

It was early evening, cold and raining, when they returned to New Orleans, and by the time Bobby pulled into the parking lot at the station house, her insides were so knotted up she actually felt ill.

As they walked to their own cars, the silence stretched on, exacerbated by the sharp sound of their echoing footsteps beneath the low concrete ceiling.

At her car, she stopped and turned. "What are we going to do next?"

"Try to think like Chloe."

Emma grimaced, and leaned back against her car. "I was hoping for something where I might stand some chance at succeeding."

He smiled, although it didn't warm his eyes. "Jacob Mitsumi did big business in drugs, so whatever he's mixing up, it'll be drug-related."

"Major badness—so why isn't Chloe acting like a hunted woman?"

"A good question, along with why ex-Dragons are dropping like flies." Bobby hesitated, then leaned back against the car beside her. "After Mitsumi's arrest, truckloads of contraband were confiscated from his properties, but a lot of shit had already been cleared out. Or so

I'm told, as I was busy bleeding in a hospital and missed the fun. Maybe we all overlooked a fortune in drugs out there somewhere, just waiting to be retrieved."

"And the *netsuke*?"

"Point the way. He said he was bored and now he's not." Frowning, Bobby rolled a pebble with the toe of his boot. "He's set the first domino in motion, and now he'll sit back to see where all the pieces fall."

"And you still believe Chloe's an innocent in all this?"

"I don't think she's innocent at all, but she's not killing people or setting up drug deals." He caught her skeptical look. "I'm telling you, it's not her style."

"People change."

"Not that much. And don't forget she hates what her brother did."

"Enough to thwart him?"

"Maybe," Bobby said slowly. "I doubt he'd turn on her after all this time, though. He didn't look too pleased when you said she was in trouble."

"No," she agreed. "But he also looked pissed off, as if she'd done something she shouldn't have and he was washing his hands of her. All that crap about her making her choice and he couldn't do anything about it . . . what *did* he mean about different lights and not watching the back door?"

"You haven't figured that out yet?" Bobby asked quietly as he pushed away from the car.

The look on his face chilled clear to the bone. "No. Have you?"

"There's a cop, or more than one, involved in this."

Denial surged through her, all jumbled with anger— and fear.

Oh, no. Please . . . not again.

"How the hell did you come up with that?" Each clipped word, in a tone sharper than she intended, ricocheted around them. "Some nut job in prison spews a bunch of nonsense, and you arbitrarily decide we have bad cops? You—"

"Emma. Keep your voice down."

Heart still pounding, she glanced around: A police station parking lot was not the place for hysterics—or talk about dirty cops. Thankfully, no one was near enough to have overheard their conversation.

"That's a serious accusation . . . you can't even begin to know how serious," she said, her voice shaking. "You better be able to back it up."

"What's the only thing Chloe's afraid of?"

"The police, with you being the exception."

"But she also doesn't want me working on the break-in at her apartment and warned me off, twice. Why would she do that?"

Emma could see where this was going—and suddenly his furious meltdown at the prison made sense. It would be a little hard to hold on to the faith after learning someone you trust might shoot you in the back. "She's afraid you'll be hurt."

"Because . . . ?"

"If you know the truth, they'd take you out to protect themselves. And the only people who could get close to you like that would be someone you'd trust—another cop. You'd never see it coming."

"Exactly. And I was after Mitsumi for years. I know how he thinks." He leaned toward her. "No one hears about this. It's between me and you, and—"

His cell phone rang. With a low curse, he fished it out of his pocket and turned slightly away.

"This is Halloran." After a moment, a bleak expression flashed across his face. "Okay, I'll be right there."

He disconnected, slipped the phone back into his pocket, and turned, looking right at her—but his eyes were blank, distant. Someplace else than here with her. "There's a problem, and I have to go. We'll talk tomorrow."

Another call-and-run? Emma narrowed her eyes. "Who was it?"

"Personal. Nothing you need to worry about."

He headed toward his car, and Emma, both alarmed by his behavior and suspicious, ran after him. "Bobby, wait!"

When he stopped, she tripped and fell into him. He quickly caught her, holding her steady. "Hey, careful . . . Emma, I know we have to talk about Chloe, but this can't wait. Please, just once, let it go."

"I'm sorry, I just . . . Never mind. Go take care of your mystery business. I'll see you tomorrow. Drive safely."

Emma got into her car and started it, but waited until his car was out of sight before reaching into her suit pocket and pulling out the cell phone she'd taken from Bobby when she'd pretended to fall into him.

Amazing, the dirty tricks she'd learned in her years as a cop.

She hated betraying his trust like this, but she smelled trouble and didn't have time to play nice. She hit the dial-back function on his phone and waited. It rang three times, then a woman answered.

Charity Trauma ICU.

Nineteen

Bobby pushed open the door to the ICU, dread crowding in with such force that his chest seemed too tight, and he tugged at the knot of his tie, loosening it so he could breathe easier.

Andrea waited for him at the desk. "Sorry for the short notice. I didn't want to call until her mother made the decision. They took her off life support five minutes ago."

Bobby nodded, running a hand through his hair. "How's she doing?"

"It's good you got here when you did."

"Her mother's here?"

"Yes. Along with the aunt."

"But not the baby or the younger kids?" When Andrea shook her head, Bobby let out his breath. Thank God for small favors. "I'll go on in, then."

"Don't be too hard on yourself." Andrea touched his arm lightly as he passed. "Considering the lifestyle this girl lived, she probably never would've made it to twenty-five."

"I know, but nobody deserves to die like this."

He headed toward Juleen's room, then slipped inside to the sound of quiet crying and labored breathing. A nurse stood in the corner, monitoring equipment and acting as a comforting presence for the family.

Clarice Moss sat in a chair by the bed, holding her daughter's limp hand. A short, thin woman with skin a shade darker than Juleen's, she was thirty-seven—his age—but she looked years older. Especially now, her face marked with grief and exhaustion. She looked up when he came in, fixing him with bloodshot, puffy eyes.

"Detective Halloran." She sounded bewildered. "What are you doing here?"

"I came to see Juleen." He spoke in a voice barely above a whisper. "If you don't mind, I'd like to stay."

Grieving people reacted with anything from numbness to violent fury, and he didn't know what to expect. But Juleen had lingered in a coma longer than anticipated, giving her family a little time to prepare as best they could for the inevitable. He didn't think they'd be angry at his presence.

"No . . . no, I don't mind. Thank you for caring enough to come see her."

The aunt—he couldn't remember her name—was sniffling, and after a brief nod toward the nurse keeping to herself in the corner, Bobby moved closer toward the bed. Not that he knew what to do; he'd delivered bad news before, more times than he cared to remember, but he'd never sat with a victim's family on a deathwatch before.

Strong wouldn't like this if he found out about it, and few cops would understand. He didn't entirely understand what drew him to this girl, either, but he listened to his instincts, and they were telling him being in this room was the right thing to do, even if it was miles beyond painful.

As he looked down at Juleen, trying not to hear her gasps for air, he noticed that her bruises had faded and a few of the cuts had healed. Without the bandages, she looked fragile and small.

Helplessness welled up inside him, dark and heavy, as he took her free hand and gave it a brief, gentle squeeze. Not so much for her sake, but for his. A touch kept her real—and served as both a good-bye and a promise.

Raymond would pay, no matter what.

As if she'd read his mind, Clarice Moss whispered, "You'll get him for what he did to my baby?"

Bobby carefully chose his words before answering. "We're still working on gathering enough evidence for a conviction."

"And a dead girl ain't enough?" asked the aunt, her voice bitter. "A girl he beat up all the damn time?"

"It's not always as simple as it looks, ma'am. It takes time, and I only have one chance to prosecute him. For Juleen's sake, I want to do it right."

The aunt nodded, a terse gesture that at least acknowledged his effort, even if the distrust in her eyes told him she didn't believe he'd follow through.

It was a look he'd seen too many times; he hated it, but understood. In their eyes, the police hadn't cared enough to protect Juleen from a violent boyfriend, and they had no reason to believe the law would serve them any better now. Everybody knew the police didn't have time for another poor black woman who hooked for the money to buy diapers, formula, and crack, and who hadn't the good sense to stay away from men who beat her.

Sometimes that was true, but not always, and it wouldn't help him any when he had to tell them the case against Raymond wasn't strong. Even the alleged history of abuse—alleged because no formal charges were ever filed—wouldn't cancel out the fact that Juleen had gone off with a john who could've had sex with her before beating her into a coma. Nor would it cancel out her past convictions for prostitution or her prior beatings; the degrading sex and violence were just a part of the job.

But how was he supposed to explain all that to a grieving family?

"I hope you do right by my daughter," Clarice said abruptly. Maybe she couldn't bear to let the silence continue—or maybe she just needed something to distract her from the sounds of Juleen's struggle. "I know she done some bad things and she had her problems, but she was a good girl in her heart, and she was good to her baby. I remember what she was like when she was just a little thing, how she was always so curious, you know . . . always talking. She never could sit still for long. I saw trouble coming, and I tried to shape her up. I even kicked her out a few times. But I always took her back. She was my little girl."

The woman fell silent for a moment, as if it had taken too much effort to say so many words at once. Then, with a tired sigh, she murmured, "I always knew this day would come. I was so afraid, and I told her and I told her . . . but it didn't do any good. Once they get so far down that road, they don't come back. But it's hard. Even knowing it's coming, it's still hard."

Bobby had nothing to say to that. Most people would look at Juleen and see the inevitable result of a high-risk lifestyle, but he wanted to see the daughter, the mother, the pretty girl he remembered, with her nihilism warring with her defiance. Her last words to him rang clear in his memory: *He'll kill me. Next time, he'll kill me, and then you don't gotta bother yourself with me no more.*

If he had any of the good fight left inside him, he couldn't let that be the end of it.

By the time she'd parked at Charity, Emma had a pretty good idea as to what was going on. All the same, as she walked into the Trauma ICU, she wished she knew more about this Raymond and his victim.

She dies, you sonofabitch, and I promise I'll be coming after you . . .

Here, presumably, would be the "she" Bobby had referred to.

A pretty blond nurse in dark pink scrubs looked up as she approached the desk. "Hi. Can I help you?"

Emma showed her shield and ID. "I'm looking for a detective. Bobby Halloran."

"Yes, he's here. I'm Andrea Thurber, the head nurse. Do you need me to get a message to him?"

"Not exactly. He's my partner." Emma paused. "And he's a friend. I'm concerned about him."

"He's with Juleen."

"And Juleen is a patient?"

"Not for much longer."

Taking in the woman's flat tone and her unsmiling face, Emma figured that didn't mean Juleen was on her way home, accompanied by mounds of flowers and cheerful Mylar balloons. "What happened to her?"

"Boyfriend beat her up for the umpteenth time. She came in almost two weeks ago and has been in a coma ever since. Her condition's steadily deteriorated, and her mother asked to take her off life support."

"How old is she?"

"Nineteen."

Oh, damn. "Are you the one who called Bobby a little while ago?"

"Yes. He said he wanted to be here when she passed on." The nurse leaned forward across the desk. "Do you want me to get him out of the room?"

Emma shook her head. "I don't want to disturb the family, or Bobby. If you don't mind, I'd like to wait here for him."

"There's a chair over by the wall if you want to sit down."

Emma thanked her and moved away. After being in a car most of the day, she didn't feeling like sitting, so she leaned back against the wall, listening to the ICU shop talk, and mulled over how she'd explain swiping his cell phone and following him here. She didn't understand why Bobby had shut her out like this, any more than she could make sense of why he hadn't simply told her the truth to begin with, but she knew he'd be furious at her interference.

His reaction wouldn't be pretty.

A young nurse walked past Emma, giving her a curious look, before stopping at the desk. "I'm back from my break. What's up? Need anything?"

"We're still waiting on Moss. But you can check the meds on Fournier and the gunshot that came in this morning. After that, you can restock the supply room. We're getting low on sterile scissors."

"Got it." The young nurse looked again at Emma. "Who's she?"

"A police detective. She's waiting for Bobby."

"He's still here, huh? That man is dedicated to his job."

It seemed Bobby was a regular around the ICU. Emma turned to the head nurse. "Does Bobby come here a lot?"

"We see a lot of police officers and detectives around this place, though I haven't seen you before. Are you new?"

"I started work a few weeks ago."

Andrea nodded, and Emma had the distinct feeling she was being stringently evaluated. "Bobby's here when he needs to be. He's stopped by to see Juleen a lot since she's come in."

Which could explain the call he'd taken the day of Alycia's picnic, when he'd bolted off like an avenging angel.

"I think he's having a hard time with this one," Andrea added.

Emma didn't reply, hoping her silence would keep the nurse talking. Instead, a flurry of activity farther down the hall caught Andrea's attention.

"I have to go. Excuse me." Andrea hurried over to the small group of people in scrubs and white coats. A doctor walked quickly past Emma, barely giving her a glance, and a moment later he said, "Okay, let's call it. What's the time?"

Halfway down the hall, to the right, a door opened and a nurse walked out, trailed by a low, keening sound. Then that same nurse, followed by the doctor and Andrea, went into the room, and the door shut, abruptly cutting off the weeping from inside.

The young nurse who'd given her a curious look a few

moments before came up to Emma. "Andrea asked me to tell you Bobby will be out soon."

"Is the patient gone?"

The nurse nodded. "A blessing, really. I honestly don't know how she survived as long as she did, poor thing."

Then Emma found herself waiting alone for Bobby, her nervous tension now colored with sadness. Finally, after what seemed like forever, the door to the room opened again. The doctor exited, only to disappear into another room. Behind him came two older women, one supporting the other, followed by Bobby. He appeared calm, but lines of weariness etched his face.

The quiet grief of the two older women was palpable, and Emma briefly looked away. She loved a lot of things about her job, but this wasn't one of them, and being caught in the middle of a stranger's pain never became routine. Or easier to deal with.

One of the women—the mother, Emma assumed— spoke to Bobby. He touched her shoulder, the gesture somehow both awkward and sincere, and in the quiet his answer came clear: "You tell your son I said he needs to take care of his sisters, and that if he wants to do right by Juleen, he better stay out of trouble. I don't want to hear him talking about killing Raymond. You tell him that's my job."

Maybe to the dead girl's family, Bobby's quiet, intense declaration sounded comforting, but Emma's blood ran cold to hear it: *That's my job.*

"You'll get him?" the mother asked. "You'll make him pay?"

"I'll get him," Bobby said flatly. "Making people pay for what they've done is what I'm here for."

Leaving the weeping women in the nursing staff's capable hands, Bobby turned toward the door—and stopped short when he caught sight of Emma.

"What the hell are you doing here? How did—"

She tossed him his cell phone. He caught it against his chest, eyes widening with disbelief before his jaw clenched. Then he closed on her, radiating hostility, and she backed up against the nurses' station desk.

Leaning forward, he said just loud enough for her to hear, "You had no right to interfere."

Emma didn't back down. "What kind of friend would I be if I didn't?"

"One that respects the other's privacy—or doesn't your code of honor cover that part?"

Placing both hands on his chest, she pushed him firmly back. "Friends don't let friends self-destruct."

"This doesn't concern you." He stared coldly at her. "Stay out of my way, Emma. I mean it."

Bobby moved past her, but she stepped in front of him. He hesitated, frowning, then shouldered her aside as if she were some bothersome insect and disappeared through the doors. Emma started after him—until a restraining hand clamped down on her shoulder.

"Maybe you should leave him alone for a while." Andrea the nurse had a vicelike grip, for such a small woman. "Let him deal with it on his own."

"I can't leave him alone. You don't understand." Over Andrea's shoulder, she caught the mother watching her, still teary-eyed, and as Emma backed through the ICU door, she added softly, "I'm so very sorry."

While Bobby had been moving fast—she couldn't see him anywhere—there were only so many directions he could go. Within a few minutes, she located him. He was hard to miss: a black-clad figure stalking through light-filled halls, past medical personnel in their white coats or brighter-colored scrubs. He looked every inch the man on a mission—and she wasn't about to allow him to start it, much less complete it.

As she followed him through Charity's halls, Emma knew better than to close the distance between them, even if Bobby had to know she was close behind him. Confronting him wouldn't be pretty; best to wait until they were outside and away from any innocent eyes and ears.

In a fast walk that matched his, she turned corners, walked down stairs, passed waiting areas—and finally he headed toward the parking garage.

Bobby slammed through the exit and took the stairs two at a time. Emma broke into a run, catching up to him as he neared his car, which was parked at the end of the row, beneath a dim, low light.

The weather had worsened, and a gust of wind whistled through the parking garage's open areas, cold and stinging against her face. Bobby had almost reached his car when she seized his coat and yanked him back.

He stumbled, then whirled around. "What the hell do you want?"

The rage on his face filled her with fear—but she held her ground. "You're coming home with me. I'm not letting you be alone tonight."

He smiled slowly, but under the pale light, it only made him look brittle and cold. "And what if I don't feel like going anywhere with you?"

"I'm not giving you a choice, Bobby."

"*You'll* make me?" He raised a brow, amused. Or maybe it was disbelief; it was hard to tell. "I'd like to see you try, darlin'."

"Don't push me. And don't argue—I'm taking you home."

"Like some stray dog you feel sorry for?" His harsh laughter rang off the concrete. "I don't need your pity or your help. Get the hell out of my way."

He pushed her aside, and after a day chock-full of ugliness, she could understand his sudden meltdown, but enough was enough. Anger flaring, Emma pushed back.

Astonishment flashed in his eyes, then his eyes narrowed and his jaw hardened. "I mean it, Emma."

"So do I."

"What's your problem, anyway? I'm just gonna talk to Raymond—a man-to-man kind of talk. That's all."

Guys like him, the only language they listen to is violence—and it's the only thing they respect . . .

"You're planning on doing your talking with a bullet. Don't you even try to tell me otherwise."

Somewhere, a car door slammed, the sound faintly echoing.

As it faded, he said, "Juleen Moss wasn't anybody's poster girl for success, but she didn't deserve to die like that."

"I never said she did."

"He'll walk free again, Emma. It isn't right."

"I know that, and I don't give a damn if that man lives or dies, Bobby, but I care about you. I can't let you do this." Spine straight, tensed, Emma stepped closer and held out her hand. "Give me your keys."

Bobby stared her down, shoulders hunched. She

didn't so much as blink, although a small shiver rippled over her, knowing she was pressing hard and he was close—so close—to losing his control.

"Try and take them," he said softly. "I could use a good laugh."

Enough.

Emma swung her arm, backhanding him across the face with her fist.

Pain burned across her knuckles as his head snapped back from the force of the blow. He'd twisted to the side, hunched over, holding his hand to his jaw. As he slowly straightened, turning his face toward her, she saw a thin line of blood trickle down from his mouth.

After a moment, he touched his split lip, glanced down at the blood, then wiped his fingers clean on his pants.

"Are you going to listen to me now?" she asked, her voice breaking as tears welled. "Am I finally speaking a language you understand and respect?"

In answer, he lunged at her. Emma raised her hands to hold him off, but his fingers closed hard over her shoulders. He spun her around and shoved her back against his SUV. Caught in the snare of the bitterness and pain in his eyes, she hardly noticed that being slammed against a car by an angry man hurt like hell.

"So." Bobby released her, but leaned forward and rested his hands against the door, on either side of her neck, effectively trapping her between his body and the SUV. "You think you can handle me?"

His breath warmed her cold, wet cheeks, and as she met his shadowed gaze, she whispered, "Absolutely."

He canted his head slightly, and the light behind him

spread a pale nimbus around his hair, like a halo, but his face was a hard, alien canvas of light and shadows, some shades deeper, darker. Sinister.

"Are you," he asked slowly, "saying what I think you are?"

"Yes."

She'd aimed for firmness, but sounded more than a little hesitant, and before she could say more, Bobby leaned full against her, thigh to thigh, hip to hip, chest to chest—and kissed her.

Emma tasted blood, then the heat of his mouth opened to her and she slipped her hands beneath his coat. She wrapped her arms around his waist, kissing him back with a sudden, hot, mindless urgency that matched his own.

Rough anger lingered in his touch and kisses, but she didn't want him tender or gentle. She wanted raw desire, the belly-deep pull of sex and passion. Digging her fingers into the broad muscles of his back, she kissed him harder, and a shudder ripped through him.

Bobby pulled back, his eyes still masked by shadows, staring at her as if seeing her for the first time. Or wondering if she were real to begin with.

"Don't stop," Emma whispered.

He brought his mouth down over hers again, possessive and hungry, tongue stroking and exploring as he pressed her back against the door. She could feel the leashed tension in the taut muscles, and the hard line of his erection against her. She moved her hips, wanting more than a touch to soothe and fill her need.

Bobby made a low sound deep in his throat, and his fingers brushed her breasts, skimming the nipples through layers of clothing. But it wasn't enough; too much separated his skin and hers, blunting his touch, and she tried to move closer, to make it better.

He lowered a hand, still kissing her, and moved his hips with an unmistakable intent and need. Emma managed to free his shirt from his pants, just enough to feel the bare skin of his back.

At her touch, he pulled back, giving her room to unsnap his pants—even as a distant, faint part of her knew a parking garage was not the time or the place for this.

An electronic chirp startled her, but Bobby had only unlocked the SUV. He opened the door, and she quickly eased to the back, where the seats had been folded flat, sliding small boxes and clutter out of her way, trying not to bump her head.

He joined her, and once he'd closed and locked the door behind him, she scooted to the side, grabbed him by his coat, and pulled him down. His mouth closed over hers, his fingers pulling at her belt as she unzipped his pants.

In the small space, each breath sounded loud, and the outside dimness provided barely enough light for her to pick up the gleam of his eye, flare of a cheekbone, and his pale hair.

Windows . . . she'd forgotten about the windows.

What if people walked by? Or some nice family with little kids, on their way home after seeing grandma at the hospital?

The panic burst over her while he worked her pants down over hips, and she dug her fingers into his shoulder, wanting to tell him to stop, but he kept kissing her, all those wonderful, deep, invading kisses . . .

"Tinted." His rough whisper sounded in her ear, his breath hot against her cheek. "The windows are tinted."

God bless tinted windows. And mind-reading lovers.

Impatient now, she pulled at his pants, and then Bobby had his hand inside her underwear, touching her, testing her readiness, and she moaned.

Bobby moved over her as she fumbled with the buttons on his shirt, wanting as much skin contact as possible. He nudged her legs apart, and she scooted closer, running her hand down his belly, hearing his sharp intake of breath as she traced his erection, cupped his heaviness in her hands.

"I want you inside me."

Inside her, filling her, full and thick and heavy, winding her up, then winding her down.

Bobby shifted her beneath him, hands rough on her hips. With so little room, every movement seemed awkward and clumsy. They were still dressed, pants pushed down just far enough to get the job done, the extra wad of clothing adding yet another obstacle.

Despite all this, Emma managed to spread her legs wider, feeling his erection nudging her, then his hand between them, guiding himself toward her. She felt the pressure, insistent and hard and beautiful, and then he slid smoothly inside, stretching her. Emma's breath caught in her throat and she squeezed her eyes shut, arching at the same time she closed her hands on his rear, pulling him deeper.

"Yes . . . yes, that right there, yes." She gasped as he began moving in her, his thrusts hard and fast, all urgency and need.

His rapid breathing heated her skin, ruffled her hair at

her neck, and she rocked with him, matching his rhythm.

So close; already so close. The second he'd touched her, his finger sliding beneath her panties, she'd almost climaxed. She could feel that inner thread pull, tugging at the knot, unwinding. Faster and faster—and then she came in a hot, sweet liquid rush, making breathy, mewling sounds, almost like sobs, as her orgasm pulsed over her, head to toe.

Bobby grunted, rasping out something that sounded like "Oh, Christ!" and then he came, still pumping her fast and hard, riding it to the end. Spent, chest heaving, he sagged over her, and she could feel the slight tremors of his muscles.

As she tried to catch her breath, Emma rubbed her palms along his lower back and rear in slow, soothing circles. A few seconds later, he let out his breath in a long sigh, and pulled out of her.

She didn't want to lose that connection, even one so rough and sudden, but already the cooler air registered along her bare skin, along with the wetness and gentle ache between her thighs.

Outside, laughter sounded close by, and reality intruded with a sharp, harsh clarity. She'd just had sex—with the man of her dreams—in the back of an SUV while in the parking garage of a major city hospital.

Quickly, she sat, her back to Bobby, and pulled up her pants as she whispered, "Oh, my God!"

From behind her, in the darkness, Bobby said quietly, "I think it's too late for prayers."

Twenty

Bobby slumped in the passenger seat, staring straight ahead as the wipers cleared away the steady rain, smearing the glow of car lights and street-lamps. Emma insisted on driving—going so far as to slide her hand inside his pants pocket to filch his keys—and he hadn't the energy to protest.

How the hell had everything gone so wrong so fast?

He didn't mind a little rough sex, although foreplay had never before included a cuff across the face, and he couldn't even remember at what point his dark rage had dissolved into a red haze of lust. But he remembered every second of what he'd done to Emma in the back of his Ford.

How could he have treated her like that? All the times he'd dreamed of making love to her, imagining how he'd pleasure her again and again—and the reality had been him going at her like an animal.

Briefly, he closed his eyes, then broke the long silence. "Emma?"

She glanced at him, her expression wary.

"Look, what we did . . . I don't usually—" he cut

himself off, frustrated and embarrassed, then finished bluntly, "We kinda fucked up the safe sex thing."

"I know. But I'm on the pill, so unless you have any evil sex cooties you need to tell me about, you can relax."

She kept her voice light, and he was almost desperate with gratitude that she didn't tear into him. It didn't help his guilt, though, or magically erase everything else that had gone all to hell tonight. "No sex cooties, evil or otherwise." He smiled halfheartedly. "I'm healthy as a plow horse, according to my last physical."

Silence returned, edged with awkwardness, and he wondered if maybe she was sharing his thoughts: He might be physically fit, but his head needed some serious straightening out.

Familiar street names and landmarks passed by outside; his cottage was only a few blocks away and he had a lot of other things to get straight besides his head.

"How I acted back there, what I said to you—" Again he stopped, trying to find his way, to make sense of it, and finally admitted, "I don't know where to begin to say sorry—me, the guy who always has the right words."

"If you're talking about the sex, Bobby, I seem to remember being an active participant."

Oh, yeah. Unbelievably responsive and passionate, hot and sweet and sexy, taking him completely by surprise. The night he'd first kissed her and she'd angrily accused him of not really knowing her, she'd been right. He didn't know the "real" Emma, but he wanted to, now more than ever.

"So you don't have anything to feel bad about." She briefly touched his mouth. "And if it's our argument you're talking about, I shouldn't have hit you. I just . . .

didn't know how else to get through to you, and I wasn't thinking clearly."

Frowning, he clenched his tensed hands, then stretched his fingers. "A lot of that going down tonight."

"Does it hurt? Your mouth?"

"I've had worse."

Emma slowed, looking for a place to park, but cars lined the street in front of the cottage and she had to drive another block before parking. They headed back to his place in silence, a cold rain drizzling down. When Bobby reached the front door, he turned, waiting. At her puzzled look, he said gently, "You have my keys."

"Oh. Right."

She handed them back, and he noticed her hands were shaking a little. After he opened the door, Bobby ushered Emma in, a hand to her back. He fumbled along the wall for the light switch, turned on the lamps, and then faced her. "You don't have to stay. I'll be okay."

"I want to stay."

To keep him penned safely inside, or because she wanted something more? Rough sex in the back of the car probably hadn't been her idea of romance, and he wasn't sure she'd give him a second chance with her—or even if he deserved one.

But, God, she was so pretty, with her solemn dark eyes and soft, full mouth. Just looking at her mouth aroused him—and at the same time made him feel like the worst kind of lecherous bastard.

Finally, he moved past her. "I'll sleep on the couch. You can have the bed."

Emma caught his hand, bringing him to a stop. "I was hoping we'd both share the bed."

Did she want him like he wanted her? Or was she just—

He couldn't finish the thought, and he pulled his hand free. "Do you mean that? And you're not just saying it to keep me here?"

"Do I look like the martyr type to you?" Her expression darkened. "And since when did you become such an idiot?"

Her indignation filled him with amazement, hope—and a healthy kick of fear that this was too good to last. "I think the question is, how the hell did I get so lucky?"

Bobby held out his hand. After a moment, she took it, and he led her toward his bedroom. He didn't turn on any lights, but left the door ajar, letting the light filter in from the living room.

This time, for her, he'd do it right. Emma deserved that much. No talk about what had happened in the hospital, or anything that wouldn't make her happy.

To that end, he let her make the first move—and she didn't wait very long. With a small smile, she took hold of his belt buckle, pulled him against her, and then leaned in for a kiss.

"The hands-on type, huh?" he asked.

"The only way to go." Emma released his buckle and trailed her hand lower, rubbing his already hard dick. He kissed her, tongue leisurely stroking hers, and for several minutes she was content to kiss him, teasing him a little, but he sensed the rising urgency in her longer, harder kisses. Before long, she'd stripped off his coat and had his shirt unbuttoned and his pants unbuckled and unzipped. He stopped kissing her long enough to get rid of her shirt and bra—and then pulled back to admire her.

"You are beautiful, Emma." He touched her breasts,

small and round, then leaned down to take a nipple between his teeth and tongue, rolling and biting until she gasped.

Looking up, he continued to slowly massage and tease her breasts. "From the way you talked, I thought maybe you'd be shy. Then I watched you play basketball, saw all that fire and passion you keep locked inside, and knew I was dead wrong."

"Some of us save our energies for the bedroom, while some of us"—she paused breathlessly—"run around on full power all the time."

"Is that a compliment?"

"As if you don't already know the answer . . . mmm, I like that." She closed her eyes as he kissed the curve of her breast, circling her nipple with his tongue. "I swear, if you keep that up, I'm going to come right here and now."

He stopped, surprised. He'd heard of women who could have orgasms with a lot of breast foreplay, but he'd never met one. "Are you serious?"

Her eyes fluttered shut. "Mm-hmm."

Well . . . damn. He nearly lost it just imagining all the things they could do to each other tonight, if she really was that incredibly responsive. "Excellent. This is gonna be fun."

Bobby grinned when she opened her eyes again, and quickly got her out of the rest of her clothes. Wearing only his unzipped pants, he walked her backward to the bed, stole a quick kiss, then eased her down. He moved over her, knees on either side of her hips, hands braced by her head, then began kissing, sucking, and biting her nipples; first one, then the other, until she came with a high, soft sigh.

And that put an end to all his grand plans to keep teasing her until she was weak and languid. All his years of practice, the self-control in bed he'd been so sure of, vanished in an instant.

While Emma lay on his bed, eyes half closed and smiling, he stripped off his pants in record time, quickly moved back over her, and entered her with a slow, deep thrust. Hot and tight, she felt so damn good surrounding him—and she immediately made it feel even better by rocking her hips, making soft little sounds that spiked his need to a fever pitch. As the hunger surged over him, he dropped his head back and swore softly, fighting to hold on to what remained of his control.

Sensing he was too close, Emma stopped her movements and pulled him down for a long, hot kiss, fingers twining in his hair, breasts brushing his chest—and he liked nothing better than the light, teasing tickle of a woman's bare breasts against his skin.

Bobby kept perfectly still until the hunger inside him faded to a manageable level. He cupped her face and slipped his tongue in her mouth, tasting and exploring—then he flexed his hips sharply upward and she arched, with a sharp, high moan.

Not in any hurry to put him out of his misery—sweet as it was—Emma took her time as she moved with him, and Bobby couldn't help admiring the play of the muscles in her long legs and her back. She was slender and strong, yet curved and soft where he liked curves and softness best.

Emma locked her hands behind his neck, kissing him with a mind-numbing passion as her sinuous, rapid movements drove him toward his climax. As a taut pleasure rocketed through him, he closed his hands hard on her hips, angling her upward so he could go deeper on his next thrust. He touched her where they joined, teasing her swollen flesh so she'd come before his whole damn brain melted down. She arched again, shuddering, and his release broke over him in a tingling white heat. With a low, long groan, he came so hard he thought he'd pass out.

After he pulled out of her and rolled to his back beside her Emma sighed—a happy, sated sigh. Tipping his head toward her, he saw her mouth curve in a dreamy smile, and a slow ache knotted his chest.

She caught his gaze, and her smile widened. "Wow . . . just wow."

"So much for that bet."

She made a deep sound of satisfaction. "Screw the bet."

"I already did." He grinned lazily. "Or was that an invitation?"

Emma stretched, languid and lithe, an eager light in her eyes. "Please."

At least there was still this thing he could do right. And in a heartbeat, her look of absolute contentment spun him down into familiar, painful terrain where he'd been too often before.

Hello, heartache. Here we go again . . .

Emma flopped back crosswise on Bobby's bed, pushing back damp strands of her hair as she glanced at the clock. "It's almost three in the morning—maybe we should try actually sleeping in this bed. We do have to work tomorrow."

"Technically, this is already tomorrow."

Beside her, Bobby stretched and Emma propped herself up on an elbow to watch: six feet of lean, gorgeous blond with slow hands, a wicked tongue, and a few techniques that had made her eyes roll to the back of her head.

Unable to resist, she ran a fingernail down his belly. He jerked, then grabbed her hand, laughing.

"Don't do that!"

She grinned. "You're ticklish?"

"Yeah, but take pity on me. I have barely enough strength to move right now, much less fight you off."

"I bet you could move if I gave you a good enough reason."

She rolled over to face him, and he did the same so that they were nose to nose on the bed. It made kissing him easy, and a few minutes passed pleasurably as they exchanged soft, playful lip nibbles.

"Girl-friendly in bed, and you like kissing, too," Emma said, her voice a little raspy. "If this is a dream, don't wake me up."

"I was just thinking the same thing."

Back to kissing, and then he looped an arm around her and pulled her close. Oh, God . . . and a cuddler, too.

"How come some woman hasn't snapped you up before now?" she asked, idly rubbing his chest, including the raised scar tissue of the bullet wound—and the scars of subsequent surgeries. Being blond, he didn't have chest hair, unlike her last boyfriend. All that skin-on-skin contact had seemed strange at first, but she liked the feel of him, all lean and powerful. All hers.

"Beats me."

"Commitment-shy?" She rubbed her nose along his chest, loving his musky, male scent—and a fresh desire swelled, low and deep inside her.

He didn't answer right away, and after a moment he pulled away and sat up. "Generally speaking, that's not been the issue."

Obviously, she'd said something wrong. Sitting up as well, she pulled the sheet over her. "Where are you going?"

Bobby stood, and she had trouble focusing on anything but his rear as he walked toward the door, scooping up his boxers as he went. He hadn't struck her as a boxers kind of guy; more like boxer briefs. Or nothing at all.

"I need to stand up and walk around, get the blood flowing to other parts of my body." He grinned at her over his shoulder, not looking upset after all. Maybe he'd just tired of cuddling. "And I need a drink. You want one?"

"Maybe. I'm going to freshen up, then I'll join you."

He used the bathroom first, and after the toilet flushed and the door opened again—it stuck a bit, and made a popping sound—she heard him in the kitchen, banging cupboard drawers and doors.

Emma went looking for a robe or baggy shirt, and stared in amazement when she opened the closet door. He had more clothes than *she* did, more shoes—and more ties than she'd ever seen in her entire life. Unfortunately, most of them verged on bizarre, with quite a few she'd classify as butt-ugly.

How on earth had one man accumulated so many ugly ties? It didn't seem humanly possible.

She managed to find an old flannel shirt, and buttoned it as she headed to the bathroom. The best sex was messy sex, and after she cleaned up, splashed water on her face, and smoothed back bed-tousled hair, she walked into the kitchen with a smile—only to linger in the doorway, watching Bobby, her smile fading as the night's earlier events came rushing back.

He stood at the counter in his boxers, a cigarette in his mouth, as he poured a glass of whiskey: a little Southern Comfort for a Southern boy who needed comfort of a sort she wasn't so sure she could give him. Or that he'd even let her.

"What are you doing?" she asked.

Startled, he jerked his hand, spilling whiskey on the counter. "Shit. I didn't hear you come in."

That was obvious. "Since when do you smoke?"

"Living the cliché, darlin' . . . great sex, now it's time for a smoke."

The mask was firmly back in place, as if their confrontation at the hospital had never taken place and he hadn't nearly gone off tonight on a personal vendetta that could've gotten him, or somebody else, killed.

Steeling herself, Emma walked over and plucked the cigarette from his mouth and the drink from his hand. After she dumped the whiskey in the sink and stubbed out the cigarette in the empty glass, she turned to face him.

He arched a brow. "So now I get a lecture on how bad these are for me?"

"You already know they are," she said evenly. "But if you think I'll kiss you after you've smoked, think again."

"Then I'll give it up for you." He smiled, stretching his split lip—and reminding her, with a pang of guilt, how hard she'd hit him. "I'll give up all my bad habits for you."

Letting out her breath in a small sigh, she asked, "What's wrong?"

His smile faded a fraction. "Nothing."

"I think there's a whole lot of something in that nothing."

The smile vanished. "And the fun comes to a screeching halt."

Emma moved to one side of his small kitchen, back against the counter, while he stood on the other side by the sink. Only a few feet separated them, but right now it might've been an ocean, and under the fluorescent lights, everything seemed brighter, harsher . . . vulnerable.

"Would you have done it if I hadn't stopped you?" she asked.

"Done what?"

He'd dodge and duck—if she let him. "Kill that man. Raymond."

"I don't know." Bobby shifted, folding his arms over his chest. "Maybe I considered it."

"He's not worth throwing away your life. It doesn't matter what he did, or that you're a cop and should know better—going after him would've been premeditated *murder*, Bobby."

"I know . . . I do, and I appreciate you were there to keep me from losing my head. I honestly don't think I'd have killed him." He paused. "But I'm pretty sure I'd have given him a major ass-kicking."

"And that would still be enough to end your career, not to mention a real possibility of getting prison time for assault."

He ducked his head. "I wasn't thinking about that."

Which summed up the problem of falling in love with

this man. Take away the incredible sex and the fact she liked him very much, their relationship faced major obstacles before it even got off the ground.

Suddenly cold, she hugged herself, wishing she'd pulled on something heavier than an old, wash-worn shirt. "I'm sorry that you don't have enough evidence to convict him, but you don't know what tomorrow, or next week, or even next year will bring. Somebody could talk, prove he lied. Sometimes it takes years to clear a case like this. You can't give up. Or take shortcuts."

"And sometimes we never catch the bastards. Sometimes people do get away with murder. You can't tell me that's not true."

"I'm not going to. I feel that frustration and anger sometimes, too. But we took an oath to uphold the law, and no matter how lame or old-fashioned it sounds to a lot of people who aren't us, it still has to mean something."

A tense silence filled the small room.

"So how do you keep dealing with it? Because I swear to God, Emma, I can't ever remember feeling this helpless and useless before."

The pain in his voice was heartbreaking, and she swallowed back the tears before answering. "By believing that even if one gets away, I'll catch others, and that makes a difference. By believing that if I can't always take the Raymonds of this world out of the game, that someday, someplace, one of his own kind will. Live by violence, die by violence."

"And that's enough?"

"It has to be. Even one life saved or changed makes a difference."

"I don't think Juleen's family feels that way."

"But we can't help or control what the families of victims feel. It's not our job, and that way lies madness, Bobby."

He looked at her sharply—and in that instant Emma recognized what really lay beneath his fears, and she could've kicked herself for not putting it together sooner.

"Did you think you couldn't tell anybody about what you're feeling?" She wanted so much to put her arms around him and hold him—but that was *not* what he needed. Not now. "Or that nobody would understand?"

His chest rose and fell as he took a long breath, and suddenly the tight, wary lines of his body melted away into weariness, and he slumped back against the counter.

"I don't know," he said slowly, his voice low, "what's wrong with me."

A lump rose in her throat. "Oh, Bobby, there's nothing wrong with you. You're just . . . a little lost right now, that's all."

"I keep trying to understand," he continued, as if she hadn't spoken. "I've seen a lot of violent, senseless death in the seventeen years I've been a cop. I'll see more. I'm not romanticizing her, like some Hollywood whore with a heart of gold. I know what she was, I know she's not the first woman who's died like this, and she won't be the last . . . but what I can't figure out is why she's different than any of the others before her. Why it got personal, how or even when—I know better, Emma. I *do*."

He straightened, frowning, focusing on the empty glass and cigarette. "And I've had to deal with people a lot worse than Raymond. I can't say why I want so badly to make him hurt."

Bobby fell silent, and she waited, giving him time to think and talk it out.

"But when I look at him, all I see is every single bastard who's walked or plea-bargained his way out of punishment, every case I've ever lost or couldn't solve, every piece of red tape that tripped me up, every brutal sonofabitch I can't touch because I wear a badge." He rubbed at his brows. "I don't know why I can't stop feeling like this."

Helpless.

He didn't have say the word, she could hear the emotion in his voice, see its toll in the lines of strain on his face, the tired language of his body.

"Drinking won't help," she said at length. "And everybody has a breaking point. You just need help in getting over it. You should see a counselor or a psychiatrist. Maybe medication—"

"Emma, I'm having trouble dealing, that's all, and it's happened before. I let myself get too close, feel too much, and I lose my objectivity. I don't need drugs; I need time to get my head straight."

The virulence of his response didn't surprise her. Most cops were strong, loyal, and dedicated—but also needed to be in control. Admitting to a mental illness, even a temporary one, made them appear weak, and everybody knew cops weren't weak. All the outreach programs in all the departments across the country hadn't made that much difference in how many cops reacted to the suggestion that they might be in trouble.

And she ought to know, since she'd been one of them. "Bobby, how long have you been feeling down?"

He shrugged with obvious discomfort. "I don't know. A few months. It's not like I've been keeping track. Once

I deal with the Juleen and Raymond thing, I'll be back to normal."

"You're sure about that?"

Bobby turned away, ostensibly to rinse the whiskey glass, but it also kept her from seeing his face—and he didn't answer. Why go through all the bother of denial or explanations when he could just ignore her?

Emma sighed. "Bobby, did it ever occur to you that you might have a short-term traumatic stress disorder? You don't have to struggle through it like this. There's help available that'll—"

"Great. You're telling me I'm mental? The guys'll love hearing this . . . as if everybody doesn't already have enough reasons to give me shit."

"You're the one who told me it doesn't matter what other people think."

"I wear a gun every day. Nobody's gonna be too wild about the idea of a crazy guy walking around with a gun. And I didn't become a cop to sit at a desk doing paperwork." He turned from the sink, his expression bleak. "If I lose this job, I don't—"

Shaking his head, he cut himself off without finishing the sentence, and Emma ached for him, wishing she could make it all better with a hug or a kiss. But it didn't work that way.

"Nobody has to know you're seeing a counselor, and nothing else matters except that you take care of yourself before your burnout heads into a full-blown depression."

"I'll cut out the drinking and quit smoking again, okay? Will that be good enough for you?"

"It'll help, but it's not enough."

"Emma, for Christ's sake—"

"I know what it's like. A year ago, my whole world fell apart. My boyfriend left me because he couldn't cope with what was happening in my life, and people I knew treated me like an enemy, even accused me of things I'd never do in a million years. I thought I was dealing with it, but all I did was start distrusting everybody, and I withdrew. I didn't sleep well, I lost weight. I wouldn't admit anything was wrong, and then one day, I started crying and couldn't stop. I couldn't even get out of bed." She walked closer to him, holding his gaze. "I scared myself, and it was enough to get me to a doctor."

He shook his head as if he couldn't believe it. "You're too tough, it's—"

"This isn't about being tough, Bobby. People aren't meant to be that hard. This is about being human and imperfect and needing help. That's all I'm trying to do here, and it's because I care about you."

The closed look on his face warned her off, but she still asked, "Answer me this: How many people have you gone out of your way to help?"

"I don't keep score."

"And you don't have to, but what's the deal with you giving everything you've got, over and over again, but feeling you can't ask for anything back? We all need help at some point. There's nothing wrong or weak in asking for it."

"It's not that bad, Emma," he said with a sigh, looking away from her.

"When you put a bullet through your head, lose your job, or finally break a law your captain can't overlook, will *that* be bad enough?"

"You're overreacting. I lost my temper for a few minutes, that's it!"

Emma returned his angry, defensive glare—and beneath it, she sensed fear. She'd pushed enough for now. She couldn't force him to make any changes overnight, and he'd have to wade through denial and anger first. Yet she'd made a clear hit. He was angry and disturbed, and although he'd dismissed her warning, he'd think about it later when he calmed down.

And if he was even half the man she knew he was, he'd come to terms with the truth with the help and support of people who cared for him and loved him.

Like her—and suddenly, all the reasons she'd concocted to tell herself she wasn't falling in love with him, and shouldn't fall in love, simply didn't matter.

"It's late, and it's been a long day," she said quietly. "Let's go to bed and catch a little sleep."

Twenty-one

Because she'd had to drive back to her apartment to change clothes—wearing the same outfit to work two days in a row was just not done—Emma arrived late. She hurried to her desk, tucking her hair back nervously, and expected to find Bobby sitting at his desk, with its messy piles of papers, files, and other assorted junk, including an always-full jar of Mike & Ike candies.

Except his desk was empty, with no sign that he'd been there at all. Relief swept over her, and she was grateful she didn't have to immediately deal with the inevitable awkwardness that came from sleeping with somebody you worked with—and not just any somebody, but the departmental black sheep.

At times like this, she wondered if some cosmic joker hadn't taped a piece of paper on her back with the words "please complicate my life" written on it. But as tempted as she might be to duck any blame, she'd managed a brilliant plunge into deep shit all by herself—and barely two weeks into her new job and new life.

Now, *that* took talent.

With a sigh, she put her coffee cup down on her desk, and pulled out her chair just as Captain Strong said behind her, "Emma. Do you have a minute? I'd like to see you in my office."

She turned, noticing right off that Strong's tie was looped around his neck, still unknotted, and he hadn't even fastened the top buttons of his shirt. He didn't look happy.

What had gone wrong now?

"Sure," Emma said casually. "Not a problem."

After grabbing her coffee, she followed Strong, and shut his office door when he'd ordered her to do so. A sinking feeling settled in the pit of her stomach, and she slowly sat in the chair across from his desk. "Is there a problem?"

"I'm hoping that's something you can clarify for me."

Knowing she couldn't possibly have screwed up bad enough to earn a reprimand, that left only one option. She swallowed, her mouth suddenly dry. "Is everything okay with Bobby?"

Strong rested his elbows on his desk, fingers laced, his expression unreadable. "That's what I was going to ask you."

"Oh." Emma covered her discomfort by sipping her coffee. "Well, if you want to know if Bobby's okay, maybe you should talk to him."

"I did. A few minutes before you came in." A small frown pulled his brows together. "Before I say any more, I want you to understand that I've been a cop for many years. Almost as long as you've been alive."

At that, Emma put her cup aside, then clasped her hands in her lap, fingers tightly laced. "That's a long time."

"Yes . . . yes, it is. I've seen a lot of changes in how departments handle business, and I've seen a lot of cops come and go. Over the years, it gets easier to read people, to see when trouble's coming."

Finally understanding where Strong was going with this, Emma nodded.

"I have to be honest with you. I didn't put you with Halloran because you were new and I wanted him to show you the ropes."

Well, well—not an admission she'd expected to ever hear. "I know."

He studied her for several seconds. "And it wasn't because I wanted to make you miserable, either, even if that's what you thought."

Emma grimaced; had her suspicions been so transparent? "I don't see what any of this has to do with Bobby."

"Bobby has a problem."

At his blunt statement, her wariness ratcheted up a notch to alarm. "I don't know what you mean."

His look—part pity, part impatience—said he didn't believe her. "When I transferred here a year ago, Bobby already had a reputation for occasionally exhibiting poor judgment. Lucky for him, those situations were resolved without serious complications. He also had a solid case record, and he was a good enough cop that his previous supervisors didn't care. Or maybe they did, but didn't know what to do. Telling an officer he's heading for a career-ending case of burnout is no picnic. I've talked to Bobby, but he insists nothing's wrong. And I'm sure he believes it. When a cop's been on a downward slide for this long, there comes a point where he can't tell anymore what's normal or not."

Strong fell silent, perhaps waiting for Emma to say something—agree, disagree, or have a quiet freakout. Not knowing Strong's intentions toward Bobby, however, she wouldn't answer just yet.

"Even after years of working this job, I still haven't figured out why some cops handle the stress better than others, or what it takes to make a good cop suddenly snap."

"I could probably give you a few ideas," she said quietly.

"Sure, with your situation, it would be enough to make anybody lose faith for a while. But with Bobby, I can't point to a specific event, or even make a guess at what's going to be the proverbial straw that breaks him."

Strong rubbed his hand over his chin, frowning. "Most people brush off his more questionable behavior as part of his personality. They've known him too long to see his recklessness for what it is: a shout for help. If nobody notices, or he can't put the brakes on himself, he'll eventually do something I can't ignore, which is to break the law. By then it could be too late."

"Is that why you had me work with him?" Emma asked coldly. "To be the unofficial department watchdog and spy? After all, I'd already ratted out a few fellow cops, what was one more?"

Strong sat forward again, not backing down from her hostility. "I was hoping you'd be a good influence on him, maybe help him self-correct his behavior. He's not unaware of his problems, but he's in denial as to how serious they could be if he doesn't get them under control."

"You should have told me."

"I would've been out of line. An officer's personal problems are not meant to be common knowledge."

"But you're telling me now."

"It was never my intention to tell you at all. I wanted to keep an eye on developments, hoping my sideways attempt at intervention would work where straightforward talking hadn't. If not, then I'd have to be more forceful about getting him help. But I was delaying the inevitable, and that was a mistake." Strong slowly let out his breath. "I changed my mind about telling you because I've been watching you and Bobby together, in the office and at the briefings."

Emma tensed, knowing what was coming next.

"I see a connection beyond a partnership. He's very protective of you, as you are with him." Strong steepled his fingers and tapped them against his lower lip. "And I didn't miss how you acted toward each other at the cookout."

Her face went hot. She'd thought she'd been so careful, but apparently she'd been as transparent as a jellyfish, with every little inner secret on display for all to see.

"I never expected that," he added. "Neither of you seemed the other's type, and even if Bobby did turn on the charm, I didn't think you'd take him seriously."

"Because it's so hard to believe he'd ever look at me and see a woman?"

Strong frowned. "That wasn't meant as an insult. You're very attractive, Emma, but you're also pragmatic."

"Even pragmatics mess up."

Such as wishing to be loved for who they were, wanting people to see their good qualities, even if they were always the quiet ones in the corner who weren't flashy or vibrant.

"Are you and Bobby engaged in an intimate relationship?"

Seeing no point in denying it, Emma nodded—but that was all. No explanations, no excuses.

Strong didn't look happy. "I never intended for it to get this far."

Stung, she straightened. "I'm an adult, sir. I make my own decisions and I accept the consequences. But I'm angry that you took this kind of risk with not only my safety, but Bobby's as well."

He nodded, making a placating motion with his hands. "I know; all I can say in my defense is that I wanted to make it easier on him—and, yes, easier on myself. But easier is almost never better."

"If it's worth working for, it's worth having and keeping. Or so my mother always told me."

"You have a wise mother." Strong gave her a small smile. "I don't believe Bobby would ever put you in danger, but I'm not convinced he'd be as careful with his own safety."

At least she and Strong were on the same page in that respect. "So what do you want me to do?"

"There's nothing you can do. I took him off the Moss and Mitsumi cases, and I wanted you to know why. You'll have to finish your case alone." He paused. "Whatever you do in your private time is your business, but because I'm the one who put the two of you together in the first place, I feel some responsibility toward you."

"How about I absolve you of that responsibility?"

"Emma, your situation and Bobby's are different, and I don't want you hanging on to false hopes. To be honest, and at the rate he's going, I'm very concerned about his continued ability to function as a law enforcement officer."

Emma started shaking her head, but Strong ignored her as he continued, "Don't get the wrong idea—I like Bobby. He's a great guy who's dedicated and has a genuine calling to help people, but I've seen too many cops with his same problems. The sad fact of our job is that we are often put in a position where we're helpless to do anything. Once a cop has difficulty accepting that, once he loses faith in himself and gives in to those feelings of vulnerability, it's too late. It's a downward cycle that can't be stopped."

Still shaking her head, she said, "I'm sorry, sir, but I don't agree. I can't believe that anybody is beyond help. There's always a chance we can change for the better if we want it badly enough. Bobby just has to want it badly enough—and I think he does. Give him a little more time. Please."

Strong rested his elbows on his desk, his expression troubled. "You have a strong streak of idealism in you, Emma, and I admire that. I just hope you won't come to regret it."

Not exactly a yes, but not a no, either. "Are we done?"

At his curt nod, she stood, retrieved her cup, and headed for the door. She'd nearly reached it when Strong added, "I'd like to help him, but he's got to want help in the first place. Without that, there's little I can do."

Emma nodded, then closed his door and made her way back to her desk, hardly noticing the lively din as detectives prepared for the day's work, joking and laughing and talking.

Not even eight-thirty in the morning, and already everything had gone to hell—and she had to talk to Bobby.

Stopping by Alycia's desk, she asked. "Have you seen Bobby?"

"Yeah. He bummed a smoke off me." Alycia looked puzzled. "What's up with that? I thought he gave up smoking. And what the hell happened to his mouth? Did he get into another fight?"

"Something like that." Emma hoped nothing in her face or voice revealed even a hint of her anxiety—or the sudden stab of guilt. "Did he go outside?"

"Probably. Is there something wrong? Because that boy was one unhappy camper."

"When I find him, I'll ask—and if Strong comes looking for me, tell him I'm in the john."

Once outside, she spotted Bobby leaning back against the building, face turned up to the dreary sky, and smoking. He saw her coming, and while he didn't encourage her to join him, he didn't tell her to get lost, either.

Taking that as a good sign, she leaned beside him and looked up at the sky as well. Not much to see, except gray, and more gray. She wished it would just rain and get it over and done with.

Finally, she switched her attention back to him. He had on black pants, a plain white oxford shirt, and a tie that had, in a row from top to bottom, a lion, a tiger, and a bear.

Oh, my, her mind filled in automatically—and not necessarily on account of the tie.

The man was almost painfully handsome, even with his damp, finger-combed hair and beard stubble. On him, the lines and shadows of too little sleep and too much stress looked good, giving his fallen-angel face a harder, leaner edge.

"Hey," she said. "It looks like another lovely winter morning in New Orleans."

Bobby smiled, his eyes lighting up in a way that nearly made her heart break on the spot. She smiled back, trying to read his mood, what he might be thinking about her after last night—and decided it was way too much to deal with this early in the morning and on only half a cup of coffee.

When it looked as if he had no intention of talking, she asked lightly, "Did I tell you I wouldn't kiss you if you smoked those things?"

He blew out a stream of smoke, then pointedly looked around at all the other cops and the usual hustle and bustle to be found outside a police station. "You weren't going to kiss me anyway."

"True," she admitted. "But the point still stands."

"Cut me some slack here, Emma. If I try giving up all my bad habits at once, I'll just screw it up."

"I can live with that. As long as you give them up eventually." She watched a group of uniforms walk past, laughing among themselves. "I hear Strong pulled you into his office this morning. How'd it go?"

He shrugged. "The way it always does. Like you, he thinks I have some 'issues' to work out. He took me off the Mitsumi case. And the Moss case."

"I know. He talked to me, too."

In an instant, Bobby's expression hardened, which confused her—until she realized he thought she'd blabbed to Strong about what had happened at the hospital, and afterward.

"I didn't tell him anything," she said, keeping her voice calm. "About last night, or about us. Except that I admitted there sort of is an 'us.' "

"Did he read you the riot act?" He sounded bitter. "And make you feel like the kid from the wrong side of the tracks heading for a smackdown because he was stupid enough to fall in love with the big boss's perfect, untouchable little girl?"

Fall in love with . . .

For a moment, she couldn't process anything beyond that. Taken aback, she glanced at him—and caught the intensity of his expression, despite his self-mocking smile.

"Yeah, you heard me," he said. "It's what I do, as everybody will tell you. I'm not ashamed to admit it. I never have any trouble falling in love."

Of all the things she'd imagined they'd discuss on the "morning after," this wasn't one of them.

"The trouble," he continued, once again communing with the sky, "is that women never stay in love with me. But like a fool, I keep falling anyway. You'd think I'd learn."

Oh, boy. "I'm not sure we should—"

"Look, it's okay. You don't have to declare your eternal love for me or anything like that. I don't expect it. I'm just telling you how it is with me."

Still a little panicky, she said, "I honestly don't know what to say."

"You could tell me you at least like me. That would help."

At that, she narrowed her eyes. "Don't be an ass, Bobby. I wouldn't have slept with you if I didn't care about you."

"I figured as much, but it wasn't all that long ago you

told me you didn't trust me." He took a final drag on his cigarette and dropped it. "Maybe I just need to hear you say it."

"I like you, Bobby. A lot."

Considerably way more than a lot, but she couldn't bring herself to say as much. Not yet.

"Then answer me something."

His pensive tone caught her attention, and she looked up from the smoldering butt. "I'll try."

"Those cops you testified against . . . what they did, was it any worse than anything I've done?"

"You didn't go after Raymond and shoot him down like a dog. You didn't falsify evidence, take a cut of any of his business, or—"

"Stop dodging, darlin'."

"I'm not—" She broke off with a sigh. "Most of them were worse, but not all. A few weren't charged with any felonies, only reprimanded, and a couple resigned from the force before the trials started."

"So why'd you turn them in, but not me?"

She didn't like where this was going. "It's not the same situation. For starts, I never made any accusations. All I did was tell the truth, as I knew it, when asked."

He was silent for a moment, and unless he was blind, he had to know this was a subject she didn't want to discuss.

And apparently he didn't care. "I'm not trying to give you a hard time, Emma. I'm just asking if you think there's any difference between them and me, and if there isn't, why you're with me at all."

She looked down. "I don't regret what I did."

"I'm not looking for excuses, either." He sounded tired. "I only want you to tell me whether or not I'm a bad cop, because I swear to God I don't know anymore."

"Don't do this to yourself, Bobby." A rush of sadness swept over her, and Emma turned. "Of course you're not a bad cop. I've seen bad cops . . . They hurt people, sometimes even innocent people, and you're *nothing* like that."

His shoulders rose, then fell, as he took a deep breath. "So why do you look like you're gonna cry?"

"I'm not going to cry, it's just that this kind of talk brings back bad memories. Really bad memories." At a sudden stinging of tears, she looked down at her feet. "Nobody really understands what it meant for me to testify against those men. They were guys who had moms and dads, wives and children . . . little children. Doing the right thing is hard when it also hurts a lot of innocent people, and *I* hurt innocent people. Those families and friends hated me for the things I said in that courtroom, but I never blamed any of them. If I'd been them, I'd have hated me, too."

Several seconds passed before he said, "I didn't know."

"And now maybe you can understand why I'm so worried about you." Not to mention fearful that a bad cop might be involved in the Mitsumi case, but that was another problem to deal with later.

Bobby shifted toward her, shaking his head. "It shouldn't be so hard to do the right thing."

"No, it shouldn't." Emma moved a little closer, brushing her fingers against his. "You're a good man, and what you did before we met is past history. The cops I testified against knowingly broke laws for personal gain, where you're making errors in judgment out of frustration. I understand why, but you're cutting it close, Bobby. If Raymond had filed an assault charge after you tossed him into that wall, and some gung-ho reporter got wind of it, you'd be kissing your career good-bye, at the very least. I don't want to see you making a mistake you can't come back from, that's all."

He returned to contemplating the gray clouds. "Strong's been on my case for a while, about the same things we talked about. Some of my friends have said a few things to me, too, and it has me thinking I might have more of a problem than I want to admit."

As much as she wanted to whoop and hug him, and tell him he'd just won half the battle right there with that admission, she kept quiet.

He sighed. "It wouldn't hurt to talk to somebody about what's going on inside my head. Like you said, nobody has to know."

"Not unless you want them to."

"I just . . . this job means everything to me. And the funny thing is, I was sure I'd never feel that way again. I thought that part of me was good and buried, and now that I know it's not, I'm scared I'll lose it all over again." He rubbed at his brows. "Maybe I don't belong on the job . . . I don't blame you for not trusting me. Hell, I don't even trust myself anymore."

"You're going to be fine, Bobby," she said quietly, because she believed it—and he needed the reassurance. "Asking for help is the right thing to do. You have Strong's support, and you have mine. I'm there for you, twenty-four/seven."

His jaw tensed, then he nodded. "I don't deserve you."

"Bullshit," she retorted irritably.

That got a smile out of him. "Okay. Then you don't deserve me."

This was more like it; the smiles, bravado, and the teasing. It ached to see him hurting so much, especially since she couldn't do much more than lend him a shoulder or a sympathetic ear.

Bobby's hand brushed hers; a light touch, but enough to send a languorous pang of desire shooting through her. Without caring who might see it, Emma closed her fingers around his, squeezing tightly. He squeezed her hand back, and when she made no move to pull away, he didn't let her go.

He rested his head back against the building, a smile playing at the corner of his mouth. "You're touching me. In public."

"It looks that way, doesn't it?"

He rolled his head toward her. "I take it this means I'll see you tonight."

"Hmmm, could be I'll just happen to find myself in your neighborhood."

"And if you find yourself in my neighborhood often enough, remember I have half an empty house, and you—"

He broke off, his body suddenly tensing. Frowning, Emma glanced around for a sign of some impending catastrophe. "What's wrong?"

"Sonofabitch." Eyes hot with anger, he released her hand. "I know where Chloe is."

Emma blinked, confused. "You do?"

"If you were in a shitload of trouble, what would be the safest place to hide and where the guys watching you would never think to look?"

As his meaning sank in, she stared at him, dumbfounded. "She wouldn't."

"Like hell. She's camped out in the empty half of my place, I bet my gun on it. That first night she came by, she told me she'd been 'in the neighborhood.'"

"This *is* Chloe we're talking about," Emma agreed. "And that woman's got brass. So what'll we do?"

"We?" He pushed away from the wall. "I'm off this case, remember?"

"What Strong doesn't know won't hurt him. Let's go check this out."

"Emma Frey . . . are you disobeying your captain's direct order?"

"Not really." She grinned at him, despite her irritation with Chloe. "You're coming with me to protect our victim, because I swear, if she's there, I'm gonna kill her. Plus, it *is* your house."

"That's right. And you don't have a warrant to search my premises." He glanced at his watch. "We gotta hustle, though. I have to be at city hall in an hour and a half."

Emma needed no further urging, and since her car was parked closest, she drove. This time, she didn't mind that she had to park a block away—no reason to alert Chloe to their presence, if she happened to be around.

As they quietly approached the empty half of Bobby's cottage, Emma asked, "What's the plan?"

"You go around to the back door and wait there while I go in through the front. If she's inside and hears me coming, she'll sneak out the back."

Emma pulled out her handcuffs, smiling. "Oh, I'm really hoping so."

She veered off toward the back, careful to make no sound, although she could hear a dog barking and children playing a few houses down. The back door opened to a small porch, and she moved to the side, out of sight. If Chloe hightailed it out the back, Emma wanted the element of surprise on her side—if for no other reason than to see a look of astonishment on the woman's face.

Several minutes passed as she waited, hearing no shouts, no running footsteps. Finally, the door opened and Bobby poked his head out—but the satisfied grin on his face chased away her disappointment.

"She's been here?"

"Oh, yeah. Come on in and see for yourself."

The empty half had a definite new-house smell: paint, glue, and freshly cut wood. She walked first through the small bedroom, then followed Bobby into the bathroom. He pulled back the shower curtain around the old-fashioned clawfoot tub to reveal blankets, a rolled-up foam mattress, a pillow, a suitcase, and a pile of clothes that were unmistakably Chloe's.

Then he opened the sink cabinet door, and Emma glimpsed a makeup bag, a hot plate and small pan, canned food, bags of rice cakes, a jar of peanut butter, and bottled water and iced tea.

"Looks like she made herself right at home. Is the electricity and water hooked up?"

Bobby nodded. "It doesn't cost me that much extra, and I only finished work in here a month ago."

"So she's living in your bathroom."

"It's the most hidden part of the house, and halfway between two exits. I also know she can fit through the bathroom window just fine."

Emma eyed the window, which was hung with inexpensive vinyl blinds. "She's a resourceful little thing, I'll give her that. Any sign of the *netsuke*?"

"Nope."

"Well, we've got her this time. Breaking and entering, trespassing . . . this gives us enough leverage to get her talking. Where do you think she is now?"

Bobby shrugged. "She also could return at any moment, though. How do you want to handle this?"

"I was going to ask you the same thing, since it's your property." She paused. "And she is your friend."

He smiled at her grudging admission, then checked his watch. "I can't sit around all day waiting for her to show up. Neither can you. We'll try to catch her tonight."

"Sounds good to me."

"When I get off work tonight, I'll come straight home. As soon as you're done for the day, come over here. If she's around then, I'll grab her. If not, we can have dinner and hang out until it's dark, then camp out here and wait for her to show up."

"So what will we do between dinner and Chloe-hunting?"

Amusement lit his eyes. "I'm sure we can think of something. You might want to swing by your place and pick up a change of clothes."

Silly her; at his husky-voiced suggestion, her heart began beating a little faster. "Dinner, sex, and handcuffing Chloe. Sounds like fun."

Bobby laughed, then leaned forward and kissed her. "A cop's guide to dating the girl of your dreams: if 'fun' includes handcuffs, she's a keeper."

Twenty-two

Bobby ended his day earlier than usual, stoked with anticipation and excitement. Considering his dark mood these past few months, and how he would've made the worst mistake of his life if Emma hadn't intercepted him at Charity, being able to feel that fire in his belly again was damn near miraculous.

And it made their argument and lovemaking, every painful word she'd spoken, easier to face. It was almost as if a huge spotlight had suddenly switched on, shining a light on what he hadn't wanted to see, and forcing him to take a long, hard look at himself. His choices were clear: the drinking and smoking had to stop, and no more punishing himself for not winning every fight. No matter what it took, he'd find a better way to channel the anger and frustration that was such a part of this job—and rediscover how to appreciate even the smallest success.

There'd been a time when he'd known how to find that balance, but somewhere along the line, he'd forgotten. All he had to do was find it inside him again—and he didn't want to contemplate how long he'd have floundered before hitting rock bottom if Emma had not come along and shone her light on this simple truth.

Lucky him, to have a woman like Emma in his life—and he meant to keep her. He couldn't wait to see her again, to watch her dark eyes grow warm, her slow smile, and the way her nose wrinkled when she laughed. He couldn't wait to get her back in his bed, either, and he was hot and hard just imagining what she could do to him with her mouth and hands, her sweet, welcoming body.

But first things first. Bobby checked to see if Chloe was in his cottage. She wasn't around, but she'd moved a few things in the tub and a pair of thong underwear were draped over the faucet drying, so she'd been by to do a little laundry.

He headed back to his place, and to help pass the time he picked up the clutter, started a load of laundry, changed into jeans and a sweatshirt, washed his dishes, and put a bottle of wine in the fridge—and all the while listened for suspicious sounds coming from next door as well as Emma's footsteps coming up his walk.

Emma arrived after six, with a bucket of fried chicken, and he hadn't realized he'd been hungry until he got a whiff of it.

His stomach growled, loudly, and Emma laughed as she leaned in for a kiss. "Sounds like your stomach's happy to see me."

"Every part of me is glad to see you." He pulled her close for a longer kiss, knowing she couldn't miss just how glad.

God, she tasted good. Dark and hot and eager, and a powerful need took hold, tempting him to haul her off to the bedroom and forget all about work. Reluctantly, he pulled away. "Kiss me like that again, and we're never going to catch Chloe."

Flushed and bright-eyed, her slow, shy smile only made him want to kiss her all over again. "Sorry."

"Never apologize for that." He ran his hand through his hair. "I checked next door earlier. No luck, but Chloe was here at some point after we left, because the clothes in the tub were moved around. She'll be back."

"How accommodating of her." Emma grabbed his shirt and pulled him close for a hug. "That means I'll have you all to myself for the next four or five hours. How hungry are you?"

Bobby smiled into her hair, liking the soft warmth of her body against his, her face nestled in the crook of his neck—he even liked the feel of her nose, cold from outside, nuzzling him. "For you, or for fried chicken?"

"Your choice."

"The food can wait. Getting naked with you can't."

Not that she needed any persuading. Halfway through the kitchen, she had his pants unzipped and his shirt partially unbuttoned. Impatient, she yanked the placket wider and the last two buttons popped free.

"Oops," she said, as the buttons bounced and rolled along the floor.

"I've got more shirts," Bobby muttered, using his foot to kick his bedroom door open.

Jesus. At this rate, they'd never make it to the bed. Then again, any stable surface would do for what they needed.

Bobby stripped off her shirt and bra and bent to taste her breasts, rubbing his tongue across their stiff tips. With a shaky sigh, she arched her back and pressed closer, threading her fingers through his hair as he worked her pants down her hips.

It was taking too long. Changing tactics, he knelt, kissing his way down her belly, and taking her pants and underwear with him. Her legs trembled where they pressed against his shoulders and the sides of his face, but she wasn't cold; not the way she was throwing off heat and a heady, female scent that burned to ashes all his self-control.

She was ready; her first climax would be fast and hard, and then he'd get down to serious business.

"Sit on the edge of the bed," he said, throwing aside her clothes.

"Why do I always get naked first?" But she sat as ordered—looking like a pagan queen: bare, strong, and graceful.

"I can fix that." Grinning, Bobby tossed his sweatshirt at her, and she batted it away, laughing. His pants followed, then his socks, until he wasn't wearing a stitch. "Better?"

"I think we're getting a lot closer," she said, breathless.

Bobby grabbed his pillows, and stacked them behind her. Her eyes dark with curiosity and arousal, she asked, "Why pillows?"

"In case you want to watch." As her eyes widened, he added, "Knowing you're watching me makes me hot . . . Now move a little closer to the edge." Taking her hips, he scooted her bottom to the edge of the mattress. "There you go. Now lean back on the pillows and put your feet on the bed, apart a bit. Just like that."

He half expected her to get shy and protest, but instead she eased back and raised her long, beautiful legs, positioning them as he'd instructed.

"Perfect," he whispered, and swallowed, mouth dry. God, she was beyond perfect, all of her. "Open your legs for me, darlin'."

"What are you—"

"Just do it."

She opened herself to him, and the sight and scent of her filled his senses. Leaning between her open legs, he murmured, "Grab the bed, Em, and hold on."

Hands on her inner thighs, Bobby spread her swollen lips with his thumbs and kissed her moist heat, then licked his tongue along her.

She jerked, gasping, and her fingers dug into the bedspread, grasping and releasing in time to his every stroke and bite, every kiss. She came right away, as he knew she would, but he didn't stop, driven on by her mewls and low moans. Her legs trembled, and she tasted slick and dark, musky and sweet. Listening to her, feeling and tasting and scenting her, made him hard and ready. Another orgasm rocked her, and she arched, climaxing with a series of shudders and a high gasp, hands fisted on the bed.

"Oh, my," she whispered, head lolling back against the bed, breasts heaving. "That was—"

He grinned at her. "A thank-you."

Emma raised her head just enough to look at him. "For what?"

As if she had to ask. "You know."

"Oh." She let out a long, shaky sigh. "Well, if I can be of help in the future, you be damn sure to ask."

Bobby stood, then positioned himself over her. He kissed her, long and deep, and feeling a kick low in his belly as her breasts pressed against his bare chest. "What do you want me to do now? Any way, anywhere, you're calling the shots tonight, darlin'."

She sat, still breathing hard, then slid a hand down his belly and touched him. He briefly closed his eyes as she circled his erection with her hand, stroking him slowly, the muted amber light of the bedside lamp highlighting her small, satisfied smile.

"I'm thinking," she murmured, hand still working him, "that you probably have a sexual-positions repertoire you could take on the road as a show, and once the newness of me and you wears off and I don't want to jump you right that very second every time I see you, I'll be happy to check out all the special features of the Bobby Halloran Show."

He laughed, though a little embarrassed, as she added softly, "But right now, I want you to make love to me. I want you to hold me, and I want to kiss you and watch your face . . . I just want to be with you."

Emma's words touched him, deep inside. Had any of his past lovers needed "just" him, rather than the steady protector or the lure of the badge and cop mystique?

"I'd like that, too," he said.

She lay down on her back, holding out her arms, and Bobby needed no further urging. He sank into her in one hard thrust, and as her legs wrapped around his hips and her hands held on to his shoulders, he made love to her the way she wanted, taking as much time as his control allowed, kissing her, showing her with his body how much he needed her. When his orgasm caught and began to build, a slow, sweet friction that slid into a frantic heat, he stopped thinking and focused on nothing but feeling her around him. Thrusting harder and faster, he came on one long shudder.

Completely spent, he rolled over onto his back beside

her, searched for her hand, then squeezed it lightly. "Jesus, I hope Chloe doesn't run for it," he said in a low, rough voice. "My legs won't be up to any running for at least a couple hours."

She sighed, then snuggled up against him. "You know what?"

"Hmm?" Damn; he didn't even have enough energy to talk.

"One of these days, we have to go on a date. A real date. Dinner out and a movie. You know, like normal people."

He smiled up at the ceiling as he stroked the smooth skin of her hip. "We can be normal people—after we bust Chloe's ass."

Stakeouts had never been Emma's favorite part of the job, and by ten P.M., she'd already been sitting on the toilet lid for an hour, waiting with mounting impatience for Madame Barfly to enter stage right and get this damn show on the road. She was beyond bored, and stiff and achy—although in a good, thoroughly loved achy kind of way, compliments of Bobby's enthusiasm and equally impressive stamina.

Bobby was in the kitchen, sitting on the floor beside the old refrigerator, and she smiled to herself, wondering if he was thinking about her, too, and the thoroughly enjoyable few hours they'd just shared.

A few hours they might've stretched out, especially since it wasn't likely Chloe would show up this early, but better safe than sorry. With any luck, their party girl would come flitting home right into their waiting, if not exactly loving, arms. Then they'd haul her off to central lockup for safekeeping for a few hours and figure out their next move.

The minutes crawled by, and as she stretched her arms above her head, yawning, she heard the sound of a key in the front door. Emma pulled her gun and edged forward, waiting for Bobby to make his move.

Careful, quiet footsteps padded through the kitchen, nearing the bathroom, and then Bobby's thick drawl boomed, "Hey, honey. I'm home."

A high yelp pierced the silence, followed by the sounds of a struggle. Emma moved quickly to the kitchen, shutting the bathroom door behind her to block Chloe's escape, and snapped on the kitchen lights.

The bright light briefly blinded both Bobby and Chloe. Emma, shielding her eyes, took in the scene: Chloe sprawled on the floor, trying to crawl away but held back by the fistful of faux mink in Bobby's hand.

"Dammit, don't move!" Bobby ordered as she tried to squirm out of the coat. "Or I swear to God I'm going to sit on you."

Emma aimed her gun. "And I'll do more than that."

Chloe froze, staring up at the unwavering barrel, then her eyes narrowed. "You wouldn't dare."

"I've spent almost two hours in a dark bathroom waiting for you, and now I'm a little cranky. Would you like to find out how cranky?"

The woman hesitated, as if tempted to push the limits of Emma's patience, then thought better of it. A look of irritation crossed her face. "Well, shit, it looks like you got me good. Now what?"

Bobby slowly relaxed his hold, ready to lunge if she made a run for it, but Chloe only sat up, rearranging her coat and skirt. He stood, then reached down a hand and helped her to her feet.

Without lowering her gun, Emma asked, "Do you have a weapon anywhere on you?"

"What do you think?" At Bobby's dark glare, Chloe sighed. "Right front coat pocket. Loaded. Pepper spray in the purse. Knife inside the left boot."

Emma arched a brow, impressed in spite of herself. "That's quite the arsenal. Do you want me to search her?"

"Bobby can do it," Chloe said. "It's not as if he hasn't been up close and personal with every square inch of my body."

A dull red colored his face. "Knock it off."

Emma imagined Bobby doing to Chloe what he'd done to her just a few hours ago—and "cranky" didn't even begin to cover her feelings right now.

"Oh, this is so good." Chloe grinned widely, looking from Emma to Bobby. "Sorry, Xena. If I'd known he was doing you, I wouldn't have said that."

"I'd almost believe you, if it weren't for the smile," Emma retorted as she holstered her gun. "Hands up, and don't you so much as twitch."

"Hey, I'm not that stupid." Chloe raised her hands lazily, gaze fixed on Emma. "Not when you're just itching to slam my face into the wall."

Emma ignored her—and was not proud of the fact that she *did* want to give Chloe a shove into the wall. She pulled a Glock from the coat's pocket and handed it to Bobby.

"Yours?" he asked irritably, as he removed all the rounds and pocketed it.

"You bet. And legally registered in my name, too."

"Which won't help you on a carrying-concealed charge," Emma pointed out as she handed Chloe's purse over to Bobby.

While he looked for the pepper spray, she searched Chloe. The woman wore a denim bustier over a white lace shirt, a short denim skirt, and fishnet stockings with knee-high black boots with platform heels and lots of buckles. She smelled of cigarette smoke and exotic, expensive perfume, and Emma got a good whiff of both.

From the boot, she pulled a small knife, but didn't find anything in the other boot, garter belt, pockets, or stashed down the bustier—and through the entire search, Emma fought off images of Chloe's small, fit body naked in bed with Bobby.

As Emma stood, she caught Chloe's dark, knowing gaze, and judging by that smug smile, the woman found the awkward situation amusing.

"Take off the coat," Emma ordered.

"Why should I?" Chloe asked, sounding bored.

"Breaking and entering. Trespassing. Withholding evidence. Carrying concealed weapons. Obstruction of justice. How's that for starters?" Emma asked sweetly.

"When you put it that way, how could I say no?" Chloe's voice dripped with sarcasm, but she dropped the coat.

Hauling out her cuffs, Emma snapped one on Chloe's wrist—and the other on her own. "Tender loving care, courtesy of the NOPD."

"I'm under arrest?" Chloe asked, staring at her wrist in disgust.

"I'd say that depends on Bobby's good graces, since

it's his house you broke into," Emma said flatly. "Besides, you have a bad habit of wiggling out of tight spots, and I'm tired as hell of chasing you through every miserable bar in town. Where are the *netsuke*? Your brother said he gave them to you."

Chloe glanced at Bobby, who stood with his arms folded across his chest, looking determined and pissed off, and then she shrugged. "They're in a red satin bag in a hidden pocket on the right-side seam of the coat. But they won't do you much good. I've been trying to figure out what they mean for a week, and I'm still coming up blank."

"Bobby?"

"Yeah, I'll get 'em." He picked the coat up off the floor. "For chrissake, why didn't you just come to me if you were in trouble? I offered to help. You didn't need to do any of this."

"I had my reasons." Chloe gave an experimental yank on her handcuff. Annoyed, Emma yanked back and Chloe, taken by surprise, stumbled a little.

"Then you'd better explain," Emma said. "Starting with what you had to do with Lew Watkins, Willie Farmer, and Stuart Yamada before they ended up dead."

"Stuart's dead?"

"Yesterday morning. Shot in the head," Emma answered.

Chloe's lashes lowered. "I didn't kill them."

"That's not what I asked."

A long moment passed before Chloe let out a sigh. "Willie gave me a message from my brother. It said that if money was tight, I should check the mink coat he gave me for my birthday. I told Willie I'd gotten rid of everything Jacob gave me, and if he'd stashed wads of cash in the pockets, then it was long gone. It was the truth. I'd forgotten I still had that coat."

Chloe raked back her hair, no longer looking so sleek and pulled-together. "Then Stuart came to see me, along with Lew. Stuart said he'd talked to Willie and had heard about the *netsuke*. It was the first *I'd* heard of this, and I said as much to him. That night Willie followed me into a bar, all upset, telling me to give him the coat or he was going to end up dead. I told him again I didn't have it. Next thing I know, Stuart says Willie is dead and Lew is missing, and I was next on the hit list. That's where you two busted in."

"Did Yamada know who killed Farmer?"

Chloe shook her head. "He didn't say."

"You're lying." Bobby flashed his amiable smile as he pulled a small red satin bag out of Chloe's coat. "The officer at the scene said you were calmly talking with him, then suddenly you were gone. Was there somebody around you didn't want to see? Like a cop?"

"I never want to see cops."

Patience wearing thin, Emma moved into Chloe's space. "But there *was* a particular cop, or cops, you wanted to avoid?"

Chloe's mouth hardened. "If you want that answer, you help me with the *netsuke* and you don't arrest me. Otherwise, no deal."

The woman wasn't bluffing. After exchanging a glance with Bobby, Emma nodded reluctantly. She didn't like bargaining, but didn't have many options left. Of the people who had answers, only Chloe was still breathing.

"Now that's settled, let's see what's in here." Bobby loosened the drawstring, looked inside, and then started laughing: belly-deep, chest-shaking laughter. "Oh, yeah . . . *this* is why I became a cop."

Hardly the reaction she'd expected. Curious, Emma plucked the bag out of his hands. "What's so funny?"

She peered inside the bag, and it took a few seconds for her to register what she was seeing. Her brows shot up. "They're erotic *netsuke*?"

"My brother is a very bad man," Chloe intoned. "What did you expect? Hallmark collectible cherubs?"

"Time to give Diana a call," Bobby said, still grinning.

Emma tore her fascinated gaze away from the bag's contents. "Who?"

"Diana Belmaine. My friend who knows a lot about old shit."

As he punched in the number on his cell phone, Emma glanced at her watch. "Isn't it a little late?"

"She owes me, considering the last favor she asked came at five in the morning." He leaned back against the wall, waiting. "Diana? It's Bobby. I've found those *netsuke* I told you about, and I need to talk to you. Now."

He glanced at Emma, smiling. "Well, that works out real nice, doesn't it? I'll be right over. Oh, and I'm bringing a couple friends to your party."

When Bobby knocked on the door of Diana's condo, it swung open to reveal her dark-haired fiancé. Jack Austin leaned against the doorjamb, looking relaxed and at home in a faded Tulane University T-shirt and sweatpants, and his ever-present smile widened when he caught sight of Emma and Chloe, still handcuffed together.

"Damn, Halloran, but I'm jealous of your sex life."
Then, at Bobby's raised brow, Jack added, "Before I became a kept man, that is. Come on in."

Diana walked into the entryway, elegant in a knit camisole and leggings, and her eyes widened. "I'm sure you have a very good explanation for this, Bobby."

Bobby grinned. "If I don't, will you kick me out?"

"Over my dead body," Jack said flatly. "Not until I get the full story."

Chloe was reveling in the attention, but Emma wasn't, and Bobby said quickly, "This is my partner, Detective Emma Frey. Handcuffed to her is Chloe, and Chloe is tonight's business."

Diana, Bobby noticed, was discreetly checking out Emma, and after a round of introductions and handshakes—a bit awkward with the handcuffs—Diana motioned everyone into the living room, where a television blared beneath the loud voices of two women.

"I have friends staying here for a couple of days." Diana spoke directly to Emma, her smile friendly. "We get together a few times during the year to go on shopping trips and just hang out, but they're here to help me pick out a wedding dress and bridesmaid gowns. Jack refuses to get involved. Hey, you guys. More company!"

Diana's two friends, casually dressed in T-shirts and sweatpants, sat on the dark leather couch: one a petite brunette who radiated energy even while sitting, and the other a fair-skinned, freckled redhead with a gentle smile. The coffee table in front of them was cluttered with pizza boxes and clusters of beer bottles and soda cans. *Monty Python's Flying Circus* played on the TV.

"These are my friends," Diana said. "Cassie Ashton is the dark-haired one, and she's a commercial fossil collector from Wyoming. The redhead is Fiona Kennedy, who owns an antique bookstore in Los Angeles."

"Oh, yeah," Bobby said. "I've heard plenty about you two from Diana."

"Honey, I assure you Diana's told us plenty about you, too." The corkscrew brunette laughed—and the redhead gave her a gentle elbow poke.

Chloe rattled the handcuffs. "Your reputation doth proceed you, Robert."

He snorted. "Yeah, and the reports of my reputation have been greatly exaggerated, so you keep your mouth shut."

Another round of introductions and handshakes ensued—complete with pointed stares at Chloe's getup and the handcuffs—and several minutes passed in casual talk as Chloe and Emma sat on the big couch next to Diana's friends, and Jack fetched drinks for everyone before he sat down on an overstuffed leather recliner. Discounting the pizza boxes and beer, the condo looked more like a museum than a place to live. Bobby didn't blame Jack for wanting to negotiate living arrangements at his more comfortable, if smaller, cottage.

"So!" Diana smiled, all bright and eager. "What do you have for me?"

Bobby tossed her the red bag. Diana caught it easily, then sat on the floor across from the coffee table. Bobby settled down beside her, and watched her remove each tiny figure—six of them, only a couple inches in size—and line them up on the coffee table.

A little mini-orgy, all rarin' to go.

Everybody in the room angled forward for a better look, then Cassie Ashton whistled loudly and nudged one of the male figures with her finger. "Looks to me like some wishful thinking in the package department. And let me tell you, if a guy with a dick that big came at me, I'd run screaming in the other direction. I mean . . . ouch."

Chloe smirked, and glanced around with an expectant expression. "Looks like fun, and here we are with five girls and two strapping boys. I can personally vouch for Bobby's prowess in the sack, and I'm sure Xena here—"

"Chloe, shut up," Emma ordered tersely.

"—would find that a nice little orgasm or two might actually improve her mood," Chloe continued, as if she hadn't been interrupted.

A short, uncomfortable silence filled the room, then Jack said, "It always works for Diana." At his fiancé's glare, he grinned. "And it always works for me, too."

Laughter and smiles followed his joke, diffusing the awkwardness, and Bobby, picking up on how Emma was avoiding him, kept his mouth shut. Anything he said would only raise more questions, and he wasn't eager to open up a speculative round of questions on his love life. Jack was already looking miles beyond intrigued to hear Chloe was an ex, and after one glance at Emma, Diana raised a brow, obviously sniffing out a secret.

To his relief, Diana focused her attention back on the *netsuke,* picked up one of the female figures—this one fully dressed—and turned it over.

Fascinated, Bobby shifted closer for a better look. "The detail is . . . damn impressive."

Not to mention arousing.

Diana frowned, then turned all the figures over. "This is interesting."

"What?" Emma leaned over the table, jerking Chloe forward—and Chloe didn't look happy about it.

"First off, they aren't worth much, maybe two, three

hundred dollars, and were made in China within the last ten years. They're on the higher end of quality for *netsuke* of this type, though. Not molded resin—they're carved out of mammoth ivory."

"How can you tell it's mammoth ivory?" Cassie Ashton picked up one of the little naked ladies. "One of my teams found this beautiful mammoth specimen in Minnesota over the summer and—" She cut herself off as the redhead—Fiona—elbowed her again. "And none of you really care about that, so just ignore my big mouth. Carry on."

"So they're not important for any financial motives." Emma picked up her 7UP—just as Chloe suddenly yawned and raised her arms in a stretch, dumping soda all over Emma's jeans.

"Whoops," Chloe said sweetly as Emma glared furiously at her. "Looks like you spilled."

"A word of advice, Chloe," Bobby said. "She's bigger than you, and wears a gun. Stop pissing her off."

Chloe leaned toward Cassie and confided in an exaggerated whisper, "Xena doesn't like me."

"I see that," Cassie said wryly. "But if I were you, I'd listen to the hottie, and tone down that inner alley cat of yours just a bit."

"More than a bit," Fiona added. "Bad kitty."

"Bad's good sometimes." Chloe smiled. "Give it a try. You look like you could use a little trouble in your life."

Fiona settled back, amused rather than offended. "I own an antique bookstore. How much trouble can I get into?"

"Well, if you want trouble," Cassie said, her raspy voice inching higher, "I've got *tons* to spare. Take my squabbling brothers, my insane staff, my cranky adolescent son, and that arrogant ass from Laramie who's got the market cornered on giving trouble to people who are just trying to make an honest buck, and I could—"

Another elbow jab, this one sharper, and Bobby grinned at Fiona. "Don't stop her on my account. I'm enjoying the show."

"Bobby, be quiet. And look at this." Oblivious to the antics on her couch, or just plain used to them, Diana turned one of the *netsuke* toward him, its bare bottom facing up. "Here's what's really interesting: numbers, scratched on the bottom of each piece."

"By the manufacturer or artist?" Emma asked. She stood, and started to walk around the table to get a better look—only to jerk to a stop when Chloe didn't budge from the couch.

With an inward sigh, Bobby rubbed the bridge of his nose. The way things were shaping up between those two, it would be a long, long night.

"Neither," Diana said, lowering her magnifier. "These are European numbers, not Chinese, and it looks as if they were scratched in with a sharp object, like an awl or upholstery needle, after the *netsuke* were carved. And here's something else: four *netsuke* have single numbers carved on their bottoms, but two of them have a double-digit number."

"Numbers for what?" Bobby checked each bare little bottom. "A lock combination?"

"Maybe it's a telephone number or address," Fiona offered.

Jack snagged a piece of pizza. "Or a license plate number."

Emma finally lost patience and pulled Chloe forward

off the couch, ignoring her colorful complaints, then
hunkered down beside Bobby. "They must have a purpose, especially if each butt matches up with another
one, in an ordered sequence."

Amused by the inference, Bobby asked, "You're sug-
gesting we connect them?"

"Excellent!" Cassie grinned, bright-eyed and perky.
"Diana, you always have the best party games. This is
way better than Twister."

Everybody laughed, which effectively eased any lingering discomfort at inserting three Tab A's into three
matching Slot B's.

"I know you all want to play, but we don't have
enough butts to go around," Diana said over the laughter. "Bobby and Emma will do the honors. It's their evidence, let them have the fun."

Emma was still acting aloof around him, which Bobby
figured was a red flag to someone like Diana. Sure
enough, a quick glance at Diana revealed a knowing
glint in her eye—which meant he could expect a phone
call and a friendly grilling tomorrow.

"The naked ones likely go together," said Fiona, with
her soft Irish lilt. "That should narrow down the possibilities considerably."

True enough—and since nobody had rushed to make
the first move, Bobby picked up one of the bare *netsuke,*
eyed the options for best fit, then zeroed in on the most
likely candidate and slid him into place.

Emma smiled. "Looks like you're a natural at this."

Briefly, she met his gaze—and the heat reflected in her
eyes reminded him of how she'd felt beneath him, straining and panting, slick and tight. Color tinged her cheeks,

and as she quickly looked away Bobby let out his breath slowly, grabbed his cold Coke, and drained it.

"This one looks like she's doing algebra equations in her head . . ." Jack took another bite of pizza. "I say she goes with the guy who looks stoned."

"Really? I don't think he's going to fit. Stylistically speaking, anyway." Scooting closer, Cassie pointed. "See? The angle's all wrong."

"Ah." Jack's expression turned thoughtful. "You're right. But it's a hell of an angle."

"Hey, knock off the editorializing." Diana tried to sound serious, but couldn't stop grinning. "Some of us here are engaged in serious police business."

"It's *art*, you pervs." Bobby skewered Lady Algebra with Smug Guy. "And anybody with even half an eye for *art* can tell the stoned dude goes with the girl who's all coy and shy."

"Like we're going to believe coy and shy when she's naked," Chloe said, as Emma connected the "coy" and "stoned" figures with a brisk efficiency.

"Well, Detective Perv is right again. They're a perfect fit. In every way." Emma eyed her newly joined couple. "It's amazing. You wouldn't know they were doing anything until you turn them over. From this side, it looks like a nice PG cuddle."

Diana sat back, hands braced on the floor. "All pieces assembled. Points to us for doing it in record time—and with a minimum of tasteless jokes."

"It's all about numbers," Bobby said, catching Emma's gaze.

Little numbers, big numbers . . . sex and greed and betrayal.

Emma nodded, her expression serious. "All we have to do is figure out the correct order."

"Maybe it's a password." Jack took a swig from his beer bottle. "And in my experience, people almost always go for easy and predictable when it comes to passwords or lock combinations. It makes 'em surprisingly easy to crack."

Bobby looked up sharply. "You haven't been adding to that experience lately, have you? Because that's something I really don't want to hear, Jack."

"Hell, no. I'm just saying."

"Is he *thief*?" Emma asked, incredulous. "Bobby, you didn't—"

"Not a thief. Just an archaeologist with a few unusual hobbies."

"When most people create a password or code," Jack continued, unruffled, "they make it easy to remember. Like the title of a favorite song, a birth date, their kid's middle name. If each couple presents a number in sequence, chances are the sequence will be the most obvious one."

"Short to tall," Emma said. "Or tall to short."

"That's my best guess," Jack agreed.

Bobby arranged the couples from short to tall—lying down, kneeling, and standing—then tipped them so he could read the numbers. "Emma, can you write these down?" When she pulled out her notepad and pen, Bobby slowly recited: "Four, eight, two, six, twenty-two, and seventeen."

Emma looked up. "That's all of them?"

He nodded. "And reverse the order, if the sequence is tall to short."

"Don't forget the numbers could be code for letters," Cassie pointed out. "My son used to write me notes like that when he was little."

Cassie didn't look old enough to have a kid, much less one that wasn't little, and although he'd already thought of that possibility, he said, "Good suggestion, thanks. And this is the point where me and Emma need to leave and try to figure the rest of it out on our own."

"You sure?" Diana looked disappointed. "You've got a lot of extra-big brains here. We could help."

"I know, but this is potential evidence in an active investigation. My boss might not appreciate me sharing that with nonpolice types. And it's not like I can afford to get into any more trouble."

After the *netsuke* were gathered and retired to their bag and everybody made their farewells, Bobby, Emma, and Chloe left the condo. Once they'd reached his SUV, he waited as they settled in the backseat, then pulled away from the curb and asked, "Do those numbers mean anything to you, Chloe?"

"Nothing about them rings a bell, sorry."

"It can't be a word," Emma said. "I converted the numbers to letters, and there's no vowels. I came up with D, H, B, F, V, and Q."

Bobby tapped his fingers against the steering wheel, thinking. "If we go the other direction, it could be a phone number: 1-722-6284."

"I don't think that's local," Emma said. "Does it sound familiar to you?"

Again, Chloe shook her head. "Off the top of my head, I'd have to say no."

As Bobby watched from the rearview mirror, Emma dialed her cell phone and waited. After a moment, she returned the phone to her pocket. "I got a recording saying that number doesn't exist."

"How about the coat?" Bobby glanced back at Chloe. "Any reason your brother would've stashed the *netsuke* in a fake mink?" When she shook her head, he added, "The coat could be a visual clue: mink, minx, fur, furry . . . what's the word for someone who sells furs?"

"Furrier," Emma answered. "We should look up any furriers in the city, as well as personal names, nicknames, and streets or public buildings with the words 'mink' or 'fur' in them."

"There's a Mink Street," Bobby said after a moment. "It's a subdivision, though. Not the kind of neighborhood where you'd stash contraband."

Chloe suddenly sat forward, tapping the side of his seat to get his attention. "There's a private marina in Mandeville, on the north side of Lake Pontchartrain, called Mink's Marina. My brother used to keep a boat there."

"A boat," Bobby repeated. "I didn't figure him for a boat kind of guy."

"He used it for private parties involving female-only guests," Chloe said.

"He's been in prison for over four years," Emma pointed out. "If he didn't pay the marina's rental fee, the boat would've been impounded or sold long before now."

"We should check it out anyway. If those last two numbers are letters, then we have a state boat registration ID number."

A short silence followed as Emma consulted her notebook. "You're right; it'd be 4826VQ. Good catch, partner." He caught her smile in the mirror. "So what could be kept on a boat for over four years? If somebody bought it, by now they would've reported finding anything out of the ordinary."

Bobby made his decision. "Here's what we're gonna do: I'll take you back to your place, and you stay there with Chloe. I'll see if I can dig up anything on a boat registered to Mitsumi. If I can't, I'll drive out to Mink's Marina and have a look around."

"I don't like the idea of you going out there alone, Bobby."

He shrugged. "No choice. We can't take Chloe."

"Why not? It's *my* brother's boat."

"We can always handcuff her to the car door," Emma said reasonably. "That way she can't run off again."

"Enough with the handcuffs already," Chloe grumbled.

"I want to do a drive-by and see what kind of security they have at the marina, and it'll raise less suspicion if I go alone," he said. "If it's minimal, I'll come back for you and we'll all go. If it's secured, it'll have to wait until tomorrow, which means you have a roommate for the night."

Chloe swore and kicked the back of his seat. "I'd rather be in jail!"

"That can be arranged," Emma said coolly.

"Girls. Behave." Bobby scowled. "And it's time to deliver on your part of the deal, Chloe. Are there cops involved in this?"

"Just one," she said after a moment. "I saw him with Willie."

"When was this?" he asked.

"A few weeks ago, at a bar. Willie was sitting with him

and acting nervous, but I didn't think much of it. He was always selling somebody information."

So it had to be a cop who'd been using Farmer as an informant.

"Do you know the cop's name?" Emma asked.

"Nope. He was just an average guy, blondish hair, and kind of quiet."

Giacomo.

Bobby glanced at Emma, and by the grim set of her mouth knew the same thought had occurred to her. "So what happened? You saw this cop in the crowd outside your apartment, and booked? Why was that suspicious? He could've been there doing his job."

"Because when I came home, I saw him crawling out my window. I was getting ready to chase him down when I recognized him, and I hid instead. Later on, I saw him in the crowd, staring at me, and I decided I'd better make myself scarce for a while."

"And you're sure the guy crawling out your window was the same guy you saw with Willie Farmer?" Emma asked, and Bobby didn't miss the tension in her voice.

Not that he blamed her. He hated the thought of one of their own gone bad, and after what she'd told him about her troubles in L.A., this must be the worst kind of nightmare for her.

"Absolutely positive. Then later that afternoon I'm calling around to find a place to stay, and bitching to one of my friends about what happened, when she reminds me I'd left some boxes of clothes stored in her basement. And *that's* when I remembered I'd packed up the fur coat with a bunch of other shit Jacob had given me. I'd had a small apartment at the time, so I'd stashed the boxes in my friend's basement. I'd just forgotten all about it."

"You should've come to me or Bobby with this information."

"I didn't think it was a good idea at the time. I thought I'd be safer if I stayed out of the way—and stayed away from cops and police stations. If this guy had killed Willie and Lew, and had even Stuart acting scared, I did *not* want him to come looking for me. So I asked for time off from work, made up the story that I was looking for a new apartment, then hid out at Bobby's, knowing it'd be the safest place in the city for me to stay until things settled down again."

"So why did you hang out in bars? Everybody knows to look for you there. And why were you prancing around wearing the fur coat, flaunting it?" Emma sounded both irritated and puzzled. "That wasn't too smart."

Chloe shrugged. "Different coats. I have two fake minks: the one Jacob gave me, and the one I wore when I saw Bobby."

"The one you had that first night was cut, like the fur had rows." He nodded, remembering. "This coat doesn't."

"Right. See, I had a plan. I'd act normal to throw off any suspicion. I was safer in crowds, anyway, and the night is my world. I know how to work it to my advantage. I'd leave the coat with the *netsuke* behind and wear the other one, because eventually Stuart or Lew would corner me. At that point, I'd protest a little to make it look good before finally giving them the coat. They wouldn't find anything, and decide it was all a stupid joke on Jacob's part, and move on. Then I'd be left alone to figure out the real deal with the *netsuke*."

Chloe sighed. "The problem was, you wouldn't leave me alone, and ended up pointing this cop right at me—and at the both of you, too. When you chased after me at Punk Amok, it forced me to leave the decoy mink behind at the coat check and hide out for real. If you would've just listened to me and stayed away, things would've worked out."

Bobby swore softly. "That's the stupidest stunt you've ever pulled! You could've gotten yourself hurt, or worse. And me and Emma can handle danger. You had no business trying to take care of this yourself."

Chloe met his gaze in the mirror, then looked out the window. "Jacob was the crime genius in the family, not me, and it was the best plan I could come up with. You know me. I'm not useful for anything but looking good."

"Don't say things like that," Emma said after a moment.

"It's the truth, just like it's true that anything my brother left behind can't be good. I don't know what everybody is after, but I couldn't let it fall into the wrong hands, or put Bobby in danger. If he knew the truth, he'd have come to my rescue because that's what he always does." She sounded faintly bitter. "But not this time. Jacob is my brother. He's my problem."

The shock of her explanation hit him like a fist, and Bobby didn't know what to say. Neither did Emma, and the rest of the ride to her apartment passed in absolute silence.

Twenty-three

Bobby had been gone exactly forty minutes, and already it felt like hours. When Emma had again asked why he had to leave Madame Barfly at *her* apartment, he'd replied, "You're on the fifth floor. If she tries to sneak out a window, she'll break her damn neck."

No arguing with logic like that.

She'd uncuffed the woman, who now roamed through the apartment, poking through books and magazines, looking in the fridge, checking out the DVDs and CDs. Then Chloe headed to the bathroom, and immediately set about rifling through the makeup.

"Leave my personal things alone," Emma said, annoyed.

"I'm bored, and we don't exactly have a lot to talk about. Except for Bobby, but you don't strike me as a kiss-and-tell kind of girl." Chloe opened a bag full of lipstick, and cooed as she poked through them. "Mmmm, there's some great colors here. How come you never wear any of this stuff?"

"I'm a cop, not a hooker."

"Meaning any woman who'd wear Tangerine Dream or Crimson Velvet is a slut? That's kinda harsh, chica." Chloe continued to rummage through the bag. "Hey, Wild Ruby. I bet only the most depraved woman on the planet would ever buy a tube of Wild Ruby lipstick."

Emma leaned back against the wall with a sigh. "I didn't mean it that way, only that wearing a lot of makeup isn't necessary where I work."

"Why?" Chloe uncapped the Wild Ruby, then checked its color against her skin tone in the mirror. "Is it against the law for girl cops to look nice?"

"A woman doesn't need to wear a ton of makeup to look nice."

"Hit a nerve there, didn't I?"

Emma debated whether to ignore Chloe, which would be the easiest thing to do, or to answer her honestly. Finally, she shrugged. "Men aren't judged by their looks. Why should women be?"

"Haven't a clue." Chloe grinned. "I like wearing makeup, so that's a good enough reason for me. I'm not trying to explore any deep philosophical issues about gender stereotypes, I'm just curious why you don't use any of this stuff. And I never would've expected you to have such a good eye for color. Lots of dark, rich shades here . . . You have a romantic streak, Detective Frey."

"You come up with this just by looking at my makeup?"

"If there's one thing I know, it's girly-girl shit." Chloe tossed back her hair. "And then there's how you look at Bobby when you think nobody's noticing."

Before she'd even finished the sentence, Emma was shaking her head. "We're not talking about Bobby."

"Why not? I can tell you're hot for him."

"I work with him."

"You sure use work a lot as an excuse for avoiding fun things."

Emma made a rude noise.

"C'mon, I'm sure you fantasize about what he looks like without clothes, about that intriguing little line of hair that runs down his belly. And about how you'd like to run your fingernail all the way down . . . and watch his face change as you touch him."

Desire mixed with embarrassment warmed her cheeks, and knowing Chloe had had her hands all over Bobby didn't help. "What I think is that you're oversexed."

"And that's a bad thing?" Chloe laughed softly. "He's an incredible lover, very generous, and so focused—"

"What's between me and Bobby is none of your business."

The sly, sex-kitten expression on Chloe's face vanished—and the coldest eyes Emma had seen in a long while stared out at her from that beautiful, doll-like face. It was creepy; like *Bride of Chuckie*.

"Maybe not, but if you hurt him, I'll make you pay."

Emma didn't know whether to be touched by Chloe's fierce protectiveness, offended by the implication that she wasn't good for Bobby, or just plain jealous. "Are you still in love with him?"

Chloe leaned back against the sink. "If I'd been a different woman back then, I might have fallen in love with him. But sometimes when the right guy comes along, you're just not ready to deal with it. And then when you are, it's too late."

It sounded more like a warning—or advice—than a yes-or-no answer. "Did he love you?"

Chloe's brows disappeared beneath her bangs. "It was

more like mutual lust, with a dose of guilt on his part. We were both looking for some kind of comfort, and it was reason enough to fall into bed together. For a while, anyway. I'm still very fond of him. I don't want to see him hurt."

"That's something we can both agree on."

Emma avoided Chloe's dark, too-observant eyes, acutely aware of the we've-slept-with-the-same-man vibe humming in the small room. To cover her discomfort, she began putting away the makeup bags.

"Ever had a makeover, Detective Frey? Because you have great cheekbones and really nice eyes. I'd love to show you what you can do with a little blush, eyeliner, and the right colors."

"You're serious?" she asked in disbelief.

"What else are we going to do, watch TV? I guess we could discuss Bobby's techniques in the sack. It used to drive me crazy whenever he'd—"

Emma huffed. "All right, fine. Anything to get you to shut up."

Chloe looked smug. "Cool. This'll be fun."

It would also be one way to get Chloe talking about non-Bobby-sex subjects. While the woman was preoccupied with the glamour routine, Emma could slip in questions about her brother and the *netsuke,* and see if she knew more than she'd admitted so far.

"And by the way, Chloe, I don't trust you."

"No climbing out windows. I pinky swear it." Chloe's sudden, wide smile made her look younger, softer. "And I promise not to hairspray your eyes, or attack you with the manicure scissors, and run away. Bobby'd kill me, and I'm kind of attached to the whole staying-alive thing. You ready?"

"Do your worst."

"Sit down on the john and prepare to be amazed . . . oooh, was that a skeptical look, Detective?"

"Let's just say I've lived with this face for over thirty years. It's a nice face, but nobody's rushing to offer me any multimillion-dollar modeling contracts."

"Beauty is eighty percent attitude. You ever see what the real Cleopatra looked like?" Chloe tipped Emma's face upward, her touch firm and cool. "Nothing like Liz Taylor, that's for sure. Yet Marc Antony gave up Rome for her."

It felt strange to have another woman touch her like this, even aside of her cop training and personal space issues.

"Why do you dress like that?" Emma asked, to start her own question-and-answer session rolling—and out of genuine curiosity, too.

"You don't like what I'm wearing?"

"I didn't say that, but if you can grill me about why I don't wear loud lipstick, I can grill you about why you wear loud clothes."

"I dress like this because it makes me feel good, period. I have a nice figure, so why not make the most of it?"

"Well, that's certainly blunt."

"Uh-huh. Don't forget arrogant." Chloe blended the dots of foundation on Emma's face. "And self-centered and shallow."

"Now that you mention it, yeah."

Chloe didn't look in the least offended. Or embarrassed. "Like you, I've lived with my face long enough to know people find it attractive. I never was big on that false modesty crap. I don't see the point, and I don't like the implication that I should feel bad just because I'm the lucky recipient of attractive DNA."

"That's one way of looking at it," Emma said dryly, though Chloe's answer had a kind of strange, practical logic to it.

"And I like attention. What can I say? I just gotta be me, and that means dressing on the wilder side of fashion."

Emma motioned to Chloe's platform boots, with their line of buckles. "Don't your feet ever get tired wearing boots like that?"

"Dr. Scholl's is a girl's best friend. Besides, I'm only five feet tall, and wearing heels is as automatic as breathing. There's nothing I can't do while I have them on—running, walking, dancing. Having sex."

The last thing Emma needed was a mental image of Bobby making love to this woman while she wore nothing but black leather boots.

Then a pleasant little thought tickled: Why not seduce Bobby herself, while wearing a pair of her hooker boots? That way she'd give him something even better and more satisfying to remember. And it would be worth it just to see the look on his face.

Chloe's voice drew Emma back from her dreamy reverie: "You're lucky to have great such skin. You don't even need foundation, and there are legions of women who'd hate you for that alone. Hold the mirror . . . right there. Now, pay attention while I show you how to bring out those killer cheekbones."

Obediently, Emma sat still as Chloe picked up a container of brown eye shadow and brushed it on her cheeks, of all places.

"Makeup trick number one, Detective Frey: Light colors raise features and dark colors create contours. So first you brush on a bit of shadow here, right under the apple of your cheek, and blend. Then you add blusher."

As Chloe rummaged with enthusiasm through the makeup bag, Emma examined her face in the mirror.

Although she was in no rush to admit it, this *was* kind of fun. It brought back memories of high school and sleepovers with her friends, experimenting with mascara and curling irons, and giggling over boys.

"Okay, this'll have to do." Chloe turned back. "Smile for me."

"What?"

"Smile. I'm sure you can do that, if you try really hard."

"Don't be such a bitch," Emma retorted, then flexed her lips.

"Oh, come on. I mean a *real* smile. You look like you're constipated. Bunch those cheeks, chica."

So much for nostalgic fun; now she felt more than a little ridiculous. But she smiled broadly, as ordered, and Chloe brushed blusher on the rounded part of her cheek.

"There. See?" Chloe asked. "It brings out your cheekbones, and you can do the same thing to make your jaw look stronger or your nose smaller. Not that you need a stronger jaw, but we can make your nose a little more slender."

She had a fat nose?

Emma sat still, her interest engaged, as Chloe fussed with the brown shadow, amazed that a dab of color here or there could alter her face so much.

"Now, most everybody will tell you that makeup

shouldn't be seen, only used to enhance or disguise. To that I say, bullshit!"

"I never would've guessed you felt that way."

"And now who's being the bitch?" Chloe asked cheerfully. "The skin is a canvas, the muscles and bones a foundation, and half the fun is making a work of art out of your face. The focal point is always the lips and eyes, but I like to play up other striking features, like cheekbones. With your face, you can carry off strong makeup."

Amused, Emma glanced away from the mirror. "You're really getting into the makeover thing."

"No kidding. God, I live for this stuff." Humming to herself, Chloe searched through the bag, then lined up brushes, compacts, tubes of lipstick, eyeliner, and mascara.

"So what kind of face do you think you have?"

"I've never been the blond, blue-eyed sweetheart." Chloe checked the color of a lipstick. "My father was Japanese, my mother's ancestry was Swedish and French, and I'm the end result. For as long as I can remember, people labeled me different. Exotic. So I play up what the girl next door never had."

"Your brother is good-looking, too."

Chloe went still, but only for a second—if Emma hadn't been looking for the reaction, she would've missed it. "You've met my brother?"

"Bobby and I drove over to Angola to talk to him."

"That must've been a blast. Bobby and Jacob hate each other's guts."

Emma let the silence lengthen as Chloe began applying eyeliner. "Do you have any idea what your brother is trying to pass on to you?"

"Something worth a lot of money."

And worth killing for. "Why tell you now, after all this time?"

"Beats me. My brother and I aren't too tight these days."

As Chloe worked, she moved closer, until Emma nearly had her nose in the laces of the woman's denim bustier. Obviously, Chloe didn't mind touching people or getting deep into their personal space.

"If you had to guess, what do you think it would be?"

Chloe glanced down, her expression unreadable. "I'd say money. If it were drugs, he knows I'd destroy it all."

Now, there was an interesting comment—and Chloe's tone of voice had been dead-on serious. "You should've gone to the police."

"I told you why I didn't and, right or wrong, that's it. Now get off my case about it." Chloe put down the eyeliner and surveyed her work. "The trick with eyeliner is not to use too much. People think it'll make your eyes bigger, but it just gives you beady piggy eyes. Not attractive. Use a little here and here, and blend. Your coloring is dark enough that black liner doesn't make you look like a raccoon. Now, here's the part I like best: putting on the eye shadow."

"Does your brother know you had an intimate relationship with Bobby?"

A slow smile curved Chloe's mouth. "Yeah, he knew we were humping like bunnies. I made sure word got back to him."

The girl had a mean streak, all right. "What did he think of that?"

"I didn't ask, and I didn't care. I imagine it wasn't nice, though."

"Would your brother order a hit on Bobby if he could?"

"I doubt it, but at the same time, I'm sure he wouldn't mind if Bobby got in the way of a bullet." Chloe settled on four colors of shadow—all dark. "Okay. I'm going to go for the glam-rock eye look for you. Shades of gray, with a dash of dark purple. Close your eyes."

Emma did so—but not completely. She still didn't trust Chloe, no matter how cooperative she was all of a sudden.

"My brother isn't crazy, not really," Chloe said at length. "I know that no sane person would do the things he's done, but he's aware of his actions. He just doesn't care. That's what makes him so scary."

"You were close to him once?"

"Years ago. After our parents died, we moved around a lot. He was the one constant in my life, and he said everything he did was so that he could take care of me."

"I'm sorry," Emma said quietly. "That must've been hard for you."

"It's okay. He changed." Chloe gently applied shadow across Emma's lids, using both a brush and her fingertips. "And I grew up. End of story."

Emma fell silent, and when Chloe told her it was all right to do so, she opened her eyes. A quick glance at the mirror gave her a start; she hardly recognized the woman looking back at her. "Um . . . wow."

"Like I said, you have a strong face. You can carry a darker, harder look and still be feminine and rank up there on the hot babe scale. Now we find the right lipstick to finish it off. I'm thinking a dark red that screams sex."

"I'm going to scare little children."

"Yeah, but their mommies will hate you and their daddies will lust after you. Give it a try sometime. It's amazing how people will act, depending on what you're wearing or how much eyeliner you've got on."

Emma was beginning to get a handle on what made Chloe Mitsumi tick, and while it wasn't exactly nice and sweet and comfortable, she admired the woman's bluntness and verve.

"Ah, here we go . . . Serengeti Scarlet. That's definitely you."

Emma peered down. A dark red, in a wet look. Like blood. "If your brother had left you money, and you found it, what would you have done with it?"

Chloe's glossy, candy-apple-red lips curved, and she looked down from beneath her heavily mascaraed lashes and gold-shadowed lids. "What would I do with a lot of money? Buy more clothes and shoes. Get a boob job. Travel around the world. Give it all away to people who really need it."

Emma straightened, surprised. "Give it away?"

"You don't believe I'd do that?"

"I wouldn't peg you as the altruistic sort."

"Yeah, but I had you going there for a minute, didn't I?" Chloe's smile widened into a devious grin. "Pucker up, Detective."

"The name's Emma," she said with a sigh, and dutifully puckered up.

"I have a name, too." Chloe carefully applied the lipstick. "And it's not Madame Barfly."

Emma detected a hint of irritation in the woman's voice—not so impenetrable to barbs, after all.

"There you go. All done. What do you think?"

Emma stood, and stared at the glamorous, striking

version of herself in the larger mirror above the sink. "I don't know . . . I sure look different," she said slowly, and then, at a flash of disappointment in Chloe's eyes, she added, "You did a great job, thanks. Even if this is not the real me."

"Sure it is. Or at least one part of the real you."

Emma smiled at her glam-girl self. She did feel sexier and more self-confident, as absurd as it seemed. True, she wouldn't be caught dead wearing all this makeup in public, as it simply wasn't her style—but for a little while, it couldn't hurt. She liked the whole "before" and "after" contrast, and, oddly, it made her look at herself in a way she never had before.

And what would Bobby say if he could see her now?

"Damn," Emma said, turning her head slightly to get a different angle. "I can be a femme fatale if I want."

"Didn't think you had it in you, huh?"

"No," she admitted. "I mean, it's not like I'm losing any sleep over it, but . . ."

Emma trailed off, not sure what point she intended to make, and Chloe finished the sentence for her: "But it's fun to play. Even if it's only to amuse yourself. I get that. No reason to feel guilty about doing something that makes you feel good about yourself. Call me hedonistic or selfish, but I just can't care what others think. I do what feels right for me."

The words had a familiar ring.

Then, realizing she'd spent almost thirty minutes in a bathroom talking about intimate subjects with a virtual stranger, Emma had a sudden need for space and distance. She headed to the living room, the least claustrophobic room in her apartment.

What on earth was taking Bobby so long?

Chloe followed more slowly. "Hey, what's the rush? I could I give you fashion pointers next."

Now, there was a truly scary thought.

"You'd be so easy to dress. With your body, you can carry off anything. You're tall, slender but curvy, and you have boobs, but they're not too big."

Emma sat on her couch and looked down at her chest beneath her sweatshirt. "I wouldn't mind if they were bigger."

"Good looks and perky boobs aren't everything."

"Easy for you to say."

"Nothing lasts forever, especially good looks. So there's gotta be something more beneath it all." Chloe flopped down on the armchair opposite Emma. "Which reminds me of a story my Grandmother Megumi told me when I was a little girl. Do you want to hear it?"

The question sounded forced, coming out of nowhere like that—and had Chloe ever been a little girl? It always seemed more likely that, like Athena, she'd just popped into existence, all bustier-wearing, fanged, and ready to plow her way through phalanxes of unwary men.

But Emma decided to play along, and when she nodded, Chloe said, "It's an old Japanese folktale. I don't remember the title anymore, but I call it 'The Twisted Sister and the Three Hot Studs.'"

"This should be . . . interesting."

Chloe laughed as she crossed her legs. "It's a typical fairy tale, with the typical beautiful, rich chick being chased by the typical three young studs, all of whom have to pass daddy's tests before one of them can get the goods. There's the usual complications—in this one, the three studs pass all the tests with equal skill, and dear old dad can't figure out what to do because, you know, life isn't supposed to throw you curves like that. But our rich and beautiful chick is also smart, and she puts on a big show. She makes sure the three studs see her pick up the bloody body of a baby, and then watch her eat its arm."

"That's *disgusting*." Emma curled her lip. "Your rich chick is bent."

Not to mention the granny. What kind of person told a little kid such gruesome stories?

Amusement sparkled in Chloe's eyes. "And that's exactly what two of the studs thought, and they split. But the third stud, he's thinking maybe something else is going down. He starts asking questions, looking deeper, thinking outside the box. And pretty soon he figures out the object of his lust and adoration didn't really eat a baby, it was just an armlike roll she'd made of mochi and rouge."

"What's mochi?"

"It's a traditional Japanese food . . . rice that's pounded into a sort of dough and cooked into round, puffy rice cakes. It's very good. Anyway, he figures out she's the real deal despite her outwardly bad behavior, so he sticks around, and our girl lands a handsome lover with a brain and common sense—and, as a bonus, a guy who also shares her unique sense of humor. A match made in heaven."

Emma got the point. Like Bobby, Chloe relied on people judging her on her appearance, taking the easy route and not looking any deeper than necessary. In Bobby's case, a sunny smile and a closetful of quirky ties and clothing made it easy for him to play people, lull them into not taking him seriously or seeing his darker edge.

And it made her wonder if most people didn't keep a

piece of themselves hidden; a little part that wasn't obvious unless someone cared enough to look.

"It's one of those stories with a moral," Emma said. "And a good one."

Chloe sat back and tapped her boot on the floor—the only outward sign that her ennui was mostly an act. "Even when I was just a little girl, I knew nobody wanted me or my brother around. I liked that story because it told me that one day the right people would come around, and they'd see me and love me even if I didn't have blond hair and blue eyes."

Chloe's admission, and the quieter tone of her voice, touched Emma. How could it not? At some point, everyone felt overlooked, misunderstood, or unable to measure up to expectations.

Even the beautiful people, it seemed.

"Also, I liked the story because it tells us to look behind people's bad behavior, below the surface, to understand why they act the way they do." She paused, then shrugged. "But sometimes there's no reason for the bad behavior."

This was the adoring little sister speaking, the girl with no constants in her world expect for her big brother, who'd done everything to take care of her. If he hadn't been forced to care for her, would he have turned out differently?

"There was nothing you could've done to help him, Chloe. You can't blame yourself for your brother's choices."

"Just more water under the bridge." Her expression grew thoughtful. "When I see you with Bobby, half the time you look like you want to jump him, and the other half like you want to run and hide. Why?"

Caught off balance by the one-eighty change in direction, it took Emma a moment to find an answer. "I've never fallen for a man like this before, so fast and so completely. I've always been careful, taking my time, but with Bobby . . . it's not like that. I care for him so much, and I'm so worried for him. It scares me. *He* scares me."

Why she'd been so honest with a woman she'd just met, Emma didn't know—but admitting the truth seemed to lift a great weight from her.

"What drives Bobby to be the incredible man he is also makes him so hard to live with. He needs somebody in his life who's strong enough to take the bad days along with the good days. But you're a lot like him, so you know that."

Emma shifted on the couch, then said quietly, "I was wrong about you, and I apologize for that."

"No need to. I don't get angry with people who don't understand me. I tell myself that, deep down, they're really just like me: They get up every morning to go to work, still holding out for that one somebody who'll walk into their lives and see them in a way nobody else can. I'm sure there's a lot of people who are just like us."

Us . . .

The phone rang, saving Emma from having to think up an even halfway intelligent response, and she snatched it up: "Hello?"

"Em, it's me."

Bobby. Thank God. Until relief rushed over, she hadn't wanted to admit how worried she'd been about him. "Hey, what's up?"

"I'm at Mink's Marina, with the security guard, and we've hit the jackpot. Ask Chloe if she knew the boat was registered in her name."

Emma turned to Chloe. "It's Bobby. He's found the boat, and wants to know if you were aware the boat is registered in your name."

"Hell, no. That bastard!"

"I figured as much," Bobby said dryly, when Emma relayed Chloe's answer. "And it explains why the boat wasn't impounded. I had the guard check the files, and the marina fee was paid up five years in advance, in cash, a couple weeks before Mitsumi was convicted."

Emma frowned. "And the five years is almost up, which also explains why Mitsumi waited until now to launch his treasure hunt. Have you been on the boat?"

"Nope. The guard won't let me on without a search warrant or the owner's permission. Which is why I'm calling."

"Ah." Emma glanced at Chloe, who was watching her intently. "And we happen to have the owner right here."

"Exactly. Bring her over, and then we can search the boat."

"I can do that."

"You might want to hurry it up, though."

Emma tensed. "Why? What's happened?"

"Nothing, so far. But the security guard called 911 to verify I'm really who I say I am, and dispatch just paged me to check my whereabouts. If Giacomo is listening in, he's going to put it together and know where to find me." He paused. "So I'd appreciate it if you were here to watch my back, partner."

Twenty-four

Although Emma made it to the marina in record time, it seemed to take forever—and Chloe's constant carping about her driving didn't help. Finally, as she turned onto the road leading to the marina, she snapped, "We can't help Bobby if we crash or run somebody over, all right? Now *stop* distracting me."

"Why do you keep looking in the mirrors? Is somebody following us?"

"Not that I can see, but I'm keeping an eye out for a tail. Be quiet."

Emma pulled into the small parking lot, noting it wasn't well lit. And at one A.M., the marina itself, nestled along the shores of Lake Pontchartrain, was dark and quiet, and offered more hiding places than she liked.

She turned off the ignition. "Stay close to me and do what I tell you. Is that clear?"

Chloe nodded. "Hell, yes. I'm scared spitless right now."

"Scared is good. That means you're less likely to do

something stupid." After locking the car, she walked toward a small gazebolike building that seemed to blaze with lights against the remote blackness by the lake. "That must be the security office."

No sooner had she spoken than a familiar figure stepped outside the building and raised his hand in greeting. Relieved, she waved back.

"That was fast." Bobby walked forward to meet them—then stopped abruptly. "What'd you do to your face?"

Damn; she'd been in such a hurry she'd forgotten to wipe off the makeup. Acutely self-conscious of how foolish she must look, all painted up and wearing ratty jeans and an old sweatshirt, she smiled ruefully. "Chloe was bored, so she gave me a makeover while we were waiting for you to call."

And as she explained all this, his focus never left her mouth. "Sorry you were so bored while I was running my ass off."

At his cool tone, her smile froze.

"Jerk." Chloe punched Bobby in the arm. "You're supposed to tell her she looks good."

"I thought she looked just fine to begin with." With a grimace, he added, "Sorry, Em. It's just—"

"You said hurry, and now I'm here. Give me an update." She tried to sound normal, not hurt, but judging by the guilt flashing across his face, she didn't succeed.

Sighing, he held the door open for them. "Let's go inside."

Chloe went through the door first, followed by Emma. The young security guard standing by his desk tried to project a professional and serious image, but came across more anxious than anything else. Or at least until he saw Chloe's buckle platform boots, and bustier/mini-skirt getup beneath her fur coat—then he perked up, alarm dissolving into bewilderment mixed with awe.

"This is my partner, Detective Frey," Bobby said. "And this is the boat's registered owner, Chloe Mitsumi."

"Hey, there." Chloe smiled and leaned closer, touching his nameplate with a long, dark purple nail. "Mr. Huntly. Pleasure to meet you."

The poor boy swallowed. "Uh, hello."

"I hear you need my permission to let the nice cops on my boat."

"Yes, ma'am." His voice cracked. "I'll also need to see some identification."

"You're thorough," Chloe murmured. "I like that in a man."

Emma was considering jabbing the woman with her elbow when Bobby, scowling, did it for her. "Quit playing, and just give him your driver's license."

Chloe pulled her wallet out of her coat pocket and tossed it to the startled guard, who nearly dropped it. After he checked her ID, he handed it back. "Thank you, Ms. Mitsumi. That's all I needed. And you're giving the detectives permission to search your boat?"

"I wouldn't be here otherwise," Chloe answered. "So that's a big, fat yes, my friend. Let them search."

"The guard gave me the boat's spare key from the file, so we're set," Bobby said as he picked up a pair of handcuffs off the desk.

"What about me?" Chloe asked, hands on her hips.

"You're staying here," Bobby said flatly. He pushed

her down on the office chair, then cuffed her wrist to the desk leg. "The last thing I need to worry about is you getting into trouble."

Chloe glared. "I can take care of myself."

Bobby leaned down, giving her a look that left no room for debate. "You've done your part, now let me and Emma do our job. You stay here until we get back. And don't give this nice young man any shit."

The guard rubbed his palms down the sides of his uniform pants. "Are you sure you don't want me to come with you?"

"Positive. You've got my cell phone number. If anybody pulls up to the office, you call me immediately."

"Yes, sir."

Bobby opened the door and ushered Emma outside, his hand on the small of her back—a casually intimate gesture that sent little skitters of pleasure shooting through her.

As she fell into step beside him, she reached inside her coat to unsnap her holster. "Which way?"

"The boat's over here." He glanced at her, lips twitching. "You look like an MTV video babe. If the guys at work could see you now, they'd be impressed."

"I feel stupid."

"Don't. I like the look on you, but I meant what I said before. You're beautiful just the way you are."

A pleasurable heat curled through her at his compliment, and she smiled her thanks as they left the paved walkway for the creaky wooden piers.

"How are you doing?" he asked.

"I'm a little nervous. Maybe nothing will go wrong, but I'd feel better if we could call in for backup."

"Already did."

Surprised, she looked over at him. "When?"

"Right before you drove up. I called Strong at home and filled him in on the situation, and that any backup he sends needs to come in quiet. If Giacomo is around somewhere, I want to catch him, not spook him off."

"Oh, boy. We're bait?"

"Gotta love the job perks." He grinned. "Turn here."

He motioned to one of the smaller piers angling off the main one, all of which were lined with watercraft of all sizes and types, from small fishing boats and sailboats to cabin cruisers, pontoon houseboats, and small yachts.

As they walked along the wooden planks, footsteps pounding, Emma spotted a large cruiser tied up at the end, behind a colorful little sailboat. The registration number painted along the hull read: LA-4826-VQ.

Excitement rippled over her. "Gotcha."

"It's a treasure hunt, all right, courtesy of a convicted felon," Bobby said, dryly, as he came to a halt at the end of the pier.

Emma didn't know much about boats, but this had to have cost a tidy bundle. "So what's the plan, partner?"

"The plan is to get back home as soon as possible and make love to you, MTV babe. I wanna lick that lipstick off you."

Despite a sharp, inconvenient tug of desire, she smiled at his light teasing. "Nice plan, but I was thinking about the more immediate problem."

"Oh, that. First, we get on the boat."

Bobby jumped onto the gently swaying deck, then turned and held out his hand. She didn't need help, but took it because she wanted to touch him. Once on the foredeck, she gave his hand a quick squeeze, then let go.

He turned, surveying the boat. "It'll take time to

search everything. How about you head below deck, and I'll take the upper deck areas and flybridge."

Emma pulled a big Maglite from her pocket. "Do you have a flashlight?"

Bobby held up his smaller one—the kind with a bendable front.

She smirked. "Mine's bigger than yours."

"But mine can get into small, tight spaces," he said in a low, suggestive tone. "That's gotta count for something. Right?"

"Smutty flashlight talk . . . we are *so* sad."

"A guy has to take his thrills where he can find them." He gave a mock sigh, then unlocked the door leading below deck. "Now go find either a pile of money or drugs so we can get the hell out of here—and preferably before Chloe scars that poor kid for life."

Emma laughed, even as she drew her gun. "Will do."

"And be careful." He frowned. "You want me to go down there with you?"

"I'm fine, Bobby. You just be careful yourself."

"Not a problem. I've got a reason to get home in one piece tonight," he said, but all the same he watched her slow descent below deck, his gun out, ready to move if she needed him.

After a moment, she called out to him, voice muffled, "Everything's clear. Nothing but spiderwebs and assorted dead bugs. It's been a long time since anybody's been down here. There's an aft stateroom, forward berth, galley, head, and a seating area. I'll start with the berth and work my way back to you."

"Okay," he called back, then started his search.

A likely hiding place would be the fuel tank, or a false bulkhead. A woman he knew in the Coast Guard had explained in great detail, one night at a bar, all the ingenious places people tried to hide contraband in boats—although what shape it would be after this long was anybody's guess.

He popped back the first of the two engine hoods and carefully poked around hoses, wires, and gauges. Down below, he could hear Emma moving around, opening and closing doors. When he didn't see anything near either engine, he moved to the fuel tank, tapping lightly to hear if anything sounded off. When he found nothing suspicious there, he worked his way through the flybridge, dinette area, and then the helm.

When it had been silent below deck for a little too long, he called down the hatch, "How's it going, Em?"

"I think I've got something. Can you come down and give me a hand?"

Surprised—had they even been searching for more than ten minutes?—Bobby headed below to the dark, musty-smelling spaces. Emma was sitting on the galley floor by a small cabinet, with one of the doors open.

Hunkering down beside her, he asked, "What is it?"

She aimed the beam of her flashlight down. "A false bottom."

But not an obvious one. He whistled. "Good job, darlin'."

"Now all we have to do is pry it open, but I haven't seen any tools."

"I've got a crowbar and hammer in my SUV, but I don't like leaving you alone to go back for them." He swung the flashlight beam around the empty galley. No pots or pans, just . . . nothing. "There must be a toolbox somewhere on the boat. Did you look in the other rooms?"

"There's nothing except a bed frame without a mattress, and all the cabinets and storage compartments are empty. It looks to me like this boat was completely cleaned out a while ago." Emma glanced up. "I'll be all right here. Go get your crowbar."

"You sure?"

She stood, and the thick treads of her boots made heavy, hollow thumps with every step toward him. "I'll be fine here for the five minutes it'll take you to run to your car and back. Come on, Bobby. I'm a cop. I've had the same training as you. Stop treating me like a helpless girl, okay?"

"You're right, sorry. All the same, humor me and lay low until I get back."

She nodded. "And watch yourself. It's dark out there."

As Bobby jumped to the pier, he glanced around, seeing only dozens of boats straining against their mooring lines and bumping up against the padded posts. The lights from the gate office still glowed. Nothing moved in the darkness except for tree limbs swaying in the breeze.

Reasonably certain the area was secure, he took off at a run for the parking lot. As he passed the security office, the guard poked his head out.

"Everything okay, sir?"

"Just fine. I'm getting a few tools, that's all." He spotted Chloe, sitting on the desk and examining her nails, glassy-eyed.

When he reached the parking lot, he slowed, listening for the sound of feet scraping on gravel, twigs snapping—or the unmistakable *snick* of a round being chambered.

After quickly retrieving his spare toolbox from beneath the passenger seat, he reached in the back for the crowbar he kept by the car jack, then ran back, armed for cabinet destruction. This time Chloe wiggled her fingers at him, still looking bored. When he reached the boat again, he quietly called Emma's name—and nearly jumped out of his skin when she emerged from the shadows of the hatch.

"Dammit! I didn't see you there."

Her lips curved—and even in the low light, he could see the sheen of her lipstick. "That's the whole point, Bobby. Whatcha got?"

He held up the crowbar and toolbox. "Everything we need . . . and can I say that, even if it's a totally bad idea, I really want to kiss you?"

She smiled slowly. "You do?"

"Yeah," he grumbled. "Instead, I have to go break things."

"Something I've noticed you're good at."

At her soft chuckle, he tossed her the crowbar, then the toolbox, and jumped back onto the boat.

With Emma behind him, he tromped below deck to the galley. He knelt, warning her to stand back. As she did so, he pounded the end of the crowbar into the wood until he'd made enough of a hole to slip the flat end inside and pry the board upward.

He pressed down with all his weight, hearing the teeth-grating shriek of nails tearing out of wood, followed by the splintering of boards. Then the plank snapped and he fell back on his ass.

"Success," Emma murmured as he rolled back to a squat.

"Hand me the flashlight." He reached back, and as

she placed it in his hand, their fingers touched, her skin smooth and cool.

"See anything?" she asked.

Bobby aimed the beam into the dark hole, and the light picked up a glint of metal. "I think so." Moving closer, he angled the flashlight—and then smiled. "Oh, yeah, baby. We got us a nice black leather briefcase."

He handed her the flashlight, then grabbed the crowbar. "Angle the light down so I can see better. I'm going to pry up the rest of these boards."

A few minutes later, he'd dismantled the false bottom and hauled out the briefcase. "It's heavy, so that means it's full of something."

"Maybe we should wait to open it. Have it checked by the tactical unit, just in case Mitsumi rigged it to explode."

"Explosives weren't ever his MO," Bobby said, hands still on the lid. Carefully, he brushed off dust and spiderwebs.

"What was his MO?"

"Guns and knives." He twisted around until he could see her. "And the occasional baseball bat. He liked his violence up close and personal."

Emma shifted uneasily. "I still think we should wait."

"If I were here by myself, I'd open it."

"I know." She smiled down at him. "But you're not alone now. No hotdogging on my watch."

"Yeah, but what if it's just confetti in here? Or moldy old donuts? The swat guys will never let us live it down."

"Tough."

"Emma, I'll crack it open just wide enough to look in-

side with the flashlight. If I see any wires or anything suspicious, I'll close it. Okay?"

She hesitated, then hunkered down beside him.
"Okay. But if you blow us up, I'm going to be really
pissed."

As Emma held the flashlight, Bobby slowly opened the
briefcase—just a fraction of an inch. Bending low,
smelling the scent of mildew and lake water that perme-
ated the deck, he peered inside. "Nothing. Just money."

Sitting back, he flipped the case open and whistled.
"There's gotta be hundreds of thousands of dollars here.
We'll have to—"

A sharp, unmistakable retort cracked across the quiet.

Bobby spun, reaching for his gun. Beside him, Emma
had already raised hers in a firm, two-handed grip.

"Gunshot." He glanced at her grimly. "Sounds like it
came from the direction of the security office."

"We need to move," Emma whispered. "If we're
caught down here, it'll be like shooting fish in a barrel."

He nodded, then climbed up the steps as silently as
possible, Emma at his heels. When they reached the
hatch, they went through together—back to back, guns
ready.

The deck, and pier, were empty.

Bobby stepped out on deck first, crouched, gaze
searching. He could feel Emma behind him, even if he
couldn't see her. Something was wrong, and a second
later he realized what.

Glancing over his shoulder, he whispered, "The office.
No lights."

She twisted around to look behind her, her expression
tight. "Shit."

Standing on the pier, they were open targets.

"We need cover." As she nodded, he added quietly, "You head right, I'll go left. Work your way back toward the office. Stay in the trees."

"Now would be a good time for that backup to arrive," Emma muttered.

She ran down the pier toward the trees, staying low. Bobby followed until they left the pier, then he veered in the opposite direction, keeping Emma in sight until she vanished into the shadows of the trees and bushes. As soon as he was under cover, he moved as quickly as he dared for the security office, already dreading what he'd find.

If Giacomo had killed Chloe and the guard, the sonofabitch would never live long enough to see a courtroom.

A funny thing, stress. And fear.

For whatever reason, the thought running through Emma's head right now wasn't tactical or strategic, but something she'd heard in the academy once, long ago: *Police work is ninety-eight percent boredom interspersed with two percent moments of sheer terror.*

Good to know the terror pounding away inside her was regulation-approved.

Crouched behind a tree trunk, she could see the darkened shape of the security office, but nothing seemed to be moving inside.

Not good.

Emma quickly searched for any sign of Bobby, Chloe, or the young security guard—any movement at all—then crept closer, trusting that Bobby wouldn't be far behind. She'd nearly reached the eerily quiet office when she heard a soft gasp.

She whirled, gun raised—and froze.

"I wouldn't do that unless you want to see her pretty face all messed up."

"*Mottson?*"

Despite the jolt of shock, Emma didn't lower her gun, and looked away from him only long enough to verify that Chloe, squeezed against Mottson's chest in a choke hold, was all right.

Or as all right as possible with an automatic rammed against her temple.

"Surprised to see me?"

"Not really." *Hell, yes!* She'd been certain her rogue cop was Gary Giacomo, but Mottson? He'd seemed far too lazy and unimaginative to put together something like this. "Where's the security guard?"

"Sleeping."

A cold, sick feeling swept over her. "You killed him?"

"What do you think?"

Emma tried to read Chloe's face, but it was too dark. "That was stupid. Stealing from an ex-drug dealer is one thing. Killing a security guard . . . they'll hunt you down. There'll be no place you can hide where they won't find you."

"Nice, but a touch heavy on the melodrama, Frey. Throw your gun in the bushes. Now." Despite the bravado in his voice, his gaze constantly darted from side to side—and he pressed the gun harder against Chloe, who flinched.

Emma's first impulse was to shoot the bastard where he stood, but did as ordered. Her gun hit the ground with a thud and a rustle of leaves.

"Good." Mottson eased the gun away from Chloe's head. He'd dressed in black, making it harder to track his movements. "Now you're going to take me to the money."

She had to stall; give Bobby time to get into position. "How do you know it's money?"

"Because Willie Farmer told me. Eight hundred fifty thousand, just waiting for one lucky guy to pick it up—and that would be me."

The final pieces clicked into place. "Farmer was one of your informants. He passed on Jacob Mitsumi's message to you, hoping you'd partner up, help him find the money, and split it."

"Willie never was too smart."

"Smart enough to tell somebody else, and they went after the money as well. To complicate your plans."

"That's what I get for trusting a weasel. But it doesn't matter, since they're dead now, too—and you can quit stalling. If Halloran tries to play the big hero, you and the cupcake will be dead before he can get to you. Show me the money, Frey."

Bobby, anytime now would be good . . .

Calmly, Emma said, "Okay. The boat's over this way."

"You lead. I'll be right behind you, with the gun to this bitch's head. Try anything, and she's dead. I know the same tricks you do, Frey. So be smart. I get the money, and you'll live."

As she walked toward the boat, Emma looked back over her shoulder and smiled. "How stupid do you think I am? You have no intention of letting any of us live. Make no mistake, Mottson, the first chance I get, I'll kill you."

His cocky smile faded. "With what, your steely glare? I'm the one with the gun."

Emma didn't answer. Let him stew, and wonder if she had another gun on her. He couldn't risk searching her; that would mean letting Chloe loose, and he didn't want that.

"You figured you could take the money and kill Farmer," she said as she led him to the pier. "And nobody would be the wiser. Plus, nobody would ask too many questions about why a loser like him ended up dead."

"Somebody gets that eight hundred grand, why not me? Like I'm ever gonna get rich on a cop's salary, and it's blood money, so it's not like I'd be stealing it from nice, upstanding citizens. None of the street punks have any business getting their hands on it. They'd just use it to cause more bad shit that you or me or some other cop would have to clean up."

"I'd say three dead men is bad shit enough—or four, if you killed that kid in the security office."

As if he hadn't heard her, he added, "I like to think of it as a reward for doing a thankless job for nearly twenty years. Nobody's losing any sleep over a few dead gang-bangers, Frey. And you know your boyfriend Halloran's no better than I am, considering some of the shit he's pulled over the years."

"Bobby's never murdered anybody in cold blood, shoved a gun against the head of an innocent woman, or betrayed a fellow cop."

"Don't tell me you wouldn't be at least tempted," Mottson said, his tone almost friendly. "There's lots of people besides me who'd want that money."

"Sure," Emma said coldly, stopping next to the cabin cruiser. "The kind that belong in jail."

Mottson chuckled, gaze darting around. "You act like

a nun, look like one, and probably fuck like one, too. I sure don't know what Halloran sees in you, but I always thought he was crazy. Is this the boat?"

"Yes."

"You know where the money is?"

"We left it down in the galley." Along with a head-crunching flashlight, a crowbar, and a hammer. "Do you want me to bring it up?"

"We all go down." He wrapped Chloe's long hair around his fist and tugged. "Together."

"Ow! That hurt, you prick."

Anger flashed across Chloe's face, and when she reached up to swat Mottson's hand away, Emma noticed a handcuff was still attached to her wrist.

Mottson gave Chloe a warning shake, then said, "Frey, I want you to get on the boat, then lay facedown on deck and lace your fingers together behind your head. Stay down until me and the cupcake climb onboard. Got that?"

Emma swung over to the deck and laid down, hands clasped behind her head, and watched as Mottson and Chloe jumped from the pier to the boat.

She didn't know where Bobby was, but he'd better show up soon. Preferably with backup.

"On your feet." Mottson ordered. "I'll follow you down the steps—and go slowly. I wouldn't want to have to hurry, then accidentally slip and send a chunk of lead ripping through her brain."

"You," Chloe muttered, "are *so* dead. Emma is gonna take you apart."

"If I go, sweetheart, you go with me."

It took all Emma's self-control to remain calm. Then,

halfway down the steps, she spotted the Maglite. "Can I pick up the flashlight? It's dark down there."

"Just take it easy."

"Yeah, yeah . . . I get it already. You can stop sounding like a nervous old lady, Mottson." Turning on the light, she slowly descended, feeling him close behind her.

In the small galley, Emma listened to Mottson's rapid breathing and smelled his fear. Casually, she moved her boot to the briefcase and the crowbar beside it, its curved end pointed upward, by her toe.

"Pick up the case, Frey," Mottson ordered flatly.

"You want it, it's yours. Let me take Chloe out of here. I'm not armed. There's nothing I can do to stop you."

"I thought you were going to kill me." His mouth curved, and in the low light, his eyes were pools of shadow. Skull-like. "Nice try, but no. We're going up together. Give me any lip, and I'll make sure both of you die real slow."

"And I thought you weren't going to kill us."

"Things don't always work out as planned, and since I've already killed a few people, a couple more aren't going to make that much difference. Are they?"

If she stepped on the crowbar's curved end, it would snap up into her hand and she could swing it around and bust his head wide open—but she couldn't be sure he wouldn't pull the trigger first, killing Chloe.

She didn't dare risk it. Moving her foot away from the crowbar, Emma slowly picked up the briefcase.

Mottson might not kill them unless forced to, and with any luck, he wouldn't notice she still had the Maglite. Also, the chances of Bobby lending a helping hand—or a helping bullet—were far better on land than inside a boat.

In silence, they climbed over to the pier, and as she led Mottson and Chloe toward the shore, Emma held the heavy briefcase in a firm grip, thinking it could also serve as a weapon. She couldn't see any movement in the darkness, except a skitter of something fast and shiny-eyed in the distance, and heard only the sounds of water lapping against the shoreline—and Chloe's boots thudding on the pier, heavy and thick and fast.

Like her heartbeat.

"Dammit, quit making so much noise when you walk," Mottson muttered to Chloe. "I can't hear if—"

"If somebody's come up behind you."

Bobby!

Emma spun, images flashing by in a blur: the whites of Chloe's wide eyes, Mottson's rigid body, and Bobby, soaking wet, rivulets running down his face, a dark pool of water widening at his feet—and holding his gun to Mottson's head.

"Now, look what we have here," Bobby said calmly. "Me with a gun to your head. Emma with a case worth over eight hundred thousand dollars—and a Maglite she can use to bust your jaw. You just have Chloe. Gotta tell you, Mottson, you're totally and completely fucked."

Emma briefly caught Bobby's gaze—and his silent signal that he was ready to back her up the second she made her move.

"We could also just stand here," Emma said, as she quickly sized up her options. "And wait for our backup to arrive."

At the mention of backup, Mottson tensed. He no

longer had Chloe in a choke hold, but held her by the collar of her coat.

"I'll kill her," Mottson said flatly, his eyes gone eerily blank. "I got nothing left to lose."

"Except *this*."

Emma threw the briefcase into the water at the same time she swung the flashlight upward. Its powerful beam hit Mottson full in the face, blinding him.

"Chloe, down!"

At her yell, Chloe dropped, head down. Mottson cursed, jerking away from the light, and Bobby grabbed his gun hand. Emma lunged forward just as Chloe rolled off the pier and into the water with a loud splash.

Mottson rammed his head back, hitting Bobby in the face and breaking his hold long enough to turn around, grabbing for Bobby's gun. Recovering quickly, Bobby forced Mottson's arm up just as Emma swung the flashlight toward the back of Mottson's head

At the last second, he shifted and she hit his shoulder instead. It hurt enough to catch him off guard, and Bobby, seizing the split-second advantage, shoved Mottson hard. The man stumbled back into Emma, knocking her off the pier and into the water.

Cold! Coldcoldcold!

Emma surfaced, gasping with shock at the frigid water. She shoved her wet hair out of her eyes in time to see Mottson's gun fly out of his hand and hit the water with a *plop*.

Spinning around, Mottson ran down the pier. Bobby followed close on his heels, shouting for him to stop.

The water wasn't even five feet deep, and Emma quickly waded back to the pier and hauled herself up as the sudden wail of sirens pierced the air and the pulsing colors of lightbars filled the night sky.

She desperately wanted to cover Bobby, but needed to be sure Chloe was safe. Spotting her a little farther out, she shouted, "Chloe, are you okay?"

"Yes! You get that sonofabitch, and I'll grab the briefcase!"

Emma ran after Bobby, slowing as she caught sight of him up ahead. He stood over Mottson, who'd dropped to his knees, hunched over, his hands cuffed behind his back, and every sagging line of his body radiating defeat.

Doing her best to ignore her chattering teeth and the icy wind piercing through her wet clothes, Emma stopped next to Bobby.

"Chloe?" he asked.

"Wading back to shore with the money. Have you checked on the security guard?"

Bobby shook his head. "Not yet, but I just asked Mottson about him, and he said he knocked the kid out and tied him up, then shot the handcuff off Chloe. That was what we heard on the boat.

"I saw him with you, and figured he'd go for the money. I cut back and waded to the boat as fast as I could. I was hoping he'd come out and I wouldn't have to go in after you. Christ, that would've been a disaster." He was shivering, too. "Good work with the flashlight. Not sure about throwing the money into the lake, but it sure wasn't what he expected."

"God, I was just reacting on instinct." From over the top of his head, she saw uniforms running their way, and yelled, "This is Detective Frey. We've got the suspect in custody, and there's an injured security guard in the of-fice. . . . Somebody check on him, please."

Now she really could relax—a good thing, because the reality of what had happened hit her hard. Abruptly, she sat down on the cold grass beside Bobby and Mottson, who was still huddled in a tight ball, as if trying to hide.

"You okay?" Bobby asked, squatting.

"My first hostage situation," she admitted, voice shaky. "How'd I do?"

"Just beautiful."

"And I've never been that close to getting killed, either."

"I don't much like that part myself." He stood. "It might be a good idea to sit there for a minute or two. Until you feel better."

The uniforms had arrived—along with Captain Strong, who stared grimly at Mottson. "Jesus. I was hoping you were wrong."

"Yeah," Bobby said after a moment. "So was I."

"What the hell happened?" Strong asked.

"Long story. Might be better told in private."

It took Strong a moment to pull himself together, then he turned to one of the officers. "Take him to my car. Don't leave him alone for even a second."

The officer nodded and with surprising gentleness hauled Mottson to his feet. Mottson never once looked up, just hung his head as he was led away.

Emma looked down, feeling an unexpected twinge of pity, then stood. "We better retrieve Chloe."

Bobby shot her a quick look, then he turned to Strong. "Mottson was using Chloe as a hostage. While I tried to take his gun away from him, she jumped into the water. Along with a briefcase full of money. Lots of it."

Strong turned to the nearest uniforms and snapped, "Hightower, MacNeil, go bring her in. And you over there!" He jabbed his finger at another cop as the first two ran toward the pier. "Get me three blankets, now!"

Without waiting for the blankets, ignoring the cold, Emma quickly headed for the boat, Bobby beside her. Strong followed behind them, with several officers, as he muttered, "This is going to be a long night. A long, and really bad, night."

Emma slowed as she spotted Hightower standing at the end of the pier, searching the water with the beam of his flashlight while MacNeil directed the bright glare of his flashlight along the decks of the boats tied to the mooring posts.

Chloe was nowhere to be seen—and no sign of the briefcase bobbing on the water, either.

"I don't believe this," Emma said, gulping for air.

"Shit." Eyes narrowed, Bobby ran a hand through his wet hair. "Chloe's gone. With the money."

"Then we'll find her and bring her in," Strong said, as one of the uniformed officers arrived with blankets.

Bobby wrapped a blanket around Emma before taking one for himself. Smiling her thanks at his old-fashioned chivalry, she moved closer to share her warmth with him. He smiled back, briefly squeezing her hand, then said, "You won't find her."

Strong looked grim—and tired. "She can't have gone very far."

"You wanna bet?" As a sudden weariness rolled over her, Emma leaned into Bobby's chest. "I swear that woman's part eel."

Twenty-five

"I didn't think this week would ever end." Through the rhythmic motion of the wipers, Emma absently watched the trees and houses flash by, shadowed by the darkness of early evening and stormy weather. "I'm glad we'll have a little extra time this weekend to kick back and relax."

"It'll be a good weekend for that." Bobby slowed for a stop sign, and increased the wiper speed. "The weather's supposed to be like this straight through Sunday."

Feeling this tired, the patter of rain and hypnotic *swish-swish* of the wipers would put her to sleep before Bobby even pulled up to his cottage. "I wish the rain would stop. I don't think I've completely dried out since I climbed out of Lake Pontchartrain the other night."

"Oh, c'mon. That was the high point of our week."

"No, the high point of the week came when I walked out of the station. I am *starved,* and this whole car smells like fried chicken."

Her stomach growled loudly, underscoring her words, and Bobby grinned. "I like a girl with a healthy appetite."

"I think you just like girls, period."

"Maybe, but every now and then one comes along with a really healthy appetite I can appreciate." And, just so she'd get his point, he waggled his eyebrows.

Smiling, she gave a gentle swat. "And this seems a good time to remind you about our talk the other day. You know, about dating. Like normal people."

"You mean normal people exist? I thought that was a myth."

"No, that's just a natural by-product of the fact we have a job that's all about deviants." She let out a long sigh, resting her head against the back of her seat. "Ordinarily, after a bad week, I'd just want to curl up and hide, but you're not off the hook. You have to take me out to a five-hanky movie, followed by an expensive dinner that's *not* fast food, then take me home to cozy up with candlelight and chilled wine and romantic music—"

"And there's sex involved somewhere in all this, right?"

"Pig." She swatted him again as he chuckled. "I'm sure there'll be sex. Especially if you're a good boy."

"If I do all that five-hanky and cozy-candle thing, I'll already be a *damn* good boy." His smile brimmed with the promise of mischief. "You sure you don't want the bad boy?"

One smile, and . . . thunk! She was a total pushover. "The bad boy is just a big ol' softie."

"Not where it counts." Again, he waggled his brows, and she giggled.

Playing the white knight with Mottson had rejuvenated his self-confidence, and seeing him so relaxed was a joy. Small worries still nagged at her, though, and she hoped he planned to follow through on his promise and at least talk to a counselor about feeling so burned out at work.

Of course, the other reason for his good mood was that Chloe had disappeared into thin air, despite a determined effort to find her.

"Will we ever hear from Chloe again?" she asked abruptly.

Bobby slowed again—the joys of residential neighborhoods, where every other corner boasted a stop sign. "Eventually."

"I still don't understand why you want her to get away."

"It's not that I want her to get away, Emma, I just don't see any need to hunt her down."

"Having her testimony against Mottson would be nice."

"But we don't need it, and as far as witnesses go, you, me, and that kid from the marina will look better on the stand than Chloe. She shouldn't have run off with the money, but I can't get worked up enough over it to chase after her. But if some cop eventually runs her to ground, that's okay with me, too."

"Don't you worry about her?"

"Sure, but Chloe's a survivor. She'll be okay." He drove slowly past his cottage, hunting out a parking spot, then swore. "I can't tell you how much I'm looking forward to the Peterson kids moving out and taking their cars with them. That family doesn't need a house, it needs a damn parking lot."

Finally, after making a U-turn and backtracking, he found a spot across the street, a little more than a block away.

Emma reached behind her and gathered the take-out

bags. "So we get wet and cold. It kind of brings the whole week full circle."

"I know the best way to heat up and chase away the chill." With an exaggerated wink, he grabbed the two bottles of wine and another bag. "And if I get my way, we won't leave the bedroom all weekend."

"Except for the five-hanky cozy-candle thing."

"Right. That's included in the plan."

Emma reached behind her, groping for the other take-out bag. "Or unless duty calls."

"Jesus, I hope not," he muttered. "The only duty I want tonight is Emma Duty, and the only justice I'm after is one satisfied woman."

Emma hurried across the street, hopping over a puddle, as hot anticipation washed over her. " 'Emma Duty?' "

"I'm a lifelong duty kind of guy," Bobby said, jogging along beside her. "What can I say? It's one of my bad habits, so you better get used to it."

And it was exactly what she wanted to hear from him—for the most part. Getting a better grip on the soggy paper of her bag, she added, "Now that we have things settled down a little, we need to talk. About us."

He grimaced, and jumped over the curb to the sidewalk. "I've heard this line before. It never turns out well."

Surprised by his response, a few seconds passed before Emma realized what he meant—and she would've hugged him, if her hands weren't full of fried chicken and biscuits. Instead, she slowed, and leaned against him in a comforting touch. "It's not *that* kind of talk, Bobby, and I'm not going anywhere. It's just that we got things a little backward, with the sex first, and the getting-to-know-you part last. And I want to get to know you. All of you."

"Why?"

Feeling suddenly awkward, she looked down at the wet sidewalk, watching the toes of her shoes kick up little rooster tails of water, and bumped her shoulder against his. She didn't know what to say that wouldn't sound silly. "You know why."

When he didn't say anything, a tickle of guilt prodded her. She knew what he wanted to hear, so why not just say it? So they'd only been a "them" for a scant two weeks, which most people would consider not enough time to know anything for certain. But it didn't matter what "most people" thought; this was about her and Bobby, nobody else.

"Well, there's that whole part about me falling in love with you, and I realize there's a lot we don't know about each other, but that'll change. I want you to let me the rest of the way inside your heart, Bobby."

He stopped so abruptly that she nearly ran into him, and then he surprised her yet again with a long, hot kiss that made her forget the rain, the bags in her hands, everything but getting him into a warm, cozy bed.

There wasn't a need to say anything more, and Emma picked up the pace as they began walking again. To hell with the fried chicken. She wanted to peel off Bobby's clothes and kiss every square inch of his body. And she'd kiss his belly button, and all the way down that thin line of dark blond hair, maybe right there in the kitchen, and watch his eyes close, his mouth go slack, and his whole face soften with passion, then she'd slip that bottle of cinnamon-flavored oil out of her purse and—

"Damn." She stopped a couple houses away from Bobby's cottage. "I left my purse in the car."

"I'll go back and—"

"No, I'll do it. You get inside and pour the wine." His old-fashioned gallantry was sweet and endearing—but she didn't want him finding the other little surprises stashed in her purse. Not just yet. "I'll be just a second. Give me your car keys."

After Emma piled her take-out bags in his arms, she jogged down the sidewalk back toward the SUV.

"Careful," he called after her.

She rolled her eyes. Like anything would happen to her while crossing a rainy, quiet neighborhood street.

As she dashed across the pavement, splashing in puddles, she smiled at one of Bobby's neighbors who was walking quickly to the other side of the road, the hood of his sweatshirt pulled forward against the rain.

He didn't smile back.

The rudeness bothered her, but of course not everybody out in the rain was in a good mood. For them, it was wet and cold. For her, it was Friday after a hellish week—and she was about to get gloriously laid.

Then she stopped, right in the middle of the street, instincts snapping alert, raising the fine hairs on the back of her neck.

Small, slight, and black . . . something about the man was familiar.

Emma turned, staring after him. As if sensing her stare, he glanced over his shoulder at her—and the light of a streetlight illuminated his face.

It was the man from the projects. Juleen's abusive boyfriend, Raymond.

"Hey, you! Stop!"

At her shout, he broke into a run. Emma followed, heart pounding as she reached for her gun—at the same moment a gleam of metal flashed in Raymond's hand.

"Bobby, look out!"

Almost at his front walk, Bobby turned. He dropped the bags and wine bottles, glass shattering, and reached for his gun just as Raymond fired three times, screaming: "*You're gonna take me down? Who's gonna take me down?*"

Bobby fell to his knees, a surprised look on his face, a split second before Emma fired two rounds at Raymond's back and another at his head. The man dropped on the spot.

She slowed long enough to glance at Raymond's crumpled body—what she glimpsed of his head assured her he'd never be a threat again—and then knelt beside Bobby.

"Oh, my God . . . are you hit? Can you talk?"

"Sonofabitch." His voice came low and strained, and he pressed both hands against the inside of his thigh. "I've been fuckin' shot *again*!"

"How bad?" Emma demanded, even as she took in his blood-covered hands and the dark pool on the sidewalk beneath him, widening much too fast.

"Pretty bad," he muttered. "I'm gonna end up in Charity again, and I hate that place."

"Bobby, let me see."

Gently touching his hand, feeling a warm slipperiness on her skin, she moved his fingers aside—and blood sprayed outward.

"Oh, God," she whispered. The bullet had hit the femoral artery—and the stark fear in his eyes told her he knew it was a fatal wound.

No. Not fatal; she wouldn't allow it.

"Keep up the pressure," she barked, shoving his hand back over the wound. "Press hard. As hard as you can."

"I am," he snapped back. "Jesus, you think I want to bleed to death on my front lawn?"

Quickly, her fingers shaking, she pulled off his leather belt, cursing as precious seconds spun by. Finally, she wrapped the belt around his upper thigh and pulled it brutally tight, forcing herself to ignore his gasp of pain.

Then she fumbled out her cell phone and dialed 911 as all around her came the sound of running footsteps and shouts of concerned neighbors.

"This is Detective Emma Frey, requesting immediate assistance." She pulled the tourniquet tighter, and as Bobby's hand closed hard over hers, she squeezed back. "I have an officer down. I repeat, an officer down!"

Twenty-six

 "Are you sure I can't get you something to drink? Coffee, maybe?"

Emma glanced at her captain, then shook her head. "No, thanks. I'm good."

"You want to take a break? Get up and walk around?" Strong looked tired and tense. "I can wait here for you. They just took Bobby into surgery, and it'll be at least a couple hours before we'll hear anything."

Hours.

And that time would pass so much more slowly than it had earlier, when the minutes had melded so quickly she couldn't even remember the ride to the ER. It had all been a frantic blur of motion and sirens and strangers. Her only clear memory was Bobby's pale face; in the ambulance, she'd insisted he keep looking at her, even as the EMT worked on him. She'd been so certain that if he closed his eyes, if he stopped looking at her, she'd lose him.

Shaking free of her thoughts, Emma realized Strong was still staring at her, waiting for an answer. "Really, I'm fine. I want to wait."

All the same, she stood, stretching her cramped, aching muscles, and tried not to look at the blood on her clothes. Not looking didn't help; she kept flashing back to what had happened, and her almost paralyzing frustration over not being able to do more. Never, ever would she forget the look on Bobby's face, full of disbelief and fear and anger. Nor would she ever forget the cops who'd raced to the scene, and the firefighters and EMT personnel, some of them off duty, who'd rushed to the aid of a fallen brother.

Blinking away a renewed sting of tears, she sniffed and turned to Strong. "Did you finally get ahold of Bobby's parents?"

He nodded. "They're on their way."

"How are they doing?"

"They sounded pretty rough, as I'd expect."

An obvious answer, but she'd had to ask. It gave her something to do. As she looked around the waiting area, avoiding Strong's concern, she noticed more cops standing around, a number of new faces among them—including Gary Giacomo, who gave her a short, respectful nod of acknowledgment.

Noticing the direction of her gaze, Strong said, "They've been coming and going since Bobby arrived in the ER, stopping by to find out how he's doing. You know cops. We're a tight bunch."

As if on cue, the door at the end of the hall opened, and Alycia hurried toward her, Car following, still in his sergeant's uniform.

"Emma!" Alycia enveloped her in a hug—not an easy thing, since Alycia was about six inches shorter—and squeezed hard. "Rosie called and told me what happened. We got here as soon as we could."

Emma closed her eyes, and a tear slipped free, followed by another, then more, until she couldn't hold back any longer. All at once, the despair and fear hit, and Emma gave in to her grief, as if Alycia's hug had quietly commanded, *Go on ahead and bawl your eyes out; we'll be strong for you until it's better.*

Alycia sniffed; all the males in the near vicinity beat a hasty retreat. Emma didn't care if she embarrassed them, or if anybody thought her crying undignified.

It didn't take long to cry herself empty, though. Exhausted but calmer, Emma pulled away from Alycia—and smiled as a large, square, dark-skinned hand appeared in front of her face, holding tissues.

"Thank you, Car," Emma murmured. "Scared you off, huh?"

"You needed a little space," he said, sidestepping the question. He patted her on the shoulder, the gesture both awkward and endearing. "I still can't believe this. Damn, but that boy has a bad habit of getting in the way of bullets. What the hell happened?"

"This guy—a suspect in one of Bobby's cases—came out of nowhere and just shot him down. I didn't recognize him soon enough. If I'd have been sharper, had just a few more seconds on him—"

"Emma, don't. It's not your fault." Strong said gruffly. "You couldn't have prevented what happened, but you did save Bobby's life. If you hadn't been there, he'd have bled to death in minutes."

Alycia dabbed at her eyes, her fierce frown matching Strong's. "How on earth did he know where to find Bobby? We never list our addresses in the phone book, and nobody at the station would've given it out."

Sighing, Strong rubbed at his brows. "I have no idea.

We'll have to ask Bobby, but he's not going to be much help for a while. Shit, what a week. One of my detectives is in jail, another gets shot . . . and it's only January."

The door at the end of the hall opened again, several uniformed officers leaving as Rosie and Lenny Delgado walked in. Her face pale, Rosie hurried over as quickly as her heavy roundness allowed.

"How's Bobby doing?" she asked.

"Still in surgery."

"You okay, Emma? You're not hurt any?"

Emma swallowed. "It's all Bobby's blood."

"I heard you got the guy." Lenny was scowling, plainly furious over what had happened and that there wasn't a single thing he could do about it. "Two slugs right through the heart. Good shooting."

"I just . . . started firing." Distantly, Emma wondered why she didn't feel something more. She'd killed a man; blew out his chest and part of his head—but she just felt numb, as if it hadn't been real.

"You doing okay about that?" Rosie asked again, her plump face and dark eyes full of concern.

"So far," Emma said. "Maybe later I'll feel . . . something. I know there'll be an investigation and all that, but right now, I don't want to think about anything unless it has to do with Bobby."

Rosie squeezed Emma's arm. "It'll work out. We're all here for you. Whatever you need, you don't hesitate to call nobody."

Car nodded. "Yeah. What she just said."

Again, tears burned at the back of her eyes, but she held them off.

"There's not much else to do but wait until he's out of surgery." Emma sat in her chair again, and Rosie and

Alycia joined her. Car and Strong wandered off with Lenny to talk to the cops who were still waiting around for news before they headed back to their patrol cars.

For the next few hours, a steady stream of cops and rescue personnel wandered by, sometimes talking to Emma, but mostly Strong fielded the updates. The press got wind of the shooting and soon showed up, but with the large number of uniforms on hand to keep them at bay, no reporters or camera crews intruded. Before too long, somebody from the department's public relations office would make an official announcement. It was their job; they could deal with the questions.

Finally, two and half hours after Bobby went into the OR, the trauma surgeon came into the waiting room, followed by a woman in dark pink scrubs whom Emma recognized as the head nurse she'd talked with the day Juleen Moss had died.

There was a sad irony in Bobby being a patient, again, in the same trauma unit where Juleen had spent her last days—and a little inner voice whispered: *What goes around comes around* . . .

Emma stood slowly, nodding a greeting at the nurse, and clasped her hands to keep them from shaking. Alycia and Rosie stood as well, and Strong and the other men hurried forward.

The doctor, in scrubs, booties, and OR cap, looked to be East Indian, with thick salt-and-pepper hair and mustache, and kind, dark eyes. "I am Dr. Randhawa. We have just taken Mr. Halloran into the recovery room, and he's doing very well."

Bless the man for getting right to the point.

As a wave of relief washed over her, Emma wavered a little. Alycia gave her another quick hug, steadying her.

"I'm Captain Derrick Strong, Detective Halloran's supervisor." Strong shook hands with the surgeon. "What can you tell me about my officer?"

"It is rather early yet to say on some matters." Dr. Randhawa had a melodic voice, and slightly rolled his *r*'s, speaking with a measured precision that sounded courtly, old-fashioned. "He is a young man and in excellent physical health, which will help him during recovery. Of course, he lost a great deal of blood and there is significant muscle and tendon damage in addition to the arterial trauma, which we repaired with a graft. It would appear that the sciatic nerve may be compromised to some degree, but it is too early to say if it will be a cause for further concern."

Emma's mouth went dry, and she swallowed several times before asking, "How long will he be in the hospital?"

"That is dependent upon his postoperative recovery course. Barring such complications as hemorrhage or infection, he could be ready to go home within seven to ten days. And he will, of course, require extensive physical therapy and outpatient clinic visits." Dr. Randhawa turned to Strong. "Typically, we expect a patient with such injuries to take up to six months for a full recovery. He won't be chasing criminals for some time."

Six months!

Dr. Randhawa must've seen the dismay mirrored in her eyes, because he smiled reassuringly. "He is most fortunate to be alive. This is what will be important to him. And because this young man has survived a gunshot wound once before, this may make his recovery easier. He will know what to expect, and that it will take time before he's back to his former self."

Considering the personal demons Bobby had been struggling with lately, twiddling his thumbs for some six months straight wasn't going to help his situation much.

"When can I see him?" Emma asked.

"In a short while. Andrea will let you know when they have Mr. Halloran settled in. The anesthesia will not wear off for some time yet, and he will be groggy when it does. And the painkillers will also keep him out of full awareness. This is normal."

Strong nodded. "Thank you, Dr. Randhawa."

"Yes," Emma said quietly. "Thank you for saving his life."

"I believe you did most of that." The doctor smiled again as he patted her shoulder. "When Mr. Halloran is awake, tell him Dr. Randhawa says he owes this young lady dinner and a dozen roses."

Strong smiled, glancing at Emma. "At the very least."

Emma lost track of time as she sat with Bobby in his room, listening to his quiet, steady breathing as she waited for him to emerge from his deep, anesthetized sleep. The nurses came in to check on him regularly, and all of them called him "Bobby," not "Mr. Halloran." They always smiled at Emma and asked if she was doing okay. She wasn't, and they couldn't really do anything to help with that, but she appreciated the kindness—there was something to be said for giving over total control of a situation to others in order to concentrate on quiet, intimate matters.

She must've dozed off, because one moment she'd been quietly enjoying the still profile of his face—longing to run her finger along his full bottom lip, but afraid to disturb him—and the next a nurse was shaking her shoulder and whispering, "He's awake."

Emma snapped alert, murmuring her thanks, and met Bobby's gaze, his pupils so dilated his eyes looked black instead of blue.

As the nurse left, quietly closing the door behind her, Emma leaned forward, smiling. "Hey. How long have you been awake?"

"I don't know. I was watching you sleep." He spoke slowly, in a whisper, the words slurring together. "I thought maybe you were a dream."

"No dream." Emma took his hand in hers, squeezing it. After a moment, he squeezed back. "I'm really here."

"That's what I decided, because if I were dreaming you, it'd be you and me in a bed that wasn't . . . this."

She smiled. "Medical equipment and nurses kind of ruin the romantic atmosphere. I agree."

"But you know what?"

"What?"

"I can't think of anyone I'd want to see, when I first open my eyes, except you."

Oh, great; tears threatened to spill over again, but she swallowed them back. "Look at you: lying in a bed all drugged up, and still flirting."

"That wasn't flirting." He briefly closed his eyes, wet his lips with his tongue. "That was me telling you . . . something I don't have the right words for." He motioned limply toward his head. "I'm all fuzzy in here."

"Don't worry about it." Scooting her chair closer, she smoothed back his hair from his forehead, feeling the coolness of his skin. "How are you feeling?"

He flashed a small grin. "These are really good drugs."

"I bet." She hesitated, then added, "And just to let you know, Strong called your family. Your mom and dad are on their way."

He nodded, frowning a little. "My mother's going to cry. I hate it when she does that. I feel like I'm six again. Or maybe four."

Emma held back her smile at his ramblings. "Mothers are emotional like that sometimes."

"Yeah, I guess so . . . I feel so far away from me, like I'm in the dark. If I start talking stupid, you'll tell me, right?"

As if he'd remember any of this tomorrow morning. "I promise."

When he wet his lips again, Emma picked up a cup of water with a straw in it, and held it up to his mouth so he could take a sip. Even that small effort was too much, and his eyes drifted shut for a few seconds.

"It happened so fast," he mumbled, brows drawing together in a small frown. "I couldn't tell . . . was it Raymond?"

"Yes." Emma put the glass down. "But you don't have to worry about him anymore. I put a couple bullets right through his heart. He's dead."

He studied her face with those dark eyes, uncomfortably lucid all of a sudden. "I'm sorry."

"It couldn't be helped, and it's not like I feel badly that he's dead. I just wish I'd moved faster, and taken him down before he shot you." Emma rubbed her thumb gently over his knuckles in a soothing gesture—as much for her sake as for Bobby's.

Forcing a lighter note in her voice, she added, "And I've been thinking that this will work out really well. I'll be on paid leave until Internal Affairs clears me of any wrongdoing, so I'll be around to pamper you and make sure you're one hundred percent taken care of."

"I don't—"

"Need any help?" She sighed, shaking her head. "Of course you will, and I *want* to. For once, would you sit back and let somebody else do the helping?"

"Look at bossy you. It's sexy." A faint smile tipped the ends of his mouth. "Does this offer involve full body massages?"

"I imagine it does. And any other bodily comforts you might require."

"I can maybe suffer through it."

She leaned over and gently kissed him, lingering a little, wanting to hold the touch as long as possible. Finally, she broke away and sat back again. "Do you have any idea how Raymond found out where you live?"

He stared past her, and she could see his struggle to think clearly through the fog of his painkillers. "Maybe he followed me home from work . . . I've had a lot on my mind and I haven't been as sharp as I could be. There's something else . . . but it's so hard to think."

Hearing the frustration in his low voice, she squeezed his hand again. "Then don't. We can talk about it when you're feeling better."

"No, I want to talk. I want to stay awake." He shifted, mouth tightening at the pain, and Emma leaned over and helped him get comfortable, careful of his IV lines. "Remember at the cookout, I got a call?"

"I remember."

"Raymond tried to see Juleen, and the nurse called me, but he was gone by the time I got here. I drove straight home. He could've followed me, and I would've been too pissed to even notice. Dammit, I should've—"

"Bobby, don't blame yourself. It's not your fault."

"No?" He spoke in a whisper, and again his eyes were uncomfortably clear. "Do you think I'd be lying here if I hadn't threatened to kill him?"

The thought had crossed her mind.

"We're not talking about this now. You're upsetting yourself, and that's not good." Something wet slipped down her cheek, but she was too upset to care. "God, Bobby, it doesn't matter. Nothing matters but that you get better . . . I was so scared," she finished in a whisper as another tear rolled down her cheek. "So damn scared I'd lost you because I wasn't watching your back. And I'd just started to get to know you, and you almost—"

Died. But she couldn't bring herself to say the word.

After a moment, he said, in an almost puzzled tone, "You're crying."

"I know. I'm sorry. I don't mean to get all weepy and freaky, and that's the last thing you need—"

"Those tears are for me?" he asked, his voice barely audible.

"Of course they are! Who else do you—"

"I just never thought I'd see anybody cry for me . . . didn't think I'd ever be lucky enough."

His rambling admission surprised her, then Emma sniffed, leaned over, and kissed him again, softly but firmly.

"Let me tell you something, Bobby. Alycia and Car waited with me all the while you were in surgery, and so did Rosie and Lenny, Captain Strong, Gary Giacomo, and a bunch of our guys, detectives and uniforms—I can't tell you how many, and I don't even know most of their names."

Gently, she continued to stroke his hand, his fingers. Just wanting to touch him, feel his warmth. "When I called for help, four patrol cars arrived in less than five minutes. Then the first fire truck and ambulance . . . I don't know how many came altogether, I was too busy holding your hand to count. But I thought you'd want to hear how all those people were there for you."

He didn't respond; only looked at her with those open, dark eyes.

"And you think you don't make a difference? That nobody would be there for you when you needed a little help yourself?" She paused. "They were all there to-night, Bobby. For you. And that means something, don't you think?"

At her quiet words, he turned his head away from her—but she didn't need to see his face, or the look in his eyes, to know he was overcome with emotion.

"And I'm here for you, too. In every way, at any time, because I care about you . . . I love you. And don't you forget it."

Epilogue

"Stop poking me with your foot. I'm trying for some manly dignity here."

"Oh, please, Bobby. I made you walk out and get the mail, but *you're* the one who insisted on leaving the cane behind."

"You got a real mean streak, girl." Sprawled spread-eagled on the living room floor, Bobby raised his head a fraction. Emma loomed over him, and from his vantage point her legs looked about a mile long. Man, if he could just get those legs bare, and wrapped around his waist, his mood would improve.

Correctly interpreting his leer, she folded her arms beneath her breasts—which looked mighty fine in a clingy shirt. But instead of looking stern, she just looked cute and kissable.

"And according to the nice physical therapist you cussed out this morning," Emma said, "I've been babying you too much."

What the hell? Scowling, Bobby hitched himself up on his elbows. "And that nice physical therapist didn't have a hole blown through his leg, did he?"

"Quit whining. He's just doing his job, and the next time you go out to get the mail, take your cane—"

"It makes me feel like that little waddling guy from *Batman,* and I'll be damned—"

"Would you stop interrupting me?" She hunkered down, her face level with his. "Anybody ever tell you that you're a real pain in the ass?"

He flashed a grin. "Well, yeah. All the time."

The comment earned him a roll of her eyes. "You need to give yourself time, and you'll be as good as new soon enough. You can go back to work in a few weeks, and come August, you'll be walking down the aisle at Jack and Diana's wedding without a limp."

"Don't remind me, because if I have to wear a tuxedo *and* limp down an aisle with a cane, I'm not going."

"You are so vain."

"Sue me."

"And cranky." She fixed him with a relentless stare. "I want you to sit up, uncurl that lip, and tone down the attitude. Then maybe I'll massage your thigh."

Bobby sat, his body responding in a heartbeat to that suggestion. "More than my thigh would be good—and I'm thinking this time you don't even have to be on top."

"It hasn't been six weeks yet, and—"

"Em, I didn't give birth, I just got shot."

"I know." She looked away. "I was there, remember?"

The silence hummed with a sudden tension. Finally, Bobby scooted back against the couch, ignoring a sharp twinge of pain, and pulled her down into his embrace.

"Sorry," he said. "Bad memories."

"It's okay." Emma snuggled into him as if she couldn't get close enough. "I just wish the memories would fade away as quickly as you're healing."

"You're sleeping better at night," he said, pushing a strand of her hair out of his way, so he could kiss her temple. "And you're back to work, with no problems. Looks to me as if things are getting back to normal."

"Really?"

"Sure. Even my neighbors have stopped staring at me."

She smiled; he could feel her cheek bunch against his chest. "You're a celebrity now. I've noticed the Johnson kids are leaving you parking spots."

"Kind of drastic, getting shot just to get a good parking spot."

"Don't make jokes about it." She poked his belly. "They're good kids. They've been a big help."

The Johnsons had sent their tribe over to help with house and yard work. Bobby appreciated it, but the constant questions from the kids wore him out. Not that he'd expected anything else; it wasn't every day that the cop living next door was gunned down on his front lawn.

"Everybody's been a big help. You, the guys at work, family, friends . . . I haven't had to do anything since I left the hospital six weeks ago."

"And you're bored."

"God, yes." He dropped his head back against the couch. "I've had nothing to do but think."

"Anything you want to share?"

He hesitated, not sure if now was the right moment, but when Emma pulled back and looked up at him, he saw only patience and understanding in her eyes.

"I've been thinking about what you said to me at the prison, that what we do makes a difference, even if it's a small one. Somewhere along the line, I got it in my head that I wasn't one of the good guys if I didn't win every fight—and then the job stopped being about what I did, and started being about who I was."

He looked down at his hand, clasping hers. In comparison, his hand looked big and rough, dusted with golden hairs. Her fingers were long and slender, her skin softer, paler—and unexpectedly strong. Just like Emma.

"This morning I told Dr. Randhawa I needed to talk about problems I'd been having," he continued. "The department would tell me to see a counselor anyway, to evaluate my fitness for returning to duty later, but I wanted to make the first call myself."

Her expression grew solemn. "How do you feel about that?"

"I'm okay with it, even if I'm still not loving the idea, but I want to do this right. I want to come back two hundred percent." He paused, rubbing his thumb over her knuckles in a soothing, circling motion. "I want it *all* back, Emma: the fire, the faith. Everything."

He waited, a little embarrassed at all those words, for Emma's response, and relief swept over him when she gifted him with a wide, beautiful smile.

"I'm so very proud of you, especially since I know it wasn't an easy thing for you to do."

"You helped make it easier by just being here, believing in me. Everything in my life should be as easy as loving you."

Emma tipped her face toward him, and he lost himself in her eyes: brown and deep, full of warmth and compassion. How had he ever thought her cold?

Those pretty eyes suddenly sparkled with tears, and he quickly changed the subject, saying lightly, "I still owe you a five-hanky cozy-candle."

His attempt to cheer her up worked; instead of looking like she wanted to cry, she stared at him like he'd gone crazy. "What?"

"You know, where we go out like normal people."

"Oh, *that*." She laughed, low and rich. "I think we need to make adjustments for the normal part, otherwise we don't stand a chance in hell."

He grinned, and slipped his hand around to cup her breast. "Speaking of chances, what's the chance of me getting you into bed before you have to leave to go back to work?"

"Back to sex, are we?"

"Darlin', sex with you is the only thing keeping me going some days. Like today."

"That makes you an easy guy to please."

"You have no idea."

To his disappointment, she pulled back, then stood. "No sex right now, sorry, but hold that thought for later tonight, then you can ravish me at your leisure."

"You've been reading those romances my sister left here."

Emma headed toward the door, and flashed a grin over her shoulder. "They're not as bad as I thought. And they've given me a few ideas about leisurely ravishing."

Bobby sighed and glanced at the clock—eleven A.M. It was going to be a long day, him with his soda, TV remote, and *Cowboy Bebop* DVDs. He carefully pushed up off the floor and onto the couch, which was a hell of a lot more comfortable, and watched Emma grab her coat, bending to pick up his scattered mail first.

Her bottom rounded out her pants, and a hot need shot through him, building fast as she turned and slowly headed back to him, sorting his mail. Just watching her walk turned him on; the way she moved, confident and proud, with enough swing in her hips to make her breasts jiggle in a way that made his mouth go completely dry.

"Hey. Kiss me," he said roughly, when she stopped in front of him.

Emma arched a brow at his order, but bent and planted a prim peck on his lips. With a low-throated growl, Bobby took her chin in his hand and kissed her hard.

Hungrily, she returned his kisses and eased between his legs, bracing her hands, still holding his mail, behind him on the couch. When she came up for air moments later, she leaned into him, pressing her breasts against his mouth.

Heaven.

"You sure about that no-sex-now part?" he asked, sliding his hands down her back to grab onto her sweet, tight bottom.

"And you say *I* have a cruel streak." She sighed, then sank down beside him on the couch. She leaned forward to drop the mail on the coffee table, which he hoped meant she'd changed her mind—until she went still and whispered, "Uh-oh."

Bobby straightened from his slouch. "What's wrong?"

Emma held up a thick envelope. "It's from Chloe—and it's a little late for a get-well card."

His gaze met hers. "Only one way to find out."

Taking the envelope, he ripped it open, and pulled out a card with a picture of a scrawny Chihuahua wearing a miniature sombrero, its bug-eyed stare embellished with plastic wiggly-eyes. As he opened the card, a thick packet of folded paper fell onto his lap: a short letter, with a bunch of news clippings.

"What's all that?" Emma asked, scooting closer.

The first clipping was from a newsletter for the Louisiana Foundation for Battered Women, and he read the headline out loud: " 'Anonymous Donation of $100,000 Received.' "

Emma stared at him in amazement. "She's giving the money away?"

"Seems so."

His surprise faded, replaced by a swell of pride, as he thumbed through the remaining clippings, mostly copies of newsletters and bulletins, and all of them from local women's shelters, inner-city day-care centers, drug rehab programs, and youth centers.

The letter was short and direct, like Chloe, and he couldn't help smiling as he read it over. When he'd finished, he handed it to Emma, then sat back and watched as her eyes gradually widened.

"She gave it away. I can't believe she did that!"

"Which would explain why she sent proof," Bobby said wryly.

Emma put the letter down. "I don't know what to say, except I'm impressed . . . and now I feel like a total bitch for thinking all those mean things about her."

His smile widened into a grin. "Who'd ever expect Chloe to turn philanthropist?"

"Um, you *did* notice the part where she wrote she'd spent some of the money on herself?" Emma picked up the letter again and read: " 'But just so that nobody thinks I've turned into some boring do-gooder, I've also blown a bundle on new clothes and shoes. I'm feeling a need to reinvent myself.' "

After a short silence, Bobby said quietly, "And I say, good luck to her."

"She got the last laugh on her brother, that's for sure." Emma hesitated, her expression troubled. "What are you going to do about this? She's still wanted for questioning."

In answer, Bobby crumpled the papers and envelope into a tight ball, and dropped it in the ashtray. When he picked up his lighter, understanding dawned in her eyes—but she didn't protest as he touched the flame to the paper. It caught at once, burning with a high, hot orange flame.

"It's breaking a few rules," he said after a moment. "But it looks like justice to me."

With a small smile, she leaned against him, and Bobby wrapped his arms around her. They watched the paper burn and curl, dark smoke drifting upward, until nothing remained but ash.

"It has a certain poetic flair," Emma said softly. "A phoenix rising from the ashes. Like Chloe, reinventing herself."

"She's not the only one starting over." He pulled her closer. "Nothing like a second chance to make a man appreciate a good thing when he sees it."

Emma peered at him, eyes full of warmth and humor—and a rawer emotion that brought a lump to his throat. "Promise me something?"

"Anything, darlin'."

"Always have a smile for me."

He lowered his mouth to hers in a soft, lingering kiss. "That's an easy promise to keep."

"Well," she said after a moment, slightly breathless. "I thought we'd start with the little promises and work our way up to the big stuff."

Bobby trailed his finger down her neck and traced her

collarbone. "Speaking of working up to the big stuff, how's the rethinking going on making me a happy man now rather than later?"

Emma giggled, a light and almost girlish sound, and slipped her warm hand beneath the waistband of his sweatpants. "I can handle any of the big stuff you've got."

He closed his eyes, smiling as her hand closed over him. "You sure about that?"

"Absolutely."

Coming in October, enjoy an Indian Summer with these hot men from Avon Books

A WEDDING STORY by Susan Kay Law
An Avon Romantic Treasure

Lord James Bennett can't forget that wild passionate moment in Kate's garden when he stole a lingering and forbidden kiss. Now the lady has asked this famous adventurer for his help in winning the Great Centennial Race—and to stick strictly to business. Will James change her mind and win a far more valuable prize: her heart?

SOMEONE LIKE HIM by Karen Kendall
An Avon Contemporary Romance

Nicholas Wright is too busy with his hectic, success-obsessed life to deal with the high maintenance pooch he inherited. So he hires a live-in "nanny." But Lavender Hart, with her sexy exuberance and charming unpredictability, is becoming an even bigger distraction. A relationship could never work between them—or is a girl like her perfect for someone like him?

FOR THE FIRST TIME by Kathryn Smith
An Avon Romance

Devlin Ryland wants to be left in peace after his heroic return from Waterloo—until he meets beautiful Lady Blythe, who wants nothing to do with him. Devlin's heroic deed—the rescue of Blythe's betrothed, who then married another—is nothing but a reminder of her heartache. Now it is up to Devlin to show her what it is like to be loved for the first time.

BELOVED HIGHLANDER by Sara Bennett
An Avon Romance

Gregor Grant was to have been the Laird of Glen Dhui. But the English took away the home that had been with his family for generations. Bitter and betrayed, the Highlander vowed never to return . . . until Margaret Mackintosh pleads for his help. The fiery lass needs a champion, and she's about to make Gregor an offer he'd be a fool to refuse . . .

REL 0903

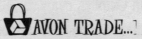